BEDLAM

WORLD FALLEN

SUSANNA STROM

THE WORLD FALLEN SERIES

Pandemonium

Maelstrom

Bedlam

Visit my website at www.susannastrom.com
https://www.facebook.com/Susanna-Strom-Author-101447404809167/

Developmental Editor: Christina Trevaskis
www.bookmatchmaker.com

Interior Designer: Jovana Shirley
Unforeseen Editing, www.unforeseenediting.com

Proofreader: Brittany Meyer-Strom
brittanym.edits@gmail.com

Cover Designer: Lori Jackson Design
www.lorijacksondesign.com

Photography: Wander Aguiar Photography
www.wanderbookclub.com

Model: Philippe Belanger

ISBN ebook: 978-1-7348292-4-2
ISBN paperback: 978-1-7348292-5-9

Published by Cougar Creek Publishing LLC

ONE

Sunny

Laughter shattered the quiet afternoon, followed by the crunch of breaking glass. I froze in place then slowly swiveled my head toward the front window of the abandoned florist shop. Across the street, two men wearing blue baseball caps stood in front of a derelict cigar store. One held a wooden bat while the other spray-painted the shop's door. A red capital letter N took shape against the white background.

Crap.

I clicked off my flashlight and dropped to my knees behind a display table.

Why were the Nampa Boys tagging a shop inside the Boise city limits? We had a treaty with them. We'd keep out of the territories they claimed—Nampa and other communities west of Boise—and they'd stay out of the city.

Holding my breath, I peered around the table at the men. They stepped back on the sidewalk, probably to admire their handiwork. One of them clapped the other on the shoulder. Both men looked up and down the street, pointing and waving their arms.

I shrank back further into the shadows and glanced longingly toward my duffel bag on the opposite side of the room. Would it be smarter to stay in place or to crawl across the room and fetch the bag? Late afternoon sunshine bathed the floor near the shop's plate glass windows. The men *probably* wouldn't see me worm my way across the linoleum, but I couldn't be sure. Better to hold still. I turned my eyes to the men again.

Please. Please. Please. There's nothing you want over here. Don't cross the street.

The men continued their animated conversation, leaving me pinned down behind the table. Dead flower arrangements—Mother's Day roses and tulips—covered its surface. The leaves and petals had long since wilted and dried, some crumbling over time into powder. The dust tickled my nose, and I pinched my nostrils together.

Don't sneeze. The urge passed, and I peeked at the men again. Still yapping.

"Time to move on, guys," I whispered.

Hidden in the shadows of a florist shop, I *should* be safe.

Within the first weeks of the flu pandemic, panicked people had cleaned out all the grocery stores and pharmacies. Liquor stores, too, so I'd heard. If the men across the street were smokers, they might break into the cigar store to see if any stogies remained. But a flower shop filled with shriveled bouquets, deflated balloons, and stuffed animals? No. It had to be the least likely place to attract looters during an apocalypse. I should know. Scavengers like me systematically ransacked stores and our dead neighbors' houses, hauling away everything of value.

I sighed. What was the number one rule for scavengers? Always use the buddy system. Never go out alone. Yet here I was—by myself—in the middle of a deserted store. Sara would pitch a fit if I told her, which of course, I wouldn't. I take that back. I'd tell her that I saw Nampa Boys inside Boise, but I wouldn't confess the precise circumstances. The head of the Haven didn't need to know about everything I got up to while I was out and about.

Dad used to reel off a quote, something about asking for forgiveness instead of permission. Who was he quoting? I couldn't remember. Once upon a time—before the pandemic—if you forgot the source of something, you turned to Google. Not anymore. Not with the power grid down and the internet dead. Now you had to hope that you'd find the right person to ask, or you'd learn to live with your unsatisfied curiosity.

"Come on," I hissed at the chatty men.

BEDLAM

The men ambled over to a red hatchback that was parked in front of the cigar store and climbed in. After another interminable moment, the driver started the engine and drove away. I blew out a long, slow breath. I waited for a couple of minutes—just to be sure—then scrambled across the room and snatched the duffel.

I was breaking the rules by foraging for supplies by myself. I had to pick up the pace, especially if I hoped to get home behind locked doors before dark. Pressing my face against the window, I scanned the street in both directions. The Nampa Boys were well and truly gone. I was safe, for now.

Lucky for me, the florist shop wasn't quite the dud that it appeared to be. Against the back wall, the owner had installed a Best of Britain selection of imported teas and biscuits, cookies to my American mind. Mom used to pick up her favorite Harney & Sons tea here. I carried the duffel to the back of the store and smiled to myself as I surveyed the shelves.

Score.

I stuffed a dozen tins of tea into the bag, followed by shortbread rounds, ginger creams, Jammie Dodgers and—joy of joys—Jaffa cakes. I cleaned the place out, shoving so many packages of cookies into my duffel that I couldn't close the zipper. I managed—barely—to hoist the bag's strap onto my shoulder and staggered out of the shop toward Daisy, my faithful van.

Fifteen minutes later, I turned in to a residential neighborhood on the west side of town. Pretty 1920s-era bungalows lined the dead-end street. I parked in the driveway of Cressida's Cottage, Mrs. B.'s name for the dove-gray house with pink shutters where she'd lived for the past forty-five years. I transferred several tins of tea and packages of cookies into a paper grocery bag and folded over the top to hide the contents, then walked up the brick pathway to her front door.

Cressida Birdwhistle opened the door before I had the chance to knock, a fluffy white-and-tan cat draped over her arm. "Sunny!" she exclaimed. A tiny woman with a crown of silver hair, she stood barely four feet, eleven inches tall. She was once "a whopping five feet tall" she'd told me, before old age compressed her vertebrae. Her bright-pink lips turned up in a welcoming smile—not even the end of the world could stop Mrs. B. from wearing her favorite lipstick—and she ushered me inside. "I was just telling Fitzwilliam that I expected you'd stop by today. We looked out the window, and there you were."

"Hey, Fitzwilliam." I scritched his massive ruff, and his blue eyes squinted with pleasure. "I have a surprise for you, Mrs. B." I dangled the grocery bag in front of her.

Her faded blue eyes sparkled, and she bounced on her toes. Fitzwilliam wriggled, and Mrs. B. gently placed him on the floor. "Off with you then." He sauntered toward the kitchen while Mrs. B. led me to her living room. Shelves crammed full of books and Staffordshire figurines lined three walls of the room, a fitting setting for a retired librarian and English expatriate. We settled down on an apple-green couch covered with pink and green pillows.

Mrs. B. clasped her hands together on her lap, giddy with excitement over her surprise. I made a show of opening the bag and slowly taking out a box of Jaffa cakes. She gasped; her face suffused with pleasure. "Wherever did you find Jaffa cakes?"

Mrs. B. was an inspiration. Despite the chaotic state of the world, she embraced moments of joy with childlike glee. Ever since she'd confessed to a hankering for the orange and chocolate cookies, I'd been on a quest to bring them to her. The Jaffa cakes made her happy, and it troubled my conscience not one bit that I'd given her every box I'd found. The cookies were a windfall, and Sara would be thrilled when I brought the rest to the Haven.

"A florist shop, of all places. Luckily, it hadn't been ransacked." There was no point in telling her about my close call with the Nampa Boys.

"Lucky for me," she agreed, tearing open the package. She tilted the box toward me. "Have one."

We munched in companionable silence. I glanced out her front window. The sun grazed the treetops on the opposite side of the street. Time to get going.

The Haven brought Mrs. B. food, water, and other supplies every Sunday, but there was never time during those trips to help around the place, so I stopped by at least once a week on my own. "Is there anything I can do for you before I have to leave?" I asked.

Mrs. B. made a face. "I pulled a muscle in my back this morning hanging sheets on the clothesline. Would you be a dear and bring them in?"

"No problem." I hopped to my feet and headed toward the backyard. After hauling in the sheets, I made up her bed, then did a quick inventory of her supplies. I'd need to bring more cans of cooking fuel for her camp stove. Mrs. B. needed her hot tea.

"Is there anything else I can do for you?" I asked, giving Fitzwilliam a final pat.

She hesitated, as if reluctant to ask for a favor. She held up her hands. "My fingers might be a little stiff, but I still love to knit. Could you keep your eyes open for yarn when you're rummaging about town?"

"Of course, I will." I hugged her, careful not to squeeze too hard. Mrs. B. had a powerhouse personality, but arthritis had left her joints and bones frail. "Especially pink yarn."

She laughed, then pulled back to smile up at me. "Jaffa cakes and pink yarn, Sunny, you're a saint."

I snorted. "My brother would laugh his ass off if he heard that." A familiar pain made my chest ache. I pushed the memory away, focusing on the present. "I'll see you in a few days." As I turned to go, a thought occurred to me. "Mrs. B., there's this saying, 'It's better to beg forgiveness than to seek permission.' Do you know where it comes from?"

"I believe St. Benedict was credited with saying it first, back in the sixth century."

I dropped a kiss on her upturned cheek. "We might not have the internet anymore, but as long as we have Mrs. B., we'll be okay."

She blushed at the praise and flapped her hands. "Get along now. I want you home before dark."

"Yes, ma'am."

I jogged to my van. I'd hoped to stop at the Haven, to tell them about seeing the Nampa Boys tag a building in town, but with night approaching, I decided that could wait till tomorrow. I headed north toward home. The light shifted as I drove, taking on the golden hue that signaled the coming of sunset. When I pulled into my driveway, I jumped from the van, unlocked the garage door, and muscled it open.

"I miss garage door openers," I muttered.

After concealing Daisy behind closed doors, I let myself into the house, making my way through the laundry room to the kitchen. Would I ever get used to coming home to an empty place? I glanced around the silent room, picturing Mom at the stove, cooking up one of her favorite curries. Or Dad at the counter, kneading sourdough bread. They'd have a fit if they saw the state of the kitchen.

In case anybody broke in while I was out, it had to be obvious that the place had been stripped bare. I'd painstakingly staged the room to give that impression. Wide-open cupboard doors revealed empty shelves. The silverware drawer lay upside down on the floor, forks and spoons scattered across the hardwood. Spice jars had apparently crashed to the counter when an impatient looter swept them from a cupboard. The pantry had been cleared out.

I'd hidden my stockpile of foodstuffs behind rows of books on the shelves in my bedroom. After fetching a can of beef and barley soup and a lunch-sized carton of applesauce from my hoard, I carried my sorry dinner to the gazebo. I popped the lid off the soup can and dug into cold, congealed beef and barley. The applesauce was a rare treat. I savored each bite as I watched the sun go down.

Night settled in around me. Stars winked in the darkening sky. The air chilled. A mosquito buzzed as it flew by my head. That propelled me into action. Slapping at my arms, I snatched up the empty soup can and applesauce container and sprinted toward the house.

After locking the patio door, I walked through the empty family room. Silence pressed in from every side. I felt my family's absence most keenly during these quiet evenings. I was a social creature and drew energy from my interactions with others. I'd taken to going to bed early, so I didn't have to face the long, melancholy hours alone.

I switched on a solar powered lantern and made my way upstairs to my bedroom. Maybe I'd read for a while before I tried to sleep. Lantern in hand, I scanned the titles on my shelf. Nothing looked especially appealing. Frustrated, I turned away, then paused. Wait a minute. Last week, Mrs. B. had lent me a copy of one of her favorite novels, the story of a time-traveling nurse and a "yummy" Highland lord. I'd left the book downstairs on the coffee table.

I started to retrace my steps back to the family room. Halfway down the hall, a sound broke the silence, the unmistakable creak of somebody climbing the stairs. I froze. Maybe I wasn't as stealthy and careful as I thought. Maybe the Nampa Boys—or some other survivor with bad intentions—had followed me home. But I'd locked all the doors, hadn't I? I hadn't heard glass shatter. How did they get in?

Good lord, get moving.

Whirling, I ran back to my bedroom. With fumbling fingers, I switched off the lantern and snatched up the trophy I'd earned for winning a spelling bee in sixth grade. Footsteps sounded in the hall. I pressed against the wall behind my bedroom door and lifted the trophy above my head, ready to strike.

The door inched open, and a tall figure stepped into the room. He cocked his head, then slowly began to turn toward my hiding place. Crap. Holding my breath, I swung the trophy.

He sidestepped the blow, then lunged at me, pinning my arms to my sides in a bear hug. I thrashed about, trying to free my arms. We staggered sideways across the room, falling heavily onto my bed. He wrestled me onto my back. The air whooshed out of my lungs and I gasped.

"What do you think you're doing, asshole?" a familiar voice growled.

TWO

Kyle

Turns out that not even the end of the world could kill my default optimism. A mile away from my old home, I rounded a familiar corner, and my heart began to pound against my chest.

Before the world fell apart, I'd rarely encountered a problem I couldn't sweet-talk, finagle, or bribe my way out of. If I'd learned anything during the four months since a new flu virus upended the world, it was that a man had to expect the worst and be prepared to deal with it. Still, the hope that things might somehow work out for the best —an emaciated but tenacious hope—clung like a barnacle to some small corner of my mind.

I rolled the pickup to a stop a few feet from the entrance to Northumberland Heights, the gated community in Boise where I'd grown up. A Tudor style guardhouse stood sentry in the middle of the road. The brick-and-stucco exterior gave the small building an appearance of grandeur, but beneath the fancy-pants veneer, it was your standard four-by-six-foot guard shack.

How many times had I driven past this checkpoint on my way home? Hundreds, no, it had to be thousands of times. Before the flu pandemic, security personnel had manned the gate twenty-four, seven. They'd wave at homeowners whose key cards tripped the swinging metal gate and check the ID of everybody else before allowing them into the neighborhood. This enhanced security was one of the reasons why my mom had insisted on moving into Northumberland Heights.

Leaning forward, I peered through the windshield at the guardhouse. Somebody had busted out its windows, and the shattered glass glinted on the surface of the road. The gate barring entrance to the neighborhood hung cockeyed from its steel post, dented, like a car had rammed it at speed.

I sighed. Yeah. I should've known that hope would kick me in the balls. That illusion of protection offered by the security guards and gate had proven as phony as the shack's ornate facade. So much for my fantasy that the old neighborhood had somehow survived the pandemic unscathed.

I took my foot off the brake, eased the pickup forward, and nudged the dinged-up gate out of the way. Turning left onto Surrey Drive, I traced the familiar route back toward my childhood home. I swung my head from side to side, scanning the street and yards for any signs of life. Survivors. Looters. Squatters. Anybody. Shoot, I'd even welcome the sight of crabby, old Mrs. Kaminski walking her Pomeranian and yelling at drivers to slow the heck down. Nothing. Not a soul in sight.

Knee-high grass baked in the front yards, and sun-scorched weeds clogged the flower beds. Eerie quiet gripped Northumberland Heights by the throat.

My cautious neighbors would've retreated behind locked doors as civil unrest spread. Maybe some of them—out of their heads from late-stage flu mania—had come out of hiding and wandered the streets. Why else would so many front doors stand wide open? Or maybe intruders hadn't bothered to close up a house when they were done ransacking it.

I braked, pausing in front of my buddy Jordan's house. The front door was shut, but looters had shattered the living room windows. Sheer curtain panels fluttered in the breach and caught on the jagged glass. A figure sprawled spread-eagle under the window. The last thing I wanted to do was to look closely at the body. Friend or foe, whoever lay there was beyond help.

The silence and stillness of the old neighborhood rattled me. I pivoted my head from side to side, searching for signs of life.

When I'd left the ranch in central Oregon early this morning, Ripper had handed me a shoulder holster and extra magazines for

Grandpa Kurt's Glock 17. "Got nobody to watch your back on the road," he'd said. "Keep your eyes open and your pistol close, brother."

I'd nodded and shook hands with the former soldier.

Kenzie had flung herself into my arms. She clutched my T-shirt. Tears glistened in her beautiful gray eyes. "Promise me you'll be careful and that you'll come back home to us as soon as you can."

"I promise, sweetheart." The back of my eyes prickled, and I blinked furiously. I wanted to keep our goodbyes low-key. No way I'd break down and blubber in front of my friends. Time to lighten the mood. I chucked her under her chin and angled my head toward Ripper. "And I expect you to keep the big guy in line while I'm gone."

Kenz cracked an imaginary whip. "You know I will."

Ripper rolled his eyes, snaked out an arm, and hauled Kenzie against his chest. "Mind your manners, Mrs. Solis."

She tossed her hair and smiled saucily at him. "Make me, Mr. Solis."

Not so long ago, the sight of Kenzie in another man's arms would have gutted me. I'd made my peace with the situation. It might strike some people as odd that I was still close with my ex—that her new man had become a trusted friend—but in this crazy, post-pandemic world, it made perfect sense. A familiar face, somebody you shared memories with, that was a gift. Moreover, reliable allies were the key to survival. And to staying sane.

Shaking my head at the memory, I reached for the shoulder holster and touched the Glock, its solid presence a comfort. "I got this," I said under my breath.

My foot tapped the gas pedal, and the truck lurched forward. I turned right at the next stop sign. Only two more blocks to go.

My pulse sped up as the pickup glided past familiar houses. The Rosens' Dutch colonial. Chelsey Rosen was the first girl I kissed, right there on the front porch. The Lavignes' French country house. Every Christmas, Mrs. Lavigne baked her famous macarons and passed them out to the neighbors. My mom loved those fancy meringue cookies and hid them from my sister and me. The Brocks' Tudor. When we were twelve, Theo Brock and a bunch of us guys built a tree fort in his backyard.

Memories assailed me from every side.

The street curved and the McAllisters' sprawling stucco house came into view, kitty-corner from my family's place. I slammed on the brakes and squeezed my eyes shut against the sight of my best friend's home. Jake. Shit. Sharp pain stabbed my chest. Jake and his girlfriend Ali had died during the first week of the pandemic. We'd been driving home to Boise from college in Portland when they fell ill. I'd sat deathwatch over them and had buried their bodies in Pendleton before heading back to Portland to look for Kenz.

I opened my eyes. I owed one last duty to my dead friend.

"I'll check on your folks, Jake," I said, pulling into the McAllister driveway. The front door was shut. Somebody—probably Jake's dad—had nailed plywood over the large picture windows, like folks did who lived in a hurricane zone. No hurricanes or tornadoes in Boise. We thought we were safe from natural disasters. Guess Mother Nature showed us, huh?

I hopped out of the truck, walked up to the front door, and pounded my fist on its surface. Holding my breath, I cocked my head to one side and listened. Nothing but silence greeted me, but that meant squat. If I'd survived the flu and somebody came knocking on my door, I wouldn't answer. I thumped my fist on the door a couple more times—to alert anybody inside—then reached into my pocket. When Jake died during our trip home, I'd planned to keep driving his pickup. Somebody had hotwired and stolen it, but I still carried my dead buddy's keys as a reminder of him and a talisman against bad luck.

I unlocked the front door and stepped into the foyer. "Naomi? Brian?" I called out his parents' names.

The hair on the back of my neck prickled at the unnatural quiet. The McAllister house was always a loud, happy place filled with a raucous jumble of music, laughter, and conversations. The family never used the built-in intercom. They stood at the bottom of the stairs and bellowed for each other. This dead air felt all kind of wrong. Creeped out by the absence of sound, I walked over to the bottom of the staircase.

"Naomi? Brian? It's Kyle Chamberlain. Anybody here?"
Silence.

Duty done, I scuttled back outside and locked the front door. I retreated to the truck, then backed onto the street.

Drawing in a deep breath, I turned my head and took my first look at my family home. Overgrown, sun-bleached grass swayed on the front lawn. Mom's prized rosebushes were clinging to life, their bare, thorny branches twisting toward the sky. Brittle leaves littered the weed-filled mulch beneath the roses.

Mom would fire the gardeners.

I choked out a harsh laugh. After everything that had happened during the past four months, *that* was my first thought. I looked past the neglected landscaping to the house. The front windows were intact and the curtains drawn, but the door stood wide open.

Another blow to my irrational, default optimism. So much for the fantasy that I'd march up the front walk, slip my key in the lock, and find my parents safe behind the sturdy door. I knew better. Of course, the virus that had laid waste to the world hadn't spared my family. I parked the pickup in our driveway, threw my backpack over my shoulder, then cautiously approached the open entry door.

Grandma's sterling silver gravy boat lay on its side on the doormat. Before the flu, a burglar could've hocked it for a pretty penny. I couldn't blame any thief for having second thoughts and ditching it on the porch. Was there anything less useful in the new world than a freaking gravy boat?

I slid the Glock from the holster and stepped inside my family home. Dried leaves crunched underfoot. Dad's laptop lay face down on the hardwood floor, another once-valuable item abandoned by somebody with looter's remorse. Freezing in place, I strained to hear anything to indicate that I wasn't alone.

"Mom? Dad?" My voice echoed through the empty halls.

I climbed the curving staircase and halted next to the double doors leading to my parents' bedroom. Old habits die hard. My sister and I were expected to knock before entering, so I automatically rapped on the door before stepping inside. The light that filtered through the curtains revealed a room devoid of life. I wrinkled my nose. Rumpled, sweat-stained sheets covered the bed. Empty water glasses and bottles of ibuprofen crowded the bedside tables. A dried substance I didn't want to look closely at clung to the sides of a bucket on the floor by the side of the bed. I stuck my head in their bathroom and closet—just in case—but found no signs of Mom or Dad.

Retreating to the hall, I gently shut the door to my parents' sanctum and leaned back against the wall. When I left the ranch this morning, I *knew* that I was unlikely to find my parents alive, but like I told Ripper, I had to see with my own eyes what happened to them.

13

From the evidence in the messy bedroom, one or both of my parents had come down with the flu.

Where were they now?

I padded down the hall and opened the door to the guest room. Another unmade bed. Somebody had knocked over a glass of OJ, and the puddle of juice had dried on the nightstand. My sister Kristen's fluffy, pink bathrobe was draped across the foot of the bed. Entering the room, I kicked aside her husband Matt's Idaho Vandals football jersey.

In early May, when reports emerged about a nasty, new flu virus making the rounds, Mom called and ordered me to come home from college. Kristen and Matt attended graduate school in Moscow, almost three hundred miles north of Boise. I guess it made sense that Mom would summon them back home, too. Gather her chicks, like she used to say.

So, where were Kristen and Matt?

Moving quickly now, I strode down the hallway, checking every room. Dad's study, Mom's craft room, the bathroom, the bonus room over the garage. All empty. I hesitated for a moment outside my bedroom, then turned the knob.

Walking into the room was like stepping inside a time capsule, a snapshot of my life before the flu annihilated the world. I hadn't been home since Easter break—when Kenzie dumped me—almost six months ago. A lifetime ago.

I dropped my backpack on my neatly made bed and glanced around the room. Photos and ticket stubs covered my bulletin board—happy memories from high school and college. My favorite books lined the shelves, the sports stories I read when I was a kid giving way to the spy thrillers I'd swiped from Dad's library. A small, framed photo of Kenzie sat on my desk. I'd snapped the picture when she was curled up on her bed, reading one of her romance novels. She was biting her lower lip, her eyes wide, totally engrossed in the story. The quintessential Kenzie.

Bet Ripper didn't have a photograph of her and wasn't likely to get one, not with the internet down and our cell phones dead. Nowadays, old school was the way to go. I slipped the framed photo into my backpack. Kenzie and Hannah were already planning our first Christmas on the ranch. The photograph would make the perfect present for Ripper.

14

I shook my head. I was stalling, postponing the inevitable. Time to find out what happened to my family. Squaring my shoulders, I steeled my resolve, then jogged down the stairs and stalked through the arched entry into the living room.

Whoever had broken into the house had no interest in the nineteenth-century Flemish landscape painting that hung over the fireplace or in the antique Chinese vase on the mantel. I skirted past Mom's pride and joy—a Steinway grand piano that cost as much as a luxury car—walked through the dining room and pushed open the swinging door into the kitchen.

Mom told me she'd sent Dad on a massive Costco run a few days before she summoned me home, before things got really crazy and the stores were picked clean. She said we were ready to batten down the hatches and ride out the virus. All I had to do was pick up Jake and Ali, and drive back to Boise, a journey that had gone terribly wrong.

I hadn't heard a peep from my family since that call in early May.

Unlike the living room, the kitchen had been tossed. Cabinet doors hung open, revealing shelves stripped bare of all foodstuffs. I pulled a penlight from my pocket and directed the beam into the walk-in pantry. No surprise there. The shelves were empty, except for a jar of pickled asparagus that apparently nobody wanted.

Stepping into the pantry, I turned the light on the whiteboard attached to the back of the door. My methodical mom kept track of everything she stored in the pantry. In neat, block letters, Mom had recorded Dad's Costco haul: three cases of chicken ramen, water, a dozen jars of peanut butter, crackers, and hundreds of cans of soup, tuna, fruit, and vegetables. Whoever raided the place struck pay dirt. They'd left behind the seventeenth-century Chinese porcelain on the mantel and made off with the ramen. That told you everything you needed to know about the state of the world, didn't it?

No food. No family. What had gone down here?

I stilled, an idea occurring to me. *Maybe...*

Kristen and I had tried for years to get Mom and Dad to join the twenty-first century, to switch from paper calendars to planner apps on their phones, but my old-fashioned parents had resisted. I dashed back into the kitchen. A calendar was tacked on the wall above the built-in desk, still showing the month of May.

Kyle and Kristen, Mom had written on the second Sunday of the month, the day I was expected home. Above my name, three red question marks. I imagined my mom tearing out her hair, unable to contact me, wondering why I hadn't showed up. On Wednesday, two words: *Kristen sick*.

My gut clenched. Kristen, my funny, smart sister. Hadn't taken the flu long to worm its way into my family's supposedly impregnable house, had it? On Thursday: *Matt sick*. Smartest guy I ever met, had been working on a PhD in microbiology. On Saturday: *Kristen and Matt gone*. On Wednesday the following week, one word, scrawled in my dad's sloppy script: *Karen*. Mom. A dozen words in total, sketching the obliteration of my family. I dropped onto the desk chair. It was one thing to presume that the virus had taken them, another thing entirely to see the stark evidence of their deaths.

Dad had been the last man standing. What would my quiet, introverted father do while the world fell apart around him, when he lost everybody he loved? I jumped to my feet and walked through the family room to the French doors that led to the backyard. Whenever he was stressed, dad retreated to his woodshop out back.

I stepped onto the brick patio. Three mounds of earth marked the place in the lawn where Dad had buried his wife, daughter, and son-in-law. He'd put his wood working skills to use, assembling and staining crosses, and carving their names into the wood.

"Nice job, Dad," I murmured as I passed by. I pushed open the door to the woodshop, then staggered, burying my nose in the crook of my elbow. I saw immediately what had happened. Dad—sick with the flu—had retreated to his favorite place to await death. He'd spread a sleeping bag on the floor in the corner of the shop and… and…

I stumbled backward, doubled over, then braced my hands on my knees. Shit. Oh, shit. Gasping for air, I forced myself to stand. I couldn't leave my dad's body in a shed. Time to nut up.

I moved like a man in a dream, going through the necessary motions, but disconnected somehow from my surroundings. One small step at a time, that was the only way I could force myself to see it through. *March to the garage. Grab a shovel. Dig a hole next to my mother's grave. Drag the sleeping bag to the hole. Tip Dad's body into the grave. Cover him up.*

That done, I sank to my knees. The mental fog that had shielded me from grief dissipated. "I love you guys," I choked out. There was some small comfort in laying Dad to rest next to Mom. Together in life. Together in death. Probably more than many couples had nowadays.

I sighed. All my questions had been answered. My family's survival had always been a long shot, the trip a likely wild-goose chase. Now I had to look forward, to focus on building a life with my new family.

"I'm okay, Mom," I told her. "I survived the flu. I've got friends and a safe place to stay. The Chamberlains aren't done, and you won't be forgotten."

I stood and glanced at the late afternoon sky. I couldn't make it back to Valhalla today; besides, I liked the idea of spending one final night at the house where I'd grown up. With a last look at my family's graves, I went back inside and bolted all the doors. Odds were nobody would try to break into the place, but I'd learned to be cautious.

I changed into a clean pair of jeans and a T-shirt, then dug through my dresser and packed my favorite shirts and pants to take with me back to the ranch. Since the pantry had been ransacked—except for the pickled asparagus—I ate my own provisions for dinner. After chowing down on a can of ravioli, I wandered the old place, taking a last look at my childhood home. Hidden at the bottom of a desk drawer in Dad's study, I found a bottle of his favorite scotch. Scotch wasn't my drink—not even this expensive stuff—but I took a couple of swigs in honor of dad. I sat down at the piano and played a halting rendition of "Greensleeves". Kristen had loved our piano lessons. I'd bitched so much about them that Mom let me quit after six months. It was sad to realize that my hands would be the last to touch this beautiful instrument.

The sun set, and I retreated to my bedroom. Might as well turn in early so I could leave at first light.

I hung the shoulder holster on the back of my desk chair and set the Glock on the nightstand within easy reach. Yawning, I peeled off my tee and tossed it onto the chair. Somewhere in the distance, a dog howled. Instantly alert, I edged up to the window and drew aside the curtain, surveying the neighborhood. Moonlight touched dark houses and empty streets. I'd never seen the place so quiet and devoid of life.

Light flickered in my peripheral vision and I turned my head. Was I imagining things? No. Across the street, a light bobbled behind the drawn shade in one of the upstairs bedrooms at the McAllisters' place.

Somebody was in Jake's house? Pawing through his family's stuff? Helping themselves to whatever they liked?

Hell, no. Adrenaline surged through my veins. I stuck the gun in my waistband—the trigger safety would keep it from discharging—and ran toward the stairs, my fingers fumbling in my front pocket.

I slipped out of the house, jogged across the street, then let myself in through the McAllisters' locked front door. I knew the place almost as well as my own, so I didn't need a flashlight to stealthily make my way up the stairs and down the hall toward the corner bedroom. Holding my breath, I slowly turned the doorknob.

The looter mustn't have expected to be interrupted; the knob twisted easily in my hand. I took one cautious step into the room, then paused. Behind me, someone panted, their panic-struck shallow breaths betraying their hiding place. I turned to confront them and sensed rather than saw an object arcing toward my head. I dodged left, then launched at my assailant, grappling them around the waist. Struggling, we shuffled across the floor, then fell across the bed. I rolled and pinned them beneath me. They bucked and writhed in a vain attempt to throw me off.

"What do you think you're doing, asshole?" I demanded.

The figure stilled. "Kyle?"

I drew back and peered down at a familiar face. Shock locked my limbs in place and robbed me of speech. I swallowed and found my voice.

"Sunny?"

THREE

Sunny

Kyle gaped down at me.
    Not so long ago, the prospect of Kyle Chamberlain sprawled on top of me, his bare, sculpted chest mere inches away from my hands, would have sent my girl parts into hyperdrive. But now—holy shitballs—with my heart thumping and my torso squashed, my girl parts couldn't care less. Instead of fondling the chest I'd secretly swooned over for years, I shoved at him with both hands.

"Can't breathe," I choked out.

"Sorry." He rolled off me, jumped to his feet, then offered a hand to pull me into a seated position. I dragged air into my lungs. We stared at each other, both wide-eyed with shock.

The brain-clouding panic subsided, and memories rushed in to fill the void. Kyle was the last person to see my brother. I clutched his arm.

"Is Jake with you?" Kyle jerked back as if stung and pain filled his eyes. The answer to my question was stamped across his face. My jaw trembled. "He's dead, isn't he?"

"Yeah." His voice was gentle. "Jake's dead."

I wasn't surprised, not really. I mean, the flu had nearly turned Boise into a ghost town. If Jake had somehow survived, he would have come home. His continued absence should have been all the confirmation I needed. Intellectually, I'd made peace with his loss months ago. Still, a tiny part of my heart had hoped that my big brother was alive and that we'd find our way back to each other someday.

"How did it happen?" I asked.

"Last May—early on in the pandemic—Jake and Ali and I were driving home from Portland."

I nodded. "I remember. It was a Sunday. Our parents said that we might lose power so we should use up the meat in our freezers. They planned to have a barbecue when you guys showed up. My dad thawed out a bunch of rib eyes, and your mom baked a German chocolate cake."

"Mom made my favorite cake?"

From his agonized expression I could tell that he knew. He knew his parents were dead, just like my parents, just like most of the people in the world. I took his hand and tugged him down to sit next to me. Skin to skin at last, his fingers warm against mine, electricity hummed along our joined hands. With his free hand, Kyle pulled a gun out of his waistband and laid it on the bed. The sparks of electricity faded, the sight of the gun like a splash of cold water.

"What happened to them?" I asked.

"Jake and Ali seemed fine when we left Portland. A couple of hours later, they started to show symptoms of the flu. We stopped in Pendleton." He paused, staring straight ahead. "They both died during the night."

I had to know. "They didn't get the flu mania?"

He squeezed my fingers. "No. Thank God. At least they were spared that."

"Thank God," I echoed, shuddering as an image flashed before my eyes. Mrs. Kaminski wandering up the middle of the street, naked, clutching a pair of bloody scissors. I'd crouched down behind a car. She'd howled like a banshee when she passed my hiding place.

Pain bit deep with every death, but you either kept going— searching for ways to connect with other survivors and do some good—or you lay down and waited to die. After all the losses of the past few months, I knew I'd survive Jake's death. I wasn't sure I could've handled hearing that my easy going brother had fallen into homicidal mania.

"Why didn't you come home after Jake and Ali died?"

"I decided to go back to Portland to look for Kenzie."

Kenzie, the beautiful ex-girlfriend. I'd overheard Mrs. Chamberlain telling my mom how relieved she was when they split up over Easter. I'd been relieved, too, although for a different reason. An entirely selfish reason.

So, Kyle still carried a torch for Kenzie.

I fixed my eyes on our twined fingers, my stomach clenching. "I thought you guys broke up."

He took so long to answer that I finally looked up at his face.

Kyle shoved a hand through dark-blond hair that touched his collar, quite a change from his usual high-maintenance taper fade haircut. Longer hair suited him. Unlike the short, fastidious style, it invited touch. The longer strands practically begged to be mussed, to be swept back from his brow when they fell across his eyes.

"We did break up," he said, "but I thought... well... never mind what I thought. Long story short, I found her. She'd fallen in love with another guy. They're immune, and they're still together."

"Really?" My gaze darted to his face. Maybe I should tell him that I was sorry that Kenzie had fallen in love with another man, but I couldn't lie. "Are you okay with that?"

He shrugged. "It took a while, but yeah, I'm okay with it. In fact, we've all settled down at Valhalla, a ranch in central Oregon."

"Together?" I asked, incredulous. "You live with Kenzie and the man she fell in love with?"

"Not just them," he said quickly. "Other friends, too." He swept out his hand, gesturing toward the outside world. "You must have seen what it's like out there. When almost everybody you've ever known is dead, you aren't going to walk away from a familiar face. You find a way to make it work."

"I get that," I said. "You're the only person alive who remembers my family and who knows our stories." My eyes filled with tears. "Mom's corny jokes. That time Dad's homemade root beer exploded all over the basement. How Jake fell off his skateboard, bumped his chin, and swallowed his loose tooth. You never feel more alone than when you realize that nobody shares your memories. I understand why you'd want to stay connected to Kenzie."

Kyle threw an arm over my shoulders and pulled me close for a hug. My heart went ka-thump. "Finding you is a miracle, Sunshine."

The childhood nickname did me in. I buried my face into his chest and held on tight. I'd fantasized about wrapping myself around Kyle, but never like this, while seeking comfort from an old friend after the world fell apart.

"So what happened in Northumberland Heights?" Kyle asked.

"Pretty much what happened everywhere else, I imagine," I said. "More and more people got the flu. The security guards stopped showing up for work. We lost power. The Home Owners Association asked neighbors to take turns watching the gate. That worked for a couple of days, until too many people got sick. Everybody locked their doors and tried to ride it out."

"Did you see my folks?" Kyle asked.

"I checked in on them on that Friday. We had a lot of bananas that were starting to go soft. Fresh fruit was going to be hard to come by, so I thought I'd share. Your dad came to the door carrying a shotgun. He said somebody broke into the house behind yours the night before. He said Kristen and Matt were sick. When she heard my voice, your mom came to the door. She asked how we were doing, then told me to get home and stay safe. Actually, she said, 'Use the sense God gave you and stop gallivanting around the neighborhood.'"

Kyle snorted. "Yeah, that sounds like Mom."

"That was the last time I saw your folks."

We sat in silence for another minute.

"How about your parents?" he asked.

"We were fine for the first two weeks." I closed my eyes and shuddered, remembering the day everything went to hell.

Kyle gently stroked a hand up and down my back. He was finally touching me, a caress I'd fantasized about for years, just not like this, not when he was offering consolation. "You don't have to tell me if talking about it hurts too much."

"No." I shook my head. "I want you to know." Kyle loved my family, and it felt right somehow that he understood what happened to them, that the memory—even secondhand—would be something we shared. "Mom woke up with a headache and a fever. By the middle of the afternoon, she was gone. Dad and I dug a grave in the backyard, next to the gazebo. Dad was sweaty and pale, and I was afraid that he was getting sick. We carried mom's body out back, and then… and then…" I paused, images from the worst day of my life rushing in. Kyle's arm tightened around me. I swallowed and pushed on. "And then Dad collapsed next to Mom's grave. A stroke or a heart attack. I tried CPR, but it didn't work."

"I'm so sorry, Sunny," Kyle murmured.

I swallowed, my throat too thick to speak. Kyle pulled me onto his lap, and we rocked back and forth, holding on to each other. I tucked my head under his chin and splayed my fingers across his chest. You don't realize how much you miss human contact until you're deprived of it. I burrowed into Kyle, savoring the warmth of his skin, the warmth of his personality. I'd made new connections since the pandemic struck but holding onto my old friend felt damned good.

"It's going to be all right," Kyle breathed. "You aren't alone anymore. I'm here."

This was almost too good to be true. Kyle's reappearance felt like the answer to a prayer, as if my imagination had conjured up my dream man. Was he really here? I bit the tip of my tongue, testing reality. The pain did nothing to banish his presence. Not an illusion then. Kyle had truly returned.

"Kyle." I sighed happily, snuggling into his chest.

"We're going to pack up your things, and you'll come back to Valhalla with me."

Pack up and go to Valhalla? Hold on. I lifted my head to meet Kyle's eyes. "I can't leave Boise. People here are counting on me."

Kyle's eyes narrowed, and he looked confused. "Of course, you can leave Boise. There's nothing left for you here, nothing left for either of us. You'll come back to the ranch with me where it's safe, where I can take care of you."

Would Kyle always see me as Jake's baby sister, a kid he had to watch out for? "You're not listening to me." Exasperation colored my voice. "I told you that people here are counting on me. I have responsibilities." I turned in his lap to face him straight on. "Tell you what, instead of me coming back to the ranch with you, how about you stay in Boise with me? It's our hometown, and people need our help."

FOUR

Kyle

"I can't believe you're still driving the Refrigerator."

Sunny huffed indignantly from behind the wheel of her ancient, white economy van and patted the dashboard. "Don't you bad mouth Daisy. She gets me from point A to point B, and she has lots of room to carry stuff."

I couldn't argue with that point. The thing had plenty of room to carry the bags of cat food and litter that companies donated to the no-kill cat shelter where Sunny had volunteered. More than enough room for the food she'd delivered once a week for Meals on Wheels. All that cargo space was the argument she used when Jake and I tried to talk her out of buying a twenty-year-old van with almost 200,000 miles on the odometer.

Most of her friends wheedled their parents into buying them a *cute* car. Not Sunny. She worked fast food part time during her junior year of high school and proudly purchased a boxy monstrosity that couldn't do fifty miles per hour against a headwind. Jake and I dubbed it "the Refrigerator." Sunny slapped bright-yellow flower decals over the rusty spots on the paint and christened it Daisy.

When my mom complained that it brought down the tone of the neighborhood, Sunny added plastic car eyelashes to the headlights. Mom had conniptions, prompting her first real fight with

Naomi McAllister. A week later, Sunny peeled off the garish car lashes. She told me that she couldn't stand to cause strife between our mothers. Sunny's always been softhearted, sometimes too much for her own good.

"All I'm saying is that you could have your pick of reliable, newer cars," I said. The post-pandemic world was lousy with vehicles whose owners had died. It wouldn't be hard to find a neighbor who'd left their car keys in a bowl on the kitchen counter or hanging on a hook.

"I like Daisy," Sunny said in a voice that would brook no further argument. She'd always been stubborn—especially when she thought she was right—so there was no point in pushing. I threw my hands in the air, giving up. For now.

"So where exactly is this Haven place we're going to?" I swiveled my head from side to side, scanning the street for any sign of danger.

"It's at a small hospital close to downtown." Sunny rounded a corner and the Refrigerator—Daisy—approached a pair of stationary vehicles that blocked the lane ahead of us. The back of the second car angled into the oncoming lane.

What would Ripper do?

Ripper would be leery of an ambush. I tugged my Glock from its holster and turned toward the window as Sunny pulled around the cars. When my fingers closed around the grip, my pulse ratcheted up, far more than the situation warranted. I shook my head, banishing the sudden memory of two staggering pillars of flame.

"Seriously?" she said. "Do you intend to draw a weapon every time we drive past a couple of parked cars? Paranoid much?"

Paranoid? I waited until we were well past the cars before turning back to Sunny and holstering the Glock. Before the pandemic, she would have been the absolute last person I'd expect to carry a handgun. But now—in a lawless world full of desperate people—even she had to see the necessity of being ready to defend herself. "Please tell me that you're not driving around town without a weapon."

"I'm not stupid," she said indignantly. "Dr. Russo—she's in charge of the Haven—she sends us out scavenging in teams of two, and one of us always carries a gun."

"How about now?" I pointed at the small pack she'd dropped on the floor between our seats. "Are you carrying a gun?"

She shifted in the car seat. "Not exactly." At my raised brows, she continued. "I carry pepper spray when I'm on my own, just in case I run into trouble."

"Pepper spray?" Before the flu laid waste to the world, that had been Kenzie's first line of defense, too. Pepper spray hadn't done Kenz a darned bit of good the first time she confronted Ripper, and it wouldn't stop a determined assailant from attacking Sunny. Pepper spray. Jesus. "Okay." I deliberately maintained a reasonable tone. "We'll ask Dr. Russo for a handgun, and I'll show you how to use it."

She shot me an irritated look. "Listen, I know that there are scary people out there, but let's not over react. Most of the folks I come across are good people just trying to get by. Nobody's pulled a gun on me. Nobody's threatened me."

"Then you're damned lucky." I scrubbed my hands over my face and sucked in a breath, calming myself. I'd always admired Sunny's idealism and her desire to help others, but the new world wouldn't cosset a bleeding-heart do-gooder. A beautiful young woman like Sunny was bound to attract the attention of some predatory asshole. The need to protect her, to keep her safe, hit me hard. "How about I teach you to shoot—just in case a situation gets out of hand—and you start to carry a real weapon. Humor me, will you?"

"What happened to make you so cynical?" she demanded, ignoring my suggestion.

"What happened to me?" My temper slipped its reins. It was past time for Sunny to face some stark realities. "Let's see. I got shot by a trigger-happy security guard. Dealt with an arsonist and a bomber. Faced down a crazy religious cult and fought a group of white supremacists." I clamped my jaw shut, biting back the rest of the story. No need to tell Sunny that I'd shot and killed three men, one of them a friend.

"Kyle!" Sunny braked, bringing Daisy to a hard stop. She whirled to face me and laid a hand on my shoulder, compassion stamped across her pretty features. "Are you all right?"

I blinked. I was anything but all right, my nights still haunted by the gruesome memories of the men I'd killed. At the sight of her kindhearted concern, my irritation evaporated. I couldn't be angry at Sunny. Until a few months ago, my life had been as sheltered as hers. Thank God she hadn't had to face the horrors I'd witnessed, but that good fortune couldn't last. If she kept tooling round town essentially unarmed, the realities of the new world would smack her upside the head soon enough.

"I'm all right, Sunny," I said. "Everybody has had a hard time during the past four months. I'm dealing."

Her amber eyes brimmed with tears. "If you ever want to talk about it, I'm here."

Tell Sunny—Jake's little sister—about all the nightmarish events I'd witnessed? No way. I stopped myself from shaking my head to reject her offer. Instead, I clasped her hand and gently squeezed her fingers. "Thanks. I'll keep that in mind."

This was why I came to Boise, I realized with a sudden clarity. To reconnect with Sunny. To bring her to safety. She was too tenderhearted and too reckless to survive on her own. The faster I could get her back to Valhalla, the better. Finding my parents alive had been the longest of long shots. I'd known that before I started the journey, yet I'd felt compelled to make the trip. Maybe divine providence guided my hand and set the wheels in motion. I hadn't been able to save Jake, but fate handed me another chance to do right by my best friend by watching out for his sister.

Sunny took her foot off the brake and drove downtown. She parked next to a side entrance to a hospital, and we hopped out of the van. When she stepped onto the sidewalk, the car keys slipped from her fingers. She bent over to pick them up, putting on display a perfect, upside-down-heart-shaped ass.

An ass I had no business noticing. What the hell was I doing? I jerked my gaze away from the enticing sight and looked at the door to the hospital. A middle-aged woman perched on a stool outside the entry, a shotgun cradled in her arms.

"See." Sunny pointed at the woman. "We have security." The woman raised a hand in greeting as we passed.

Inside the double doors, to our left, a wall of windows illuminated a former waiting room. Instead of neat rows of chairs filling the space, privacy curtains tacked to the ceiling divided the area into treatment rooms. It was a smart use of natural light now that the power grid had collapsed.

To our right, more windows spilled light across a former coffee shop. Half a dozen people sat at the tables, sorting through piles of stuff. A man with a clipboard was apparently cataloging a mountain of canned food. Two tables were heaped high with clothing and shoes. At another table, a powerfully built man—his forearms covered with tattoos—examined bottles of prescription medicines, a pen and ledger at his side. He lifted his head and flashed a smile at Sunny.

"Hey, Rocco," Sunny called, waving at him. "Rocco was an obstetric nurse. He keeps track of our meds."

I lifted a hand in greeting. "I doubt many nurses survived. You're lucky to have him."

"We are and not just because he knows about medications. He's a great guy, super friendly, always willing to help out."

I frowned. Why did her enthusiastic praise for the man rub me the wrong way? People bonded quickly at the end of the world, but it hadn't occurred to me that Sunny might have found love during the past four months. I thought of Sunny as Jake's kid sister, but at twenty-one—only thirteen months younger than Jake—she was no kid. Men outnumbered women in the post-pandemic world. An attractive young woman like Sunny would have no shortage of suitors.

"Are you two..." I pointed between Sunny and Rocco, leaving the question hanging in the air.

A pink flush crept across her cheeks. She shook her head. "No, Rocco and I are friends. That's all."

The tension in my chest eased, replaced by a jolt of relief.

"Good," I said.

Sunny glanced at me, her brows raised, before moving on.

An elderly man sat at the reception desk in the middle of the foyer, several file folders stacked neatly in front of him. "Hi, Ed." Sunny smiled at the gray-haired man. "This is my friend, Kyle."

"Kyle." He nodded at me, his gaze reassuringly sharp and assessing. I was glad to see his wariness. He should be cautious of any stranger.

"Nice to meet you, sir."

Sunny touched Ed's arm. "We couldn't do without Ed. He keeps track of everybody who comes in for treatment or supplies."

"I was an accountant," Ed said. "I'm older than dirt, so paper records are nothing new to me."

"Sounds like you're the right man for the job," I said.

"That I am."

"Do you know where Sara is?" Sunny asked. "I need to talk to her."

Ed pointed toward the curtained cubicles. "Dr. Russo is setting a broken arm."

"I'll show Kyle around while we wait for her to finish up."

Ed handed her a solar powered lantern—the kind Miles had stockpiled. Sunny grabbed my hand and led me around the reception desk toward a hallway. "All of our storage rooms are along this corridor." She opened the first door. "Our pharmacy. Our scavengers bring back all the pill bottles and first aid supplies they come across. Combined with all the meds from the hospital pharmacy, we have a good supply."

I followed her inside the room. Metal shelving units held boxes full of both over-the-counter and prescription medications. I glanced at a box on a shelf near the door. Somebody had written *prenatal vitamins* on the front with a black Sharpie. Next to it, a box labeled *childrens vitamins*. Another box marked *adult vitamins*. The place appeared well organized and well stocked.

"Come on." Sunny tugged my hand and pulled me back into the hall. A wiry man with a reddish beard bustled past us carrying an armful of heavy winter coats. "Hi, Gavin," Sunny called. "Gavin is second-in-command around here," she explained.

He tossed a smile over his shoulder, then awkwardly shifted the coats to one arm while he reached for the doorknob of a room marked Community Closet.

"Let me help." I jumped forward and opened the door.

"Thanks, man." He tilted his head at the pile of coats. "We're expecting a cold winter. Want to make sure we have enough coats for everybody who needs one."

Confusion furrowed my brow. "Back in Portland, survivors cleaned out the grocery and liquor stores fast. Pharmacies and weed shops, too, but the department stores still had plenty of clothes left. I mean, how many winter coats does one person need? Is it really likely that you're going to run low on them?"

Gavin and Sunny exchanged a glance. Gavin dropped the pile of coats on a table inside the door of the community closet, then he turned to me. "Sounds like you don't have anybody like the Nampa Boys in Portland."

"The Nampa Boys?"

"That's what they call themselves," Sunny said. "They're a group of teenage flu survivors from Nampa who banded together. They all wear blue baseball caps with NB written on the front."

"They tag a building with their name to warn other survivors to keep their hands off whatever is inside," Gavin added "Our scavengers first bumped into them when we went to check out a pharmacy in Meridian. They've laid claim to Nampa, Caldwell, Meridian, most of the cities close to Boise. We signed a treaty with them. We stay out of the places they've claimed, and they stay out of Boise. The arrangement has worked, mostly."

"Mostly?" I asked.

"In the last couple of weeks, we've started to see the words Nampa Boys spray-painted on some buildings inside the Boise city limits." Gavin shook his head. "Violating the treaty makes no sense. It's benefited both sides. But who knows what's going on with them. Maybe their leader is losing his grip on his people."

"I saw two Nampa Boys downtown yesterday," Sunny said. "They were breaking windows and tagging buildings. That's what I need to talk to Dr. Russo about."

Holy hell. What was going on in my hometown? Was war brewing between rival bands of survivors? If so, the Haven would need more than one woman with a shotgun standing guard over their stockpile of supplies. I glanced at Sunny. The danger she'd so far escaped might be heading her way.

"We haven't had any direct confrontations with the Nampa Boys," Gavin said.

"Yet," I muttered, my imagination spinning with dire possibilities.

"Anyway," he continued, "our scavengers are making sure to pick up everything we might need, just in case things escalate between our groups."

"You were asking to see me, Sunny?" A young woman wearing a white lab coat walked toward us. Her dark hair was pulled back in a messy ponytail that had slipped sideways on her head. Purplish smudges stained the skin under her bloodshot eyes. Despite her obvious exhaustion, she smiled at us as she approached.

"Yes." Sunny hugged the woman. "First things first, Dr. Sara Russo, meet Kyle Chamberlain. Kyle and I grew up on the same street, and he was my brother's best friend. Kyle, Dr. Russo was a third-year resident in emergency medicine when the flu struck. She runs the Haven."

"Call me Sara." Dr. Russo extended a slim hand to me. She tilted her head and studied me with a quizzical expression. "You weren't in Boise when the pandemic started?"

"No." I shook my head. "I was going to school in Portland. I came back to town yesterday to check on my parents. They're gone, but I found Sunny."

"I'm sorry about your family, but you and Sunny finding each other is amazing," she said. "Most of us never get the chance to reconnect with an old friend."

"We're lucky," Sunny agreed. "Now I'm trying to convince Kyle to stay in Boise and help out here."

Trust Sunny to blurt out whatever was on her mind. The girl couldn't do subtle or subterfuge if her life depended on it. All right. I'd match her forthright declaration with one of my own.

"And I'm trying to convince Sunny to come back to Oregon with me." All eyes turned toward me. "I'm staying with friends at a ranch in the central part of the state. We've got food, water, weapons. The ranch is way off the beaten track. She'd be safer with me than in the city dealing with the Nampa Boys."

"Sunny saw Nampa Boys tagging a building downtown yesterday," Gavin said.

"Dammit." Sara shook her head. "We've coexisted for months. Why would they break the treaty now?" Her expression clouded, and she touched Sunny's shoulder. "Maybe you should think about Kyle's offer. We'd all miss you like crazy if you left, but it would be good to know you're someplace safe."

"Nope. I'm part of the team. I'm not bailing on you guys."

At her intransigence, my heart sank. Valhalla was my home. I'd no more abandon Ripper and Kenzie and the others than I'd turn my back on my family. If Sunny felt the same way about the Haven, we'd end up butting heads. There was absolutely no way that I'd walk away from this spirited woman who already made me feel more alive than I had in months. Shit. Why couldn't she see reason and put herself first?

Commotion at the hospital entrance drew our attention. Two men staggered through the double doors. The taller of the two had slung his arm around his companion's shoulders, leaning heavily on him. Sara ran toward them, with Sunny, Gavin, and me close behind.

"What happened?" the doctor demanded, easing the tall man into a chair. Pale and dripping sweat, he slumped sideways, pressing a hand against his chest.

"The Nampa Boys," the shorter man gasped. "Two pickups blockaded our car. Men wearing blue baseball caps fired shots in the air. One guy shouted, 'Boise belongs to us.' Then they pulled away." He pointed at his companion. "I think Larry is having a heart attack."

FIVE

Sunny

"I'm coming with you," I said to Kyle's back.

Kyle slid extra ammunition into the pocket of his shoulder holster. He turned to face me, his expression tight. "You're not coming with me. Jake would have my head if I put you in harm's way."

After stabilizing Larry, Sara met with Gavin and Ed, the other members of the Haven's executive committee. They were drafting a message to the Nampa Boys, and Kyle volunteered to deliver it.

"We're dropping off a note, not going into battle," I said. I waited a few seconds for him to respond. He didn't. "I've done it before, you know. Left messages for the Nampa Boys."

That got his attention. "Are you telling me that they've sent you *by yourself* to a deserted park close to enemy territory?"

Enemy territory? Good grief, Kyle was over reacting. Planting my hands on my hips, I gazed up at him. He loomed over me, his face set in stern lines. Heat flushed my cheeks. Indignation battled with reluctant exhilaration. His over protectiveness got under my skin in more than one way.

I poked his chest. "First, the drop-off spot is on neutral ground. We've agreed not to confront each other there. Second, we use the buddy system around here. Scavengers, messengers, we never go out alone and unarmed." My conscience pinged. Except for on the rare occasions when I made a quick stop by myself, but yesterday was the first time that even threatened to go wrong. "And third, we aren't at war with the Nampa Boys. The truce has held for months."

His brows angled up. "Tagging buildings? Blockading cars? Firing shots in the air? You telling me that those are the actions of a friend?"

"Of course not. That's why Sara is asking for a meeting, to figure out what's going on. Maybe they *are* backing out of the treaty. Or maybe they have discipline problems, and some Nampa Boys are going rogue. We don't know what's going on, hence the parley."

"I don't like it." Kyle scowled and crossed his arms over his chest, an action that made his biceps bulge, which distracted me no end. Not fair.

"Leaving a note at the drop-off spot is a low-risk operation." I pointed at his gun. "But if anything goes wrong, you're armed. And I know the exact spot where to leave the message. We'll be in and out fast."

Conflicting emotions danced across his face, his knee-jerk desire to protect me at war with reason. "All right," he muttered, his expression unhappy.

Mom always said that it never hurts to be gracious in victory. I smiled. "Thanks."

I knocked on the door of the conference room. Gavin stepped into the hall and handed me the envelope. "Check back at the hospital once you've delivered the message."

"Will do. Afterward, I'd like to take Kyle with me on a scavenging run, so he can see what I do around here."

Gavin clapped me on the shoulder, then handed me a pair of the red vests all the Haven scavengers wore to identify ourselves. "Good idea."

Kyle and I walked back to Daisy. I tossed the red vests onto the back seat.

Twenty minutes after we left downtown Boise, we arrived at the small park on the east side of Meridian. The place appeared desolate, the basketball courts, baseball diamond, and playground equipment empty. Between the bathrooms and the picnic shelters, a dozen public barbecue grills dotted the knee-high grass. With their rusty grates and piles of ash, even before the pandemic, these public grills struck me as kind of yucky. After months of neglect, they now looked even the worse for wear.

I led Kyle to the most decrepit grill, the one with a charred brick supporting one side of the grate. Brushing aside the mountain of ash that covered the bottom of the grill, I pulled out a thin hinged metal box and popped the lid. It was empty.

"Our message drop," I said. "If we need to communicate with the Nampa Boys, we leave a note here. Both sides check the box on Saturday and Wednesday late in the afternoon." I folded the envelope from Gavin in half, slipped it into the box, and buried it under the ash. "It's Wednesday. They'll see the invitation to the meet-up within a couple of hours."

Kyle scanned our surroundings before turning his eyes back toward me. "Meridian is Nampa Boys territory, right?"

"Yes, but the park is a no man's land. Unless things have completely gone to hell, we shouldn't have any trouble."

"I feel eyes on us," he said, reaching for his gun. "Let's get out of here."

The happy-go-lucky charmer I'd grown up with was gone, wasn't he? The new Kyle had an edge—a hardness—that the old Kyle never possessed. It made me shiver, but not in an unpleasant way. He was still Kyle, still charismatic and a bit cocky, but the amiable, easygoing young man was no more. Whatever he had experienced during the past months had changed my old friend.

We climbed into Daisy and sat in silence as I drove west to the Haven headquarters. Kyle kept his gun on his lap and his gaze on our surroundings. His vigilance was unnerving. Boise was almost empty. We'd found no more than two hundred people alive in the city. Until yesterday afternoon, I hadn't had any close calls. I assumed that the few survivors meant me no harm. I felt safe behind the van's locked doors, with the pepper spray on hand. Had I been too careless? Too unwary of danger?

I parked next to the hospital's entrance. "You might as well wait in the van. I won't be a minute," I said. Before Kyle could protest, I jumped out of the van and jogged inside. Ed was back behind the reception desk. The executive committee's meeting must be over. "Tell Gavin that we dropped off the message, please."

"Will do." Ed glanced at my face, frowning. "You all right, honey?"

"Kyle thinks that I need to learn how to shoot and that I should carry a gun. What do you think?"

"I'd say it's about time."

"Really?" I hadn't expected such a simple, straightforward answer. Ed was the guy who balanced pros and cons, looking at both sides of every argument when the Haven debated a course of action.

"Yep."

I glanced over my shoulder. Kyle watched our conversation intently. "Thanks, Ed. I'll think about it." I waved at Rocco and the others, then hurried back to the van.

"You up for some scavenging, Haven style?" I asked, fastening my seat belt.

Kyle tilted his head. "What does Haven style mean?"

"We wear red vests to identify ourselves. We always knock on the doors in case a survivor lives in the house. If we find a survivor, we write down the address for Ed's records, and we tell them about the Haven. Most places are empty. Some have already been hit by looters. For the past week, we've been working our way up and down the streets on the west side of town."

"Sounds simple enough. So, we're looking for nonperishable foods, medicine, and weapons?" he asked.

"Yeah, and we check the garages, too, for gasoline and motor oil, stuff we need to keep our cars running."

I drove to a residential street about a mile from Mrs. B's place and parked in front of a blue house. Three houses on the street sported red X's spray-painted on the front door. Kyle glanced at the red X's and raised his eyebrows.

"The X means we've checked the house." I tossed him a vest and slipped into my own, then picked up empty cardboard boxes from the back of the van, a can of spray paint, and a crowbar. "Grab some more boxes, will you?"

"Sure." He tucked the boxes under his left arm, leaving his right hand free. His piercing gaze moved up and down the quiet, tree-lined street before settling on me. "I'll go first." Without waiting for my reply, he led the way up the walk toward the blue house. He pounded his fist on the door and cocked his head, listening intently. After a minute, he pounded on the door again. No sounds came from inside the house.

Kyle twisted the doorknob. Locked. The homeowners had installed a heavy entry door with a dead bolt. There might be an easier way inside. "Sometimes people leave their back doors unlocked," I said. "And even if the doors are latched, a lot of times the wood is flimsier, and the locks are easier to break."

Kyle smiled down at me, and butterflies danced in my stomach. "Never would've pegged you for an expert on breaking and entering."

"I got mad new skills," I purred, only half kidding. "You'd be astonished."

"Is that right?" he said slowly. Kyle tilted his head and studied me through narrowed eyes. "What other talents have you been hiding from me?"

"Wouldn't you like to know?" I fluttered my eyelashes.

"Sunny," he said in the exact same reproachful tone he and Jake used when I was fifteen and said something that scandalized them.

It was past time for Kyle Chamberlain to figure out that I wasn't a kid anymore. I stepped close and laid my palms on his chest. "Ask yourself, after all these years, why are you just now wondering about my hidden talents?"

He blinked and his Adam's apple bobbed. Good. I'd confounded him. It was a start.

Whirling around, I started toward the side yard. Kyle caught up and led the way through a gate in the fence. His walk had changed during the past months, his stride purposeful as he stalked toward the back porch. Were his shoulders wider, too? I mentally fanned myself.

We walked around an overgrown flower bed until we came to a small patio. A single step led to a wooden back door. Four glass windowpanes filled the top half of the door. The interior shades were drawn, blocking our view into the house.

"If we can't jimmy the lock, we can break the glass," Kyle said. He tried the knob and when it didn't turn, I handed him the crowbar. He took a credit card from his wallet, pried open the door with the crowbar, and slid the card through the latch.

"Talk about mad new skills," I muttered. The old Kyle would never have used a credit card to break into a locked house.

He flashed a self-satisfied grin, one that made my toes curl. "You're not the only one with hidden talents, Sunshine." Triumph turned to aggravation when he tried to push the door open. "Something is jammed under the knob." He grunted, shoving hard against the wood. After a minute, whatever it was gave way, and the door swung open. We stepped inside and found a kitchen chair lying on its side on the linoleum.

"Somebody blocked the door from the inside," I observed. If the homeowners had barricaded the house before succumbing to the flu, the place would have reeked of death. I sniffed. The air smelled musty, not putrid. I scanned the room. Mason jars filled with canned fruits and vegetables covered the counter. A spoon protruded from an open jar half full of peaches.

We weren't alone.

Catching Kyle's eye, I angled my head toward the counter. He reached for his gun.

"Ahhh!"

A small figure brandishing a baseball bat burst through the arched opening to the hallway. Matted reddish-blond hair tumbled around the shoulders of a little girl who rushed straight for Kyle, wielding the bat like a war club.

Kyle pivoted toward her, raising his weapon.

Oh, crap.

SIX

Kyle

"No," Sunny shrieked, launching herself between the girl and me. She grabbed the bat, wresting it out of the girl's hands and tossing it onto the floor.

I shoved the Glock into the holster. Oh, man, that was close. All my lessons with Ripper—all his reminders about keeping my finger off the trigger and making sure of my target before I fired—really paid off big-time. I'd come *this* close to shooting a kid.

I leaped forward and grappled with the girl, locking her arms against her sides in a bear hug. Hissing and spitting, she flailed against me.

"Nobody is going to hurt you," I gritted out. "I promise."

"Lemme go." The little spitfire writhed in my grip. Hard to believe that a kid who barely reached my chest could put up such a fight. I tightened my hold, careful not to squeeze too hard. The last thing I wanted to do was to hurt her or let her hurt herself while she fought against me.

"I'll let you go as soon as you calm down," I said.

She stomped on my foot.

"Sweetheart," Sunny said in a soothing tone. "It's all right. We don't mean you any harm."

SUSANNA STROM

Ignoring Sunny's comforting words, the girl continued to struggle. She banged her head against my chest and kicked at my shins. "Cut it out," I grunted.

Sunny stepped forward and caught the child's face between her palms. "Hey. Look at me." When the kid stopped thrashing, Sunny offered a reassuring smile. "You're okay. We're nice people. We want to help."

"Don't need help," the girl muttered, her brows drawn down in a scowl. "I can take care of myself." Her grubby appearance gave the lie to that assertion. Dirty, tangled hair hung past her shoulders. Her clothes could use a wash. Shoot, *she* could use a wash. The kid positively reeked.

"My name is Sunny, and this is my friend Kyle. Do you promise to hold still if Kyle lets you go?"

I wasn't so sure that I trusted any promise the kid made, but I didn't want to contradict Sunny after she got the girl to stop squirming.

"Okay," the girl said, her tone begrudging.

"Kyle." Sunny shot me a pointed look.

I released the little girl but braced myself to grab her if she struck out again or tried to run. She backed up against a cabinet.

"What's your name?" Sunny asked gently.

A long pause. The kid's inner struggle showed on her face, and her gaze darted between Sunny and me. "Ever," she finally said.

"Ever," Sunny repeated. "That's a pretty name."

The girl nodded, agreeing with Sunny. "Mom said they named me Ever because I'm the best girl ever."

The *best girl ever* had just tried to bean me with a baseball bat. She blinked and shifted from foot to foot, like a jackrabbit ready to bolt. Crap. I could only imagine what had happened in the past few months to make the kid so skittish.

I dropped down on my haunches so I wouldn't tower over her. "Where's your mom now, Ever?" I asked.

Wrong question. Her face flushed, then crumpled. Tears welled in her eyes. She bent forward, hugging her stomach while she gasped for breath.

Sunny rushed to her side. She stretched out a hand, as if she wanted to comfort the girl, but hesitated before touching her. "I'm sorry, sweetie."

42

Ever lifted her head and studied my friend's face. Maybe the girl recognized genuine kindness and concern. Maybe she was worn down by loneliness and deprivation. Whatever the reason, with a sob, she flung herself into Sunny's embrace. Sunny dropped to the floor and wrapped her arms around the weeping child. Rocking back and forth, Sunny murmured soothing words to the little girl.

Sunny had a big heart. She was the girl who sat by an unpopular kid on the school bus, or who smiled and patted a chair, welcoming a new student to join her table in the cafeteria. The end of the world brought out the worst in some people—hardened folks and turned them against each other—but it hadn't changed Sunny. Not entirely sure that was a good thing. I'd witnessed some crazy shit during the past four months, seen good people victimized by predators. How long until my kindhearted friend found herself face-to-face with the wrong person? Protectiveness roared through me. If somebody hurt her… if she had to carry the memories of the kind of violence that kept me awake at night…

Valhalla called me home. I'd head back today if I could, but leaving Sunny behind in Boise was impossible.

Ever finally cried herself out. She wiped her nose on the sleeve of Sunny's shirt, then looked at me, her red-rimmed eyelids puffy.

"Have you been living here all by yourself?" I asked, trying again to connect with the girl.

Ever sniffed and bobbed her head "This is my grandma's house. She came to stay with us when she got sick. She died, and then mom and dad died." Her eyes filled with tears again, and she trembled. Sunny rubbed the girl's shoulders.

What a freaking nightmare for the kid. Alone with three bodies. No wonder she fled her home. "And you decided to come back to Grandma's house," I guessed.

"I couldn't stay there," she said in a low voice. "I found Grandma's keys in her purse. My red wagon—the one I played with when I was little—was in the garage. So, I filled it up with food and clothes and stuff. I got my softball bat, and I pulled my wagon to Grandma's house."

My blood chilled at the thought of the girl pulling a wagon full of food through a dying city with nothing but a softball bat to defend herself.

Sunny's eyes met mine, her expression revealing the same horror I felt. "And you've been living alone at Grandma's house ever since?" she asked.

"Uh-huh."

"You're a brave little girl," I said.

"I'm not a little girl," she said, indignation stamped across her face. "I'm nine."

I dipped my head apologetically. "I beg your pardon."

"What about food?" Sunny asked. "What did you do when you ran out of food?"

"I used to help Grandma can fruits and vegetables and meat," Ever said. "Grandma wouldn't let me touch the pressure canner, but I'd fill the jars and wipe the rims. There's lots and lots of jars of food and juice in the basement. Peaches are my favorite."

"You've done an amazing job taking care of yourself," Sunny said.

"The way you used a chair to block the door was really smart," I added.

Ever's gaze moved from Sunny to me. "Is Sunny your girlfriend?"

At the innocent question, my shoulders stiffened. Before today, I'd never considered it, never wondered what it would be like if Sunny were mine.

"Kyle and I are friends," Sunny said quickly. "We've known each other since we were your age."

"Yeah, but is he your boyfriend?" Ever persisted.

"No, he's not my boyfriend," Sunny said. "But he's one of the people I love best in the whole wide world."

I cast a sideways glance at Sunny. The McAllisters were unabashedly demonstrative. Jake had ended every conversation with his parents with an "I love you." I guess I shouldn't be surprised that Sunny declared her love for an old friend.

Still, illogical disappointment punched me in the gut. When she laid her hands on my chest and talked about hidden talents, I thought—shit—I wondered if maybe Sunny was flirting with me. I must have read that exchange entirely wrong. Not her boyfriend, but one of the people she loved best in the entire world. Friendzoned before it ever occurred to me to make a move.

"Okay." Ever shrugged, accepting the answer at face value.

44

"Now that we've found you, Ever, we don't want to leave you here all alone," Sunny said.

"Do you want me to go home with you?" Ever asked, a hopeful expression on her face.

"No, sweetie, that wouldn't work. I have a better idea," Sunny answered. "Let's pack up your clothes and a box of your grandma's canned food, then we'll take you to meet a very nice friend of mine."

Twenty minutes later, Sunny steered the van onto a dead-end residential street. She parked Daisy in the driveway of a single-story, slate-colored house with garish pink shutters. "Grab your backpack," she told Ever with a smile. "Kyle and I will carry the boxes."

We climbed out of the van and walked to the front door. In a window, a lace curtain twitched, and someone peeked out at us. The front door flew open, and an elderly woman stood in the doorway, a huge smile wreathing her face. An enormous cat rubbed against her leg.

"Sunny, you brought me company!" she exclaimed. She clasped her hands together and beamed at Ever. "Who is this young lady?"

I suspected that after months alone, Ever might turn shy and hide her face against Sunny's side. Instead, the girl stepped forward, extending her hand for a formal handshake. Somebody had drilled manners into the kid. "Hello. My name is Ever van der Linden."

The elderly woman seized the child's hand. "Pleased to meet you, Ever van der Linden. Sunny calls me Mrs. B. Why don't you call me that, too? Now come inside and have a biscuit."

"Okay." Without a backward glance, Ever tagged along behind Mrs. B. Sunny and I deposited the boxes in the foyer, then followed the pair into the living room.

Yowza. The old lady loved pink, didn't she? Pink shutters on the house, a pink front door, pink curtains covering the living room window, and so many pink pillows on the sofa that you'd have a hard time finding a place to park your butt. Ceramic figurines—each one sitting on a fancy doily—crowded the tabletops and dotted the many bookshelves that lined the room.

Ever's legs dangled from a wicker rocking chair that she'd set in motion by throwing her weight back and forth. Sunny parked her adorable butt on a needlepoint-covered hearth bench. Mrs. B. perched on the edge of a sofa. The tiny woman patted the cushion next to her. "Come sit by me, young man. It's been too long since I last had a handsome fella to keep me company."

I shoved a frilly pillow out of the way and dropped down next to Mrs. B. The fluffy cat hopped onto the coffee table, extended a hind leg, and began to groom itself, keeping one eye firmly on me.

"My name's Kyle," I said, remembering my manners. "Nice to meet you, Mrs. B."

She turned to Sunny, her eyes wide. "This is *the* Kyle?"

The Kyle.

Sunny's cheeks flushed a bright pink that rivaled the curtains. "Yes," she said quickly. "You remember, I told you that Kyle was my brother's best friend."

"Oh, I remember everything you told me about Kyle, dear." Mrs. B. picked up a box of shortbread cookies from the coffee table and offered me one. "Biscuit?"

"Thank you, ma'am." I took a cookie and glanced at Sunny, who was studiously picking at a loose thread on the needlepoint bench. Wheels turned in my head. Sunny had talked to Mrs. B. about me, and whatever she had said made her turn a beautiful shade of pink. Maybe she *had* been flirting after all.

Ever stopped rocking. "What's the kitty's name?"

"His name is Fitzwilliam." Mrs. B. extended the box of cookies toward Ever, who stood and helped herself to one before plopping back in the chair. "If you pat your legs, Fitzwilliam might decide to sit on your lap. Or not. Cats are willful creatures, and they don't always do what they're told."

Ever giggled. "I'm a willful creature, too."

I smiled to myself. Ever and Sunny both.

Mrs. B.'s eyes sparkled. "As am I. I suspect that you and I are going to be great friends, Ever van der Linden."

"Yup," Ever agreed. She patted her lap. Fitzwilliam turned his head and studied her for a moment before returning to his ablutions. "Willful creature," Ever repeated with a grin. She stuffed the cookie in her mouth and recommenced her energetic rocking.

I looked at the books piled next to the cat on the coffee table. *Pride and Prejudice*. No surprise there. Who else but an Austen fangirl would name her cat after Mr. Darcy? A biography of Napoleon. Huh. *The Art of War* by Sun Tzu. My brows drew together at that title. Odd choice for a flirtatious little old lady obsessed with pink.

I glanced over at Sunny and imagined her curled up in bed on a pile of pillows. What did Sunny like to read before she fell asleep? Romances, like Kenzie? Biographies? Or something else? Curiosity stirred in me. There was still so much to discover about my old friend.

"Ever has been living by herself for months," Sunny said. "I'm not at home during the day to keep an eye on her, so she can't stay with me. I *could* take her back to the Haven and ask Dr. Russo to find a place for her—"

"Nonsense," Mrs. B. interrupted. She leaned forward. "Ever, would you like to stay here with Fitzwilliam and me? I have a pretty guest room where you could sleep and lots of books and games. Do you know how to play gin rummy? Or five-card draw?"

Wait. Mrs. B. was offering to teach Ever how to play poker?

Ever stopped rocking and shook her head. "Is that a video game?"

"No, dear. It's a card game. If you stay, we'll keep each other company, and we'll have lots of fun. And I promise to take good care of you."

Ever turned to Sunny. "Will I still see you sometimes?"

"You'll see me all the time, I promise," Sunny said. My heart sank. First, problems with the Nampa Boys and now this. Another commitment binding Sunny to Boise. "I visit Mrs. B. at least twice a week," Sunny added. "I work for a place called the Haven, and we bring her food and water and anything else she needs."

"More cookies?" Ever asked hopefully.

Sunny laughed. "I'll bring cookies whenever I can."

Fitzwilliam stretched and jumped off the coffee table. He sauntered toward Ever, his tail swishing back and forth like a plume. He leapt onto her lap and head-butted her arm, like he was trying to win her over, to tip the scales in Mrs. B.'s favor.

Ever stroked his fur. "He's soft like a bunny." She glanced at Mrs. B. "Okay. I'll stay."

Mrs. B. clasped her hands together. "Excellent."

Sunny and I helped Ever carry her things to her new room. Like Mrs. B. said, it was a pretty room, with rosebud wallpaper and an antique brass bed. We left the two chatting like old friends while Mrs. B. warmed bathwater for the girl.

"Looks like she'll be in good hands," I said, as Sunny and I walked toward the van.

"The best," Sunny concurred.

"I want to get back to Northumberland Heights before sunset," I said.

"Me, too," Sunny agreed.

We fastened our seat belts, but instead of starting the van, Sunny turned to me. "You'll spend the night in Jake's room again, won't you? You'll stay with me?" The vulnerability in her voice cut me to the quick.

"Of course, I will."

No way I'd sleep at my family home while Sunny stayed at hers. Nowadays, safety in numbers was the rule. And I *wanted* to stick close to her. Jake, our parents, our neighbors, our friends, they lived again in our shared memories. Sunny was unselfish and kind, endangered qualities in the post-pandemic world. Infuriatingly reckless, too, liable to rush headlong into any situation where she thought she might be of help. The need to protect her, to bask in her inherent warmth and goodness, clutched at me. I'd never abandon her to the crazies who roamed the new world.

She started the engine and headed back to Northumberland Heights. We drove in silence. I glanced sideways at Sunny. Yesterday life was simple. No, that was wrong. Nothing had been simple since the pandemic emptied out the world, but life had been *simpler*. Yesterday I believed that Sunny was off-limits. And now? Now I had to rethink my assumptions and what that meant for our future.

You'll stay with me?

Of course, I will.

I hadn't just promised to stay in Boise, had I?

SEVEN

Sunny

Mom always said that I could sleep through the Second Coming. Once upon a time that was true. For my sixteenth birthday, Jake gave me an alarm clock with pulsating lights and a 100-decibel siren alarm. Then he complained that the new alarm clock woke him, too. Well, what did he expect, with his bedroom right next to mine?

Sleeping like the dead wasn't a problem anymore. Not since flu survivors started breaking into vacant—or presumably vacant—houses. Now the slightest sound would rouse me from my slumber.

A muffled cry startled me awake. I sat up in bed. Without electricity, my 100-decibel alarm clock had been kaput for months, but the old windup alarm clock with glow-in-the-dark hands said it was nearly 3 a.m. Cocking my head to one side and holding my breath, I strained to listen.

Another indistinct shout. Half-awake, I swung my legs over the mattress and stood, trying to pinpoint its source. A mumbled protest followed by more strangled gibberish sounded through the wall I shared with Jake's bedroom.

Kyle.

I stumbled toward the door, stepped into the hall, then cracked open the door to Jake's room. Pale moonlight fell across the bed. Kyle had kicked off the blanket and lay flat on his back, one arm thrown over his head. Sweat glistened on his bare chest, and his legs twitched.

"No." His head thrashed from side to side. "No, Miles." He gasped for air, then lapsed into unintelligible mutterings.

Who's Miles?

I tiptoed to the side of his bed and stretched out a hand to touch his shoulder, then paused. Should I wake him or not? A psych professor told my college class once that nightmares allowed people to process painful events, and that the best thing was to let the dream run its course. Unless the sleeper looked like they were extremely agitated or like they might hurt themselves, that is. Whatever Kyle was processing, whatever memory his subconscious had dredged up, he was clearly distraught.

Kyle groaned and raised his arms, as if fending off an imaginary assailant. "Miles… don't… don't…" His hands pummeled empty air. He arched his back, sucked in a deep breath, and froze.

I stared at him, counting off the seconds.

Come on, Kyle. Exhale. Move.

He collapsed against the mattress, the air whooshing from his lungs. "Miles," he choked out. The pain in his voice clinched it. I lay down on the bed, then rolled onto my side, facing him.

"It's all right," I murmured, stroking the hair back from his sweaty forehead. "Nothing bad is happening. We're safe. Everything is all right."

Kyle's eyelids fluttered open, and he looked around the room in confusion before focusing his gaze on me. He jerked his head back, then raised up on his elbows. "Sunny?"

"You were having a nightmare," I said quickly. Despite all my lurid fantasies, unless it was an emergency, I'd never climb into bed with Kyle uninvited.

"A nightmare? Dammit." He sat up and shoved his hands through his hair. Squeezing his eyes shut, he shook his head. After a few seconds, he opened his eyes again and squared his shoulders, visibly composing himself. "Thanks for waking me, Sunny. I'm fine now."

Nope. He wasn't fine, and he didn't get to brush me off while he indulged in a show of manly fortitude. Jake had been an overprotective big brother. The last thing I wanted was for Kyle to assume that mantle, to act like a tough guy who took everything on his own shoulders. He had to cut himself some slack. Survival in the new world required community and connection, not machismo.

"Everybody has bad dreams, especially now," I assured him.

"That's true. They're nothing special, so let's not make a big deal out of it."

"That's not what I meant." I sat up and faced him. "Every person on the planet has been traumatized by the pandemic. Nightmares aren't a sign of weakness."

He shrugged, dismissing my assurances.

I poked him in the chest, and his eyes grew wide. Good. I had his attention, so I poked him again.

"Cut it out," he protested, batting my hand away.

"Don't act like you're not entitled to feel bad," I said. "Nightmares are normal; they're a sign of your humanity. So stop with the *they're nothing special* crap."

He opened his mouth as if he was going to argue, then snapped it shut. After a moment, he started again. "You're right, but when everybody's been traumatized by the pandemic, it feels whiny and self-indulgent to bitch about what I've gone through."

"You told me that you've dealt with seriously bad stuff." I hesitated. "An arsonist, a cult, white supremacists." Should I ask him about Miles? No. Whatever had gone down with Miles—whoever that was—Kyle would share the story when and if he felt ready. "You don't get over bad stuff by pretending it didn't happen."

"When did you get so smart?" he asked.

I snorted. "I've always been smart, dumbass." Jake and Kyle used to call each other dumbass when they bantered. The familiar jibe got a smile out of him, a smile that didn't quite reach his eyes.

He sighed. "Okay. The truth is, I've been dealing with insomnia and nightmares for a while now. But it's all right. I can handle it."

"It might help if you talk about the bad dreams, you know, drag the boogeyman out into the light of day," I suggested.

Kyle rested his elbows on his bent knees and studied me, moonlight slanting across his handsome face. "Thanks. I'll keep that in mind; I promise." It was a rejection, a gentle one, but still a rejection.

You can't nag someone into confiding in you. I bit back a protest. "Okay."

"You got any idea what time it is?" he asked.

"A little past three," I answered. There were hours to go until daybreak, plenty of time for the bad dreams to lay siege to Kyle again. He might not be willing to open up to me, but he shouldn't be alone. I should be here to wake him if the nightmares returned. "I'd like to stay in here with you, to wake you up in case the bad dreams come back."

He made a face. "What am I, five?"

"Please, Kyle." I widened my eyes and jutted out my lower lip in the way that always got Jake and Kyle to cave when we were kids. Shameless manipulation, sure, but he'd shot down my direct approach.

Concern creased his brow. "You scared, Sunshine?"

"Not exactly." I wouldn't lie to Kyle to get my way. "But I've been alone for a long time, and I'd feel better if we were together." That was the absolute truth, a truth that coincided conveniently with my desire to stand guard against the nightmares.

"All right, Sunny, I give." He lay down and patted the pillow next to his. "Let's settle in."

I stretched out on my back next to the man of my dreams. Suddenly I didn't know what to do with my hands. This platonic bed-sharing was nothing like my fantasies. In my daydreams, I was an irresistible siren, desirable, confident, totally at ease. In reality? My breath caught in my throat, and my limbs locked up, my legs straight and my arms ramrod stiff at my side. God. I must've looked like I was afflicted with rigor mortis.

I'm such a dork.

"You cold?" Kyle pulled a sheet over us. "Come here." He raised an arm, inviting me to cuddle. I sidled close to him and laid my head on his shoulder. As if it had a will of its own, my hand fell across his chest. I narrowed my eyes and stared at my wayward hand.

Don't you dare pet him.

"Better?" he asked.

"Uh-huh."

"Good." He squeezed my shoulders. "Now go to sleep."

Seriously? Sleep was the farthest thing from my mind.

EIGHT

Kyle

Sleep eased its grip on me, and my senses stirred awake. Something smelled good. Eyes still glued shut by slumber, I inhaled slowly. What was that? A citrusy aroma filled my nostrils, grapefruit with a hint of honey. Nice. I burrowed my face into the source of the scent. Soft hair tickled my nose, and somebody stirred in my arms.

A warm, feminine body pressed against mine. We lay on our sides. Our bodies curved together to form an S shape, my arm wrapped around her waist, my hand cupping her breast, and my nose buried in her hair.

Who was I spooning?

Memory flooded back. My eyes flew open. I lay plastered against Sunny McAllister, her soft breast filling my palm, her bottom tucked against my groin. Beneath my boxers, I was rocking morning wood. If she woke up, no way she'd miss the erection shoving against her ass.

How effed up was this? What kind of a perv gropes a woman in her sleep, his dead best friend's kid sister nonetheless?

Well, not exactly a kid, thank God. At twenty-one, Sunny was a full-grown woman, but still... I shifted, breaking contact between my cock and her ass. Sunny murmured something in her sleep and wriggled backwards, molding herself against me once again. Biting back a moan, I stilled. I hadn't slept next to—or with—a woman since Kenzie and I broke up last spring. I missed sex, of course, but if a man's got two hands, he can get by.

Sex was one thing, emotional intimacy another. In a lawless world, trusted allies made the difference between survival and death. Friends kept you sane and helped you hold onto your humanity. I had people waiting for me back at Valhalla who were both friends and allies. Ripper and Kenzie. The good doctor, Sahdev. Bear, the rodeo star and rancher. The crazy-ass tattoo artist, Nyx. And a pair of lovestruck teenagers, Hannah and Levi. Good people all.

Mom used to call me her golden boy, and for most of my life I was fortune's favorite child. My family loved me. Friends, good grades, and athletic achievement all came easily to me. Girls, too, at least until Kenzie dumped me. And like Kenzie used to say when I flashed my Am Ex card, I had a *stoopid* amount of money at my disposal.

Not even the flu pandemic could make this golden boy completely lose his luster. I had everything that mattered: friends, provisions, and a place to call home. Don't get me wrong. I had to work like hell to get and keep what I had, but I was still luckier than most. I'd survived the flu and found my people.

Yeah, I had the essentials, but I didn't have *this*. Somebody to fall asleep with at night, our limbs tangled as we held each other close. Somebody to nudge me awake when the bad memories haunted my sleep. Somebody to be there when we woke up feeling frisky. I imagined my hand drifting lower, my fingers brushing over the soft curls at the apex of her thighs, then gliding through the slick folds of her sex.

And *this* wasn't mine.

Get your mitts off Sunny.

Holding my breath, I gently lifted my hand from her breast and pulled my arm back. I inched away from her again. She muttered a protest, and her eyelids fluttered. I turned onto my stomach and folded my arms under my head, like I'd spent the night keeping my hands to myself on my side of the bed.

She stretched, arching her back, then rolled over to face me. I squinted at her, letting her know that I was awake, too.

"Good morning," she said.

"Morning." I yawned. "How'd you sleep?"

"Good. You?"

"Slept like a log," I answered.

"A log, huh?" She smirked. "So *that's* what was poking me."

Busted. Looked like we'd be having an awkward *sorry I groped you while we were sleeping* conversation after all. "Shit, Sunny. I'm sorry."

She laughed. "You copped a feel in your sleep. I won't hold it against you."

Was that a double entendre? Not a clue. Instead of answering, I flashed a smile.

Sunny sat up, and I got my first real look at the yellow camisole and striped shorts she'd slept in. The ribbed cami clung to the curve of her breasts, breasts I had no business touching last night. Perfect, pert nipples poked against the fabric. Balling my fists to resist the urge to touch, I resolutely lifted my gaze to her sleep-tousled hair.

Jesus Christ, I had to get a grip.

Sunny had always sported a chin-length choppy bob. Before the flu, we shared both a favorite stylist and a love for expensive hair products. Her chestnut-brown hair now touched her shoulders. Sleepy eyes—the same golden amber shade as Jake's—met mine.

"You drink coffee in the morning, right?" she asked.

"Yep."

"I'm a tea drinker, but I have a box of those instant coffee packets from Starbucks that Dad liked."

"Perfect." I sat up and nonchalantly placed a pillow on my lap.

"I'll meet you downstairs in five," she said, climbing out of bed.

As soon as she left the room, I fixed stern eyes on my crotch. "Down, boy," I growled. I counted to one hundred—that's how long it took—then threw on jeans and a T-shirt. I made my way to the kitchen, where Sunny was bringing water to a boil on one of those alcohol camping stoves that's safe to use indoors. A box of whole wheat crackers and a jar of peanut butter sat on the counter next to two mugs.

Sunny pointed to a small bowl of cherry tomatoes. "Fresh tomatoes from the patio planter. Enjoy."

"We're living large," I said, popping one into my mouth.

"You know it." She poured boiling water into the mugs, dunked a tea bag into one, and emptied a packet of instant coffee into the other. "Although I really miss Mom's Swedish pancakes."

I groaned at the memory. "With lingonberries and whipped cream. Best pancakes ever."

"Whipped cream." Sunny sighed. Her tongue darted out and swept across her lips, as if the mere mention of pancakes triggered a sense memory of the experience. I stared and imagined myself licking a dab of cream from that full lower lip, tasting her mouth before pressing my lips against hers.

Shit. I wrenched my gaze away from her mouth and accepted the cup of coffee she offered me. I took a sip. "What's on the agenda for today?"

"I thought we could go back to Ever's grandma's place and pack up all the canned food, then take it to the Haven," Sunny said.

"Sounds good."

I knew better than to mention Valhalla again. With trouble from the Nampa Boys brewing, there was no way that Sunny would pack her things and head to the ranch with me. If the meeting between the Haven and the Boys went well—if they reestablished a détente—then I'd bring the subject up again, use my persuasive skills to change her mind. If Ever was the sticking point, we could bring her along with us. And what about Mrs. B.? Could I show up at Valhalla with three new people in tow, including a child and an elderly woman? Knowing Ripper and Kenzie and the rest, I thought I could.

After breakfast, we drove the van to grandma's house. Ever hadn't been exaggerating when she told us that there was "lots and lots" of canned food in the basement. Miles would have approved of the old woman's industry. Hundreds of jars filled the basement shelves. By the time Sunny and I finished carefully packing up the boxes and carrying them to the van, it was noon. We stopped at Mrs. B.'s place to check on Ever and found her trying to teach an indifferent Fitzwilliam to play fetch. After a cup of tea and a cookie, we said goodbye, promising to return soon. A little before one, we pulled up to the Haven. I hopped out of the van and opened the sliding passenger door. Sunny rounded the front of the vehicle. I reached inside and lifted a box of canned food to hand off to her.

Before I took two steps, Ed rushed outside, agitation stamped on his face. He waved his hands and limped toward us. I set the box down on the sidewalk. Ed clutched at Sunny's arms.

"I'm worried about Sara and Gavin and Rocco," he said.

"Why? What's going on?" I asked.

"That note you delivered yesterday. Was a request for a meeting with the Nampa Boys. This morning at ten." A sheen of sweat covered the older man's forehead, and his words came in a disjointed rush. "Sara and Gavin went to represent the committee. Rocco went as extra security."

"What makes you think there's a problem?" Sunny placed a hand on Ed's shoulder and spoke in a quiet, steady voice, clearly trying to calm the man down.

"Sara said—" He gulped, then began again. "Sara said the meeting would take no more than an hour. Max. That they'd be back by 11:30. That's ninety minutes ago. I've got a bad feeling about this."

"Maybe the meeting ran long," Sunny said. "Maybe they got a flat tire on the way. We can't know for sure that something is wrong."

"Did you send somebody to check on them?" I asked. If the man was worried, he shouldn't just sit around wringing his hands.

"I'd have gone myself, but I can't drive with this." He pointed to the cast encasing his right ankle. He nodded at the woman guarding the entrance. "Margie is a good shot, and we need her at the door. There're a couple of young people inside sorting food, but neither one of them ever learned how to drive. Everybody else is out scavenging. And they're either not picking up or are out of radio range."

And we spent the past hour drinking tea and watching Ever play with the cat.

"I'll go." I turned to Sunny. Ed was probably overreacting, but I didn't want to drag Sunny into any potential danger. "Why don't you stay here and help sort food while I go see what's up."

She cast me a scathing look. "The buddy system, remember? You don't go anywhere without a partner."

"But—"

"Forget it." Sunny cut me off. "I'm going with you." She pointed at my Glock. "And if there is a problem, you can take care of it, Mr. Armed and Dangerous."

Sunny still didn't take the possibility of danger seriously enough, did she? I pressed my lips together, biting back further arguments. Odds were, nothing was wrong, but if things did go south, I guess I'd rather have Sunny at my side than anywhere else. My experience with the cult showed that bad things happen when you're separated from your people.

"Let's go," I said.

"We'll report back as soon as we know anything," Sunny assured Ed, touching his shoulder again.

We hopped back into the van, and Sunny navigated toward Meridian.

"Mr. Armed and Dangerous, huh?" I said as we pulled onto the freeway.

She glanced sideways at me, her beautiful golden-brown eyes sparkling. She pointed to the Glock. "It does feel weird to see you carrying a gun."

"Took me a while to get used to it," I confessed. "But now it would feel weird to go around unarmed."

We drove in silence for a few minutes, the only car moving on the freeway. In the early days of the pandemic, a lot of people had fled the cities. Sometimes they ran out of gas. Sometimes they pulled over when the flu symptoms struck, and they died in their vehicles. The freeway shoulder was littered with abandoned cars. I scanned the freeway's edge, keeping my eye out for Sara or Gavin standing next to a broken-down car. No sign of them.

When Sunny took the exit for Meridian, I leaned forward, studying our quiet surroundings. Once upon a time, the absolute stillness, the absence of people going about their business, would have felt unnatural and eerie. Now it was par for the course. We pulled into the same parking lot we'd used yesterday and drove slowly toward the picnic grounds.

"That's Gavin's car," Sunny said, pointing at a green sedan parked in front of the public bathroom. She pulled Daisy up next to the vehicle.

"No sign of our people." I frowned, craning my neck to examine the picnic area and the barbecue grills beyond.

"They've got to be here." Sunny unfastened her seat belt and opened the driver's door.

What would Ripper do? He'd proceed with caution.

"Hold on." I grasped her wrist. "Where do the meet-ups take place?"

She angled her head. "Over there, by the picnic tables in that grove of trees."

"I figure you'll refuse to stay in the van, so we'll go together, but I want you to keep behind me."

"Okay." Sunny's brow wrinkled, but she didn't argue. She slipped out of the driver's seat and met me in front of the van. We kicked through overgrown grass as we walked toward the grove of trees. Before the pandemic, the shady spot must have been prime picnicking real estate on hot summer days. Now, it appeared as empty as the rest of the park. Still, we approached with caution. My hand automatically moved toward my Glock, and I kept two paces ahead of Sunny.

That tingly sense that something was wrong—a warning from what Ripper called the back brain—grew as we tromped through the grass. I pulled my gun from the holster and rounded a pair of cedar trees.

Gavin lay flat on his back on the ground, his arms akimbo. Blood soaked his white T-shirt and pooled at his sides. His mouth hung oven, ruby droplets spattered his beard and cheeks, and his sightless eyes were fixed vacantly on the sky. My heart thumped, and my breath constricted. For a few critical seconds, I froze as ghosts clambered up from the depths of my memory.

Get a fucking grip.

I gritted my teeth and raised the Glock. Stalking forward, I swept the area, past picnic tables, a couple of barbecue grills and a rusty garbage can. No sign of life. No sign of Sara or Rocco. I turned back to the body.

Sunny dropped to her knees beside Gavin and pressed her fingertips on the side of his neck. Shaking her head, she leaned over and placed her ear close to his lips. She lifted dazed eyes to mine. "I don't feel a pulse or hear a breath. I think... I think he's dead."

No shit.

Shoving my gun into the holster, I rushed to her side. She stared at her red-stained fingers, then frantically wiped the bloody residue on the grass.

I sank down onto my haunches next to Sunny. "We need to get out of here. The Nampa Boys might still be around."

"Why would they do this?" Her voice broke. "Why?"

"We can't worry about that now." I stood and tugged Sunny to her feet. "We need to clear out in case they come back."

"We can't... we're not going to leave Gavin here." Hysteria touched her voice.

"No, we're not going to leave Gavin here." What was it Sahdev always said? The living take precedence over the dead. "We'll make sure that somebody picks up his body, but right now we need to clear out."

She stared at me, her expression blank. "But..."

"Sunny." I cupped her face. She fixed tremulous, shock-filled eyes on me. "This was a declaration of war. Gavin is dead. Sara and Rocco are missing. We have to get back to the Haven and warn the others."

Confusion cleared from her delicate features, and she shook her head, as if forcing herself to wake from a dream. "You're right. We have to get back to the others."

"Can you drive?" I asked. Shock had bleached all the color from Sunny's face, and her hands trembled.

She hesitated, then squared her shoulders as resolve filled her expression. "I'll drive. You keep your eyes out for the Nampa Boys."

"Yeah. Good."

I led the way as we jogged back to the van. We hopped in and sped toward the freeway. The trip back to downtown Boise crawled by, even though Sunny floored the gas pedal and raced around everything in her path. The tires bounced over the curb as we careened onto the drive up to the emergency room.

Sunny slammed on the brakes, bringing Daisy to a skittering stop. "Oh, shit," she whispered.

Glass from the wall of windows sparkled on the sidewalks, as if somebody had sprayed the place with an automatic rifle. Margie lay on the cement with her cheek pressed against the shattered glass. No need to worry that she'd cut herself. The woman was clearly dead.

Sunny threw open the driver's door and slipped from the high seat. As soon as her feet touched the ground, she was moving, running full tilt toward Margie's body.

"Sunny, no!" I bolted after her, scanning the area for any sign of the attackers. Sunny crouched next to Margie, then recoiled. I grabbed Sunny's arm and hauled her to her feet.

"Ed." She turned her head to look inside the building, then tugged on my restraining hand.

"After me," I said. Gun drawn, I tucked Sunny behind me and stalked toward the reception desk. Ed lay on his side behind the desk, his head and chest a bloody pulp.

Sunny gaped, her eyes wide in a bloodless face. Nothing would obliterate the image of a friend's body—I knew that from experience—but staring at it would only burn the grisly details into her memory. I pulled her into my arms and pressed her face into my chest. Shuddering, she wrapped her arms around my waist. After a few seconds, she yanked her arms back.

"The others," Sunny gasped, stumbling toward the sorting room. "Maybe they had time to hide."

Two bodies lay crumpled on the floor between tables that just yesterday had been piled high with clothing and canned food and medicines. No more. All the surfaces were bare. I bent over and checked the bodies for pulses. Meeting Sunny's eyes, I shook my head.

"The rest of the supplies," I said through stiff lips. What was the chance that the assailants had left behind anything of value? Practically nil, but we had to know for sure. I took Sunny's hand and strode up the hall, glancing in each room as we passed. The well-organized medicine room was stripped clean, all the shelves bare. Same with the food pantry. The clothes closet. And all the other rooms.

"Ed's ledger," Sunny cried, running back toward the reception desk. "All of the survivors' addresses are in the ledger." We pawed frantically through the drawers—maybe Ed had had time to hide it—and swept aside papers on the desk. I knocked over a mug of coffee. The liquid was still warm. Jesus. We'd barely avoided a bloodbath. "Crap. They took it."

The fuckers who killed everybody here knew where the survivors lived? The time for debate was over. "Listen to me. Boise isn't safe anymore. We're heading back to Valhalla. We'll get my truck, pick up Ever and Mrs. B., and head out of town."

"Sara and Rocco?"

"God knows what happened to them, but we have to get real. Even if they're still alive, the two of us won't be able to save them. We *can* save Ever and Mrs. B."

"I don't understand... why would the Nampa Boys do this?" Sunny wrapped her arms around her waist and rocked. She stilled. "Wait. There are teams of scavengers out in the city." Sunny glanced around the desk and at the floor. "Ed's radio is missing, too. We have no way to warn them."

"Sunny." I gripped her arms. "When they report back in, they'll see what happened. They'll decide what to do. Most of them will probably take off, too. It's out of our hands. We can only do what we can do. But we have to get moving."

Tears filled her eyes, but she nodded jerkily. "Okay." She leaned into me, and I pressed a kiss to her forehead.

"Come on." I grabbed her hand and pulled her toward the emergency room entrance. Broken glass crunched underfoot. Sunny turned her face away from Margie's body as we marched toward the van. "I'm driving. Throw me the keys," I said.

Sunny reached into her pocket, then she froze, her gaze fixed on something over my shoulder. I whirled around.

A young man wearing a blue baseball cap stomped toward us, his face contorted with rage. A Nampa Boy. His lips moved, although he was too far away to make out the words. His arms hung at his side, but he held a gun in his right hand. I grabbed Sunny's shoulder and shoved her to the ground, then quickly drew my Glock and settled my stance, ready to shoot.

"That's Robbie, the Nampa Boys' number two," Sunny said, lifting her head.

"Stay down," I barked. I kept my eyes on his advancing figure. If he pointed his gun at us, I'd fire.

Robbie threw his arms in the air, gesticulating wildly, and I tensed. Was the man planning to shoot or not? He took another step. A sharp retort cracked the air and Robbie pitched sideways, blood spurting from his head.

NINE

Sunny

K yle threw himself on top of me, another fantasy come to life in the most perverse and ungratifying way. Air exploded from my lungs, and my chin smacked onto the concrete. Ignoring the pain, I twisted my head and peered out from under his arm.

A black SUV peeled around the corner and squealed to a stop next to Robbie. Gold letters were inscribed on the door, but I couldn't make out the words. Two men wearing jeans and gray T-shirts jumped out. They carried guns. They had to be the men who shot the Nampa Boy. The taller of the two bent over and checked Robbie's body while the shorter man turned to Kyle and me.

A second identical SUV pulled up next to the first. No one climbed out, and I couldn't see inside through the tinted glass.

The gray T-shirts sparked a memory. Last week a pair of scavengers—Lily and Frank—reported that they'd run out of gas on the south side of town, out by the airport. Two men wearing gray T-shirts had stopped to help. They'd poured a gallon of gas into their tank and told the pair to be careful on the road. Were those good Samaritans these same men?

"You two okay?" the man called.

I was anything but okay. Scared. Overwhelmed. Bewildered. Queasy from the sight and smell of blood. *Okay* figured nowhere in the equation.

"Stay down," Kyle said in a low voice. He rolled to his feet, gun in hand. He didn't brandish the weapon; instead he lowered his chin and squared his stance in a way that showed that he meant business. Kyle had always been self-confident and assertive, but this was the first time I'd seen him look dangerous. My old friend had turned into a badass.

Who are you and what have you done with Kyle?

The taller man stood up straight and looked our way. A whoop erupted from his lips. "Kyle? Kyle Chamberlain? And is that Sunny?"

"Brody?" Kyle tucked his gun into its holster and pulled me to my feet.

"It's good to see you, man." Brody bounded toward us, a gleeful smile on his face. Thirty seconds ago, he was checking out the bloody corpse of a man he'd probably shot. Now he was zeroing in on us like we were long-lost friends he spied from across the room at a kegger.

Without thought, I grabbed Kyle's left hand, entwining my fingers with his. Kyle glanced sideways at me, a small dent between his brows. He untangled our fingers and slung his arm around my waist, drawing me to his side.

"Good thing we came along when we did," Brody said, pumping Kyle's hand. "That Nampa Boy fucker meant to take you down." His gaze shifted to the demolished entrance to the Haven. "Whoa." He rocked back on his heels. "A scout reported the sound of gunfire, and we came to check it out. What the hell happened here?"

"We weren't here when it went down," Kyle said. "But it looks like the Nampa Boys coordinated an attack on both the Haven headquarters and their top brass. The head of the Haven, Dr. Russo, is missing. So is Rocco, their nurse. Everybody inside the headquarters is dead."

"The bastards. We'd heard that the Nampa Boys were looking to expand into Boise, but who would have thought they'd do something like this? We're living in dangerous days, my friend." Brody shook his head, then his gaze shifted to me. "Hey, Sunny. Glad to see that you survived the great flupocalypse."

"Hi, Brody." I inclined my head, acknowledging his greeting, and my gaze fell on his white sneakers. My stomach lurched. He must have stepped in Robbie's blood. A wavy, bright red line crept up the sides of his otherwise pristine shoes. I looked behind him. Bloody shoe prints marked the concrete, the kind of incriminating forensic evidence that would close the case for any TV detective.

I glanced over my shoulder at Margie's body. A trembling took hold in the pit of my stomach, and my knees wobbled. Without a word, Kyle pulled me in front of him, so my back pressed against his chest. He wrapped both arms around my waist and rested his chin on the top of my head, a gesture both comforting and possessive. I knew better than to read too much into it. He was holding me up so I wouldn't fall, and he'd probably picked up on the fact that I didn't much like Brody.

A pair of men wearing gray T-shirts climbed out of the second SUV. Brody looked over at them and raised his palm. They obediently stayed in place. One of them pulled out a two-way radio.

Why were these guys taking orders from Brody Allsop?

"So how come I haven't seen you around before today?" Brody asked Kyle.

Kyle shrugged. "I was going to school in Portland when the flu hit. After a while, I came back home, and Sunny and I found each other."

Brody waggled his eyebrows. "And you two hooked up?"

"We're in love," I blurted out. Behind my back, Kyle jerked. Great. Way to put my old friend on the spot. It was just... crap... Brody was a notorious flirt, and Sara had told me that men outnumbered women after the flu. I'd rather Brody saw me as partnered up with Kyle. Wasn't there some sort of Bro Code that made poaching a buddy's woman off limits?

"Something like that," Kyle said slowly. I stifled a relieved sigh, grateful that he didn't set Brody straight.

Brody's gaze raked my body. "Can't say I blame you, brother."

Kyle's grip tightened on my waist. "You aren't hitting on my girl, are you, *brother*?"

"Nah." Brody slapped him on a shoulder. "Just messing with you. Sunny and I are old friends."

Old friends. Sure. The last time I saw Brody was at a party a few months before the pandemic shut down the world. He was sprawled in a chair, holding court, when I walked by. He'd held out a red plastic cup to me and winked. "Get me another beer, will you, babe?" I'd backed away from him, giving him the finger with both hands.

Brody wasn't a bad guy—exactly—he was more your run-of-the-mill douche. He wore entitlement like a crown, not surprising since his father was the self-styled "king of the leveraged buyout." I once heard Dad refer to Elliot Allsop as a corporate vulture. Our families might have belonged to the same country club, but they didn't socialize beyond polite greetings at club functions.

"What have you been up to?" Kyle asked. "What's with the matching SUVs and T-shirts?"

Brody laughed, scratching the back of his neck. "Dad and I have been putting together a security force—"

"Hold up," Kyle interrupted. "Did you say, 'Dad and I'? Your dad's alive, too?"

My mouth fell open. In all my months working for the Haven, I'd never come across two survivors from one family. The flu was a mass murderer, cutting down nearly everybody in its path. If you survived its rampage, you found yourself alone in the world. I'd thought that reconnecting with Kyle was a miracle, but this—a father and son both alive—this was beyond astonishing.

"Yeah, Dad's alive. He never got sick, so we think he's immune. I got the flu. It was touch and go for a while, but I pulled through."

"Me, too," Kyle said. "I got it and recovered. Not many people do. We're lucky."

I glanced at Kyle. I had no idea that he'd had the flu. According to Sara, only a tiny percentage of people survived it. Sweet Jesus. I'd come close to losing him, too.

Brody grinned. "You can't keep good men down." He raised his hand. Kyle released my waist and fist bumped Brody, then settled his arm around me once again.

"Seriously, man. What have you been doing since the pandemic hit?" Kyle asked.

"You know we have a vacation place in Ketchum, on the Big Wood River, don't you? Big estate with two guest houses, a tall stone fence, and a locking gate?"

"Yeah," Kyle said. "Remember in high school, a group of us stayed there when we went skiing in Sun Valley."

I'd never visited the Allsops' Ketchum place, but I'd heard of it. A 10,000 square-foot vacation house. Nothing ostentatious about that.

"That's right. Anyway, as soon as word got out about the pandemic, we packed up a shit ton of supplies and caravanned to

Ketchum. Dad brought his security team from the company, set them up in the guest houses. We were sitting pretty for a while, snug as a bug in a rug, like Grandpa used to say. We'd brought everything we needed, and we caught fresh trout from the river every day." He paused, smiling at the memory.

"What went wrong?" I asked.

"One of the guards got sick. Then Mom and my sisters. Next thing you know, everybody came down with the flu, everybody except Dad. They fell like dominoes." He flapped his hand, imitating a domino toppling over. "Jonesy—he's the head of security for the Allsop Corporation—he and I were the only ones to pull through."

"I'm sorry, Brody. That's tough," Kyle said.

"It is what it is," Brody said.

I winced. Coming from the lips of another man, I might write off the flip words as an attempt to be stoic in the face of a worldwide disaster that spared nobody from pain and loss. Coming from Brody, the words felt more cavalier. Or maybe I was allowing my dislike for the man to color my interpretation.

"I'm sorry, too," I said.

"Thanks, babe," he said.

Kyle ran a hand up and down my arm, then gently squeezed my hand. "What did you guys do next?" he asked.

"Well, once Jonesy and I got our strength back, we all went out and started to look for other survivors. Dad knew that everything would go to hell after the pandemic burned out. Our only chance to stay safe, to maintain law and order, would be to band together with other survivors. If we're going to rebuild society and protect the American way of life, then we need good men to—"

"And women," I chimed in.

"Of course, sweetheart." Brody's eyes twinkled. "We need good men *and* good women to pitch in and do their part. We recruited in Twin Falls, Pocatello, Idaho Falls, Missoula, Coeur d'Alene, Spokane, Walla Walla. We came back to Boise a couple of weeks ago. Dad wants to make Boise the capital of the new Pacific Northwest Republic. He's going to send feelers out to Portland and Seattle."

"Portland is gone. Maybe Seattle, too," Kyle said. "Burned to the ground by a religious cult. The same group blew up The Dalles Dam and flooded the freeway west."

"Holy fuck." Brody shoved a hand through his auburn hair. "Are you telling me there's some wackjob cult running around setting fires and blowing shit up?"

"Not anymore," Kyle said.

Brody's eyes narrowed. "Not anymore, huh. You have something to do with stopping them?"

Kyle shrugged. "I helped."

Over Brody's shoulder, I glanced at the three men from the Allsop security force. They stood-stock still wearing stern expressions on their faces. Their muscular arms were crossed over their chests as they watched us talk. They posed quite the contrast to Brody. With his perfectly styled hair and easy smile, he looked more like a frat boy than a member of a security team. Yet the men deferred to Brody.

Brody was silent for a moment. "Listen, Kyle," he said slowly, excitement glinting in his eyes. "You *have to* come talk with my father, tell him what went down with the cult. You're exactly the kind of man we need in our ranks. A man who believes in law and order, a man who knows how to get things done. And you're one of us. I've known you—you and Sunny—forever."

"Why didn't you guys reach out to the Haven as soon as you got to town?" I interrupted before Kyle could reply to Brody's suggestion.

Brody turned another smile on me. "We needed to get the lay of the land before we reached out to anybody. Can you imagine if we'd approached the Nampa Boys, thrown in with them, only to find out later that they're a bunch of homicidal assholes? No. It's only smart to do some basic reconnaissance before contacting any group."

"I guess that makes sense." My head was spinning. This was too much to take in. The attack on the Haven. The revelations about Kyle. The reappearance of Brody Allsop. The prospect of a new Pacific Northwest Republic.

Brody glanced at the cluster of men and snapped his fingers. The man who'd asked if Kyle and I were okay jogged over.

"Yes, sir?"

Brody pointed to the emergency room entrance. "Make sure that everybody inside the Haven headquarters gets a decent burial."

"Will do."

"When the Nampa Boys ambushed Sara and Rocco, they killed the Haven's second-in-command," I said. "His body is in a park in Meridian. Can you guys bury him, too?"

The guard glanced at Brody, who nodded his permission.

"Thanks, Brody," I said. I gave the guard the name of the park and the location of Gavin's body.

"You know, maybe we could help you find out what happened to Sara and Rocco," Brody suggested. "If they're being held by the Nampa Boys, we could use our muscle to stage a rescue or to force the Boys to negotiate for their release."

Twenty minutes ago, at Kyle's urging, I'd been ready to grab Mrs. B. and Ever and flee the city. I saw the logic behind the move, but damn, it would've haunted me to abandon all the people in Boise. Could the Allsops and their forces rescue Sara and Rocco? Assuming they were still alive, of course. Could they protect the other survivors in town from the Nampa Boys?

Dad had dismissed Elliot Allsop as a ruthless corporate raider. That meant he was a man who got things done. The stock market and big corporations were things of the past. Brody said that his father wanted to rebuild society and maintain law and order. Those were worthy goals. Nobody wanted to end up living in a *Mad Max* world. It might take a man of his drive and determination to pull it off.

I turned around in Kyle's arms and laid my hands on his chest, the way a girlfriend would. Maybe I was being paranoid, but I wanted to continue the charade, especially if we accompanied Brody back to meet with his father. "What do you think?" I asked in a low voice. I'd rather have this conversation in private, but with Brody hovering nearby, that was impossible.

Kyle met my eyes. "Let's hear the man out," he said.

It couldn't hurt to talk to Elliot Allsop, especially if there was a chance that he'd save Sara and Rocco. If the conversation didn't go well, if anything felt hinky, Kyle and I would go on our way. "Okay."

Brody whooped again. He kissed me on my cheek and thumped Kyle on the back.

"Great to have you on our team."

TEN

Kyle

I glanced at Sunny, then did a double take. With both hands she lifted the gilded dessert plate to her lips and shamelessly licked the last of the cheesecake from its surface. Her tongue flicked a cherry into her mouth. Sighing with pleasure, she returned the plate to the linen tablecloth, then settled back in the chair.

She met my startled gaze and smiled unapologetically. "Cheesecake," she said, as if the word alone justified what my mom would consider an egregious violation of good manners. If I'd licked my plate at the table when I was a kid, my mom would've taken away my dessert privileges for a month.

"You want to lick mine?" Brody called from across the table. Smirking, he held up a plate smudged with graham cracker crust and creamy filling.

I bristled. What the hell was my old buddy thinking?

Sunny shot him a saccharine smile. "That's sweet of you, but no. I don't want to lick yours."

"You're out of line, Brody," I said. "The innuendo isn't cool."

"Kyle's right." Elliot Allsop spoke from the head of the table.

All eyes turned toward the former CEO. He had hardly spoken during dinner, but I'd felt the weight of his scrutiny as he took our measure throughout the meal.

"Maintaining our standards of behavior is important, now more than ever," he continued.

He must have been in his fifties, but only the fine lines around his eyes and the gray at his temples gave away his age. Tall, with an athletic build, he was what my sister Kristen would have called a silver fox. If he commanded a boardroom as easily as he commanded a dining table, he must have been a force to be reckoned with.

"Yes, sir." Brody turned to me. "Sorry, brother. No offense meant. I was just joshing."

"Kyle isn't the one you should apologize to," his father said, swirling the pinot noir in his crystal wineglass.

Brody sucked in a breath, then smiled at Sunny. "I got carried away, and I'm sorry if I offended you."

"Apology accepted," Sunny said.

I shifted in my seat, glancing between them. An uncomfortable silence descended on the table. After a moment, I pointed at Sunny's chin. "You've got some cherry goo under your lip."

Her tongue darted out and swiped at the sticky red liquid. She tilted her face up for my inspection. "Did I get it all?"

With her chin angled up, I could see a bruise under her jaw. Frowning, I reached over and gently touched the purple splotch. "How did you get this?"

"My chin smacked the pavement when you pushed me down." She shrugged. "It's no big."

I did it? My chest tightened. "Sunny, I'm so sorry."

She waved a hand, dismissing my concerns. "Bullets were flying. You're forgiven."

"Why don't you kiss her owie and make it better?" Brody suggested, snickering.

Mr. Allsop cleared his throat and carefully placed his wineglass on the table. "You're not yourself this evening, Brody. Perhaps you should retire early and see if some extra sleep restores your equanimity."

Brody's jaw tightened. Can't say I blamed him. Yeah, he was acting like an ass, but at twenty-two, he was way too old to be sent to bed early for misbehaving. Not even my persnickety mom would have humiliated me that way.

"You're right, Dad," he said, making light of his obvious embarrassment. "I am tired." He tossed his napkin on his plate and stood. "Sunny, Kyle, I'll see you guys in the morning." Back stiff, he retreated from the room, leaving another awkward silence in his wake.

"Please forgive Brody's lapse in manners," Mr. Allsop finally said. "He hasn't been the same since he lost his mother and sisters. He's a young man who needs the civilizing influence of good women."

The old-fashioned sexism of that phrase was sure to raise Sunny's hackles. I widened my eyes and shot her a warning look.

She dipped her head. "I understand, Mr. Allsop. Brody and I are fine. And I want to thank you for a lovely dinner. I haven't had a steak or salad or cheesecake in forever." She looked up at the bright chandelier that illuminated the room. "I've missed electricity. This has been a real treat."

He inclined his head, acknowledging her thanks. "We have generators and fuel to power the house," he said. "Water. And sources in the countryside to keep us supplied with fresh meat, milk, and vegetables. You and Kyle could live very comfortably here. I hope you'll decide to join our team."

"We appreciate your generous offer, sir," Sunny said politely, her expression giving away nothing about her thoughts on his proposal.

"Why us?" I asked. "Why would you want a couple of college students on your team? What do we have to offer?"

Mr. Allsop leaned forward. "Society needs to rebuild after the pandemic. People crave stability and security. Protection from ruffians like the Nampa Boys. One might argue that people like us— people with our shared values and background—are best suited to restore and lead a law-abiding society."

"That sounds a lot like an aristocracy," Sunny observed.

"What is an aristocracy other than rule by the best and brightest?" he asked.

Oh, that wouldn't fly with my socially conscious friend. Not with me, either, but this wasn't the time or place to argue it. I kicked Sunny under the table. She kicked me back but didn't pursue the point.

"I'd like you to meet with my head of security tomorrow morning to go over plans to search for your missing friends," Mr. Allsop said.

Sara and Rocco. With the Haven in ruins, if anybody had the power to challenge the Nampa Boys, it was Allsop and his men. A well-armed, well-organized force could calm the chaotic situation and bring Sara and Rocco home. With Allsop running security and Sara getting the Haven back on its feet, stability would return to Boise. And a stable Boise meant that Sunny and I could go to Valhalla with a clear conscience.

"I'm looking forward to it," I said.

"Breakfast is at eight. You'll meet with Jonesy directly afterward." Allsop dropped his napkin on his plate and stood, a clear cue that dinner was over. "There's a whirlpool tub in the guest suite's bathroom. You might as well take advantage of the hot water and electricity, Sunny."

She offered him a genuine smile, her eyes bright with excitement. "That sounds like heaven." Hopping to her feet, she held out a hand. "Come on, Kyle. Let's fire that thing up."

Hand in hand—like a real couple—we retreated toward the guest suite on the second floor.

The Allsops lived large. Their estate occupied forty acres of land on the east side of town. The mansion clung to the side of an arid ridge. Before the pandemic, extensive landscaping turned the property into a lush, green oasis, complete with a big indoor pool. During the family's absence, the shrubbery had withered from neglect, but it was still an impressive place. Our guest suite rivaled the fanciest room at any luxury hotel. Even with a king-sized bed along one wall, there was plenty of room on the opposite wall for a pair of overstuffed chairs to face the stone fireplace. French doors led to a private deck offering a view of downtown Boise in the distance.

I switched on a light when we entered the room, dropped into one of the overstuffed chairs, and pointed to the other. "We need to talk."

She made a face and perched on the edge of the chair. "We do."

"You want to tell me what's going on, *my love?*"

She winced at the endearment. "I ambushed you with that declaration, didn't I?"

"Yeah, you did, but I figured you had a reason. You have history with Brody?"

"Not really," she said. She smoothed back her brown hair, tucking it behind both ears—a tell—something she did when she was nervous. Her diamond stud earrings caught the light, the earrings her parents had given her for her eighteenth birthday. At that party, I'd wished her happy birthday and kissed her cheek. She'd blushed bright red. "Brody and I never dated," she said, the words pulling me out of the memory. "He asked me out a couple of times, but I said no. When he got insistent, I may have told him that I had no interest in going out with a spoiled fuck boy."

"He got insistent?" I sat up straight. "Why didn't you tell Jake and me?"

She rolled her eyes. "Because I could handle it. I didn't need my big brother and his best friend to come home from Portland to tell Brody Allsop to back off."

"So, there's bad blood between you two?"

"Honestly, I don't know. Is Brody the kind of guy who holds a grudge?" She paused, biting her lower lip. "Our friends were murdered today, then Brody rolls up with a bunch of armed men. I wanted him to think that I'm off-limits. I told him we're in love. It was a spur-of-the-moment impulse."

I squatted next to her chair. "It's okay, Sunny. You did right. If Brody harbors any fantasies about getting with you, telling him we're in love should put the kibosh on that. And I want to stay close. I'd rather share the guest suite with you than be in separate rooms."

Sunny's gaze swept over my face and lingered on my mouth before she lifted her eyes to meet mine. "Me, too. I feel safer when I'm with you."

Her lips parted and she inhaled a slow, shaky breath.

It struck me then; if she'd stayed behind in the Haven this morning, the way I'd asked, she would have died when the Nampa Boys attacked. I would have found her body alongside Margie's and Ed's. Survival hung on the flimsiest of threads. One wrong move, one wrong decision, and she could be lost forever.

"I'll always protect you," I vowed. "You can count on it."

I touched her chin. The purple bruise under her jaw stood out against her pale skin. I was responsible for that; the knowledge a bitter blow. Life was fragile, something to be cherished.

"Maybe Brody was right." The words tumbled out before I could stop them. "Maybe I should kiss your owie and make it better."

Owie. I half expected her to wrinkle up her face and laugh at the ridiculous word. Instead, her beautiful amber eyes focused solemnly on my mine. "Maybe you should." She angled her head, exposing her throat. Leaning forward, I pressed a gentle kiss against the bruise.

Sunny turned her head, and my mouth grazed hers. Electricity sizzled along our lips and zinged all the way down to my toes.

Sunny gasped and her head reared back. Her eyes grew wide. We stared at each other, our breath coming in shallow pants.

My conscience reasserted itself. What the hell was I thinking kissing Sunny?

"No," she said, shaking her head. "Don't you dare be sorry. Because I'm not." For once, my silver tongue, my easy way with words, totally failed me. A knowing smile turned up the corners of Sunny's mouth. She stood. "If you need me, I'll be in the tub." She whirled around and sauntered toward the bathroom, glancing back over her shoulder before she closed the door.

My heart thudded against my ribs. Jake's little sister had turned into a woman who left me speechless.

I'm in so much trouble.

ELEVEN

Sunny

I stood next to my van, tapping my toes with impatience. Mr. Allsop had promised that one of his security team would meet me out front in ten minutes, but I'd been pacing in the driveway for at least twenty. Early afternoon sun beat down on the stone surface, and sweat trickled down my neck.

A tall, muscular young man jogged around the side of the garage. He wore the familiar gray T-shirt and jeans that all Allsop's men sported. At the sight of Daisy, he stopped short. He slowly circled the van, his forehead crinkling as he touched one of the flower decals that covered a rusty spot.

"It could be worse," I said. "She used to have plastic eyelashes on her headlights."

He chuckled. "Seriously? Eyelashes on a van?"

"Yep."

"Huh." He huffed out a breath, shaking his blond head. "Like lipstick on a pig."

Smiling to himself, he walked over to the garage door, where a wireless keypad was mounted on the frame. He flipped up the cover and pressed in a series of numbers. A once-familiar tone sounded with each number he pressed. I gawked as the third garage door rolled up.

Man, I miss garage door openers.

The young man walked into the garage and emerged a minute later pushing a hand truck weighed down with cases of bottled water. The wheels rattled and the boxes jumped as he guided the hand truck over the uneven cobblestone driveway. He stopped next to Daisy's sliding door, then began to heave the cases of water into the van.

"Do you need help?" I asked.

"No, ma'am. I got this."

"Come on," I protested with a smile. "I'm not old enough to be a ma'am." I had to be younger than him by at least a couple of years.

He paused in his exertions. "You're Mr. Allsop's guest. That makes you a ma'am in my book."

Mr. Allsop was a stickler for good manners. If he'd chastise his own son's behavior, who knew what he'd do to an employee who breached his standards of decorum. I liked the blond guy; he struck me as much more easygoing than the rest of the security team. I wouldn't want to get him in trouble.

"Okay." I shrugged. "Ma'am it is."

He finished loading the cases of water, returned the hand truck to the garage, and climbed into the passenger seat. I turned the key and the engine started. It ran rough for a few seconds—that happened every now and again—then it smoothed out, and I threw the van into reverse.

"We can take one of the SUVs if you like," the young man suggested. "I don't mind switching the boxes to another vehicle."

"No need," I said. "Daisy always gets me where I want to go."

"Daisy," he repeated with a grin.

"You going to make fun of me for naming my van after a flower?" I demanded.

"Nope. I like it. I had a horse named Daisy when I was a kid."

"You're a farm boy?" I asked, squinting against the bright light. That would explain the ease with which he slung the heavy cases of water into the van. Working a farm—tossing bales of hay around, or whatever else they did—had to develop some serious muscles.

"Born and bred."

Up ahead, the heated surface of the road shimmered. I flipped down the visor and slipped on my sunglasses. "Did you work for Allsop security before the pandemic?"

"Nope," he said. "I came across Mr. Allsop a few weeks ago near Walla Walla. When the flu struck I was still working the family

78

farm. After my parents passed..." He paused, as if caught short by emotion.

"I'm sorry," I murmured.

"Thanks." He inclined his head. "After I lost my folks, I came down with the flu, but I recovered." Glancing sideways, I caught him staring into the distance, his brows drawn down. I held my tongue, waiting for him to speak again. "My mom and dad were good people," he said slowly. "I don't know why the Almighty saw fit to take them and spare me."

"I think we've all asked ourselves that," I said. "My mom and dad were the best."

"Mine, too," he said. "You have any brothers or sisters?"

"One brother. The flu took him. How about you? Did you have any siblings?" I asked.

Pain creased his features. He turned away, his face flushing. I got it. Sometimes, out of the blue, memories of loss ambushed you. The only thing you could do then was to wait for the pain to retreat. Nothing I could say would comfort the man. I touched his arm, and we lapsed into silence.

As we approached the outskirts of the city, he leaned forward, scanning our surroundings. His gun was within reach, tucked into the same type of shoulder holster that Kyle wore. Kyle hadn't wanted me to go into Boise today to make deliveries, but Mr. Allsop assured him that I was unlikely to run into trouble from the Nampa Boys. He had patrols crisscrossing the city, and he offered to send an armed guard with me.

"Where to first?" he asked.

I sighed. "The Nampa Boys took our registry when they attacked the Haven, so I don't have a list of addresses for all the people we serve. I'll have to rely on my memory, at least until I can meet up with other scavengers. We'll head to the west side of town and start there."

"What exactly does the Haven do?" he asked.

"We take care of survivors. Bring them food and water, whatever they need. Give them a place to go for medical treatment," I said. "I'm a scavenger. I go through houses and businesses looking for food and medicine. Sara Russo is our doctor. She runs the place. The Nampa Boys took her and Rocco; he was a nurse."

"They spared people with valuable skills," he observed.

I frowned. Technically, he was right. Not many doctors or nurses survived the flu. Sara and Rocco possessed vital skills, but the notion that anybody would consider one person inherently more valuable than another rubbed me the wrong way.

"They killed good people," I said.

He turned toward me, his expression serious. "I'm sure they did. Didn't mean nothing disrespectful by my comment."

"I know you didn't. It's just..." I shook my head. "They all mattered, and they're gone. And if Kyle and your security team can't rescue Sara and Rocco, they'll be gone, too."

On his lap, his hands clenched into fists, then relaxed. He cleared his throat. "Wouldn't make sense to kill your friends. I got a feeling they're still alive. Keep your hopes up."

"Thank you," I said, touched by his genuine sympathy. It was reassuring to see that Mr. Allsop's law and order crusade attracted nice guys.

"Where did you meet your boyfriend?" Was he trying to change the subject, get my mind off Sara and Rocco?

"I met Kyle when I was seven years old. His family moved into our neighborhood, and my brother invited him over to play video games. They were best friends ever since."

"No shit?" He blew out a low whistle. "I don't know anybody from before the flu. You're lucky to still have each other."

"Yeah, we are." I brushed my fingers over my lips, remembering our kiss, the sudden surge of pleasure that tap-danced through my body when our mouths touched. Sometimes a first kiss throws cold water on a romance. Not with Kyle. The reality was better than any fantasy, and I'd fantasized about kissing him for years. And from his sudden inhalation of breath and shocked expression, he'd felt it, too.

"I think you missed your exit." A voice interrupted my reverie.

Crap. I reeled in my thoughts and took the next exit, navigating toward western Boise. For the next couple of hours, we dropped food and water off to a half dozen survivors. I told everybody about the Nampa Boys' attack on the Haven and assured them that Allsop security was protecting the city from further incursions.

"One last stop before we head back," I said when we climbed into Daisy. I drove to a familiar dead-end street and parked in the driveway of Cressida's Cottage. The front door flew open, and Ever skipped down the front walk, Fitzwilliam in her arms. Mrs. B. appeared in the doorway, a huge, welcoming smile on her face.

We jumped out of the van. Ever paused when she saw the stranger at my side.

"Hey, kiddo. Who's your friend?" he asked, dropping down on his haunches, so he was eye to eye with the cat.

"His name is Fitzwilliam, and I just taught him how to fetch a paper airplane."

"You did?" He offered the girl an easy smile. "That's one smart cat you got there."

"Uh-huh," she agreed. She looked him up and down. "My name is Ever. What's yours?"

"Pleased to meet you, Ever. My name is Finn, Finn Rasmussen."

TWELVE

Kyle

"It's not a big deal." I stood in the doorway to the bathroom, tucking the gray Allsop security T-shirt into my jeans.

From her perch on the end of the bed, Sunny tilted her head and pulled a face, her expression skeptical. Yeah. In her mind, it clearly *was* a big deal.

"You don't think wearing their uniform might look like some kind of statement?" she asked. "Like you're all in?"

No danger of that. I had an agenda. Rescue Sara and Rocco. Help Elliot Allsop neutralize the Nampa Boys and stabilize Boise. Get the Haven up and running again. *Then* head back to Valhalla with Sunny in tow, leaving the Allsops in my rearview mirror. Shouldn't take more than a couple of days, should it?

Who was I kidding? That could take freaking forever.

If we found Sara and Rocco and brought them home, that *might* be enough to convince Sunny that Boise was in good hands. That she wouldn't be abandoning her friends if she came back to Valhalla with me. It *had* to be enough because I couldn't leave Sunny behind.

And that's all it took for my mind to snap back to our kiss. I'm no player, but I've kissed plenty of women. Nine times out of ten, it's good. Great even. Occasionally, it's a dud. You can't fake chemistry, and when your body says a big nope, your libido—and everything else—shrivels. On rare occasions, a first kiss is mind-meltingly spectacular, sending sparks raging throughout your body.

Who would've thought a simple kiss from my best friend's kid sister would almost knock me sideways? I've lived by a code: your buddy's sister was off-limits. If Jake were alive, I'd never risk our friendship by making a move on Sunny. But Jake wasn't alive, and Sunny had grown into the most delectable woman I'd ever met.

"Um... earth to Kyle."

Shit.

"Mr. Allsop asked me to wear the tee, in case we come across any survivors," I explained. "He said they need to start associating the gray T-shirt with helpers, with people they can trust."

"Right," she drawled.

"You don't trust him?" I asked. "Brody can be a tool, but has Mr. Allsop said or done anything suspicious?"

"If you can get past the idea of the best and brightest running the world, you mean?" She shrugged. "I don't know. Something doesn't feel quite right, but I can't put my finger on it. He's saying the right things about protecting Boise from the Nampa Boys. About restoring security and stability. About finding Sara and Rocco and saving the Haven. And I guess a man with good intentions, a man who has all the resources to keep the peace, that *could* be a good thing."

"It could be a very good thing," I said. "I want Boise to be a safe place, but don't worry. I'm not swearing allegiance to the Allsops. As soon as possible, I'm going home to Valhalla, and you know I want you to come with me."

She nodded. She knew I wanted her to stick with me. Wasn't the same thing as agreeing to, was it? If the Allsops restored order in Boise, she might feel compelled to stay with her friends. My cheeks puffed when I blew out a slow breath. Sunny *would* decide to stay with me. She had to.

"You'll be careful?" she asked. "If you guys run into the Nampa Boys?"

"We're going out loaded for bear, and the SUVs are armored," I said. "I just hope to God we find some sign of Sara and Rocco."

"Amen to that," Sunny said. "And you'll keep your eyes open, won't you? Just in case something more is going on than we can see?"

"Of course."

"And while you're gone, I'll spend the afternoon dropping off supplies," she said.

"Still wish you'd wait and go with me tomorrow."

"Mr. Allsop is sending an armed guard with me, remember?"

I remembered. I also remembered how often things went to shit when I got separated from my friends. How we thought we'd lost Kenzie. And Sahdev. Nowadays, every goodbye could be the last one.

Sunny hopped to her feet and walked over to me. "We'll both be careful, and I'll see you tonight."

Hugging a friend was totally normal under the circumstances, right? I slung an arm around her shoulder and pulled her close. Jeez, it felt like one of those weird side hugs you saw on reality TV shows featuring super-conservative religious families. I shifted and wrapped both arms around Sunny, hauling her against my chest. She slid her arms around my waist, returning the hug. Her breasts pressed against my chest, and I inhaled, remembering how perfectly those enticing mounds had filled my hands, how her ass had pressed against my cock. I shuddered and forced my arms to release her. We disentangled and stepped apart.

"See you at dinner." I dropped an awkward kiss on her forehead and immediately regretted it. What was I, her favorite uncle? I faced her, my arms hanging awkwardly at my side.

Sunny's mouth tipped up at the corners in a knowing smile. She laid her palms on my chest, rose on her tiptoes, and placed a quick kiss on my lips. "See ya."

I stood stock-still as she whirled and walked out of the room. My buddies would howl if they could see me now, flustered by a girl I've known most of my life.

"Smooth, Chamberlain," I muttered. "Real smooth." Shaking my head, I shrugged on my shoulder holster, then strode to the garage.

Brody stood with a cluster of Allsop security men. He clapped me on the shoulder with a friendly grin when I approached. "You all set, brother?"

I patted my Glock. "I'm good to go."

"All right. You and I will ride with Jonesy. We'll drive through town, show ourselves, so the good citizens of Boise can see that we're on the job. If the Nampa Boys think the city is wide open and defenseless, they'll learn otherwise."

"All right," I said, climbing into the back of an SUV. "How about searching for Sara and Rocco?"

"If we run into any Nampa Boys, we'll try to take one alive to interrogate. If not, we'll head west into their territory and scout around."

Scout around? Kind of a vague plan, wasn't it? I frowned.

"We have it well in hand, Mr. Chamberlain." Jonesy spoke from the driver's seat. I met his eyes in the rearview mirror. Deadly serious. No nonsense. He exuded an aura of lethal competence that reminded me of Ripper.

Three black SUVs pulled out of the garage and headed toward downtown Boise. We cruised up and down the streets. Occasionally, the two-way radio Brody carried crackled as men reported in.

"Do you mind if we drive past Haven headquarters?" I asked.

They'd promised to bury the bodies, and I wanted to see if they'd honored their commitments.

"Mr. Allsop?" Jonesy inquired.

"Do it," Brody said.

Jonesy swung the SUV around, and our caravan headed toward the hospital. We pulled into the emergency entrance, pausing in front of the double doors leading into the Haven headquarters. The bodies were gone, the broken glass swept up, and the puddle of blood scrubbed clean. Only the jagged glass along the window frames gave evidence of yesterday's attack.

I turned to Brody. "You guys took care of their bodies."

"Of course, we did. The Allsops keep their word. We buried your people and cleaned up the mess."

"Thanks, Brody," I said. "Sunny will be grateful."

I winced. I'd provided the perfect opening for one of Brody's crude comments. *Yeah, just how grateful will Sunny be?* Nudge, nudge. Instead of seizing the opportunity, Brody bumped his shoulder against mine. "Come on, man. It's only common decency to give your friends a proper burial."

Brody Allsop had stepped up. Maybe I'd underestimated the man.

We drove away from the headquarters and continued north. Turning a corner, we came upon a disheveled elderly man climbing out of a busted-up storefront. He stilled when he saw us, gripping a bottle of mouthwash in both hands.

"Pull over," Brody ordered. When Jonesy obeyed, the other SUVs followed suit.

Brody jumped out of the SUV, and I trailed closely behind him. The old man blinked and stumbled backward. Arms outstretched, palms up, Brody slowly approached the man.

"Sir, we mean no harm," Brody said in a gentle voice. "We're friends."

The man clutched the mouthwash as if he thought we'd steal it from him. His hands trembled, his knees wobbled, and he leaned against the battered storefront. His gaze darted from Brody to me. I smiled, trying to look nonthreatening.

"Do you need help?" Brody asked. "Food or water? Medical care?"

The man licked his lips. "I'm doing fine. Don't mean no harm. I'll just be on my way."

Brody pointed at the man behind the wheel of the second SUV, who jumped from the vehicle and joined us on the sidewalk. "Clint, this gentleman needs a ride home. Give him a case of water and a box of rations. Write down his address so our people can check in on him later."

"Yes, sir." Clint walked up to the elderly man and took his arm. "Come with me, sir. We'll see you safely home."

"Who are you people?" the man asked.

"Allsop security," Clint said, leading the man to the second SUV. "We're here to help."

I stared at Brody. I never would have guessed that Brody Allsop would be a force for good in the world, but then I'd totally misjudged Ripper when I first met him, too. If an outlaw biker could turn out to be a stand-up guy—a hero—maybe there was hope for a spoiled rich kid like Brody. Sometimes disaster changes people for the better.

"Radio Jonesy when you're finished so we can meet up," Brody called. He turned to me. "I'm not giving up on finding your friends today. Let's go."

We climbed into the SUV and pulled away from the curb, recommencing our journey through the city.

Fifteen minutes later, Brody's radio squawked.

"Yes?"

"We dropped off the old man at his house," Clint said. "Then we spotted a Nampa Boy outside of a pawn shop, and we gave chase."

"And?" Brody barked.

"We got him."

Brody whooped and shot me a thumbs-up. "Where are you?"

"A block off Main Street." Clint relayed the address.

"Hold him. We'll come to you." Brody turned to me. "And now we'll get some answers about your friends."

We raced to rendezvous with Clint and his team. Their SUV was parked diagonally across a sidewalk, as if they'd jumped the curb in order to cut off a man fleeing on foot. As we climbed out of our vehicle, I spied the Nampa Boy, sitting on the pavement, surrounded by Allsop's men.

He was young, no more than twenty, wearing the blue baseball cap that signaled his affiliation with the Boys. Somebody had slapped a pair of handcuffs on him. He must have resisted his captors. Blood trickled from the corner of his mouth, and the skin around his left eye was puffy and discolored. Jaw set, he scowled defiantly as we approached.

Brody dropped to his haunches next to the young man. "This can go one of two ways," he said, his tone perfectly amiable. "You cooperate, you tell us what we want to know, and we'll part as friends. Then you can skedaddle back to your buddies in Nampa." Brody angled his head to one side, and his voice took on a menacing edge. "Refuse to cooperate, and things will get ugly. Oh, we'll make you talk, no doubt about that." He cocked his thumb at Jonesy. "My security chief is an expert at getting men to spill their guts." He paused, probably for dramatic effect. *Spill their guts.* The double meaning raised the hairs on the back of my neck. The kid's Adam's apple bobbed when he swallowed. "You'll talk, and then we'll let you rot in a cell in the old state pen," Brody continued cheerfully. "The easy way or the hard way. Your choice."

"You think I'm stupid?" the young man sputtered. "No matter what I say, there's no way you'll let me go."

Jonesy crouched down next to Brody and drew his gun from its holster. "Let's make this simple, boss." He flashed his teeth, then pointed his weapon at the young man's leg. "What's your name, kid?"

The young man's brows drew together. "Daniel."

"You got a choice to make, Daniel. Answer Mr. Allsop's questions, or we'll see how you like a bullet in the knee."

Daniel's gaze darted from Jonesy, to Brody, to Clint, to me, as if he couldn't believe what he was hearing and sought validation of the words in our eyes.

"Brody," I said in a low voice. I didn't sign on to kneecap a kid.

Brody raised a hand, silencing me, then he sighed. "You're right, Daniel. We're not going to let you go, but we are willing to let you live. Here's the deal. Answer one question, one simple question, and I guarantee that Jonesy won't put a bullet in you."

"Fuck, man. You've already admitted that you lied about letting me go," Daniel cried. "Why should I believe you now?"

"Boss?" Jonesy tapped the barrel of the gun on the kid's knee.

"One simple question," Brody repeated.

Silence, then a grudging, "What?"

"The woman and man you took from the Haven, the doctor and the nurse, where are they being held?"

Daniel snorted. "Them? They're not being held anywhere." He shook his head, his mouth twisting bitterly. "It was a total shit show, and Pete's in big trouble for it."

"What happened?" I demanded.

"Pete was bragging, told them that we'd attacked the Haven, killed everybody there, and took all their stuff. 'Boise belongs to us,' you know? Then later, when he was walking them to lockup, the doctor chick did some kind of karate move on Pete, and the big guy punched his lights out. They took his gun, his keys, and his car."

"They escaped?" I gasped, scarcely able to wrap my head around the good news.

"Yeah. They're in the wind."

THIRTEEN

Sunny

I practically skipped down the stairs and along the hallway leading to Brody's basement man cave. Not even the prospect of spending the evening in the company of one of my least favorite people could dampen my joy. The two bottles of French champagne we downed after dinner only added to my giddiness.

Sara and Rocco had escaped. All wasn't right in my world—not even close—but this was the best news I'd heard in forever. I was so stinking happy that when Brody invited Kyle and me to hang out in his man cave, I said yes without a second thought.

"Hold up, Sunny," Kyle called from behind me.

"Okey dokey." I spun around and lost my balance, wavering on my feet until Kyle caught up with me. He slung an arm around my waist, and I leaned against his chest, smiling to myself as we swayed back and forth.

"You sure you're up for this?" he asked in a low voice.

"Yep," I said. "Brody said he has a pool table. I want to play pool. I bet I'll beat your socks off." Wait. That wasn't right. What was I trying to say? "I mean, I'll knock your pants off."

"And she's at point of the bacchanalia where she starts mixing up her cliches." He chuckled.

The double doors to the man cave swung open, and Brody poked his head out. "I thought I heard voices. Come on in."

"Hi, Brody," I called.

Kyle took my hand, and we followed Brody into his private retreat. My eyes turned immediately to a corner of the large room, where a Tiffany-style chandelier cast a circle of light on a carved mahogany pool table.

"Fancy," I said, letting go of Kyle's hand and lurching toward the pool table. I took three steps, then something in my peripheral vision snagged my attention. I swiveled my head and froze in place.

Not ten feet away, a full-grown cougar sprawled on the hearth of a stone fireplace, his massive paws outstretched, and his long tail curled upward at his side. Fur in shades of brown and cream covered his powerful body. Although in repose, he looked ready to pounce. Implacable yellow eyes bore into mine. I blinked. Did his pink nose just twitch?

I staggered backward, unable to tear my eyes from the beast.

"Sunny, you haven't met LeRoy, have you?" Brody asked, dropping to his haunches. He held out a hand toward the cougar. "Here, kitty kitty."

"Are you crazy?" I hissed. Not even Brody Allsop would keep a pet mountain lion, would he?

Brody laughed so hard that he fell backward onto his butt. "No worries," he said, gripping the side of a coffee table and hoisting himself to his feet. "He's not alive. Not anymore."

My panic retreated, and an odd combination of relief and horror roiled in my gut. I looked more closely at the cougar—a dead animal stuffed and mounted, frozen forever in a lifelike pose. Goose bumps skittered across my shoulders and down my arms.

I turned my face away, and my gaze fell upon another dead beast. A brown bear reared back on his hind legs, so tall that his head almost touched the ceiling. Enormous claws slashed at the air, and he bared his teeth in a menacing rictus. Dead, yet wearing a convincing mask of life.

"Dad and I shot the cougar in Texas," Brody explained. "And we bagged the bear in Alaska."

Maybe I shouldn't be surprised that a douche like Brody was a fan of trophy hunting and taxidermy, but Jesus, killing and stuffing big animals? For fun? It absolutely boggled my mind.

"Dad and I were supposed to hunt in Africa this summer," he continued. "The damned flu messed up our plans."

Seriously? Brody was whining because the pandemic that wiped out most of the world's population messed with his plans to shoot animals in Africa.

"But one of Dad's friends—a doctor in town—was a big game hunter, too. I've seen his safari room. Dude had some primo trophies. I had a couple of the security guys move the best ones over here."

Brody swept out his arm. Along the back wall of his man cave, the doctor's *primo trophies* occupied a place of honor. A black-maned lion tackled a zebra, his mighty paws digging into the zebra's striped back. Wearing what looked like a hairy gray shoulder cape, a baboon perched on a wooden ledge. A spotted dog-like creature—I think it was a hyena—posed on a rock. A gold-and-black leopard skin rug, complete with a snarling head and pointed teeth, draped across the back of a sofa. I gaped, open-mouthed. *Was that even legal?* At the sight of a giraffe's head, mounted to the wall by its shoulders, my eyes welled with tears. It had to be seven or eight feet tall, its beautiful lifeless eyes framed by heavy lashes. The curve of its mouth gave the illusion that it was smiling. *Smiling.*

I whirled on Brody. "What the hell is wrong with you?"

His shoulders shook with laughter. "Aw… is Sunny afwaid of the widdle animals?"

Right. I was *afraid* of the dead animals. *That* was my problem. I wanted to knock that mocking expression from his face. I took a step toward him, my hands clenching into fists.

Kyle pushed between Brody and me and wrapped his arm around my shoulders, halting me midstep.

"Remember, Sunny used to volunteer at animal shelters. You can't expect her to be a fan of trophy hunting."

Brody rolled his eyes. "Tree-hugging hippie," he muttered under his breath.

I tugged against Kyle's restraining arm, and he shot me a warning look. Closing my eyes, I mentally counted to ten. Nothing I said or did would change Brody's mind about his precious trophies. Moreover, it couldn't be a good idea to alienate a man whose father controlled a private army, an army they promised to deploy to protect Boise from the Nampa Boys.

"I'm going to shoot some pool," I said, swallowing back my anger. "Anybody want to join me?"

"Before that, I want to show you guys something else," Brody said, his tone eager.

I couldn't help myself. "More dead animal trophies?"

"Nah, but this is just as good." He led the way past the pool table, pausing next to a wall covered with mounted weapons. "You guys ever take a school field trip to the old state penitentiary? Did you see the weapons exhibit there? I had a bunch of the collection moved over here."

Brody pilfered stuff from a museum? Yeah, of course he did. I couldn't even pretend to be shocked.

"Check this out." He pulled a curved knife from an ornately carved scabbard. "It's an Arab jambiya knife. This sucker's really old." Laughing, he brandished the knife, stabbing an imaginary foe. He returned it to its scabbard, then pointed at the corner of the room. "A Civil War Gatling gun. I've got a German Howitzer, too. And a Tommy gun, like the gangsters used during Prohibition. And an Uzi."

The last of my happy buzz completely dissipated.

"And Kyle, you'll like this." He waved his hand at a dozen swords mounted on hooks on the wall. "You were on the fencing team, right? Maybe we could spar sometime," he said eagerly.

Kyle's brow wrinkled as he studied the precious historic weapons. If he was tempted to say something about the wisdom of fighting with museum-quality antique swords, he decided to keep it to himself. He shrugged. "Maybe we could." He touched my shoulder. "You want to shoot some pool, Sunny?"

"Yes, please," I said, relieved that he changed the subject.

The three of us played for about an hour, until I began to feel sleepy.

"You can't go to bed now," Brody protested. "I have a surprise for you coming at ten o'clock."

"For me? What kind of surprise?" I asked, yawning.

He made a face. "It wouldn't be a surprise if I told you."

"Okay." I curled up on one of the leather recliners—definitely not the sofa with the leopard skin rug—and watched Brody and Kyle play a game of one-pocket pool. At 10 p.m. precisely, according to the clock on the wall, somebody knocked on the door to the man cave.

"Come in," Brody called.

The door swung open, and a middle-aged woman stood in the doorway. She was wearing a gray housekeeping dress with a crisp white apron tied around her waist. With one hand on the doorknob, she balanced a wide silver tray on her hip.

"Let me help you." Kyle dashed across the room, took the tray from the woman, and carried it to the coffee table.

She followed him, her hands fluttering nervously. "It's quite all right, sir. I can manage."

"No problem," Kyle said.

"That will be all, Hildy," Brody said.

Hildy bobbed her head and exited the room.

The tray held three silver, dome-shaped cloches. With a flourish, Brody lifted a cloche, revealing a bowl holding a mound of vanilla ice cream topped with hot fudge sauce and a cherry. Tucked on either side of the ice cream were walnut-studded brownies.

"Jake told me once that brownie sundaes are your favorite dessert," Brody said. "I had Hildy make them special for you."

Brownie sundaes *were* my favorite dessert, and I thought they were a thing of the past, that I'd never taste another one. *Jake* had told Brody that I love them, and Brody had remembered. I swallowed, the pain from Jake's absence striking me anew. And Brody. Why had Brody gone out of his way to do something nice for me? One minute I was certain that he was an irredeemable creep, then he went and had his private chef make my favorite dessert.

Kyle took my hand and gently squeezed it. "That was a really thoughtful thing to do, Brody," he said.

"Yes, it was." I remembered my manners. "Thank you, Brody."

He grinned and lifted the two other cloches. "Let's dig in."

I dipped a corner of a brownie into the ice cream and hot fudge, then moaned when the decadent chocolate touched my tongue. "I've missed this."

"If you and Kyle stick around, you can have brownie sundaes every day," Brody said. He took another bite. "Now that we know that Sara and Rocco have escaped, we can focus on taking down the Nampa Boys. We won't have to worry about your friends being hurt when we move against the bad guys."

"Thank God for that," I said.

"How about if you help us try to find the other scavengers, the ones who were out in the city when the Haven was attacked? They need to hear that the doctor and nurse got away, and we need to make plans for getting the Haven back on its feet," Brody said. "You know where they live, don't you?"

"Not all of the scavengers, but some of them," I answered.

"That's a start," Brody said. "Tomorrow we'll begin rebuilding Boise."

FOURTEEN

Kyle

The bedroom door rattled in its frame as a heavy body slammed against it. I squinted, struggling to raise my head.

"No, Miles." My lips hardly moved as I spoke the words.

The flu had stolen every ounce of strength from my body, leaving my limbs leaden and weak, but I had no choice. I had to pick up the shotgun in my lap. I had to stop him before he killed me. Before he killed Kenzie.

A knife blade pierced the flimsy wood, then retracted. A momentary reprieve.

Shit, not again. My head swam. I knew what came next, still I held my breath. Maybe this time... this time...

The blade tore a jagged hole in the door as he savagely pounded against the wood.

"Miles.. Miles... don't..."

My fingers curled around the shotgun, and I strained with all my might, but I couldn't lift it. Which was worse, if I succeeded in lifting the weapon, or if I failed? I knew what it would cost me to succeed, but failure had to be worse, didn't it?

The door splintered, and a hand reached through the hole. God. I pressed back against the chair, readying myself for what came next, for what always came next.

"No... no... Miles."

My entire body jostled as someone roughly shook my shoulder. "Kyle, wake up. Wake up!"

I sucked in a startled breath, and my eyes flew open. In the dim light I saw Sunny leaning on her elbow, one hand still on my shoulder.

"You with me?" she asked.

Nodding, I forced myself to sit up, then scrubbed at my face with my hands. "I had another bad dream." I snorted. Talk about stating the obvious.

Sunny sat up, too, and gently rubbed my shoulder. Without thought, I leaned toward her, allowing her touch to comfort me. After thirty seconds or so, I straightened.

"Who's Miles?" Sunny asked.

I jerked and turned my head her way. "What?"

"Whenever you have a nightmare, you call his name."

I gulped. I couldn't tell Sunny what went down with Miles. I couldn't plant those images in her brain. "It's okay, Sunny. I can deal."

"It's not okay," she said. "And clearly you can't deal. Maybe it would help to talk about it."

I shook my head frantically back and forth, rejecting the notion of spilling my guts to Jake's little sister.

She sighed. "I'm getting tired of your bullshit, Kyle. I'm not a little girl you need to protect from the world. Let me help you."

God, it was tempting to unburden myself, to allow someone— to allow Sunny—to console me. Maybe I could share a sliver of the memory without burdening her with all the gory details.

She must have seen the uncertainty flicker in my eyes, because she pressed her advantage. "Come on, Kyle. It's not working for you to carry this by yourself."

"Miles was my friend." I spoke quickly before I could relent. "A truly good guy. We both came down with the flu." I closed my eyes against the memory, then snapped them open, meeting her compassion-filled gaze. "He developed symptoms a day before I did, and the disease ran its course more quickly in him than in me. I was weak, barely able to lift my head, but Miles… shit… Miles…"

"The flu mania," she guessed.

"Yeah. My friend was gone. All that was left was a crazed shell of a man intent on doing violence. It came down to him or me. And if he killed me, there was a good chance he'd turn on Kenzie next."

Sunny's eyes widened at the mention of my ex. "Kenzie?"

"Miles was her cousin," I said. "I couldn't risk him attacking her. And I couldn't leave her to defend herself against a man she loved. So I did what I had to do. I shot him."

"Oh, Kyle." Sunny's voice broke. She wrapped both arms around me and pressed her face against my neck. Her tears soaked into my skin. "I'm so sorry."

Did it make me a wimp that it felt damned good to be held? Ripper had become the gold standard in my mind for how a man comports himself in the post-pandemic world. A man took care of business. He protected his people. He kept his word. If Ripper ever showed weakness or vulnerability, I never saw it. Didn't mean that it never happened, I supposed. Who knew what went down between him and Kenzie when they were alone.

"Thanks, Sunny," I murmured, savoring the warmth of her soft, feminine body. "I know I did the right thing. I know that Miles would never blame me, but man, it hurts." She tightened her embrace. After a while, she lifted her head and studied me with watery eyes. I smoothed back the hair from her face. "I'm happy you're here with me, Sunshine."

She smiled at the old endearment, then her expression faltered. "Do you still love Kenzie?"

"I'll always love Kenzie." Sunny stiffened in my arms. "But I'm not *in love* with her anymore. Our friendship survived the breakup." I paused. "I mean, it took a while, but we're good now, and I'm happy for her and Ripper."

"Really?" A note of skepticism—or hope—lingered in her voice.

"Yeah, really. It all worked out for the best."

"I'm glad," Sunny said, her eyes luminous in the dusky light.

"Me, too."

We lapsed into silence. She laid her head on my shoulder. I nuzzled her hair, breathing in the scent of honey and grapefruit shampoo. Man, honey and grapefruit was fast becoming my favorite smell.

Sunny lifted her head. "It's still early. Do you want to try to get some more sleep?"

I have a better idea. I almost said the words out loud, but stopped myself. We needed to wrap our heads around our evolving relationship, figure out what we're doing before we jumped into sex.

I glanced at the alarm clock on the nightstand. "It's 5:30, and I'm too wired to fall back asleep, but you go ahead."

"No." Sunny hopped out of bed, extended a hand, and pulled me up. "Let's go down to the kitchen, make cups of coffee and tea, then go out on the balcony and wait for the sun to come up," she suggested.

We put on the terry bathrobes we'd found in the closet and tiptoed down to the kitchen, a huge room full of top-of-the-line stainless steel appliances. Appliances that worked, thanks to the house's generators and solar panels, a fact that still boggled my mind. I'd never take electricity for granted again.

I found the coffee and tea and brewed a cup of each while Sunny poked around in the kitchen. Swinging open a door, she gave a low whistle. "Check this out," she called. I followed her into a large walk-in pantry lined floor to ceiling with shelves crowded with foodstuffs. Another refrigerator and a huge freezer stood along one wall.

"Reminds me of Miles's basement," I said. At Sunny's quizzical expression, I explained. "Miles was a survivalist, and he had a ton of food set aside for the end of days."

"Sounds like a smart guy."

My chest ached, the way it always did whenever I spoke about my friend. "He was."

"Excuse me," a voice called. Sunny and I turned around. Hildy stood behind us. Despite the early hour, she was wearing an immaculate gray dress and a white apron. Her hair was pulled back in a neat bun. "I'm sorry that I wasn't here to make your coffee and tea," she said.

Sunny smiled. "It's not even six in the morning. You don't need to get up to make us coffee."

Hildy frowned. "Mr. Allsop wouldn't like that his guests had to fend for themselves."

"Then we won't tell him." Sunny winked and laid a conspiratorial hand on Hildy's arm.

"If you ever need anything, please don't hesitate to wake me." Hildy pointed toward a short hallway leading from the kitchen. She blinked rapidly, appearing flustered. "First door on the left."

"You were up late last night making those delicious brownie sundaes," Sunny said. "Then I bet we woke you up early rattling around in the kitchen."

"Oh, no," Hildy said quickly. "Mr. Allsop likes to have fresh pastries with breakfast. I'm always at work by six. I'm baking croissants this morning."

Sunny's eyes grew wide and hopeful. "By any chance are you making chocolate croissants?"

"I am now."

Sunny squealed and hugged Hildy. "Do you need help?"

Hildy patted Sunny's shoulder and offered a genuine smile. "No, miss. The dough is in the refrigerator. All I need to do is shape the rolls and give them a final rise. You and the gentleman should enjoy your drinks while I get to work."

"Okay, we will." Sunny picked up her cup of Earl Grey tea. "Thanks for making chocolate croissants. I appreciate it."

"My pleasure." The woman beamed.

Sunny's kindness and warmth had worked its magic on Hildy. I took my cup of coffee and followed my old friend—friend, yeah right, the jig was up on that one—onto the wide balcony that overlooked the city. She settled onto a cushioned outdoor sofa and patted the spot next to her, inviting me to sit.

I'd missed her during the past crazy months, missed her gift for drawing people in and making them feel valued and seen. The new, dangerous world hadn't dulled her spirit, made her cautious or less openhearted. I wasn't entirely sure that that was a good thing. The urge to cherish her and keep her safe burrowed deep in my chest.

"The Allsops run that woman ragged," Sunny said as I took a seat next to her.

"They sure do," I agreed.

In the distance, the skyline of downtown Boise slowly grew visible in the lightening sky.

Sunny shivered. I threw an arm around her shoulders and drew her close. She snuggled against me, clutching her cup of hot tea to her chest.

"We can go inside if you're cold," I suggested.

"No, I like this. I like sitting with you waiting for the sun to come up."

"Me, too." I dropped a kiss on her temple, and she sighed, her lips tilting up in a small smile.

We fell into silence. Birds twittered in the nearby trees. In the distance, a coyote yipped, then a second joined in. A cacophony of sharp barks and yelps erupted.

"I hope they didn't find a dog," Sunny said, turning her face toward the sound.

"Probably a rabbit." I *hoped* it was a rabbit.

"Probably," Sunny repeated, her voice uncertain. She shivered again, and I rubbed my palm up and down her arm. "I wonder where Sara and Rocco are right now."

"Do you think they'll come back to Boise?" I asked.

"Maybe," she said slowly. "I know that they feel responsible for the people here. But if the Nampa Boy told them that everybody at the Haven is dead and that they'd taken control of the city, Sara and Rocco might decide that it's too risky. They might go into hiding or take off."

"At least they got away," I said.

"Thank God for that." She snuggled against my shoulder. "You still want to go back to Valhalla right away, don't you?"

I shouldn't be surprised that my forthright friend brought up the subject that I'd been wondering how to broach.

"Yeah, I do. It's my home, and the people there are my family." I caught her chin and tilted her face up to mine. I needed her to see the conviction behind my words. "I want you to come with me, Sunny. I couldn't bear to leave you behind."

Her beautiful amber eyes glistened in the pale morning light. "I want to be with you, too."

Something shifted inside of me, and certainty settled in my chest. I dipped my head and brushed my lips against hers. We weren't playing for an audience. We weren't selling our roles as boyfriend and girlfriend. It was just the two of us. No witnesses. No ghosts from the past.

What would Jake say if he could see us now? Would he be glad that his friend stood by his little sister's side as she faced the post-pandemic world? I hoped so.

Sunny moaned and shifted, curving her body against mine. Her tongue darted from her mouth and teased my lips apart. I tasted bergamot and lavender as we deepened the kiss. Her fists clenched on my terrycloth robe. She slowly pulled the collar apart, baring my upper chest. Delicate fingers traced my collarbone then dipped into the notch in my throat. Sunny yanked her mouth away from mine. We stared at each other, panting.

"You want to stop?" I choked out.

"Nope."

"You sure?"

She laughed softly. "I've fantasized about kissing you since I was fifteen. So, no, I don't want to stop."

My brain short-circuited. Sunny had wanted to kiss me since she was *fifteen*?

Her gaze dropped to my chest, and she bit her lower lip.

What was the woman doing?

With half-closed eyelids, she lowered her head and pressed open-mouthed kisses against my pecs. When her fingernail scraped over my nipple, I bucked. Seizing her hips, I pulled her across my lap. She straddled my thighs. I tangled my fingers in her hair and tugged, dragging her mouth back to mine. My body rioted, my nerve endings set ablaze.

Behind us, somebody cleared their throat. Sunny and I jerked apart. I twisted my neck, scowling. Brody leaned against the wide-open French doors. He lifted a cup of steaming coffee to his mouth and took a sip, his eyes dancing. "Sorry to interrupt, brother. I'm heading to the gym to get some cardio in before breakfast. Hildy told me you're up, so I thought I'd invite you to join me."

Sunny swung off of my hips and stood. If I'd guessed that she'd be embarrassed that Brody Allsop caught us making out, I would've been wrong. Bending over, she pressed a quick kiss on my mouth. "Later, babe," she said. Chin held high, she sauntered past a smirking Brody.

"You want to come, Sunny?" he called after her.

Pausing, she glanced back over her shoulder. "No, Brody, I don't want to come. At least not now."

He barked out a laugh as she disappeared into the kitchen, then he turned his eyes toward my lap. "You... uh... need a minute, buddy?"

Yeah. I needed a minute. Dammit.

He's lucky I don't strangle him.

FIFTEEN

Sunny

I resisted the urge to lick the melted chocolate off my thumb, although now that I thought about it, wouldn't it be smarter—less wasteful of resources—to clean up with my tongue rather than smearing dark chocolate on a white linen napkin?

"Thank you for the croissants, Hildy," I said to the housekeeper, who was bustling around the breakfast table refilling coffee cups. "They were perfect."

She bobbed her head, acknowledging my thanks, and glanced at Mr. Allsop. "That will be all, Hildy," he said. "You may go."

"Yes, sir." Clutching the coffee pot to her chest, she scurried from the room.

Mr. Allsop dabbed at his mouth with his napkin, then settled back in his chair. "Now that we know that the doctor and nurse have escaped, we can begin to plan an assault on the Nampa Boys headquarters. Kyle, I'd like you to join Jonesy, Brody, and me in the war room."

War room? The Allsops have a war room?

Kyle looked as startled as I was by the request, but he recovered quickly. "Of course, Mr. Allsop."

"And Sunny. We need to get the word out about your friends' escape. I'd like you to take one of my men and visit your fellow scavengers."

"Sure," I said. "Could you send the same guy who went with me yesterday? We got along great."

He inclined his head. "As you wish."

"Maybe they could stop at Northumberland Heights when they're finished," Kyle spoke up. "Sunny could use some more clothes, and I'd appreciate it if your guy could drive my pickup back here."

"Of course." Mr. Allsop tossed his napkin onto his plate and stood. "Sunny, my man will meet you out front in ten minutes. Now gentlemen, follow me to the war room."

"One sec." Kyle hopped to his feet and dug in his jeans pocket. "You'll need my keys." His hand closed briefly over mine when he handed me the fob. I tilted my face up, and he dropped a quick kiss on my lips.

"You taste like chocolate," he murmured.

I smiled. "You taste like coffee and chocolate."

Mr. Allsop cleared his throat.

"Later." Kyle backed away, smiling a farewell.

"Later," Brody echoed, following his father from the dining room.

After a quick trip to the bathroom to brush my teeth and attend to business, I met Finn in the driveway. "Hey, Sunny." He greeted me like an old friend. Most of Mr. Allsop's people maintained a painfully polite distance. I appreciated Finn's relaxed manners. He waved a small spiral notebook in the air. "I'm supposed to write down as many addresses as you can remember, so we have a record of where the scavengers live. It'll come in handy once we get the Haven back on its feet."

I doubted that I could remember them all, but maybe if we put our heads together, the other scavengers and I could compile a comprehensive list. Finn and I climbed into Daisy. This time, when the engine hesitated Finn didn't comment. We drove into town. Within a couple of hours, we'd visited the homes of five of my fellow scavengers. The last man—Josef—directed us to two more of our people. Finn dutifully wrote down everyone's names and addresses.

"You ready to see my old neighborhood?" I asked him when we were done.

"Sure thing," he said.

I steered Daisy toward Northumberland Heights. Finn gave a low whistle when we drove past the guard shack. "Guess I should have figured you were rich, being friends with the Allsops and all."

"I wouldn't exactly call us friends," I said. "More like acquaintances. Mr. Allsop knew my parents and Kyle's. We all belonged to the same country club."

"Country club." He laughed. "Like I said. Rich."

I could have argued the point. My family had never been Allsop rich—with live-in staff and a private jet—but we'd undoubtedly lived a life of comfort and plenty. Growing up, I'd been damned lucky, and more for my family than for our material possessions. I sighed.

"What is it?" Finn asked.

"Just missing my parents and my brother," I confessed.

He reached over and patted my arm. "I know. Me, too."

When we parked in my driveway, I turned to Finn. "My food supply is hidden upstairs. I won't need it. Would you mind if we box it up and take it to Mrs. B. and Ever?"

"Not at all. I'd like to see that little rascal again."

I glanced his way with wide, shocked eyes. "I'm going to tell Mrs. B. you called her a rascal." I mock gasped. "Even though she deserves it. What did she call you, a 'tall drink of water'?"

"No, ma'am. You will not tell that sweet old lady that I called her a rascal." His voice was firm, but his blue eyes twinkled with humor. "You know darned well that I was talking about the little girl."

I grinned. "Knowing Mrs. B., she'd probably prefer that you call her a rascal rather than a sweet old lady."

He snorted. "That may be."

Finn carried an empty box into the house and followed me upstairs to my bedroom. I pointed to my bookshelves. "The food is hidden behind the rows of books. Can you start packing it up? I'm going to go grab a suitcase from my parents' closet."

"You bet."

I crossed the hall to my mom and dad's bedroom, then faltered before stepping across the threshold. I hadn't stepped inside the room since the day they died. The messy bed sheets were rumpled and stained, the air in the room so sour that my nose stung. In my mind's eye, I saw my father lift Mom's body from the bed, knocking both a pillow and a glass of water onto the floor as he staggered under her slight weight. Was his heart already failing when he lifted her? Was that why he stumbled? Or was it grief? I'd never know.

"Shit," I whispered, overcome by memory.

Finn appeared at my side. "You need help?"

I almost asked him to fetch the big, black suitcase from their closet, but changed my mind. If Kyle and I left Boise, this might be my last time in this room, in this house. I'd never forget my parents, but I wanted to take a few tangible reminders of them.

"No," I said. "Thanks, but I got this." He clasped my arm, then silently returned to my room. Squaring my shoulders, I marched toward the closet, lifted the suitcase down from the shelf, and rolled it into the hall.

I walked over to the dresser, to the inlaid wooden box where Mom kept her treasures. I pushed aside a diamond bracelet and the emerald earrings Dad gave Mom for their twentieth anniversary. I was looking for something far more precious.

There. My fingers brushed over Grandma's charm bracelet. Grandpa had given grandma the 14 karat-oval linked-bracelet on the day they wed, with a single heart-shaped charm attached. They'd been in college at the time, and he'd worked extra shifts at his part-time job in order to afford the gift. Over the years, as his business grew and flourished, he'd added to the bracelet. Dozens of charms now adorned it. A cat with sapphire eyes purchased for their fifth anniversary. A gold baby rattle to celebrate my mother's birth. The Eiffel Tower to commemorate their first trip to Paris. An hourglass engraved with the words Grow Old Along With Me. They *had* grown old together, lived a long and happy life. Something the damned flu had denied my parents and millions—maybe billions—of other souls.

I fastened the charm bracelet around my wrist, then walked to the dresser. In the bottom drawer I found Dad's favorite sweater, an army green, Irish knit cardigan with leather patches on the elbows. When I was little, Dad read me storybooks every night before bed. On chilly evenings, perched on his lap, I'd snuggle into that sweater, warm and safe in my daddy's arms. I folded the sweater over my arm and picked up the framed family photo that sat atop the dresser.

My gaze traveled slowly over the room. The bracelet, the sweater, the picture; I didn't need anything else. No wait. I jogged to the closet, lifted Mom's favorite scarf from a hook, and wrapped it around my neck. She called it "her signature fashion statement," and she wore it all the time. A 1960s Pucci print scarf sporting a jarring kaleidoscope of pink, green, and orange swirls.

I carried the suitcase back to my room. The cardboard box full of food sat in the hallway outside my door. Finn watched in silence while I packed up clothes and a few mementos. I stuffed my heavy winter parka into the suitcase; I bet I'd need a warm coat on the ranch. And some sturdy boots.

"Almost ready," I told Finn. "Kyle's duffel is next door in my brother's room."

"I'll carry your suitcase and the food downstairs while you pack up Kyle's stuff," he said.

Jake and Kyle had been about the same size, so I threw a few extra shirts and pairs of jeans into the duffel. Maybe Kyle would like to wear my brother's clothes. Before zipping the duffel shut, I slipped a childhood photo of Jake and Kyle wearing their Little League uniforms into the bag.

Finn waited for me in the hall. Without a word, he took the duffel and carried it downstairs to Daisy.

I pointed at the Chamberlain's house kitty-corner across the street. "Kyle's pickup is in the garage. You can follow me to Mrs. B.'s house."

"Sure thing."

We crossed the street. Finn took the keys from me and wrestled open the garage door. At the sight of the black truck, he frowned. Trailing his hand over the side of the truck bed, he slowly approached the driver's door.

He cocked his head and glanced at me. "Valhalla Ranch?"

"Yeah. Kyle borrowed his friend's truck for the trip."

Finn was silent for a long moment. "I thought Kyle was a city boy," he said slowly.

"He is—or he used to be. Early on in the pandemic, Kyle was hitchhiking to Portland after somebody stole his ride. A rancher—Bear—picked him up on I-84 and told him to come to Valhalla if things got bad in the city. Things got very bad in the city. Kyle and his friends headed to Valhalla. Found that it had been taken over by a group of white supremacists. Real bad guys. They were holding Bear prisoner. Kyle and his friends helped Bear take the ranch back from the bad guys. And now they all live there."

Finn touched the letters spelling out Valhalla Ranch. "That's quite an adventure Kyle had."

"It is. As soon as Boise is stabilized, he and I are going to Valhalla. Kyle said it's his home. Bear and his friends there are his family."

Finn swung his startled gaze my way, his expression serious. "Mr. Allsop says that you and Kyle are signing on to help him run Boise."

Oh, crap. How could I be so stupid? I was so comfortable with Finn that I forgot that he was Mr. Allsop's man, that he would report back what I said. "Mr. Allsop wants us to stay. He has some idea that because we grew up with Brody—because he knew our parents and our background—that we're the right kind of people to work with him."

"Mr. Allsop has some strong opinions about the right kind of people," Finn conceded. "But you don't want to join up?"

"We want Boise to be safe from the Nampa Boys. We want the Haven back up and running. We want to see law and order restored, so survivors can live in peace and rebuild their lives. That's what the Allsops are working to achieve, but as soon as we know that Boise is secure, Kyle and I are going to Valhalla."

Hands on his hips, Finn stared at the floor, deep in thought.

"Please don't tell Mr. Allsop that Kyle and I will be bailing on him. We'll tell him. I promise. Just not yet."

He lifted his head and met my eyes. "You're asking me to keep a secret from my boss."

"I am. I'm sorry to put you in that position." I faltered. I was asking a good man to compromise his integrity. "If you need to report this to him, I understand. I guess there's no real reason to keep our decision from him, it's just that he seems so set on us staying. We want to keep the focus on stopping the Nampa Boys, not the fact that we're leaving."

"I understand," he said. "Guess it wouldn't hurt to keep the news from Mr. Allsop, especially since you'll be telling him eventually." Despite his assurance, Finn looked troubled, lost in thought. His fingers drummed on the gold lettering on the driver's door.

"I'm sorry," I repeated.

He ran a palm across his face. "No need. You're going to Valhalla. Sounds like a fine plan. Can't say I blame you."

His voice sounded wistful. It made sense. He grew up on a farm, and he probably missed it. An idea occurred to me. Finn understood everything required to raise crops and tend livestock. With his work ethic and character, he'd be an asset wherever he settled. Kyle said that Valhalla was a big place, that his friends would welcome Ever and Mrs. B. Maybe they'd have room for a hardworking farm boy.

"Are you committed to sticking with the Allsops?" I asked. "Maybe you'd like to come to Valhalla with us."

A pained expression crossed his face. I'd guessed right. He did miss farm life. "Now that's a tempting offer. I can't think of any place I'd rather go, but I have work to do that will keep me here." He blew out a breath. "But tell you what, when things settle down, I'll do my best to come to Valhalla."

I smiled. "I'm going to hold you to that."

He opened the driver's side door. "I'll meet you at Mrs. B.'s place."

I jogged across the street and climbed into Daisy. Finn had already pulled out of the Chamberlain's driveway. I backed my van onto the road and headed for Mrs. B.'s, Finn following close behind.

As I was climbing out of the van, the pink front door of Cressida's Cottage flew open. An agitated Mrs. B.—her silver hair unkempt and her eyes wild—raced down the front walk. She came to a stop, gasping for breath and pressing a hand to her chest.

Finn parked the pickup, jumped out, and ran over to us.

"What's wrong?" I asked.

"It's Ever." Mrs. B.'s voice trembled. "She's missing."

SIXTEEN

Kyle

One of the Allsop security men opened the door to the war room and stuck his head inside. "Sir, we have a problem."

I looked up from the map of Nampa that I was studying.

Mr. Allsop rose from his chair on the opposite side of the table. "Jonesy, with me." The two men stepped into the hall, shutting the door behind them.

Brody and I exchanged glances. "Wonder what that's about," he said, arching his brows.

A minute later, the two men returned.

"What's up, Dad?" Brody asked.

Ignoring his son, Mr. Allsop turned to me. "Sunny's security detail radioed in."

"Did something happen to Sunny?" I interrupted, my stomach clenching.

"No, Sunny is fine," Mr. Allsop assured me. "My man reports that they were visiting..." He frowned and glanced at Jonesy. "What was it?"

"Cressida's Cottage, sir," Jonesy said.

"That's right, they were visiting Cressida's Cottage, and learned that the little girl—Ever—is missing."

"What?" I jumped to my feet, alarmed. "What happened?"

"The elderly woman who lives there said that yesterday evening the cat knocked the screen out of the kitchen window. He went outside and hadn't returned by bedtime," Mr. Allsop said. "The little girl was distraught and after the old woman went to bed, the girl decided to go search for the cat. She left a note saying that she wouldn't come home until she found him."

Sunny and Mrs. B. must be frantic with worry. "I've got to get there," I said.

"Jonesy will assemble a search party and drive you to the house. In the meantime, my man has taken your pickup and is scouring the neighborhood looking for the child."

"Can you be ready to leave in ten minutes?" Jonesy asked me.

"Of course."

"Good. Meet my team out front."

I dragged my hands through my hair. Shit. This was a nightmare. The spunky kid had wormed her way into my heart. If she were lost, or hurt, or taken... all of the horrible possibilities raced through my mind.

"Don't worry, son." I hadn't noticed Mr. Allsop approach until he spoke. He squeezed my shoulder in a reassuring, fatherly gesture. "My team will find her. After the flu, every child is precious, especially girls. My men won't rest until they bring her home."

"Thank you, sir." I glanced around the room. "Brody, do you want to come?"

"Sure." He shrugged. "I can help."

"I'm going to my room to get my weapon—just in case. I'll meet you out front." Without waiting for a reply, I dashed from the war room and up the stairs to the guest suite. Shrugging into the shoulder holster, I patted the magazine carrier, confirming that I had extra ammo. I raced downstairs and met Brody in the driveway. Two black SUVs pulled up. The passenger door on the first slid open, and Brody and I jumped in.

Twenty minutes later, we parked in front of Cressida's Cottage. Sunny and Mrs. B. sat on the front porch, holding hands. Sunny leapt to her feet and ran to me. Sliding my arms around her waist, I held her close.

"I can't..." she whispered. "If anything happens to Ever... I just can't."

"I know, Sunshine, but we'll find her and bring her home. I won't rest until she's back where she belongs." I'd experienced enough to understand that it was a promise I had no business making, but it was one I wouldn't allow myself to break. Whatever it took, I'd find Ever, even if it meant searching every house and looking under every bush in the whole damned city.

"I want to help." Sunny's face was pale, and her chin trembled.

"I know you do," I said gently. "I think that the best thing you can do right now is to keep Mrs. B. company. Look at her." I pointed. Mrs. B.'s fists were clenched over her stomach, and she rocked back and forth in her chair, her lips moving as she talked to herself, or maybe prayed. "She shouldn't be alone."

"You're right. Mrs. B. needs me. I'll take her inside and make her 'a nice cuppa' like she always says."

"Good. And who knows, maybe Ever will surprise us all by coming back home on her own, Fitzwilliam in her arms."

"Oh, Fitzwilliam came home this morning. Pleased as punch with himself. According to Mrs. B., he sauntered across the yard with a mouse in his mouth."

"If only Ever had waited," I said.

"Yeah, if only she'd waited."

"I gotta go," I said firmly, stepping back from Sunny. "Take Mrs. B. inside for a cup of tea. I'll check in later."

"Okay. Good luck." Sunny whirled around and returned to the porch. One arm thrown protectively around the older woman's shoulders, Sunny escorted Mrs. B. back into the house.

Jonesy appeared at my side. He unfolded a map of Boise—who would've guessed that paper maps would ever again be a thing—and pointed to a star that indicated our location. "Instead of teams, we're splitting up and going out individually, so we can cover more ground before it gets dark." That made sense. "We'll check every house and every yard on every street, working our way out from this location. You'll take a crowbar, in case you need to break into a place. Each man will carry a radio and check in with me once an hour." His finger sketched a rectangle on the map. "This is you."

I memorized the street names in my search zone, grabbed a crowbar and two-way radio from the back of the SUV, and took off at a jog. The first house was only a quarter mile away. I checked the yard first, looking behind every bush and inside every outbuilding before approaching the house. The place had been ransacked, and the front door stood open. Gun in hand, I stalked through the house, calling Ever's name. Unless she was hiding from someone, it was unlikely that Ever would take refuge in an abandoned house. But on the off chance that she had been injured and crawled away to safety, I'd search every damned house on my list.

One frustrating hour passed. I checked in with Jonesy, who reported that none of the searchers were having any luck. During the second hour, I turned a corner and approached a house with a swing set and a child's inflatable pool in the backyard. The pool stood upright, its three plastic rings full of air. How likely was it that the pool had been baking in the sun all summer without deflating? Child-sized pink and lavender shirts and shorts hung on a clothesline, along with adult-sized bras, panties, and a nightgown.

The back of my neck prickled. Was somebody alive in the house? Somebody with a kid whose clothes needed to be laundered? What were the odds that both a parent and child would survive the pandemic? Brody and Mr. Allsop were the only ones I'd heard of. And Sahdev had told us that women never recovered from the flu. The clothing appeared to belong to both a little girl and a woman. Something was off here.

I hopped over the short picket fence surrounding the backyard and approached the clothesline. If the clothes had been hanging there since the outbreak of the flu, the sun would have bleached the colors, and they'd be coated with dust stirred up by the wind. Instead, the pinks and purples were still vibrant. I rubbed the woman's panties between my fingers. The fabric was soft, supple, and freshly laundered. The clothes hadn't been baking in the blistering Boise sun for months.

Somebody *was* alive inside the house.

I crept up to the patio and peered through the sliding glass door into the family room. Nobody was in sight.

All right. Think.

What would a person do if she saw a stranger lurking outside the house, spying through the windows? Freak out. Grab a gun. If there was a survivor inside the house, I didn't want to scare her or goad her into attacking me in a misguided sense of self-defense. A direct approach might be better.

I prowled around to the front of the house, marched up to the door, and tapped the old-fashioned knocker against the wooden surface. Nothing. Not a sound came from inside. I repeated the action and again was met with silence.

"Hello! Is anybody there?" I pounded on the door with my fist. I waited for thirty seconds. Still nothing. "I have a crowbar. I'm coming in to check the place out for survivors. We have a missing child, too, who might be hiding. If somebody's in there, I mean no harm. I'm here to help."

I pried the front door away from the frame, then carefully pushed it open. Taking one cautious step inside the house, I swept my gaze over the hall and living room. The Haven's scavengers hadn't been here. There was no X spray-painted on the front door. And the place hadn't been tossed by looters. It looked neat and orderly, the hardwood entry swept clean. An entry table held a collection of those Precious Moments figurines that my great-aunt Beverly collected, all free of dust and grime. Through an arched doorway I spied a tidy kitchen. A full glass of an orange-colored drink sat on the counter next to a plate of crackers and an open jar of peanut butter.

Somebody was here.

"I mean you no harm," I repeated. "I'm working with the Allsop Corporation. We're here to help. We're making a list of all the survivors in town, and we're working to make the city safe again."

A woman's narrow face peeked out from the entry to the kitchen.

"I don't need any help from a pervert," she declared, her voice wavering.

My head reared back. *Did she just call me a pervert?*

"Ma'am?"

"I saw you fondling my panties on the clothesline."

The sheer absurdity of the accusation stopped me in my tracks. Jesus. I don't get off on fingering strange women's panties.

"Don't try to deny it. I saw you with my own eyes."

"Ma'am," I said again, with as much dignity as I could muster. "I was trying to figure out if the clothes on the line were recently washed, or if they'd been hanging outside for months."

She sniffed, a sound that conveyed both skepticism and disdain.

A thump from upstairs brought me back to the matter at hand. "Are you here alone?" I asked, glancing up the stairs.

"My daughter is in her bedroom," she said. "She's been sick, and I won't have her disturbed by the likes of you."

The thump sounded again, and she took a step into the front hall. A gaunt woman with dirty hair and dark circles under her eyes, she faced me defiantly. From behind her back, she pulled a pistol. She pointed the gun at me, her hand shaking. "Get out of my house," she ordered.

Well, crap. Still holding the crowbar, I raised my hands. "I'm here to help," I said again.

On the floor above us, a series of thuds erupted.

"Sophia," the woman cried, worry filling her voice. She dashed to the bottom of the stairs, turning her back to me, concern for Sophia overriding her paranoia about my intentions.

I sprang forward, taking advantage of the distraction. No way I'd hit the woman with the crowbar. Instead, I dropped it to the entry floor and tackled her, shoving her face-down onto the stairs. She bucked beneath me, her frenzied desperation lending her an unlikely strength. I locked my fingers around her narrow wrist.

"Sophia," she howled. "Hide. Hide from the bad man."

Bad man. Pervert. What a shit show. What must the poor kid be thinking? The situation had gone totally off the rails.

I planted a knee in her back. "Drop the gun," I snarled in her ear.

"Sophia," the woman shrieked, ignoring my command.

"Drop the gun, dammit."

Jesus, why wouldn't she let go? Jaw set, I twisted the pistol from her hand and tucked it in the waistband of my jeans. I might have her weapon, but the fight hadn't gone out of the woman. She kicked and threw her head back, thwacking my nose.

Shit, that hurt.

Eyes stinging, I seized both of her wrists and leaned forward, pressing my full weight onto her. She gasped for breath.

"You done?" I demanded.

"Sophia," she whimpered.

"I'm not going to hurt Sophia," I growled. I pulled her arms behind her back, clamping one hand around her wrists. "We're getting up." I dragged her to her feet and shoved her forward. We stumbled up the stairs, pausing on the landing. I swiveled my head, examining the layout of the second floor. Two hallways branched off from the landing; the one to the right had three closed doors, the one to the left had four.

First things first. I needed to make sure that the woman couldn't attack me again. "Where's your bedroom?" I asked. She had to have a belt or scarf in her closet that I could use to bind her hands. She tilted her head at the first door on the right. "Let's go." We shuffled toward the room. I opened the door and pushed her inside, glancing around the gloomy interior. My gaze traveled over a bed and dresser before landing on another closed door. That had to be the closet.

The woman shuddered, her face turned toward the bed. "Please don't rape me."

I froze. Holy fuck. She thought I brought her into her bedroom to assault her. Guess I couldn't blame her. After all, I was a *pervert* and a *bad man* in her eyes, a man who used a crowbar to break into her house. I swallowed. "Lady, I swear to God that I'm not going to rape you. I just wanted to get a belt or scarf to tie your wrists so you won't attack me again."

"I won't attack you again," she said in a small voice. "I promise. You have my gun. Just don't hurt me or Sophia."

"Okay," I agreed, feeling like a total shit. "Okay, I won't tie your hands." I released her wrists and stepped back, raising my palms in the air so I'd look less threatening. "Listen, I am really sorry that I scared you. I meant it when I told you that I work with a group that helps survivors. I'll send men to fix your front door and bring you anything else you and Sophia need."

Silent, she stared at me with suspicious eyes. Another series of thumps rattled a door up the hall. I glanced over my shoulder toward the sound.

"Maybe we should go check on Sophia," I suggested.

She shook her head. "She's fine. You've done enough." Her voice was bitter. "You should go."

I stepped backward into the hall. A narrow table held a vase of artificial flowers and more Precious Moments figurines. A loud thud sounded, and one of the doors shook in its frame. Three long strides and I was outside the closed door. I twisted the knob. It was locked, but I heard a muffled sound from inside the room.

"What the?" I muttered. Someone threw themselves against the locked door. "Stand back," I barked. I kicked out, striking the weak place below the doorknob, just like Ripper had taught me. The frame splintered and the door flew open.

Not three feet in front of me, Ever stood. Zip ties bound her wrists and a knotted cloth gag filled her mouth. She frantically shook her head back and forth, making unintelligible grunts. I took one step into the room, and something struck me from behind. Staggering, I whirled around and caught the woman's arm just before she clocked me a second time with a porcelain statue. I wrapped both arms around the woman's torso, pinning her arms to her side. The porcelain statue clattered to the carpet. The assault had done more damage to the figurine than to me—knocked the head clean off the figure of a little boy holding a teddy bear—but it would probably raise a lump on the back of my head.

I didn't give a shit. The only thing that mattered was the little girl watching me with wide, tear-filled eyes. Behind her on a dresser, I spied a pile of zip ties.

"Ever, grab me some of those zip ties, will you?"

Despite her bound wrists, she managed to snag a few zip ties, then dropped them into my palm. I bound the woman's hands behind her back and pushed her toward a rocking chair sitting in a corner of the room. She sat and I fastened her legs to the chair.

"Come here, sweetheart." I untied the gag, snapped open my pocketknife, and cut Ever free from the zip ties. She smacked her lips and made a face, then rubbed wrists banded with red indentations from the tight ties. I thought Ever might break down now that she was free, but the girl marched over to the bound woman.

"You're not my mama and my name isn't Sophia."

The woman smiled indulgently, a smile that chilled my blood and raised the fine hairs on the back of my neck. "I knew the doctor lied, baby," she cooed. "I knew you'd come back to your mama. I kept everything ready. Your clothes. Your toys. I even saved a bag of your favorite animal cookies."

Whoa. Grief can really divorce some people from reality, can't it?

"I'm not Sophia," Ever insisted, stamping her foot. "My name is Ever van der Linden, and my mama is dead."

The woman twisted her lips into a moue and tut-tutted Ever's assertion. Ever flushed and crossed her arms over her chest.

"Hey, Ever." I touched the girl's shoulder. "You're right. You're not Sophia and that lady isn't your mother. I'm proud of you for standing up for yourself. But right now she's mixed up, and I don't think she's going to listen to you."

"You mean she's sick in the head?" Ever asked.

"I mean she's so sad that she can't think straight."

"She kidnapped me," Ever said indignantly. "I asked her if she saw Fitzwilliam. She lied and told me he was inside her house eating a can of tuna fish."

"Yeah," I said. "She lied and she did a bad thing."

"Uh-huh." Ever's angry expression smoothed out. She spun around and wrapped her arms around my waist, hugging me tight and sniffing back tears.

"Let's get you back home to Mrs. B. and Sunny," I said, patting her shoulders.

Ever lifted her face to mine. "Is Mrs. B. mad at me?"

"Mad? Maybe a little bit." I didn't want to lie to the kid. "But more than anything she's scared and worried. We've all been scared and worried. She'll be super happy to have you back home."

"Me, too. I want to go home. I wish... I wish I'd found Fitzwilliam. He's an indoor kitty and he's not supposed to go out by himself... just like me, I guess."

"Good news," I said. "Fitzwilliam came home this morning."

Ever grinned and tugged on my hand. "Let's go."

"We can't leave the lady by herself tied to a chair," I said. I pulled the two-way radio out of my pocket and called Jonesy. "I found Ever. A grieving mother took her. Looks like as a replacement for her dead daughter. I have the woman secured. She shouldn't be left here alone."

"Where are you?" he asked.

I gave him the address. "Could you get Sunny for me?"

"Sure."

A minute later, Sunny's voice came on the line. "Kyle?"

"Ever's with me. She's fine."

"Oh, thank God. Mrs. B.—" Sunny's voice faded as she called to her friend. "Ever's okay. Kyle has her." In the background, Mrs. B.'s exclamation of joy filled the air.

"Hurry back," Sunny said.

"We will," I said. "Jonesy will be heading our way any moment."

"And... thank you, Kyle. Thanks for saving Ever. I think losing her would have broken me into a million little pieces."

"Sunny," I breathed. "No matter what, we'll keep her safe. I love the little twerp, too."

"Hey, did you call me a twerp?" Ever protested. I ruffled her hair and she lunged at me, hugging me once again.

"Jonesy wants his radio back." Sunny laughed. "See you in a few, baby."

"See you."

When we disconnected, I stared at the radio for a good minute. How was it possible that my life had changed so much in less than one week? I was one hundred percent committed to the well-being of a little girl I'd met three days ago. Mrs. B.? I'd do anything to keep that woman safe and happy. And Sunny... I shook my head.

Sunny was my miracle, our reunion a life-changing stroke of luck. If I hadn't looked out my bedroom window at that exact moment on Tuesday night, I wouldn't have seen her light moving in the McAllister house. I would have returned to Valhalla the next morning without ever discovering that one of my oldest friends had survived the pandemic. A woman whose kisses made me feel alive again. A woman who called me baby as if it were the most natural thing in the world. Gratitude almost dropped me to my knees.

Brakes squealed outside and I shook off my reverie. I offered Ever my hand. We ran downstairs and opened the door to the Allsop security team. Within ten minutes our group had split into two. Jonesy and Brody took the bereaved mother in one SUV. The Allsops had set up a facility in town where people who needed help could be cared for, and Jonesy would take her there. The other SUV carried Ever, three additional security men, and me back to Mrs. B.'s place.

The Valhalla ranch truck pulled onto the street a few seconds before we did. The pickup came to a stop in front of Cressida's Cottage, and a tall, blond young man jumped out.

"That's my pickup," I told the man driving the SUV. "Can you give that guy a ride back to the Allsop place. I'll drive the truck back later."

I climbed out of the SUV, then offered a hand to Ever to help her out.

The blond guy rushed toward us. He dropped to his haunches and held out his arms. "Glad to see you back, sweet pea." Ever hugged him. The front door flew open and Sunny and Mrs. B. ran outside. With a happy squeal, Ever raced toward them.

"Sunny and I are going to spend some time with Ever and Mrs. B., so I'll need my truck. You mind riding back with the rest of the men?"

The blond man stood and looked me over from head to foot. He'd spent the past couple of days in Sunny's company. He was probably wondering if I was good enough for her. Had I passed muster? He offered a slow smile. "No problem. Suppose you'll be needing your keys." He tossed the keys and I caught them. "'Night," he said, tipping an imaginary hat.

"Good night."

I turned toward the house and strode up the path where Sunny, Mrs. B., and Ever waited for me.

SEVENTEEN

Sunny

We hadn't intended to stay so late at Cressida Cottage, but both Mrs. B. and Ever had been jittery and wired after the little girl's rescue. Ever insisted she was A-okay, but her actions said otherwise. She clung to Kyle's side, imploring him to sit next to her at dinner. They played gin rummy together for a solid hour. After her bath—two inches of warm water in a claw-foot tub—Ever begged him to read her a bedtime story. Fitzwilliam sprawled at the foot of the brass bed while Kyle and Ever leaned against a mountain of pillows at the headboard. He read *Anne of Green Gables,* nodding patiently every time Ever pleaded for one more chapter. By the time she finally drifted off to sleep, it was a little past eleven.

"You're her hero, you know," Mrs. B. said. Rising up on her tiptoes, she pulled Kyle's head down and soundly kissed him on the cheek. "Mine, too. Thank you for bringing our girl home."

"Would you like us to stay?" I asked. "Kyle and I could bunk out in the living room."

"No, I'm fine. There's a glass of sherry with my name on it in the kitchen cabinet. I plan to read for a while then toddle off to bed. You two scoot."

We scooted. The moon rode high in the sky when Kyle parked his truck in front of the Allsop's garage. Hand in hand, we walked into the dark house. The guards standing sentry outside the front door nodded to us as we passed.

"You want anything from the kitchen before we head to our room?" Kyle asked.

"No. I'm good. You?"

"Nah."

We climbed the stairs in silence and made our way to the guest suite. Once inside, I switched on the nightstand lamp on my side of the bed, casting a pool of light over the midnight-blue silk coverlet. Kyle lingered at the door, eyes intent as he watched me. An awkward silence hung between us.

When did I ever have trouble speaking my mind? Jake used to tease me, saying I blurted out every thought in my head, but now, when it mattered the most, I couldn't find the words. I plopped down on the edge of the mattress and buried my face in my hands.

Instantly, Kyle was at my side, kneeling in front of me, his palms warm where they rested against my thighs. I lifted my head and gazed into his serious hazel eyes. Reaching out with one hand, I traced along his jaw. Stubble prickled my fingertips and I smiled at the sensation. Kyle returned my smile, his eyes crinkling at the corners. I ran my thumb over his mouth, outlining the firm bottom lip, then sweeping across the cupid's bow on his upper lip. His lips parted and his teeth closed around the pad of my thumb, his warm mouth encircling the digit down to the knuckle.

I gasped, then sighed. "Kyle..."

His mouth released my thumb and he angled his head, his expression serious again. "What's going on in that head of yours, Sunny?"

Too many things.

"It's been a day," I said.

It had. Instead of keeping a stiff upper lip, Kyle had confided in me, had allowed me to comfort him. Allowed me to act like an adult, an equal, instead of the kid sister of his best friend, a person who must be sheltered from all of life's harsh realities. We'd shared the best kiss of my life. Then Ever disappeared, and sheer panic held me in its grip until Kyle found her and brought her home. Life reminded me once again how quickly we could lose the people we held most dear. How very fragile was our existence. It struck me deep down in my bones that I would do whatever was necessary to hold onto those I loved.

"Are you tired? Do you want to sleep?" Kyle asked.

"I feel like I've been through an emotional wringer," I said. "We came so close to losing Ever. The experience made me step back and take a look at my life. I decided that you're right. That we need to go to Valhalla. Now. Before anything else bad happens. I want to pack up Ever and Mrs. B. and Fitzwilliam and go someplace safe. Even if it means leaving behind my responsibilities in Boise. I'm ready to be selfish and take what I want."

"You're the least selfish person I know," Kyle said, taking a seat next to me on the bed. "You're not abandoning Boise. The Allsops are going to turn things around here. They'll take care of the people, the way they took care of that deranged woman who kidnapped Ever. You can leave town with a clear conscience."

"I hope so," I said. "But that's not everything. I want to talk about us."

I closely watched his expression for any reaction, positive or negative. How would Kyle respond to my assertion that *we need to talk?* Isn't that a conversation that most men dread?

"What about us?" He took my hand in his, and his thumb massaged the center of my palm.

Spill it, McAllister.

I sucked in a breath, then exhaled slowly, searching for the words. "When I was a teenager, I'd lie awake at night fantasizing about you, my big brother's impossibly cool best friend. You were everything I wanted: handsome, smart, athletic. And I mean, you *had* to know how I felt. You had to see the way I blushed when you caught me staring at you..."

He offered a rueful smile. "Trust me, Sunny, if there was anything I was determined *not* to notice, it was my best friend's little sister crushing on me."

Fair enough. The Bro Code and all that.

"I was convinced that I was in love with you, and I kept hoping that someday you'd see that I was all grown-up. And that you'd declare your undying love for me."

His lips quirked. "How did you imagine that? Would I burst into the room carrying a dozen red roses and spouting poetry? Would I hire a skywriter to spell out the words Kyle Loves Sunny?"

I punched his shoulder. "Shut up."

He rolled his eyes and his expression sobered. "Sorry. I'm being an ass. I do that sometimes when I'm anxious."

I smiled. "Anyway, I compared every guy I met to my vision of you, and they all came up short. I wasn't a nun. I dated, but you were always there in the back of my mind. The perfect guy."

He winced. "Shit, Sunny, I am *so* far from perfect."

"My point is that I thought I was in love with you, but I see now that I didn't really know you back then. I didn't see you for who you really are."

"Okay." His face turned thoughtful. "So what are you saying?"

"I'm not a kid with a crush anymore. Tonight, when I watched you reading to Ever, I saw a kind man taking care of a traumatized little girl." Tears welled in my eyes, and I brushed impatiently at them. "And I understood that the real Kyle is so much better than any fantasy I had when I was a teenager. I could fall in love with the real Kyle. Really, truly in love. In fact, I'm halfway there already."

Kyle said nothing and my pulse stuttered. Crap. Had I read too much into our kiss? Was he trying to think of a way to let me down easy? I focused my eyes on the opposite wall for a few agonizing seconds. Screw it. Life was too short and too uncertain to play it safe. I turned my gaze back to Kyle. If he couldn't see any kind of future with me it would sting, but I could deal.

"I didn't see the real you either," he confessed. "I put you in a box. Jake's little sister. A naive do-gooder with a heart of gold. I actually thought that you'd grow out of it. I was wrong to be so dismissive. These past few days I've seen the real you, too. More than ever, the world needs good people like you. I'm halfway there, too, Sunshine." He pushed my hair away from my face. With one finger, he gently traced the shell of my ear, a caress that sent shivers to my core.

I stared at him unblinking while his words sunk in, then I pinched myself, hard on my upper arm. "Nope," I said. "Not asleep."

Kyle laughed softly and pulled me onto his lap, turning me so I straddled him. He brushed his knuckles across my cheek. My lips parted and I dragged in a slow, tremulous breath, quivering beneath his touch. He cupped my face with gentle hands.

"It's been a day." He repeated the words I'd spoken minutes ago. "It's after midnight on a long, stress-filled day. I'd like—shit, I can't believe I'm actually saying this—but I'd like our first time to be something special. Not something we do late at night when we're exhausted and still reeling from almost losing Ever."

"I get it," I said. "I'd like my first time to be something special, too."

Kyle stiffened and his brows drew down. "Sunny, you said your *first* time?"

He didn't need to look so shocked. At twenty-one I was definitely late to the party, but not ridiculously late. Suddenly, I couldn't meet his eyes. Did Kyle think I was some kind of freak of nature for waiting for the right moment? For the right man? For him?

I squirmed. "Yeah. My first time."

"Well, hell, Sunshine. We're definitely going to make it something special." He grinned, setting my mind at ease. "Tomorrow night. I'm going to tell Hildy that we'd like to have dinner in our room. We'll take the entire evening. Candlelit dinner. Champagne on our balcony. Rose petals in the whirlpool tub. Make it a night we'll never forget."

I glanced up at him, my embarrassment forgotten. "I'd like that."

Strong fingers caught my chin and angled my head back, forcing me to meet his eyes. The lines of his face shifted—a subtle transformation that held me in thrall—his lighthearted expression morphing into something intense, something that held a hint of dark promise. My eyes widened even as Kyle's lids slid down and his hooded gaze honed in on my mouth.

Time hung suspended between us. I gulped. My chest constricted, my heart slamming against my ribs. I felt light-headed, giddy, as if I couldn't draw enough air in my lungs. Kyle slid his hand to the back of my head, cupping my nape. His fingers tightened in my hair, holding me in place as his mouth swooped down to cover mine. My lips trembled against his. I fought for breath. Digging my fingernails into his shoulders, I pressed my aching breasts against his chest. He shuddered and yanked his mouth away from mine. He panted, his breath warm against my tingling lips.

Kyle lifted glazed eyes to meet mine. "I'll be gentle the first time, Sunshine. I promise. But after that—" He paused. The world stopped spinning while I waited for him to continue. He lowered his chin. "After that, I'm going to wreck you."

This was Kyle? My old friend? Damn. Not once in my teenage fantasies had he threatened to *wreck m*e, but I was dying to discover exactly what that meant. I lost the ability to speak. I nodded once, a jerky motion that delighted him, if the sudden, self-satisfied curve of his mouth was any indication.

I had to say something. I shook myself, searching for words. Any words. "Won't you have to explain why we're eating in our room?" I asked. "Brody will have a field day."

"Brody can think what he wants. And he'd better keep his damned mouth shut," Kyle said.

"This means that we can't leave for Valhalla immediately," I reminded him.

"Not a problem. We can take a day to get ready. Tell the Allsops our plans. Talk to Mrs. B. and Ever. Give them time to pack. We'll have our evening, then we'll take off for Valhalla the following morning."

Too good to be true. It all felt too good to be true.

"Wow," I marveled. "Dreams can still come true."

"Our happily ever after is just getting started," he said. "You're going to love Valhalla and all my friends there. Kenzie. Ripper. He might look intimidating at first, but he's a truly good man. We've got our own doctor, Sahdev. Hell of a great guy. Bear. Nyx. Hannah and Levi. They're all great people, and I can't wait for you to meet them."

I could get over my antipathy for Kenzie now that she no longer held Kyle's heart. Maybe we could even become friends. "It sounds like heaven." I sighed.

"Well, yeah. It ought to. It's Valhalla. Viking heaven."

I laughed. In Norse mythology Valhalla was a hall of warriors who had died in battle, who were preparing to fight the big battle at the end of time. Not exactly a traditional view of heaven, but I was too stinking happy to quibble. "I can't wait. Can you imagine Ever growing up on a ranch? With chickens and horses and cows? She'll love it."

"And sooner or later there will be other kids to keep her company," he said. "Ripper and Kenzie want to have children someday. Nyx has her eye on Bear. That cowboy doesn't stand a chance. Maybe Hannah and Levi when they're older. Who knows, maybe even us."

Maybe even us. A future full of promise stretched out before me. A week ago such happiness would have been unimaginable.

I pinched myself again, just to be sure.

EIGHTEEN

Kyle

Knowing how Sunny felt about Brody, no way in hell would I ask him if he had any condoms. Even if he was willing to share, I wouldn't put her in the position of hearing any unwelcome comments about her sex life. Nope. I was on my own. Pharmacies had been picked clean. Grocery stores, too, but I had a couple of ideas where I might get my hands on them.

I rolled out of bed a little past 9 a.m., leaving Sunny curled up on her side making the cutest little snuffling sounds. She wasn't snoring—I knew from Jake's sad experience with his girlfriend never to accuse a woman of snoring—the sound was a cross between a snort and a sniffle. Like I said, a snuffle, and it was absolutely adorable.

The heavy gold charms on her grandma's bracelet clanked together whenever she rolled over or tossed her arm over her head, which she did. A lot. I'd better get used to it because Sunny told me she was never taking off the bracelet. Snuffles and clanks made for a noisy night.

I'd gotten out of the habit of sharing my bed and woke up hot a couple of times. It had nothing to do with my quest for condoms. I wasn't *hot and bothered* like Mom used to say. No, I woke up sweaty because I wasn't used to sleeping next to a warm body. And Sunny was a cuddler, throwing her leg over mine or burrowing into my chest.

I passed a hot and noisy night. Was I complaining? Hell no. I hadn't felt this happy in God knows how long. Not since Kenzie and I split up, and the pandemic burned its way through the world. And no nightmares disturbed my sleep. Life was full of promise.

I snagged a cherry Danish and a cup of coffee on my way out the door. The pickup sat where I'd left it in the driveway, but somebody had filled its tank with gas and deposited three five-gallon gas cans on the floor of the truck bed. I scratched my head over that. I had no clue who'd do that for me, or why.

One of my high school friends had decided to stay in Boise for college. He'd mentioned that the vending machines in his residence hall sold condoms. On a hunch, I drove across town and parked in front of one of the largest residence halls. I carried a crowbar—in case I had to break in—but the main door was unlocked, and I walked right in.

An eerie sense of deja vu snuck up on me as I made my way down a long hallway, my flashlight beam bouncing off a seemingly endless line of closed doors. This was how the nightmare began four months ago. A new flu virus was sweeping across the globe. Rumors were rife that the governor was about to declare a state of emergency. Stories spread of flu victims falling prey to a homicidal mania. Kenzie and I, along with Jake and his girlfriend Ali, had fled the dorm. Kenzie took refuge with her cousin, Miles. I took off with my friends for an ill-fated drive home to Boise. On that one day, everything began to go to shit.

Now I carried both a gun and a crowbar as I made my way through another dorm. I was ready to defend myself from anything, anything except the memories triggered by the walk down the long corridor. My footsteps echoed in the empty hall. Nobody was dying behind the closed doors. Still, I picked up the pace, jogging until I came to a communal bathroom.

People might have emptied the grocery stores and pharmacies, but nobody had thought to raid the vending machine in the residence hall bathroom. I pried it open with the crowbar and took every single package of condoms.

I smiled to myself. Ripper would rib me if he could see me shoving dozens of foil packets into my pockets. *Big plans tonight, brother? Sure you got enough there?*

"Soon," I said out loud. "We'll be home soon." I couldn't wait to introduce Sunny to my friends. Ever and Mrs. B., too. With any luck, we'd be in Valhalla by tomorrow night. That thought propelled me into a sprint. I ran back to the truck, started up the engine, and drove straight for Cressida's Cottage.

"It's Kyle," Ever shrieked when she opened the front door. She leapt. I hoisted her into the air then settled her around my waist like she was a toddler instead of a nine-year-old. I spun around three times, then deposited the girl back on the floor.

Mrs. B. emerged from the kitchen, wiping her hands on a towel and smiling a warm welcome. "I just put the kettle on. You'll have tea?"

"Yes, thank you."

Ever chatted happily about Fitzwilliam's latest tricks while Mrs. B. bustled around her sunny kitchen, brewing a pot of English breakfast tea. I glanced around her cheerful home, crammed full of books and framed prints and embroidered cushions. Would she be willing to abandon it all to move to a ranch that was—in Ripper's words—"at the ass end of nowhere"? I hoped so. I'd known Mrs. B. and Ever for only a few days, but already I'd be bereft without them.

"I need to talk to you about something important," I said, accepting my mug of hot tea.

"Ever, dear, can you go play in your room for awhile so I can chat with Kyle?"

"Okay." Ever slung Fitzwilliam over her shoulder and pranced down the hall toward her room.

Mrs. B. took a seat on her bright-green sofa and patted the cushion next to her. I sat down. Three foil-wrapped condoms slipped from my bulging front pocket and fell on the carpet at our feet. Mrs. B. leaned forward, studying them.

"Magnums," she pronounced with a delighted tone.

Jesus Christ. I hadn't blushed since I was fourteen, yet there it was. A hot flush crept up my cheeks. Dammit.

"Are you here to ask my blessing to woo our sweet Sunny? Dear boy, I say go for it. A little bird told me that she'd be very receptive." She pushed a condom toward me with the toe of her shoe, then the woman actually waggled her brows.

I cleared my throat, bending to pick up the condoms and stuff them back in my pocket.

"Mrs. B... ma'am—"

133

"Oh dear, this sounds like the start of a serious conversation." She placed her teacup on the coffee table and folded her hands in her lap, giving me her full attention.

"Tomorrow morning Sunny and I will be leaving Boise. We're going to Valhalla. It's a cattle ranch in central Oregon where I've settled with some friends. A safe, out-of-the-way place."

"I see." Mrs. B. twisted her hands together in her lap.

"We want you and Ever to come with us," I said quickly. "Sunny's been reluctant to leave town before things here stabilized, but the scare with Ever changed her mind. We want to move someplace safe. All of us. Together."

Mrs. B. looked stunned, staring into the distance, her forehead furrowed. "Leave Boise. Live on a cattle ranch."

"I say yes," Ever cried, poking her head in from the entryway. Apparently she'd snuck back to the front hall where she'd been eavesdropping. "I want us to live with Kyle and Sunny. Please, Mrs. B."

"Back to your room, young lady," Mrs. B. ordered. "I want to talk privately with Kyle."

"Okay." Ever frowned. "But remember I vote yes." She stomped back down the hall, every loud footstep a protest at being excluded from the conversation.

"Sorry about that," I muttered.

She waved her hand, dismissing my concerns. "Do you and Sunny really want to live with an old woman and a little girl? Your friends, they would welcome us?"

"Yes and yes," I assured her. "They're good people and Valhalla is a beautiful place. Ever could gather eggs and pick carrots. Learn how to ride a horse, if she liked."

A squeal sounded from the hall.

"I take it that's a yes to horseback riding lessons," Mrs. B. said dryly.

"Please, Mrs. B., Sunny and I really want you with us."

Her gaze traveled around the cozy pink room. "I've lived here for more than forty years. So many memories of my late husband, Jack, are woven into these walls. I love this little house." She turned her eyes to me. "But a house isn't a home. A home is the people you love. And Ever and I love you and Sunny." She stood, her eyes sparkling. "Besides, a cattle ranch in central Oregon sounds like a real adventure, and I'm not too old for a new adventure. Maybe *I* could learn how to ride a horse."

I seized her hands, my grip gentle because of her arthritis. "Mrs. B., you've made me a happy man."

She smiled. "Pshaw, young man. Thank you for including us. Ever will be over the moon."

"Is that good?" Ever asked, sticking her head back into the room.

"I give up." Mrs. B. held out her arms, and Ever rushed to her side, hopping up and down as she hugged the woman.

"I've got some time," I said. "We have room in the bed of the truck to bring some of your things. Clothes and toiletries, of course. Maybe a couple of boxes of books and your favorite knickknacks. I can help you pack."

"I'd like to bring my mother's tea set and my grandmother's quilt," Mrs. B. said.

"And Fitzwilliam's toys and bed. And his cat food," Ever added.

"Good thinking," I said. "Fitzwilliam is part of the family, and we'll pack up what he needs."

I hauled several empty boxes up from the basement. For the next couple of hours, I helped Mrs. B. pack. She stood in the middle of her living room, tapping her chin as she deliberated, then pointing at the books she wanted me to pack. I carried three heavy boxes of books to my truck. Mrs. B. carefully wrapped up her mother's tea set in her grandmother's quilt, then placed a Staffordshire figure of Queen Victoria on top of the box.

We gave Ever two empty boxes to fill with books and games. To my surprise, she put a Staffordshire figure of a zebra into her box. "His name is Jeff," she explained. "I want to keep him in my new bedroom." At the top of the box she placed a beaded pillow embroidered with a blue bird of happiness. Mrs. B. and Ever each packed a suitcase full of clothing and shoes.

"We'll be here around 8 to pick you up," I told them as I unrolled the waterproof truck bed cover and snapped it in place over the boxes and gas cans.

"We'll be waiting with bells on," Mrs. B. said, smiling.

"We will?" Ever demanded. "Where are we going to put the bells?"

"Just an expression, dearest." Mrs. B. dropped a kiss on top of the girl's head.

Ever and Mrs. B. stood side by side in the driveway, waving as I drove away. I sang an old country music song while I navigated back to the Allsop estate—a Garth Brooks love song—both hands tapping a rhythm on the steering wheel as I crooned. Sunny should be up and dressed by now. I smiled, imagining her delight when I told her that Mrs. B. and Ever had agreed to come to Valhalla with us. My chest ached, I was so freaking happy.

I pulled off the main road and followed the long, curving driveway up to the house. When I turned the key and jumped from the pickup, the front door flew open. Brody jogged toward the truck, his face twisted with stress.

"Shit, man, why didn't you take a two-way radio with you?"

"What's wrong?" My limbs locked and dread constricted my breath.

"It's Sunny," he said. "She's gone."

NINETEEN

Sunny

I woke up face-down on the mattress, drooling onto my pillow. I swept out my arm, patting the sheets, feeling for Kyle. He was gone. I was alone in the big bed. Prying one eye open, I mumbled and swiped at my damp cheek. Blech. I must have slept like the dead. I fumbled for the clock on the nightstand, squinting as the numbers swam into view. 11:14 a.m. Good lord. How had I slept so long? My bleary gaze settled on the wall of windows. Kyle had closed all the curtains, leaving the room bathed in darkness, probably so the morning light wouldn't awaken me.

I smiled to myself. My man—I could think of him as my man, couldn't I—he was taking care of me. He'd told me to sleep in, and he'd made sure that it was possible. Arching my back, I stretched and sighed happily, burrowing into the sheets.

All was well in my world. And tonight... tonight... I'd finally discover what it was like to make love to the man of my dreams.

I sat up and spied a note on the nightstand.

Good morning, Sunshine. Hope you got a good night's sleep. You're gonna need it! I'm off to talk to Mrs. B. and Ever and to get some things ready for this evening. Should be back early afternoon. Kyle

I jumped out of bed and began stripping the sheets from the mattress. I wanted everything to be perfect this evening, including clean sheets and pillowcases that weren't crusted with dried drool. Hildy probably changed the sheets on a schedule, but I was certainly capable of finding the laundry room and washing them myself.

Tomorrow Kyle and I would be walking away from this life of luxury, from a house powered by electricity and full of all the amenities of modern life. From brownie sundaes and cheesecake. This might be my last chance to use a washing machine. I didn't care. I could move on without a backward glance because I'd be sailing into the sunset with Kyle.

I'm such a sap.

I took a quick shower, threw on a pair of jeans, sandals, and a white embroidered top in the floaty boho style I loved. I wrapped mom's wild Pucci scarf around my neck. Grandma's charm bracelet jingled on my wrist as I gathered up the dirty sheets and headed off to search for the laundry room.

The thick carpeting muted my footsteps as I traipsed along the hall and down the stairs. At the bottom of the steps, I paused, hearing voices from the kitchen.

"You and Brody took care of that unfortunate woman?" I recognized Elliot Allsop's voice.

"Yes, sir," Jonesy answered.

"And disposed of the body?" Mr. Allsop's voice was bland and uninflected, as if he was talking about nothing more exciting than the weather or what he ate for breakfast.

"Of course."

"Prepare to start culling the herd next week," Elliot Allsop said.

"Have you decided the cut-off age, sir?"

"I have. We need to balance a person's productivity against available resources. We can't afford to subsidize leeches. I've decided that we'll cut off access to food and water at sixty-five."

"Very good, sir," Jonesy said.

"Unless there are mitigating circumstances, of course," Mr. Allsop added. "Someone who is of continuing value to society—doctors, engineers, perhaps some particularly fine musicians or artists—they'll warrant an extension. And the converse is true. Those with no potential to ever contribute to society will be cut off, regardless of age."

I stood stock-still, my arms full of sheets, my mouth hanging open. This couldn't be real. Culling the herd? Deciding which survivors lived or died based on their ages? Jesus Christ. Mrs. B. was eighty, as vibrant, as full of life, as valuable to the world as anyone. And whose body had Jonesy disposed of? Were they talking about the woman who'd kidnapped Ever, the mother driven mad by grief? Kyle told me that Jonesy and Brody had driven her to a facility in town, a place where she could be taken care of. Did Jonesy take care of her with a bullet?

What the hell was going on? What kind of stable, law-abiding society were the Allsops trying to create?

Holding my breath, I turned to tiptoe back up the stairs.

"Hey, Sunny. Where you going?" Brody asked, leaning casually against the arched entrance to the living room.

Could I bluff my way out of this, pretend I hadn't heard a thing?

"I forgot that I wanted to wash Kyle's T-shirts with the sheets. I'm heading back upstairs to get them," I lied.

Brody grinned, a gleeful expression filled with such malice that my blood chilled. I took a step backward, tripped on the bottom stair, and sat down hard, still clutching the sheets. "Nice try," he scoffed. He raised his voice. "Dad, Jonesy, we got a problem." Brody took the balled-up sheets from my hands and threw them on the floor. Seizing my elbows, he hauled me to my feet and shoved me ahead of him to the kitchen, where Mr. Allsop sat at the counter with a cup of coffee in his hand. "Somebody was snooping," Brody announced.

Dread curdled in my stomach.

"What did she hear?" Mr. Allsop asked his son.

"That Jonesy disposed of the body. That we plan to cull the herd."

"How unfortunate." Mr. Allsop took a sip of his coffee. "This was not how we intended to introduce Sunny to our new order."

There was no way to defuse this powder keg, was there? I couldn't bring myself to pretend that I sympathized with his *new order*. "You're out of your minds if you think that people come with an arbitrary expiration date. If you believe that some people are more valuable than others. Your plans for the new world are barbaric."

That got a rise out of Mr. Allsop. He thumped his coffee cup on the counter. "Barbaric? On the contrary. We are in a life-and-death struggle for the survival of civilization. I'm trying to protect all the best that humanity has achieved over the past millennia. We can't afford to be ruled by sentiment."

I could argue until I was blue in the face, and Elliot Allsop wouldn't budge. The man had an agenda I wanted no part of. He'd amassed an army and an arsenal of weapons. What troops could I rally against him? He held all the power here. Retreat—even a dishonorable retreat—was my only option. Stick to the new plan. Kyle and I would take Mrs. B. and Ever and flee to Valhalla.

"Listen," I said. "There's no way that Kyle and I can be a part of your new order. We've already decided to move on. We were planning to tell you that today. To tell you that we appreciate everything you've done for us, how you offered us a place with your organization, but we want to live somewhere quiet and out of the way."

"You planned to tell me that today?" Mr. Allsop dabbed his mouth with a napkin.

"Yes."

"You were ready to walk away, to abrogate your responsibility to your class, to your upbringing?" Mr. Allsop said. "I thought better of you."

"See, Dad, I told you she has a shitty attitude," Brody said. "Fat lot of good being nice to her did. Making her brownie sundaes." He snorted. "She's got poor Kyle wrapped around her little finger. She's always hated me, and she probably poisoned Kyle against us."

"So I see," his father said. "What do you propose we do with her?"

"Let's get real, Dad. We don't want to kill her. Let's put her in lockup. Let her stew in her own juices for a while. She'll come around. And even if she doesn't, we still have another shot with Kyle."

Mr. Allsop sighed, the bone-weary sigh of a man burdened with too many responsibilities. "And what will we tell Kyle about her disappearance?"

Brody laughed. "That's easy. Tell him that our favorite boogeymen took her."

Finn sauntered into the kitchen carrying a manila folder. "I got those reports you were asking for, Mr. Allsop." He halted, probably cuing into the tension in the room. He glanced at me, frowning, then looked at Mr. Allsop. "What's going on, boss?"

"It seems we have a traitor in our midst."

Finn stiffened, his eyes darting from Mr. Allsop to Jonesy and then to Brody, before settling on me. "Sir?"

"Miss McAllister overheard a conversation she had no business listening to. She finds our plans for the future of Boise objectionable. And apparently, she's persuaded Kyle to abandon the city."

"Used her feminine wiles," Brody said in a mocking tone.

I shot the creep a dirty look but said nothing. I'd never throw Kyle under the bus, never tell them that leaving Boise was his idea.

But I'd told Finn that. Shit. I glanced at the farm boy, waiting for him to rat Kyle out. He remained silent, although his jaw was clenched, like he was biting back words. The tension in his face suddenly eased. He scratched the back of his head and offered one of his slow, easy smiles. "Guess you just can't tell about people, can you, sir. You think you can count on 'em, that they'll do right, then they go and disappoint you. What do you want to do with her?"

He was throwing *me* under the bus. That good-old-boy country charm was entirely bogus, a realization that pained me more than it should under the circumstances.

"I liked you," I said bitterly, glowering at him. I couldn't believe that I'd invited the dick to come to Valhalla.

"I liked you, too, darlin'. Too bad you turned on the boss."

I screwed my eyes shut so I wouldn't have to see his stupid face.

"Jonesy," Mr. Allsop said. "Take Finn and Brody and escort Miss McAllister to lockup."

Opening my eyes, I glanced frantically around the room. My gaze landed on a plate of cherry Danish on the counter, next to the coffee maker. Hildy must have been up at 6 a.m. to bake pastries. Now that I'd been deemed a traitor, fresh pastries were a thing of the past, weren't they? My panic-addled brain fixated on nonsense. I choked back a hysterical laugh. No more pastries. I sobered. No more Mrs. B. and Ever. No more Kyle.

Past Jonesy's shoulder, Hildy stood in the hallway, her hand pressed over her mouth. Sympathy and horror reflected in her eyes. I gave a slight jerk of my head, encouraging her to retreat before Brody and Mr. Allsop tore their eyes from me and saw her. "I'm sorry," she mouthed before slinking away.

A small smile touched Brody's lips as he watched me flail. Bastard. I lunged at the stove and grabbed the handle of a small cast-iron skillet. I had no delusions. There was no way I could take on four men with a frying pan. But the satisfaction of smashing it against Brody's smug face—of watching blood spurt from his broken nose—that would keep me warm at night after they'd put me in lockup. Wherever that was. I raised the pan over my head and swung with all my might.

A pair of strong arms interrupted its downward arc. Finn's right hand captured my wrist, and his left arm snaked around my waist, hauling my back against his chest. "Drop the pan, sugar." I defiantly tightened my grip on its handle. He twisted my wrist, forcing me to let go.

"Ow." I scowled, rubbing my wrist.

"You gonna be good?" he demanded.

"Screw you," I spit out, stomping on his foot. Fat lot of good it did. My flimsy beaded sandal didn't stand a chance against his heavy work boot.

Finn chuckled. "Feisty little filly, aren't you?"

"Such histrionics are beneath you, Sunny," Mr. Allsop said. "Jonesy, bring the SUV out front. You need to leave before Kyle gets back."

Kyle. They were taking me away from Kyle. Oh, God. Would I ever see him again? I slumped against Finn's restraining arm, a trembling taking hold deep in my bones. They planned to lie to him, to tell him that I'd been kidnapped. Kyle would be mad with worry. He'd probably turn to his old pal Brody and Brody's dad to help rescue me. Fat lot of good that would do.

Get a grip. Think.

It sounded like they intended to give Kyle the benefit of the doubt, to assume that I'd led him astray with my dislike for Brody. That implied that they still hoped they could bring him around to their cause. At least he'd be free. As long as Kyle was free, there was hope.

Five minutes later, Finn and Brody were hustling me into the back of an SUV. Mere minutes after that, Jonesy pulled up to a place familiar to everybody who grew up in Boise: the defunct Old Idaho Penitentiary, a former prison built in the late 1800s. Jonesy's rough hands pulled me from the SUV. Brody led the way toward the women's annex of the prison where two Allsop security men stood guard outside the entrance.

A sturdy door was built into the tall stone wall that surrounded the complex. Inside the wall, dead grass and a few scraggly trees surrounded the Women's Ward. When I visited the place as a child, the small stone building reminded me of a medieval castle, complete with crenellations and a battlement.

I stumbled on the uneven walkway leading of the entrance to the Women's Ward, and Jonesy caught my arm. How had I ever imagined the place as a castle? Now it resembled nothing more than a dismal hellhole, a place where the Allsops would hide me away from the world. Away from Kyle.

The four of us stepped inside the small building. Sunlight from a skylight illuminated the central hall. Jonesy shoved me down onto a bench.

"Sit," he ordered while he fumbled in his pocket for a set of keys.

I turned my head, surveying the place. It hadn't changed since my school field trip. Seven narrow prison cells surrounded the hall. Instead of bars, a grid of metal straps and mesh covered the doors to the cells. Depressing mint-green paint covered the walls. If I remembered correctly, each cell held a bunk and a toilet. God knows if the toilets worked.

"Sunny?"

I jerked at the sound of a familiar voice. Dr. Sara Russo peered at me from inside a prison cell. Her face was pale and her eyes exhausted.

"Sara!" Ignoring Jonesy's order, I jumped up and ran to my friend. "Are you all right?"

"Rocco's here, too," she said quickly as Brody bore down on me.

He dragged me away from the cell door and pushed me back onto the bench. "Sit means sit, sweetheart."

I glared at him. "You," I sputtered. "You kidnapped Sara and Rocco. You attacked the Haven."

"Well, yeah." Brody shrugged. "If we're going to make Boise our center of operations, it makes sense to get rid of any groups that might stand in our way. We dressed some of our men up like Nampa Boys and made sure they were seen around town. We hit the Haven and the Nampa Boys at the same time, and let the survivors blame each other while we rounded up the stragglers. Thanks for leading Finn to the rest of the scavengers, by the way."

Finn grinned and patted the pocket holding the spiral notebook. Bastard.

I swallowed back the guilt that threatened to swamp me. Brody was chatty and I had more questions. "But Kyle was there when you captured the Nampa Boy. The one who said his group took Sara and Rocco. That they escaped."

"Daniel? He works for us. Earned himself a nice steak dinner for taking a punch to the face."

"Why?"

"We needed Kyle to stop searching for the doctor. Telling him they escaped did the trick."

I clutched my head, overwhelmed, trying to put all the pieces together. "You couldn't have known that Kyle and I would show up after you attacked the Haven."

"You're right. We had no fucking clue," he said cheerfully. "But Dad and I always liked Kyle. Dad wants to put the right kind of people in positions of power in the organization. People like us. We still have hopes for Kyle. You were always a long shot. Didn't pay off, but we tried."

"Then why keep me alive?"

Brody smirked, that patented douchebag grin that always raised my hackles. "The flu took more women than men. Dad never wastes assets. Every woman of childbearing age is valuable. Why would we kill you? Makes more sense to breed you. The new world could use a passel of Brody juniors, don't you think?"

My jaw dropped and I gaped at the man.

Nope. *Hell* to the nope.

"Later, babe." Chuckling to himself, Brody strolled out of the Women's Ward. Jonesy and that rat fink Finn followed closely behind.

I freaked out and tore apart my cell looking for something I could use to defend myself. At first I thought that the metal box springs held promise, but my bare hands couldn't pry apart the metal strips. The porcelain lid to the toilet tank proved to be my best bet. It was heavy, and if I hit him just right, it could crack his skull. Would he close his eyes and hold still while I took a swing at him? No, he would not. As an offensive weapon, it sucked, but it was the best I could come up with under the circumstances. I hid the toilet lid under a blanket on the pathetic excuse for a bunk, then took a deep breath. Knowing I had some kind of plan—lame though it might be—allowed me to calm down enough to think.

I walked over to the cell door and gave it a good shake. It rattled, but the padlock held.

"We've tried. There's no way out," Rocco called from a cell across the hall from mine. His tall frame filled the small doorway. "The windows don't open and they're barred outside."

"They give us food and water twice a day." Sara was in the cell next to mine. I could hear her voice, but I couldn't see her. "The guards always come in twos. One of them stays in the hall with a gun trained inside the cell."

"Shit, shit, shit," I muttered, shaking the door again.

"Where's Kyle?" Sara asked.

"He's free for now. The Allsops want to recruit him to their side, so they're still making nice. They gave up on me and put me in here."

"They're hoping that Rocco and I will agree to work for them, too. They said a doctor and a nurse are valuable assets, so they'll give us time to come around to their way of thinking."

And I was still in the land of the living because Brody wanted to sleep with me. Because he wanted to make babies for the post-apocalyptic world. I shuddered. Tonight was supposed to be something memorable and wonderful, my first night with Kyle. Instead, I'd be listening for the jangle of a key in a lock, wondering when Brody would decide to make his move. He might station one of his men outside the door—with a gun trained on me—to make sure I cooperated. Maybe it would be Finn. Pain sliced across my heart again. How had I managed to so completely misjudge the man?

"The guards said that the Haven was destroyed." Rocco's voice interrupted my thoughts. "Is it true? Did they kill our friends?"

"While you were at your meeting with the Nampa Boys, Allsop's men hit the place. They killed Margie and Ed and everybody inside. They took everything, including the ledger, so they know where all our clients live."

"Fuckers." Rocco threw himself against the door. The hinges held. He punched the door then stepped back, growling in frustration.

"The Allsop men were waiting for us when we got to the meeting with the Nampa Boys," Sara said. "It was all a setup. They intercepted our message. They killed Gavin in cold blood." Her voice broke. "He was kneeling on the ground with his hands in the air."

"Bastards laughed and told us their men were attacking the Nampa Boys headquarters, too," Rocco added. "Said they'd get the word out to any survivors in Nampa that the Haven had broken the truce."

"You heard what Brody said. They want to get rid of any competition," I said. "Blame the violence on the Nampa Boys and the Haven. Ride into town like heroes promising to restore law and order. Then they'll take over and implement the agenda for their new order."

"What agenda is that?" Sara asked.

"I don't know many of the details, but I did overhear plans to stop giving food and water to anybody over sixty-five. They called it 'culling the herd.'"

"Jesus..." Sara cried, horrified.

"I thought they were good guys at first," I confessed. "That's why I helped one of Allsop's men compile a list of all the scavengers. I turned our people over to them." The knowledge was bitter acid and the guilt would gnaw at me forever.

"Oh, sweetie. We know that you'd never betray them on purpose," Sara said.

True, but not much of a consolation.

Sara and Rocco fell silent. I whirled around and paced to the far end of my cell. I'd never suffered from claustrophobia, but I felt the walls closing in on me. The cell was so narrow that the fingertips of my outstretched arms could touch opposite walls. Stepping on the toilet seat, I ran my fingers along the window frame. If I managed to shatter the thick pane, could I wriggle through? I pressed my eyes to the opaque glass and could just make out the exterior bars Rocco had mentioned. Damn.

No more than a mile or two separated me from Kyle, but it might as well have been a million miles for all the good proximity did us. Had Mr. Allsop told Kyle that I was dead? Right now, at this very minute, was Kyle coming to grips with that lie, absorbing it, making it part of his inner reality? If so, the man who blamed himself for his friend's death from the flu mania would surely think that my so-called death was his fault, too. That he'd failed me. I'd become another nightmare—like Miles—a specter that haunted his sleep and stole his joy.

No. I pounded both fists on the unforgiving cement walls.

I'm here. I'm alive.

I plopped down onto the bunk. The ancient bed frame squeaked and shifted under my weight. A thin, ratty old mattress—one that must have been left behind when the prison shuttered in the 1970s—provided next to no cushioning against the metal springs. It was beyond me how Sara and Rocco managed to sleep in this place. Not that I anticipated sleeping. Not with Brody liable to show up at any moment.

"Think!" I hissed, rocking back and forth, an old soothing mechanism I hadn't resorted to since I was a child.

A creaking sound from a nearby cell indicated that Sara was on her bunk, too. I'd read someplace that political prisoners often sleep their days away, their minds' way of protecting them from boredom or fear. If Sara could find any respite in sleep, it was a good thing, and I wouldn't disturb her.

Resting my chin in my hands, I closed my eyes and allowed my thoughts to wander. Sometime later, a clattering at the door to the Women's Ward brought me to my feet. Two Allsop men entered. While one guard held his weapon at the ready, the other delivered our dinner: two bottles of water, a teriyaki flavored jerky stick, a package of cheese and peanut butter sandwich crackers, and a plastic cup of diced pears. Quite a step down from rib eye, Caesar salad, and cheesecake. Sighing, I chowed down. I had no appetite and wasn't tempted by the processed fare, but I hadn't eaten today, and I'd need my strength to face whatever was coming.

After dinner, Sara, Rocco, and I sat cross-legged at the doors to our cells carrying on a desultory conversation, a halfhearted attempt to keep each other's spirits up. We even played a few rounds of twenty questions. The light spilling from the overhead window gradually faded, and darkness seeped into every corner of the Women's Ward. I rested my forehead against the metal mesh, fighting back despair.

"You should try to sleep," Rocco called in a low voice.

"Good idea," I replied. Impossible notion, but no reason to say that to a man who was only trying to help. Metallic creaks told me when Sara and Rocco sprawled on their bunks. A short time later, Rocco's snores punctuated the silence. The springs rattled when Sara rolled over. Drawing my knees to my chest, I sat on the cold cement floor. And waited.

Hours later, keys jangled in the door to the ward. I hopped to my feet and grabbed the heavy porcelain tank cover with both hands. My heart raced. I wouldn't go down without a fight. A tall man holding a flashlight stepped inside the Women's Ward. The flashlight beam swept over the room before stopping on my cell door. Blinking against the sudden brightness, I squinted as my eyes adjusted to the light.

Finn stood inside the door. My heart sank. The man I'd trusted would be standing guard while Brody came for me. Betrayal bit deep and only stubborn pride kept me from sobbing. My fingers tightened on the tank cover. I'd let Brody have it, then I'd clobber the traitor Finn. I'd steal their keys and take their weapons, then Sara and Rocco and I would break free. We'd find Kyle and Ever and Mrs. B. and—

A dark figure appeared behind Finn, and I sucked in a breath, readying myself to fight. He stepped around Finn and the world came to a shrieking halt.

TWENTY

Kyle

Half a dozen men followed Brody outside the house, including Jonesy, Elliot Allsop, and the blond man who'd driven my pickup yesterday.

"What do you mean Sunny is gone?" I demanded, a block of ice taking up residence in my chest. "Where did she go?"

Mr. Allsop placed a hand on my shoulder. "There was an incident downtown, son. A truly horrific incident. Prepare yourself."

"I don't understand," I said, looking from one man to the next as if their solemn faces could help me make sense of Mr. Allsop's words.

"Sunny asked to go downtown to visit one of her Haven friends," Mr. Allsop said. "I sent my man with her, of course." He pointed toward the blond guy. "They were ambushed by the Nampa Boys. During the ensuing scuffle, Sunny was shot in the chest."

I stared blankly at him.

"Dude, I'm sorry, but she's dead," Brody said. His chin trembled and his brows were angled at a downward slant, but his eyes were dry.

What's he talking about? Sunny can't be dead.

"I need to see her body," I said. That's the only way I'd believe this was real.

"Unfortunately, that's impossible." Mr. Allsop patted my shoulder. "The Nampa Boys threw her into the back of their car and drove away."

They killed her and then took her body? Unless they were into necrophilia, that made absolutely no sense. Warning klaxons went off in my brain, and my bullshit meter pinged. I'd been through this before, after all, when Pastor Bill claimed that Kenzie had died from the flu. All so he could steal her away from Ripper.

What the fuck is going on?

I was either in a state of denial so deep that my brain simply refused to entertain the truth, or the Allsops were up to something. My eyes met those of the blond guy, the security man who supposedly accompanied Sunny to the fateful encounter. Not a scratch on him. Not a drop of blood. Not even his shirt was rumpled. If Sunny died on his watch, he should look racked with guilt—or sad—maybe numb with shock. Instead he regarded me with a level, imperturbable gaze.

Jonesy was an unflappable hard-ass. If the Allsops had told me that Jonesy was at Sunny's side when she was shot, I might not have questioned such a callous demeanor afterward. But the blond guy? The man who dropped to his knees to hug Ever, who called her sweet pea? Nah, that guy wouldn't stand there like an unfeeling statue while the Allsops broke the news of Sunny's death.

Yeah, something is up.

What was it Sunny had said? Brody had grown insistent when she refused to go out with him. She'd wondered if he held a grudge after she flipped him off. I swung my eyes toward my old buddy, whose face wore a perfect mask of grief. Crocodile tears, that's what Mom would call his exaggerated expression. Had he made another move on Sunny while I was out, and had she shot him down again?

Where is Sunny?

I had to get to the bottom of this, but for now, they were all watching me. I moaned, then swayed, as if overcome with anguish. Staggering sideways, I braced both hands against the side of the truck. "Shit. I'm think I'm going to puke."

"Brody, help Kyle to his room," Mr. Allsop snapped.

"Let me do it, boss." The blond guy stepped forward. "Don't want to risk Mr. Chamberlain upchucking all over your son's fancy shoes." Brody stepped back, his mouth twisting in disgust.

Elliot Allsop waved a hand. "Very well."

"Happy to do my bit, sir." The blond slipped a shoulder under my arm, supporting me as I stood.

I stumbled toward the front door, hamming it up, acting like grief and nausea left me barely able to walk. Once inside, I shut the door, whirled on the stranger, and jabbed him in the chest. "You're going to talk."

"Not here," he said under his breath. Then, in a loud cheerful voice, "Let's get you upstairs, sir."

Side by side—in case somebody was watching through the window—we climbed the stairs. Once in the bedroom, I locked the door and led him to the bathroom. To muffle the sounds of our conversation, I switched on the overhead fan. Crossing my arms, I waited for him to speak. The faint scent of Sunny's grapefruit shampoo lingered in the air.

"You know my brother," he said, crossing one ankle over the other as he leaned against the door. "Bear Rasmussen."

"Finn? You're Finn?" Holy shit. Now that I looked for it, I saw the resemblance. Both tall, blue-eyed blonds. The same cleft in their chins. They even struck a similar pose when they leaned. "Bear has been going crazy trying to figure out what happened to you after the Wilcox Brigade stole the ranch."

"They winged me when I ran." He touched his shoulder. "Then I came down with the flu. Listen, we don't have much time." His voice was low and urgent. "I'm undercover, spying on the Allsop organization for Major Marcus Havoc. The major's gathering survivors in Pendleton. He wants to make sure that when society rebuilds in the Pacific Northwest, it'll be a democratic republic based on the US constitution. Not a white supremacist state like the Wilcox Brigade dreamed of. And definitely not the kind of hereditary oligarchy the Allsops are trying to set up."

Too many questions tumbled through my brain, but I zeroed in on the most pressing one. "What happened to Sunny?"

"That story that the Nampa Boys shot her?" He snorted. "Bullshit. She overheard Allsop and Jonesy talking about cutting off food to people over sixty-five, and she made it clear she'd never be down with that. They still seem to think that you might come around, though."

I'd come around, huh? I'd process that insulting piece of news later. "Where is she?"

"Allsop is keeping prisoners at the Women's Ward at the Old Idaho Penitentiary. Jonesy, Brody, and I locked her up there, right next to the doctor and Rocco."

"Wait. The Allsops took them? Not the Nampa Boys?"

"Yep. I'll fill you in later. What you need to know now is that Brody has designs on Sunny, and we need to get her out of there tonight."

"What do you mean designs?"

Finn sighed. "He's talking about using her like a broodmare."

My head almost exploded. "I'll fucking kill the bastard."

Finn raised a hand to stop me from rushing out of the room. "It won't do a damned bit of good to rush off half-cocked. I got a plan."

"Tell me."

"Far as everyone knows, I'm a trusted Allsop man. Even Sunny thinks I'm a no-good son of a bitch. I can walk right up to the door of the prison, and nobody will think twice about it. That's our way in. We go tonight. Take out the guards. Spring Sunny, the doc, and the nurse."

"And then what?"

"My cover will be shot. We'll head to Pendleton so I can report to the major. I filled the tank in your truck and put extra gas cans in the back for your trip back to Valhalla. Should get us to Pendleton with no problems."

My mind raced. So many questions I didn't have time to ask. "We have to get Mrs. B. and Ever. They're going to Valhalla with us," I said.

"That's a darned good idea," Finn said. "The old lady would be a goner once Allsop finishes consolidating power."

"Unbelievable," I muttered. The notion of Allsop starving Mrs. B. to death—because she was over sixty-five—filled me with a murderous rage.

He blew out a breath. "I'm gonna tell Brody that you want to lie down for awhile. In an hour or two, get up and ask him for a bottle of booze. Let him think you plan to get wasted up in your room. At nine o'clock, sneak downstairs. I'll move your truck to the far side of the garage, out of sight of the house. We'll go get Mrs. B. and Ever. We'll park a couple of blocks from the prison. Leave the keys with Mrs. B. If things go sideways, they can take off for Pendleton and tell the major what's up."

"Yeah. Let's do it."

Finn stood upright and opened the bathroom door.

"Finn?"

He glanced over his shoulder at me and raised a single brow, the exact same quizzical gesture Bear always made.

"Your brother is my friend and one of the finest men I know," I said. "You have to come home to Valhalla."

He smiled, his teeth flashing white against tanned skin. "I will. Soon as I can. That's a promise."

Once Finn left the room, I turned on the bedside lamp and stretched out on the bare mattress. Sunny must have been in the middle of changing the sheets when she was caught. She was probably planning to make things nice for our first night together. Dear lord, what must she be thinking now? No doubt Brody had bragged about telling me that she was dead, about using her as a broodmare. I shuddered. She had to be feeling scared and hopeless.

A soft knock on the door jolted me from my thoughts. I answered the knock. Hildy stood outside my door, holding a silver tray bearing a steaming mug of tea. Instead of a napkin, a piece of paper folded in two sat under the mug. "I thought you might like some ginger tea to settle your stomach," she said, glancing pointedly at the paper.

I played along. "How thoughtful. Thank you, Hildy." When I took the tray, her hand closed over mine, giving it a squeeze before she turned and retreated down the hallway. I shut the door and set the tray on the dresser, then picked up the paper.

Mr. Allsop lied to you. Sunny is alive. He is an evil man. If I find out where she's being held, I'll let you know. God bless you and God keep Sunny safe.

I tore the note into tiny pieces and flushed them down the toilet. Mr. Allsop must never suspect Hildy's betrayal. No doubt Jonesy would take care of her the way he'd taken care of Ever's kidnapper. The woman was risking her life to help Sunny, a commentary both on her courage and on Sunny's gift for connecting with people.

I took a shower, maybe my last hot shower ever, as if that mattered under the circumstances. I threw on jeans and one of my old navy-blue T-shirts, definitely not an Allsop gray tee.

What could I do right now to maximize our chances for success? I checked my shoulder holster, confirming that I had extra ammo. Once I left the estate at 9 p.m., I wouldn't be coming back. I scanned the room, checking for anything that Sunny might want to take with her to Pendleton. Pendleton, not Valhalla. The reunion with my friends would have to wait.

She'd set her family photos on her nightstand. I stuffed them into my duffel, along with her dad's cardigan, a few items of her clothing, her favorite shampoo, and some of my own stuff. All the condoms. When it came down to it, it was surprising how little of your old life you needed to carry with you when you moved on. If Sunny and I escaped with just the clothes on our back, I'd count us as among the blessed.

I stuck the duffel into the closet, ready to grab as I headed out of the house to meet Finn.

Now what? It was hard not to focus on Brody's threats against Sunny. I had to do whatever I could to keep him in the house and away from Sunny this evening. I glanced at the clock. A few minutes past 6 p.m. Mr. Allsop was a creature of habit. The Allsop men met in the library for a before-dinner cocktail at 6. I combed my hair and made my way there.

"Kyle, will you be joining us for dinner?" Elliot Allsop inquired from his seat in a leather club chair, an unconvincing expression of solicitude on his face.

"No, sir. I'm not feeling up to it. I hope you understand."

"Of course." He inclined his head. "If you change your mind, Hildy can bring a plate up to you. She retired to her room with a migraine, but don't hesitate to knock if you need her."

She probably retired to her room to avoid facing the Allsops, but sure, I'd agree to disturb a woman with a migraine so she could make me a sandwich. "Thank you, I'll keep that in mind. Actually, though, I was hoping that Brody might do me a favor," I said.

Brody glanced at his father. "What do you need, man?"

"If I want to talk later, will you be around? I could use a friend." I almost choked on the words.

Brody frowned. Was he planning to visit Sunny in her prison cell tonight? If that was the case, I had to swallow my pride and pour it on.

I dropped heavily into a chair and buried my face in my hands. "I don't know, Brody. I'm not sure I can keep going without her. I loved Sunny, you know?" Out of the corner of my eye, I saw Mr. Allsop jerk his head, silently ordering his son to reply.

"No problemo," Brody said without enthusiasm. "If you need me, I'll be down in the man cave after dinner."

Problem solved. Like it or not, Brody was in for the night. I lifted my head. "Thanks, man. I appreciate it. One more thing."

"Yeah?"

"Do you have a bottle of vodka or tequila I could take back to my room? Something to help take the edge off?"

"Sure." Brody fetched an unopened bottle of premium vodka from the bar cart. "Here you go, buddy."

I tucked the vodka under my arm and shook hands with both men, fighting the urge to bash them over the heads with the bottle. Back in my room, I locked the door. On impulse, I stuffed the bottle of vodka into the duffel, then I crossed to the private balcony overlooking downtown Boise. My hometown. I sighed, sinking into an upholstered patio chair. My eyes picked out the tallest buildings on the Boise skyline. The US Bank Plaza. Eighth and Main. The Capitol dome. After tonight, would I ever see the city again? Probably not. I shrugged. Life moved on and so would I.

I lingered on the balcony until the sun went down, then I strode to the bathroom and splashed cold water on my cheeks. Time to put my game face on. Time to ready myself for battle. I'd done it before, fought and defeated Pastor's Bill's cult and the Wilcox Brigade. I had it in me to do violence to protect those I loved, even if the violence ended up costing me.

At five minutes till 9, I cracked open the door to my room and scanned the hall. No one in sight. Duffel in hand, I silently padded down the hall and stairs. To avoid the guards who stood sentry outside the front door, I exited the house through the garage. At precisely 9 p.m., Finn appeared from between the trees lining the driveway.

"Coast is clear to the road," he whispered. "We'll need to push the truck to the end of the drive, so nobody hears the engine or sees the lights." We both shoved against the truck to get it moving, then I hopped in and steered it down the drive.

We drove straight for Mrs. B.'s place, parked, and ran to her front door. The house was entirely dark. No surprise there. Nobody with a lick of sense called attention to themselves by lighting up their house at night. Instead, they pulled the blinds and huddled around candles or lanterns in a back room. Besides, Mrs. B. probably retired early in preparation for our departure for Valhalla.

I pounded on the door. After a few minutes, a curtain was pushed aside, and Mrs. B.'s face appeared in the window. The front door opened. Mrs. B. greeted us, a small revolver clutched in her hand.

"Whoa, what do you got there, ma'am?" Finn asked.

"Jack's service weapon. A Smith & Wesson .38 Special. A lady can't be too careful these days," she said primly.

"You can shoot?" I asked.

Mrs. B. preened. "I can."

"Good. Pack your gun. We're leaving now."

A sleepy-eyed Ever appeared behind Mrs. B. "What's going on?"

"Change of plans," Finn said. "We need to take off right now. Can you get dressed real fast, sweet pea?"

"Okay." Ever yawned, then staggered to her room.

"Mrs. B., Sunny is in trouble," I said in a low voice. I quickly filled Mrs. B. in on the situation. She ran to her room and exchanged her nightgown for slacks and a blouse. Returning to the front hall, she slipped her revolver into a shiny black purse.

"Kyle, there's a case of Fitzwilliam's food in the cabinet next to the kitchen sink, and the cat carrier is on the back porch."

"Got it," I said.

She hustled behind me into the kitchen and filled an old paper grocery bag with tins of tea and boxes of cookies. "Leave no Jaffa cake behind," she said, smiling even as her chin trembled. It had to be hard to leave the home she'd shared with Jack.

"It'll all be okay," I said. "We're going to rescue Sunny, and then we'll get to safety."

"You're absolutely right." She lifted her chin. "Let's blow this joint, sonny boy."

Despite everything—despite my fears for Sunny—despite the danger hanging over our heads—I coughed out a laugh. "Mrs. B., where have you been all my life?"

She winked, then without a backward glance, she marched to the front door. "Ever," she called. "Come along, dear."

Ever emerged from the back hallway, struggling under the weight of a bed pillow and a pink rosebud quilt. "I want to be comfy in the truck," she explained.

"Good idea," Finn said, taking the bedding from her arms. "We've got a long drive ahead of us. We'll make you a cozy little nest in the back seat right next to Mrs. B. and the kitty."

Ever glanced around the front hall. "Where's Sunny?"

BEDLAM

Finn and I exchanged a glance. "Don't you worry," Finn said. "We're going to pick up Sunny on our way out of town."

"Okay," Ever said agreeably. She yawned again, her eyes sleepy. Apparently the stress we all felt about Sunny's absence had gone right over the little girl's head. Good.

While I hauled the cat food and carrier to the bed of the truck, Ever and Finn piled the bedding on the rear seat. He helped her fasten her seat belt while I walked back to the house.

Mrs. B. stood inside the entry, Fitzwilliam in her arms, taking a last look at her home. "I've been happy in Cressida's Cottage." She sighed. "Now it's time to be happy somewhere else." She squared her shoulders and stood up straight. "Let's go get our girl."

TWENTY-ONE

Sunny

The porcelain tank cover slipped through my fingers and shattered into a million tiny pieces when it struck the cement floor. I blinked, unable to trust my eyes. Shock robbed me of my voice.

Kyle. Kyle stood in the doorway to the Women's Ward.

He took the keys from Finn and rushed toward me. Cursing to himself, he fumbled with the padlock. A click. The cell door flew open, and Kyle dragged me into his arms.

"What?" I gasped, unable to make heads or tails out of the sudden reversal in fortune. "How?"

Finn snatched the keys from Kyle's hand and ran to Sara's cell.

Kyle's arms tightened around me and he grinned. "Finn's a good guy. Ever and Mrs. B. are waiting in the truck. We'll explain everything on our way out of town. For now, we have to haul ass."

Sara and Rocco stumbled from their cells.

"We knocked out the entry guards, tied them up, and stashed 'em behind a bush," Finn said. "With any luck, it'll be at least an hour before any of Allsop's men figure out that something's wrong."

We ran out of the building and toward the door in the fence. Kyle and Finn stepped through first. Once they'd confirmed that the coast was clear, they signaled for us to follow. We jogged through the darkness, past the Bishop's House and defunct state offices, until we came to a residential street.

Kyle's black pickup was parked under the canopy of a tree. "Sorry, you'll have to ride in the truck bed," Kyle said to Sara and Rocco.

"You kidding? No problem." Rocco climbed into the back and offered a hand to Sara to help her in. Mrs. B. jumped out of the driver's seat and patted Kyle's shoulder before he took her place behind the wheel. She flashed me a smile and Ever waved excitedly at me through the window. Finn boosted Mrs. B. into the back seat, next to Ever, then he climbed in after her. I took the front passenger seat.

"We did it. Woo-hoo!" Kyle cried, pounding on the steering wheel. He turned the key and drove the truck to the end of the quiet street.

"Are we going to Valhalla?" I asked, craning my neck to look for any sign of pursuit.

"Eventually," Kyle said. "But for now we're heading to Pendleton so Finn can report in to the major about what the Allsops are up to."

Pendleton? The major? Questions jostled for priority in my mind, but one rose above all the others. Turning around in my seat, I fixed my eyes on Finn. "Who are you?" I demanded.

"Finn Rasmussen. My family owns Valhalla Ranch. After the Wilcox Brigade killed my folks and ran me off, I met up with the major. He leads a group out of Pendleton. They're working to make sure that any new government does right by people and follows the constitution."

"Why were you working for the Allsops?" I asked.

Fitzwilliam jumped onto Finn's lap and stretched out, belly up. "Hey there, buddy," Finn said, scratching the cat under his chin. "Word got out that the Allsops were moving through Idaho, Montana, and eastern Washington, recruiting men for their private army and offering protection to everybody else. For a price." Fitzwilliam began to purr loudly. "Got quite a motor on you, don't you?" Finn chuckled.

"Finn?" I persisted.

He glanced from the cat back to me. "The major sent me to Walla Walla to wait for them to show up. When they did, I signed on and came to Boise with them to gather intel."

"You're a spy? Like Agent Cody Banks?" Ever inquired, her eyes wide.

"Don't know no Agent Cody Banks, sweet pea, but yeah, my job was to spy on the Allsop organization and to report back to the major." Sharp eyes—at odds with his lazy drawl—scanned the road behind the truck. Certainty struck me. His laid-back demeanor was an act, a ploy to keep Ever calm.

"Cool." Ever bounced in her seat.

"And you abandoned your mission to help Kyle rescue me?" I asked.

"We're friends, remember?" he said. I winced, recalling how I'd thrown those words in his face.

"I'm sorry I doubted you," I said.

He laughed. "Sunny, if you hadn't doubted me, I wouldn't be very good at my secret agent job, now would I?"

"No, you wouldn't. I guess not everybody who works with the Allsops is a creep." I frowned, remembering my only other friend in the Allsop household. "Hildy is a good person, too."

"She seems like a nice lady," he agreed. "She owned a popular restaurant in Walla Walla. When Allsop came through town and discovered that she was alive, he told her she'd be working as his private chef. Didn't give her a choice about it, either."

"So she's trapped?" I shook my head. "Forced to work for him? Poor Hildy."

"She tried to help us," Kyle said, reaching over and squeezing my hand. "When Allsop told me that you were dead, Hildy risked everything to give me a note saying you're still alive. She said he's a bad man and a liar, and if she found out where he was holding you, she'd let me know."

"Allsop's not a forgiving man," Finn said. "She took a big risk there."

"Oh, Kyle." Guilt took my breath away. We were hightailing it out of town to safety, and Hildy was stuck slaving away for the Allsops. "We can't leave her behind. Not after she put herself in harm's way to help us."

Kyle pulled the truck over onto the side of the road. He peered ahead of us into the darkness, then turned and looked at the roadway behind the truck. "No sign of pursuit," he said. "No sign of any commotion. Could be the Allsops haven't found the guards and figured out that we're gone."

161

"What are you thinking?" Finn asked. "We go back to the house and get Hildy?"

"No," Kyle said. "*I* go back to the house and get Hildy. I owe her. Drop me nearby then get away. Hildy and I will take Sunny's van. We'll all meet up later in Pendleton."

"No," I interrupted, clutching at his hand. "If you go back for Hildy, I'm going, too. I'll hide by the street so nobody sees me, but I won't be separated from you again."

"Listen up." Finn raised both hands. "We've got a narrow window of opportunity here, and it's getting smaller as we speak. Sunny, we can't risk any of the Allsop security team laying eyes on you, not when you're supposed to be in prison."

Kyle nodded his approval. "That's right."

"Kyle, you're supposed to be out of your mind with grief, drunk as a skunk in your room," Finn continued. "You can't just sashay up to the front door and walk in past the guards. Not without raising a lot of questions. You can't, but I can."

"No—" Kyle protested.

"Listen up." Finn voice was hard, his tone unrelenting. "Far as anybody knows, I'm still a loyal Allsop man. I can march right up to the front door and nobody will say boo. Brody will be down in his man cave. Mr. Allsop spends his evenings in his library, usually drinking or with one of his lady friends. I can get Hildy, go out through the garage, and we'll drive away. Nobody will challenge me."

"You can't risk it," Kyle said. "You need to report back to the major."

"I'm the *only* one who can risk it," Finn insisted. "But if we don't get a move on, it will be too late."

"Shit." Kyle pounded the dashboard, clearly torn.

"There's a church not half a mile from the house." Finn pressed his advantage. "Park behind it, out of sight. Give me twenty minutes to rendezvous with you. I'm not back by then, you'll know things have gone south. You take off and get to Pendleton. Don't fret about me. I've gotten out of tougher scrapes."

"Finn's right," Mrs. B. said, laying a hand on the cowboy's shoulder. "I don't want to risk either of you, but under the circumstances, the plan stands a better chance of success if he goes."

"Thank you, ma'am," Finn said solemnly.

"Don't you dare thank me for encouraging you to put yourself in danger," she said, with more fire in her voice than I'd ever heard. "And Kyle, pull your head out of your ass and drive."

Kyle pulled a U-turn on East Warm Springs Avenue and raced back toward the Allsop estate.

"If I run into trouble, tell the major that Allsop's assembled close to four hundred men," Finn said. "About half are with him in Boise, the rest are stationed in Coeur d'Alene, Spokane, and Bend."

"Bend," Kyle exclaimed. "He has men in central Oregon?"

"Yep. He plans to create a northwest nation state out of Oregon, Washington, Idaho, and the western parts of Wyoming and Montana. Boise will be the capitol."

Kyle pulled into the church's parking lot and brought the truck to a stop behind a small building marked Offices.

"Please be careful," I said. "We don't want to lose you."

Finn handed me the small spiral notebook where he'd recorded the names and addresses of all of the Haven's scavengers. "Just in case," he said.

"You sure?" Kyle asked.

"No worries. I got this." Finn passed Fitzwilliam to Mrs. B.

"Be careful." She kissed Finn on the cheek, leaving behind a smear of pink lipstick.

"You be good, sweet pea." He winked at Ever, then opened the door. "Twenty minutes. No longer." With a final nod, he hopped out of the truck and ran away into the darkness.

"I'm scared for Finn," Ever said in a small voice.

"Finn's a secret agent, remember?" I reminded her. "He's good at this spy stuff."

"But what if the bad guys are good at bad guy stuff, too?" she asked.

I had no answer for that question.

Mrs. B. hugged Ever. "Worrying won't do a lick of good, sweet girl. Our job is to hope for the best and to wait." Her eyes met mine, and I saw fear in their hazy blue depths. She'd maintain the proverbial stiff upper lip for Ever's sake, but the woman was clearly sick with concern for Finn.

A sharp rap on the driver's window nearly made me jump from my skin, until I turned and saw Sara and Rocco standing there. Of course they'd wonder what was going on. Kyle rolled down the window and filled them in.

Seeing Sara reminded me of how we passed the time in our prison cells. "Hey Ever, how about we play twenty questions?" I suggested. "You can go first."

"Okay."

The minutes crawled by as we played round after round of the guessing game. Finally, Mrs. B. held up a slim wrist and tapped the face of her watch. Twenty minutes had passed. I looked at Kyle and raised my brows.

What do we do?

Conflicting impulses warred across Kyle's expression. Reason demanded that we follow the plan and abandon Finn. Emotion required us to wait for our friend. Either option could spell disaster. If we split just seconds before he arrived... or if we stuck around too long... Kyle glanced into the back seat, his gaze lingering on Ever's face.

I saw the instant he decided. The child's safety came first. He frowned, clearly unhappy, but resolute. Grinding his teeth together, he fired the truck's engine and eased cautiously toward the road.

I craned my neck and stared in the direction of the Allsop estate. No signs of unusual activity signaled trouble. No flashing lights. No voices. No squealing tires. Darkness—a quiet, heavy, imperturbable darkness—surrounded us. The absence of commotion made the decision to flee even more painful, bailing on our friend when there was no hint of peril.

"Shit," Kyle whispered, clearly as conflicted as I was.

"We're doing the right thing," Mrs. B. said in a low voice. "Drive, Kyle."

"Yeah." He sighed and turned east onto the road, heading toward the freeway. The pickup glided along quiet streets, its headlights punching holes in the darkness. We'd traveled no more than a couple of miles when a distant whirring sound broke the night's silence. I scanned the roadway behind us, but saw no signs of pursuit.

"Pull over. Cut the engine and turn off the headlights," I said on a hunch, dread creeping up my spine. The truck coasted to a stop, and Kyle turned off the engine. The whirring sound grew louder. We pressed our faces against the windows, staring into the blackness. Overhead, a beam of light sliced through the night sky. The chuff-chuff-chuff of rotors raised goose bumps across my shoulders.

Holy shitballs. Who knew that Elliot Allsop had a freaking helicopter?

TWENTY-TWO

Kyle

"Is that helicopter chasing us?" Ever piped, pressing her nose and hands flat against the window.

The chopper whooshed by overhead, its sharklike silhouette giving it the appearance of a deadly predator on the prowl. Man, that fit. I definitely felt like prey. It kept right on going, its circular searchlight beam dancing back and forth over streets and buildings. If it spotted us, wouldn't it hover above the truck, keeping eyes on our vehicle while the Allsop men on the ground tracked their target? At least, that's what would've happened on TV, which I admit is a piss-poor way to predict how a helicopter chase would go down in real life. I was so far out of my element here.

What would Ripper do?

Ripper would probably bring down the whirlybird with one well-placed shot from his trusty Colt. Me? Not a chance. I'd gotten waaay better at hitting a moving target, but I wouldn't have a clue where to place a kill shot on a helicopter.

"They might be chasing us, but they haven't found us yet," I answered Ever, keeping my eyes on the sleek machine.

Think.

My goal was simple. Get on I-84 west toward Pendleton. The Allsops had no inkling about our destination. As far as they knew, we could literally be heading for the hills, escaping into the rocky terrain north of Boise. Or maybe we were taking off for Salt Lake City to the southeast. We could be driving west into the Malheur National Forest and central Oregon. Or maybe we'd set our sights on Nevada.

There lay our best bet for evading capture. They had no idea where we were going, so they had to cover every route out of town. The odds were still stacked against us. Finn said Allsop had a couple hundred men in town, two-way radios, and a fleet of SUVs. I had a sturdy ranch truck, some extra gas, and a powerful motivation. To keep my people safe. To deliver Finn's message to the major. To organize a rescue, because there was no way in hell I'd go back to Valhalla and tell Bear that he'd lost his brother twice.

I ignored the small voice in my head that said Finn might already be dead. Nope. Wouldn't go there. Allsop would keep him alive. For information. As a bargaining chip. No way would I write Bear's brother off as a casualty of this war.

We had to cover as much ground as possible before the Allsop SUVs spread out over town. What first? I opened the driver's door. "Sara, Rocco, you need to get in the back seat." While they clambered out of the truck bed, I slammed my door and turned to Mrs. B. "Can you and Ever share a seat belt? It's not ideal, but Sara is at least five feet nine, and Rocco is bigger than both of you combined."

"We can snuggle up, can't we dearest?" Mrs. B. smiled at Ever, unfastening and then looping her seat belt around both of them. She placed Ever's rosebud quilt and bed pillow across their laps and shifted Fitzwilliam to the soft surface. By a stroke of pure luck, the cat sprawled contentedly on the pillow. Thank God. I'd rather not have a disgruntled Fitzwilliam howling and writhing in protest or launching himself at the back of my head while I navigated the city. Sara and Rocco climbed onto the back seat.

I switched off the truck's automatic headlight function, allowing me to control the headlights manually. We'd have to drive dark in order to evade the chopper and the SUVs.

Here goes nothing. I confirmed that the headlight control was in the off position.

"Everybody buckled in?" I asked.

A chorus of yeses greeted my question.

"Help me watch the road," I said. "And call out if you see any Allsop vehicles."

I turned the key and pulled onto the road, my path forward illuminated by nothing more than moonlight. Odds were no innocent survivors were out and about, but I'd still look out for pedestrians. And black SUVs. Shit. We were in for a hair-raising ride across town.

"I'll keep an eye out for the helicopter," Sunny said. "Mrs. B., you look to the right. Sara, watch behind us. Rocco, look to the left."

"How about me?" Ever demanded.

"You can help me watch straight ahead," I suggested. "Two heads are better than one."

Ever giggled and some of the tension in my stomach eased, replaced by a calm self-possession. Maybe some of Ripper's levelheaded stoicism finally wore off on me. Lives were on the line here, and I'd do everything in my power to see my people to safety. I touched the Glock in my shoulder holster. Better not come to a shoot-out.

"What's the plan?" Rocco asked quietly.

"We need to get onto I-84 West before Allsop has time to get all of his men into position. If I were him, I'd barricade the major roadways and entry ramps to the freeways first. We'll head west, stick to secondary streets that run parallel to the freeway. Try to get on I-84 out toward Caldwell or maybe Sand Hollow. That far out, his men should be stretched thin."

"Sounds good," Rocco said.

"Chopper at 9 o'clock," Sunny cried.

I pulled into the open bay of a car wash, out of sight of the helicopter when it passed overhead.

"You don't think the helicopter has infrared, do you?" Sara asked while we waited for it to disappear from sight.

"If it does, we're screwed," Rocco said.

"It's a corporate helicopter, not a military one." Sunny shot Rocco a dirty look, then angled her head toward Ever. "I saw the company name on the side. If they'd added infrared capability, I think we'd know by now."

Rocco glanced at Ever, looking abashed. "I bet you're right."

We had a close call at an intersection downtown, when Mrs. B. spotted an SUV heading south one street over. And the helicopter got too close for comfort twice more. Our luck held. We pulled under a restaurant awning once and beneath a tree the second time. Less than ninety minutes after we began our flight from the city, we were rolling along Old Highway 30 outside of Caldwell. With no Allsop vehicles in sight, we took a left turn then merged onto I-84.

I knew this stretch of the interstate well. It was the route I traveled several times a year, driving back and forth to college in Portland. In the summertime—once you got past the businesses offering RV storage, auto auctions, and truck equipment—you'd find yourself surrounded by bright-green cornfields. Not this year, not when the pandemic left few people alive to plant or manage crops. I didn't need to turn the headlights on to know that dried-up browns instead of emerald green now dominated the countryside.

Reasonably certain that we were safe, I finally turned on the truck's headlights. It was close to midnight. Ever dozed against Mrs. B.'s shoulder, but the adults appeared wide-awake, if not wired. All except Sunny, who struggled to keep her eyes open, not surprising after the day she had. Imprisoned, threatened, rescued. The adrenaline spikes would wear anybody out.

"I'd like to stop for the night somewhere around Baker City," I said in a low voice. "It's less than a hundred miles away, but far enough from Boise that we should be safe. We'll keep our eyes open for Allsop men, but Finn didn't say anything about them being stationed in Baker City." Sunny stifled a yawn. "Why don't you close your eyes and get some sleep?"

"I think I will." Within minutes her head lolled back against the seat.

With the headlights on, we picked up speed, flying past a sign for military surplus vehicles. Huh. Had either Allsop or the major checked the place out? Or would they have their pick of vehicles at any military facility? I frowned. I hadn't thought along these lines before. Were tanks just sitting around waiting to be driven away by anybody who wanted one? How about the big guns? How about nukes? Now *that* was a chilling prospect. But wouldn't the government have somebody stationed underground—far away from contagion—keeping an eye on the nuclear arsenal? No clue. Great. Something new to worry about.

We crossed into Oregon, and the freeway rose as we drove into the hills. We sped past a sign for the Lost Dutchman Mining Association and past an old cement plant. The freeway angled downhill again as we approached Baker City. I took Exit 306 and headed toward the city.

The truck's headlights caught the sign for Wagon Wheel Motel, one of those old-style motor courts from the middle of the last century. I turned into the parking lot and stopped the truck in front of the office. The place looked undisturbed. Most looters probably figured that a bare-bones motel wouldn't have much worth taking.

Rocco jumped out of the truck and fell in by my side as I approached the office door. It was locked. Rocco threw his shoulder against it, and it gave way, swinging open into a small lobby. The flashlight beam revealed nothing alarming. A chair. A dead plant. A display case full of brochures for local attractions.

A piece of paper taped to the reception desk caught my eye. A black-and-white image of a Harley and below it the words Street Spawn Approved. The Street Spawn had to be a motorcycle club. I'd never heard of them, but I bet Ripper had.

"Street Spawn," I whispered, committing the name to memory, so I could tell Ripper that we slept at a motel with an MC stamp of approval.

Keys for the motel rooms hung on hooks behind the desk, very old-school. Rocco selected keys for three consecutive rooms while I poked around behind the desk.

"Look." I nudged Rocco, pointing to a full five-gallon water bottle, a refill for one of those upright water dispenser stands.

"Nice," he muttered.

On the shelf next to the water bottle sat a box full of trail mix snack packs and an unopened bag of dried apple slices. Looked like whoever used to work the desk had a serious case of the munchies. I tested the flashlight I found under the desk and it worked. Score, score, score.

We took three rooms at the back of the motel. Rocco carried a sleeping Ever into the middle room that she'd share with Mrs. B. Rocco and Sara chose the room on the left, the one with two queen-size beds. Sunny and I would take the room on the right. I nudged Sunny awake, grabbed my duffel from the truck bed, and followed her into the utilitarian room.

The rooms hadn't been touched since May when the pandemic struck, but the beds were neatly made—if musty—and cleanish towels hung in the bathrooms. We removed the cellophane wrapping from all the disposable glasses, then filled the glasses and the three ice buckets with water.

Sara, Rocco, Sunny, and I huddled together outside the door to our room.

"I'm thinking we should be up and on the road by nine," I said. "We need enough sleep so we won't be punchy, but we want to get there as quickly as possible. We have no way of knowing if the Allsop men will be blockading the freeway, or if they'll have given up by now. We'll have to be ready for whatever comes."

"We will." Rocco ripped open a package of trail mix and tossed a handful into his mouth.

"Sounds good. Good night, guys," Sara said. With a sleepy wave, she retired to her room, Rocco on her heels.

Sunny took my hand and pulled me inside. She locked the door and tugged the curtains closed, leaving only filtered moonlight to illuminate our spartan motel room. And it truly *was* spartan. One bed, covered with a plaid spread. A dresser. A useless television set. A small round table and two chairs. My mom would never have consented to stay in such a humble place, but it felt like heaven to me. Sunny and I were together, safe—for now at least—and alone.

Sunny snaked her arms around my waist and pressed her cheek against my chest, hugging me tight. After a long moment, she tilted her head back and met my eyes, her expression defiant and full of resolve.

"Enough is enough," she said. "I'm not dying a virgin."

"What?" I barked out a startled laugh.

"Look what happened after we decided to wait until everything was *perfect*." She made air quotes around the word. "Everything went to hell. The Allsops locked me up and told you I was dead. And Brody threatened to—" Her voice hitched, and she shuddered.

"Brody's never getting anywhere near you," I said firmly. "If he tries, he's a dead man." Simple truth there. I'd killed before and I'd do it again, especially to keep Sunny safe from a bastard like Brody.

"My point is, we have no idea what the future might hold. We didn't see any of this coming. The only thing that's certain is the here and now."

"And right here, right now, you want to have sex?" I asked skeptically. "When you're exhausted and traumatized?"

"I don't need perfect," she said, her fingers digging into the small of my back. "I need you." She spoke with such earnest conviction that I couldn't point out that she'd accidentally dissed me. I knew what she meant, and this was no time to make a joke.

"I need you, too, Sunshine," I said, touching her cheek. Her eyes glimmered in the dim light.

She grabbed the hem of my T-shirt, jerked it up over my head, and threw it onto the small table. Her fingers went to my belt. "Let's do this."

TWENTY-THREE

Sunny

Kyle's hands gently closed over mine. "Hey, slow down."
I stilled, cursing under my breath. After Kyle expressed reservations about the timing, I'd wanted to demonstrate that I was one hundred percent ready and on board. Instead, apparently, my enthusiasm came across as inept and overzealous fumbling.

"Sorry," I mumbled, blushing.

"No... shit... *I'm* sorry," he said. He took a step back and shoved a hand through his hair. "I was trying to say it's not a race to the finish line, that we have time to enjoy it. Instead I made you feel self-conscious. I'm a jerk."

Self-doubt and self-recriminations. This was off to a promising start, wasn't it?

"I don't know what to do," I confessed.

"Every couple has their own way of doing things, their own rhythm, their own tempo," he said. "We'll figure ours out together."

I bit my lips.

He arched his brows. "So, you want to try again?"

For an answer, I stepped close and twined my arms around his neck. He slid both hands around my waist, his palms warming my skin through the gauzy fabric of my peasant blouse. I brushed the fingers of one hand along his jaw. He must have showered and shaved this morning in our luxurious suite at the Allsop estate. Five o'clock shadow now darkened his jaw, the bristles a sandpaper caress against my fingertips. "I like your stubble," I murmured. "I've fantasized about you dragging it across my breasts or over my thighs."

His fingers tightened around my waist, and his eyes hooded. "You have?"

"Mm-hmm." I considered all the other things I'd fantasized about Kyle doing to me—or me to him—and my face heated.

He laughed softly. "You know, nothing's off-limits. Well... nothing we're both into, that is."

"May I touch you wherever I want?" I asked.

"Hell, yes." He grinned. "I'm all yours."

Permission to put my hands anywhere on Kyle Chamberlain. My dream come true. All the enticing possibilities rendered me momentarily mute, unable to form a coherent sentence or thought. I swallowed, my mouth suddenly dry.

I'm all yours.

Emboldened by his declaration, I stood on my toes and lightly bit his chin, my mouth soft and pliant against coarse whiskers that scraped against the delicate flesh of my parted lips. Nice. Humming in my throat, I licked under his jaw. My tongue sought the spot where his heartbeat pulsed against his skin, a violent thudding that telegraphed his growing desire.

My breath quickened and feminine power coursed through my veins. I might lack experience, but I didn't need to be a skilled seductress to sense Kyle's mounting excitement.

Arching my body against his, I nipped his earlobe. Goose bumps erupted across his shoulders and skittered down his arms. I flattened one hand against his chest, then brushed my thumb across his nipple. His pectoral muscles rippled beneath my palm. He stood stock-still, allowing me to take the lead, ceding control over these first moments of intimate contact. Through his jeans, I cupped his erection, my hand spanning the bulge. I sucked a nipple into my mouth then squeezed his cock.

"Sunny," he gasped.

I lifted my head. My eyes sought his, then I threaded my fingers through his hair and yanked, angling his head to one side. It was a power move, one I saw a favorite singer perform during a concert when she marched over and tugged on her guitarist's hair. Impressed the heck out of me at the time, and I had filed it away in my folder of *Things to try someday*. What would Kyle make of it? Would he indulge my little show of force?

Curiosity tinged with a hint of amusement flickered across his face.

"Strip me," I ordered, feeling very worldly.

Kyle's head reared back and a small smile curved his lips. "Yes, ma'am." He slowly unwound the Pucci scarf from around my neck and draped it across the back of a chair. Eyes locked on mine, his nimble fingers worked the buttons down the front of my blouse. Slipping it from my shoulders, he tossed it onto the small table next to his tee. He pulled my camisole over my head and threw it next to my blouse. With both hands on my hips, he maneuvered us over to the bed, slight pressure from his fingers urging me to sit.

"Not on the bedspread," I blurted out. I'd read horror stories about all the vile things that stained hotel bedspreads and didn't want to be stripped naked on a surface covered with... well... yuck.

Laughter erupted from his throat. "Okay, Sunshine. Not on the bedspread." Still smiling, he peeled back the offensive coverlet and threw it onto the floor. He pushed the blanket out of the way then nudged me down onto the edge of the bed so I sat on a reasonably clean sheet. He paused, lifting one brow.

I bowed my head graciously. Yes, this met with my approval.

"High maintenance," he muttered, not quite under his breath.

Kyle dropped down on his haunches and slipped the beaded sandals from my feet. Standing, he reached for the button on the waistband of my flared jeans. I leaned back on my elbows and lifted my hips so he could tug the jeans down my legs. They joined my blouse and camisole on the table. Wearing only a white lace bra and boy shorts, I lolled back on the bed.

What would he do next?

Kyle toed off his shoes, then worked the buckle of his belt. He shoved his jeans and boxers down his legs and kicked them off. Naked. He was naked. I was waaay too sophisticated to gape at my first penis, so I lay back and crossed my arms beneath my head, staring resolutely at the ceiling.

Could I be less cool?

Good lord. I actually said that out loud.

The mattress dipped and Kyle stretched out beside me, adopting the identical pose. We lay in silence for a long moment, studying the cracked ceiling.

"Sunny."

I squirmed. "Yes?"

He rolled on his side to face me. After a beat, I did the same.

"I don't know what to do," I repeated my earlier words.

In the movies when people had sex for the first time, they were swept away on a tide of passion, with none of this awkwardness or false starts. I wasn't usually self-conscious. I was no prude. Maybe I should have hooked up with one of the guys from college so I wouldn't act like such a clueless nimrod in front of the man I most wanted to impress.

"Performance anxiety," I added unnecessarily.

Kyle tucked a strand of hair behind my ear. "Let's see if we can get you out of your head and back into the moment." He curved a hand around my nape. "And keep in mind that even if tonight turns out to be a complete bust—which it won't—we've got forever to get it right."

Some of the tension leeched from my chest. My anxiety retreated, morphing into background noise rather than the center of my focus.

Be in the moment.

I reached for him again. With one finger, I traced the outline of his mouth. Kyle closed his lips around the tip of my finger and sucked it into his mouth, his tongue swirling around the point. I shivered and slowly withdrew my finger before plunging it once again into the wet heat. He lightly bit my knuckle, then released the digit.

"Got an idea about how to get you out of your head," he said, pressing me onto my back. He swung a leg over my hips. Straddling me, he ran a finger over the lacy edge of my bra. "Pretty, but this has to go." I started to sit up, so I could remove my bra. He gently pushed me back down. "I got this." He slid one hand beneath my back and undid the clasp, then pulled the straps down my arms. He tossed the bra over his shoulder. It flew across the room in a graceful arc and landed atop the lamp on the dresser. The lace cup hooked on the finial, and the straps dangled down on either side of the pleated lampshade.

I bit back the ridiculous urge to giggle at the sight.

"Pretty," Kyle repeated. I turned my eyes back to his face. He stared at my breasts, his expression unreadable. I gulped in air and my chest swelled, my breasts suddenly aching. My nipples puckered, tightening into sharp points. Kyle made a noise deep in his throat. He reached with both hands out and ran his fingers over the curves of my breasts.

I moaned, then arched my back when he scraped the rough pad of his thumb against a nipple.

Kyle bent forward and kissed me, a long, soul-satisfying kiss that left me breathless and trembling. He smiled against my mouth, then sketched a chain of kisses along my chin and throat. He latched on to that sensitive spot where neck meets shoulder. I wriggled when his lips formed an O, and he sucked hard, so hard that capillaries had to burst beneath my skin.

"A hickey?" I gasped. "You gave me a hickey?"

He chuckled softly, his tongue teasing the spot. Tilting his head back, he dragged his chin over the fresh mark, the bristles raising goose bumps across my entire body. I shuddered. He shifted positions, now lying on top of me, supporting his weight on his elbows. He caught a nipple between his teeth and tugged, elongating the tip. He sucked, drawing my entire nipple into his mouth, his tongue circling the point.

Kyle slid a few inches lower on my body. He scraped his jaw across my breast, the whiskers rasping over the tender flesh. My fists clenched in the sheets. God. This was exactly what I'd fantasized about, only… better. I'd suspected that I'd welcome the rough sensation of bristles scratching skin, but I'd had no idea that the sting would be so sweet.

He kissed the hollow between my breasts, his lips warm as they molded against my skin, sucking here, biting there. His tongue found my navel as he shifted lower.

His head reared back. "You pierced your belly button?" He gently touched the flower-shaped charm that dangled from the bottom of the rose gold navel ring. Studded with diamonds, it had been a twentieth birthday present from my mom.

"You like it?" I asked.

"Yeah. I do." He glanced at my face, frowning. "It doesn't hurt if I touch it, does it?"

"Not a bit." I laughed. "For a hot minute I considered piercing my nipple, but chickened out. Now it's too late, I suppose. Even if I change my mind, what's the chance of finding a body piercer anywhere?"

"Not as slim as you might think," Kyle said. "Nyx ran a tattoo shop and she's an experienced piercer. Just saying."

"I'll keep that in mind."

I closed my eyes, full of happy anticipation as Kyle stroked my breasts and belly, reanimating all the delicious sensations that had left me limp with pleasure. Once again, desire flared. He rained soft kisses across my stomach, then slipped lower down my body. Clamping his hands on my thighs, he urged my legs apart.

My eyes flew open when stubble grazed the soft flesh of my inner thighs. Kneeling between my legs now, he dragged his cheek over my right thigh, pausing to nuzzle the dark curls at the apex, before scraping his bristles down the left.

"I'm dying to taste you, Sunny." Kyle groaned. "That all right?"

"Yes," I breathed.

Strong fingers teased apart my lips, and a flat, wide tongue slowly licked over my clit. Once, twice, three times. I tilted my hips, pushing closer to his mouth. That must have been all the encouragement Kyle needed. The tip of his tongue fluttered across my clit, then sketched clockwise circles around it.

Of their own accord, my hands tangled in his hair, and I pressed his mouth against my sex, encouraging him to go harder and faster. He did. I shed any lingering inhibitions and devolved into a creature driven by need, whimpering and thrashing my head from side to side.

He slid a finger inside me, then lifted a glistening face to meet my eyes. "Jesus Christ, you're tight and hot."

"Don't stop." Was that desperate, breathy voice mine?

Moaning—a glorious rumble that penetrated to my core—he wrapped his lips around my clit and gently sucked it into his mouth. He slipped a second finger inside me. I gasped, my back bowing, thighs spasming, as the best orgasm of my life crashed down on me, a tsunami of pleasure. When Kyle gave a final lick to that now oversensitive bundle of nerves, I shrieked and pushed his head away.

Panting and resting his cheek on my thigh, he grinned up at me.

"You taste so freaking sweet, Sunshine."

I found the strength to lean up on my elbows. With one arm, I reached for him. "Come here, baby."

Kyle crawled up between my legs, until we were face-to-face. He smiled down at me with unabashed warmth and genuine affection in his eyes. My heart turned over in my chest. Kyle Chamberlain was a good man. Some of my friends thought you had to choose between a boring nice guy and a hot bad boy. Fate had handed me a hot nice guy, a considerate badass who rescued me from a genuine villain. I was one lucky girl. And we weren't done yet.

Holding his weight on his forearms, he dropped his head and kissed me. I tasted the metallic tang of my excitement on his tongue. His heavy cock lay against my thigh. Thirty seconds ago I felt limp and spent, drained of energy, but now something stirred to life. Desire, curiosity, and tenderness coalesced into a feverish arousal. Once again, I burned for him.

"Now, please, Kyle."

"Hold on." Kyle rolled off the bed and walked over toward the door, where his duffel sat on the floor. I watched him through slitted eyes, my fingers stroking through my slick and puffy folds. He dug through the duffel, then stood, brandishing a foil-wrapped condom. His gaze fell on my hands, and his expression morphed, from triumph to a blazing need that matched my own.

Three quick steps brought him to the bed. I reached out with eager hands and dragged him back to me. My heart thundered in my chest, and my limbs trembled with anticipation, yet we kissed as if we had all the time in the world.

Kyle dropped his forehead to mine. "Ready?"

"Yes."

Rising up on his knees, he tore open the foil packet. I watched, fascinated, as he rolled the condom down his erect cock. I gulped. Would that thing really fit inside me? It was bigger than I imagined, but people had been doing this since the dawn of time, so it had to work, right?

He settled once again between my legs. Reaching between us, he eased the tip of his shaft into position. I slowly undulated my hips. My wet heat slid over his length. I held my breath when he pressed his cock inside me. I squeezed my eyes shut, sorting through the sensations—tissues stretching, an unfamiliar fullness, a bite of not-unwelcome pain. I opened my eyes and glanced down at our joined bodies. Whoa. Only the tip was inside.

Relax.

Kyle supported his weight on his arms, his shoulder and bicep muscles corded with tension as he held himself immobile. Was he giving me time to adjust? Probably. I touched his face, tracing a

finger over the lines of tension that bracketed his mouth as he fought
to hold still. Sweat beaded his forehead and dampened the hair at his
temples. He turned his head and kissed my palm.

"Move," I whispered. "I want you to move."

He dropped his mouth to my ear. "You want me to fuck you,
baby?"

*Oh my God. I never imagined I'd hear those words coming from Kyle's
mouth.*

"God, yes," I whimpered. His fist clenched the sheet by my head
and his cock twitched inside me.

With a groan, he pushed, driving forward until his cock was
seated deep in my core. He stilled once again, his breath coming in
shallow pants. I felt... breached, impaled... but beyond the
undeniable throb of pain I sensed something tantalizing just out of
reach, something that only Kyle could help me find.

"Move," I breathed, certain that this was the only path forward.

"You sure?"

In response, I raked my nails down his back, goading him on.
That was all the encouragement—all the permission—Kyle required.
With a low growl, he pulled back, then slammed home.

I gasped, absorbing the incursion. Heat flared in my sex, zinging
out across every fiber of my body. My fingers curved into claws, and
I dug my nails into his ass, pulling him closer. I clenched my muscles,
allowing myself to feel how completely he filled me. Holy hell, how
he filled me. I rocked my hips, encouraging him to thrust. With a
groan of undisguised relief, Kyle did just that, tentatively at first, then
with increasing vigor.

I danced a fine line between pleasure and pain. Only when I
embraced it—permitting my senses to spiral out of control—did the
balance shift decisively in favor of pleasure. My world contracted to
a pinpoint. The only reality was the immediate, the tangible.
Everything else retreated. Nothing existed beyond the circle of
Kyle's arms.

He reached down and brushed his thumb over my
hypersensitive clit. That's all it took. An orgasm rocketed through
my core. Everything clenched. My nails must have clawed furrows
into Kyle's ass. To my surprise, tears sprung from my eyes.

Kyle must have held off his own orgasm until I found mine. As
my muscles contracted around him, he let himself go, jerking and
shuddering inside me. I collapsed, physically and emotionally spent.

Kyle sprawled next to me. We were silent as our heart rates and breathing returned to normal. Sighing, he rolled on his side. He twirled a damp tendril of my hair around a finger, then ran his palm across my sweat-slicked breasts and stomach.

"Got to admit, Sunshine, I never expected to see you like this. Trembling with exhaustion. Drenched with sweat. Smelling like sex."

I batted at him with a limp hand. "Are you complaining? Are you going to accuse me of leading you astray?"

His shoulders shook. "Hell, no. No complaints. Probably sounds crazy to say—the way the world is—but I don't think I've ever felt happier." He frowned, reality clearly rushing back. "If we can avoid the Allsops, get to Pendleton, and find a way to rescue Finn, that is."

"Shhh." I laid a finger across his lips. "A smart guy told me once to be in the moment."

"Yeah? Sounds like a *really* smart guy. A genius."

"Eh." I waggled my flat hand in the classic maybe-yes, maybe-no gesture.

"Hey." Lunging at me, he blew a raspberry on my belly button. I shrieked, then covered my mouth, remembering Mrs. B. and Ever next door. Laughing, Kyle hopped out of bed and disappeared into the bathroom. He reappeared a minute later—sans condom—and carrying a washcloth. He poured water from the ice bucket onto the washcloth. He knelt next to me on the bed, then gently wiped the damp cloth over my face, my breasts, my stomach, and my thighs. He pressed the cool cloth over my sex.

"You're good?" he asked, his expression serious.

I smiled. "I'm perfect."

"Eh." He mimicked my skeptical hand gesture. I burst out laughing, unable to contain my happiness. Grabbing his hand, I pulled him back down on top of me.

TWENTY-FOUR

Kyle

I fell asleep late—a good hour after Sunny drifted off—but still managed to wake up early, well before our scheduled 9 a.m. departure time. I stared at the ceiling, listening to Sunny's quiet, steady breathing. I'd worn her out last night. That knowledge filled me with a crazy sense of pride. She laid curled against me now, one leg thrown over my thigh, her fingers flat against my stomach. If I shifted positions—wriggled a few inches higher on the bed—her hand would brush against my cock. Thinking about it made me hard. Maybe I could wake her up and go again.

"Don't be a dick," I muttered. Dick. Ha ha. Groaning at my own lame humor, I carefully lifted her hand off my stomach. Sunny had been a virgin and having sex again so soon after her first time might hurt. Sure, I'd promised to wreck her, but said wrecking wasn't supposed to cause actual pain. Untangling my legs from hers, I slid out of bed. I hiked up my jeans and pulled on my tee and my shoulder holster. One hand on the doorknob, I paused and looked back at Sunny. Her brown hair fanned out against the pillow, and her pretty face was relaxed in sleep. Smiling, I stepped outside into a crisp, sunlit morning.

Mrs. B. waved at me from the middle of the parking lot where she'd dragged one of those flimsy plastic chairs piled up next to the motel's outdoor pool. Wrapped up in her quilt, she held a steaming cup of tea. Her shiny black purse sat next to her chair. Good. Mrs. B. was packing. I walked barefoot over to her, careful to avoid anything sharp on the asphalt on my way.

"Pull up a chair and let me make you a cup of tea." Her small camp stove sat on the asphalt, next to her box of tea things.

I fetched a second chair while she put a tea bag in one of her mother's antique cups. As soon as the water came to a boil, she poured it over the tea. Wrapping my hands around a porcelain cup covered with—what else—pink rosebuds, I sat back in the wobbly chair.

"Sleep well?" she asked archly.

Shit, she'd heard us, hadn't she?

"Yes, ma'am." I brazened it out. "You?"

She ignored my attempt at deflection, and her expression grew serious. "You'll be good to Sunny, won't you?"

I met her eyes, hoping that the truth radiated from mine. "I will. I promise."

She smiled. "Well, now that that's settled—biscuit?" She held out a box of ginger cremes.

We sipped our tea in comfortable silence. Eventually, Sara and Rocco joined us. A few minutes later, Ever poked her head out of the motel room door.

"I need to pee and the toilet is icky," she called.

No way we'd let the little girl out of our sight, not until we were well out of danger.

"I'll take her." Sara hopped up. She grabbed a roll of toilet paper from the motel room, then led Ever around a corner of the building to attend to business.

"Don't look." Ever's voice carried across the parking lot.

"I'm not looking," Sara said. "My back is turned."

They emerged from the side of the building. Ever grumbled when the doctor insisted that she wash her hands, but did as she was told, rubbing a tiny bar of soap from the motel's bathroom over her fingers while Sara poured water from a cup. Mrs. B. held out the box of ginger cremes, restoring Ever's good spirits. The girl skipped across the parking lot and took a cookie.

Cookies for breakfast. Unless you were the Allsops—or you lived on a ranch like Valhalla—apocalypse chow left a lot to be desired. Fingers crossed the major had found a way to bring healthy foods into the city. What I wouldn't give for a plate of scrambled eggs or some fresh fruit.

"Fitzwilliam slept with me all night," Ever announced. "Right on my pillow. I rolled over once and got a mouth full of fur."

The door to our room cracked open, and Sunny peeked outside. She was dressed and, unlike me, she'd put on her shoes. "I thought I heard voices." She crossed over to us, smiling a greeting. I watched her approach, alert for any sign of morning-after-the-first-time awkwardness.

She dropped a kiss on Mrs. B.'s cheek. "Good morning, Mrs. B. Love you."

"I love you, too, sweet girl," Mrs. B. said. "Tea?"

"Yes, please."

"How about me?" Ever demanded, hands on her hips. "Do you love me?"

Sunny laughed and kissed the girl on the cheek. "I love you, too, sweetie."

Rocco crossed his arms and huffed, widening his eyes in mock offense.

"And I love you guys," Sunny said to Rocco and Sara.

"But don't hold your breath waiting for a kiss," I warned him. I snagged Sunny's hand and pulled her onto my lap. She came unprotesting and wrapped her arms around my neck. The chair swayed precariously under our combined weight.

"Aren't you going to tell Kyle that you love him?" Ever asked.

Sunny bit her lower lip and tilted her head, a tiny furrow between her brows. Was she hesitating because two days ago we'd confessed that we were halfway to being in love? We hadn't crossed the finish line, so to speak. A lot had changed during those two days. Her disappearance clarified a lot of things, at least in my mind.

"I love you, Sunny McAllister," I said speaking my truth.

A smile crept across her face. "And I love you, Kyle Chamberlain."

That was that. In a motel parking lot, perched on rickety chairs and surrounded by friends, our first declaration of love. I set my empty teacup on the ground and wrapped my arms around her waist.

"Shouldn't take long to get to Pendleton." Rocco tore open the bag of dried apple slices and passed them around.

"No more than an hour and a half, assuming the roads are clear," I agreed.

"I imagine the major controls access to the town with blockades and checkpoints," Sara said.

"Probably," I said. "We'll use Finn's name to talk our way in to see him."

"Finn." Sunny sighed. "I hope he's all right."

"Will the bad guys hurt Finn?" Ever asked.

"I imagine that they'll put him in jail, dearest," Mrs. B. said. "Like they did with Sunny."

Probably true, but Mrs. B. was leaving a lot out, wasn't she? Any child living in the post-pandemic world had to face some scary realities, but I had no idea where you drew the line. What was too much for a young mind to process? I'd defer to Mrs. B. on this one.

"Sunny escaped from the bad guys," Ever said, ignoring the fact that Finn played a big part in gaining Sunny's freedom.

"I did," Sunny said. "And I'm okay. We'll have to hope that Finn will be okay, too. And remember, Finn works for the major. I bet the major will want to rescue him."

"And then Finn will go to Valhalla with us?" Ever asked.

"That's the plan," Sunny said.

"Did you hear that Finn grew up at Valhalla?" I asked Ever. "And that his brother, Bear, is my good friend?"

"Well, then he *has* to escape from the bad guys so he can go home." Ever spoke with absolute conviction. A clear and simple truth, with no room for terrifying what-ifs.

From her mouth to God's ears, like my grandma used to say.

Rocco topped off the gas tank while the rest of us packed up our things. Sara and Ever raided the motel's bathrooms for more bars of soap and tiny bottles of shampoo. Mrs. B. supervised Fitzwilliam as he followed the call of nature. Sunny and I checked the office again and found a stash of kids' juice pouches—the kind you poked open with a straw—tucked behind a pile of old phone books under the register.

We climbed into the pickup, crowding Mrs. B., Ever, Sara, and Rocco into the back seat once again. Ever settled in happily with Fitzwilliam on her lap and a pouch of orange juice in her hand. We headed north into downtown Baker City, past a beautiful historic hotel and a grand old stone cathedral. We turned right onto Campbell Street, heading back toward I-84.

"What's that funny-looking swing set thing?" Ever asked as we drove past a city park.

I slowed the truck to a crawl so I could check it out.

"That's not a swing set, dearest," Mrs. B. said in a strained voice.

No. I swallowed. Not a swing set. Someone had constructed a raised wooden platform in the park, fifteen or maybe twenty feet wide. A dozen steps led from the ground to the platform. Atop it, four evenly spaced upright posts supported a crossbeam. Heavy wooden brackets attached to the top of the posts stabilized the beam. From the beam, hung three thick ropes, each one wrapped several times around the timber. It was a fucking gallows. The only thing missing were the nooses, but it looked like somebody had sliced through the ropes, cutting down the unfortunate souls who had been hanged there.

Who erected a gallows in a city park? Shit, when did the world turn into a horror novel?

Sunny's fingers dug into my arm. "Let's get out of here."

"Yeah." I stomped on the gas pedal, racing toward the freeway entrance. A few blocks past the park, out of the corner of my eye, movement. A man stepped out from behind a parked car. He threw something across the roadway, something black that uncoiled across the surface. Before I could react—with the slightest of bumps—the truck passed right over it.

"What was that?" Sunny cried, turning around to look behind the car.

At first, nothing seemed wrong, then within about ten seconds, thump-thump-thump. A flat tire. No, *four* flat tires.

"Spike strip," Rocco said grimly.

I eased the pickup to a stop in the middle of the street, all of my senses on high alert. Pivoting my head, I scanned our surroundings. A liquor store and bank to our left. A pharmacy and grocery store to our right. A thick row of bushes edged the grocery and liquor store parking lots, creating a divider between the parking spaces and the once busy street.

"What's happening?" Ever asked.

"Hush, dearest," Mrs. B. whispered, wrapping both arms around the girl.

From behind the bushes on both sides of the street, six people stood, weapons in hand. Stalking toward us from every direction, they converged on the truck. I reached for my Glock. My hand paused, inches away from the grip. We were surrounded and outgunned. People would die if bullets started flying.

"Everybody raise your hands," I said. "We've got no choice. We're surrendering."

TWENTY-FIVE

Sunny

Part of me wanted to throw myself in front of Ever and Mrs. B., snarling at anybody who threatened them. Another part wanted to duck under the dashboard and hide from the strangers brandishing guns or to burrow into Kyle's arms. This was not the time to either indulge in heroics or to act like a complete chickenshit. Instead, I lifted both hands in the air, assuming the classic *you're under arrest* pose. I glanced into the back seat. All of the adults had raised their arms in a similar fashion. Ever clutched Fitzwilliam against her chest, her freckles standing out against a face bleached of color.

I smiled at the girl. "You're going to be okay, sweetie." Not even the Allsops would hurt a child. Morality had nothing to do with it. As far as I knew, only a handful of children had survived the flu. Children were assets—and like Brody told me—the Allsops never wasted assets.

I met Kyle's eyes. "I love you," I mouthed. If this was it, if the Allsops were dragging us back to Boise, I needed to say the words again before they separated us, or worse.

"Love you, too, Sunshine." He reached for my hand and squeezed my fingers reassuringly. His expression revealed neither fear nor despair. Instead, he looked deadly calm, ready for whatever was coming.

All four truck doors flew open at the same time. "Get out," a man barked.

With shaking fingers, I unfastened my seat belt. I climbed out of the truck and stood next to the open door, my arms raised above my head.

"Move." With a jerk of his gun, the man closest to me ordered me to walk to the front of the pickup. Mrs. B. and Ever stepped away from the truck the same instant I did.

Ever gazed wide-eyed at the man with a gun. Her chin trembled. "Sunny," she cried, hurling herself at me. She threw one arm around my waist and buried her face in my chest, squashing Fitzwilliam between us. I dropped my arms to hold her. I couldn't stop myself. I glared at the man with the gun.

"Proud of yourself?" I hissed, almost choking on my anger. "Scaring a little girl?"

He was young, no more than sixteen. He took a step back, confusion creasing his features.

"Come along, Fitzwilliam." Mrs. B. took the cat from Ever. Head held high, betraying not the smallest sign of fear, the tiny, silver-haired woman marched to the front of the truck. Ever's arms were locked around me as we stumbled along behind her. Sara and Rocco stood side by side, arms raised, expressions sullen and defiant. Ignoring the guns that tracked his every move, Kyle rushed to our side. He touched my cheek, then lifted Ever up into his arms. She clung to him like a monkey, wrapping her legs around his waist and hiding her face in his neck.

"I got you, sweet pea," he said, borrowing Finn's nickname for the child.

Silence descended as the two groups took each other's measure. I'd assumed at first that the Allsops had caught up with us, but these people were far too motley a crew to be part of that team. Instead of the official gray security T-shirts, they wore a hodgepodge of colors and styles. Allsop's men were neatly groomed. *Standards must be maintained.* Elliot Allsop said that more than once.

The man who appeared to be in charge here—the one the others kept glancing toward—wore a plaid shirt, faded jeans, and scuffed work boots. A scraggly beard covered half his face, and his salt-and-pepper hair was pulled back in a low ponytail. Not a stylish man bun—there was nothing stylish about this guy—but a plain old, utilitarian ponytail.

"Who are you people?" he demanded.

"Stop waving those weapons in our faces, young man," Mrs. B. snapped, her upright bearing and English accent lending a certain *je ne sais quoi* to her words. The fluffy purebred cat she held in her arms only added to the confusion.

The man blinked. He had to be at least sixty. Bet it had been a long time since anybody referred to him as a young man, especially in that tone of voice. "Um..." he said, clearly at a loss.

Mrs. B. raised a haughty eyebrow. "As I was saying, lower your weapons and we can discuss this unfortunate situation like civilized people."

I bet this was the tone of voice she adopted with miscreants back when she was a librarian, putting firmly in their place anyone who dog-eared a page or misshelved a book.

"We're on our way to Pendleton," Kyle said, patting Ever's back. "We stopped and spent the night in town."

"Yeah, we saw you camped out at the Wagon Wheel," the teenage boy said.

"Where you coming from?" the bearded man asked.

"Boise," Kyle said.

"Boise?" The man spat on the ground. "You work for that bastard Allsop?"

"We're running from that bastard Allsop," Rocco said, lowering his hands. "We escaped from Boise by the skin of our teeth. We thought *you* were Allsop's men, chasing us down."

"Well, if that's not the most insulting thing I ever heard." The man spat on the ground again. Mrs. B. cleared her throat and fixed him with a steely scowl. "Beg pardon, ma'am," he mumbled, kicking some loose gravel over the gob.

"How do you know the Allsops?" Kyle asked.

"They came through town a few weeks ago, talking big about restoring government and maintaining law and order. Larry Schultz—he was a city council member who survived the flu—he started asking some hard questions about how the Allsops planned to do it. What they'd expect from us in return. He didn't much like their answers."

"And then he—" the teenage boy started.

"Little pitchers have big ears," Mrs. B. said, interrupting him midsentence.

"Huh?" The teenage boy looked blankly at Mrs. B. She pointed to Ever, who still held tight to Kyle. The proverb escaped the teenager, but he got her meaning. Not in front of Ever. He nodded.

"Looks like we have a common enemy," the bearded man said, signaling his people to lower their weapons. "Don't make us friends, but it suggests that it might be worthwhile to talk."

"We're not going anywhere anytime soon," Kyle said, frowning at the four flat tires on the truck.

"Drew." The bearded man spoke to the teenager. "You and Charlie head over to the tire place. Look for replacement tires for the truck."

"Yes, sir." The boy bobbed his head and jogged toward a red sedan parked next to the liquor store, another young man on his heels.

The bearded man scratched his head. "My name's J.R. Dreyer. I run things around here since we lost Larry. We set up a community center for survivors at the armory, a couple of blocks back." He jerked his thumb in the direction of the park. "How about we go there and swap stories? We got a children's room with games and puzzles and stuff where the little girl can play while we talk."

"Sounds good," Kyle said.

"I'll just get my purse." Mrs. B. offered her best helpless little-old-lady smile while she fetched her gun from the truck.

Ever lifted her head. "Are there many kids in town?" she asked hopefully.

J.R. rubbed his beard while he considered her question. "Let's see. There's Tommy Vasquez. He's seven. And Jayden Fisher. He's eleven."

"No little girls?"

"Not right now, but Lori Murphy's going to have a baby in the next couple of weeks. We might get a little girl here someday soon."

"I'm an emergency room doctor," Sara spoke up. "Rocco is an obstetric nurse."

J.R.'s brows shot up. Few people would guess by looking at him that Rocco—a six-foot-four tattooed behemoth—was a highly respected obstetric nurse who taught classes on newborn care before the pandemic.

"If you don't have a doctor, we could examine Lori and see how her pregnancy is progressing," Sara added.

"Sara and Rocco used to run the survivors support group in Boise, before the Allsops came to town and destroyed it," I said.

"We lost all of our doctors to the flu. I can send somebody to Lori's place to ask her if she wants a checkup," J.R. said. "Thanks for the offer."

Since it was only a couple of blocks away and our truck was grounded, we walked to the armory. We weren't all buddy-buddy. J.R.'s people followed close behind us with weapons still in their hands, but the tension had eased considerably.

The Baker City survivors had established their version of the Haven in the armory's assembly hall, a huge, sunny room with a high vaulted ceiling and a stunning black-and-white patterned floor. Like the Haven, they had set up sorting tables and rows of shelving units full of supplies.

My chest tightened at the sight, at the reminder of everything we'd lost, of everything the Allsops had taken from us. Of our murdered friends and stolen supplies. Of the Allsops' plans for their infernal *new order*. If the Allsops had their eyes on Baker City, would these people stand a chance against them?

While Kyle and the others took seats around a table, Mrs. B., Ever, and I checked out the children's play space, a small room right off the assembly hall. Mrs. B. offered to stay with Ever and I didn't try to dissuade her. We hadn't told her about the Allsops' cut-off age for supplies yet, and I didn't want her to hear such shocking news in front of an audience. I left them putting together a puzzle.

I took a seat next to Kyle as he was finishing telling the Baker City people about what the Allsops were up to in Boise.

"That's twisted, trying to turn survivors against each other like that," J.R. said.

"They're devious and deadly," I said, taking Kyle's hand. "And they killed good people."

"They killed good people here, too," a young man with a buzz cut called from the end of the table.

"That's Wade," J.R. said by way of introduction.

We exchanged nods.

"What happened here?" Sara asked.

"The Allsops rode into town with a fleet of black SUVs," Wade said. "Acted like they were the Second Coming. *Your problems are over. We're here to save the day.*" He snorted. "We *thought* we had problems

193

before they showed up. Food, water, medicine. Making plans for winter. Hah!"

"What did they do?" Kyle asked, squeezing my hand.

"At first they made all their requests sound perfectly reasonable, perfectly rational," J.R. said. "All of the food and water and medicine had to be turned in at a central location. So everybody could get their fair share and nobody could hoard. Then they told us that the penalty for hoarding was death. And, by the by, the Allsop organization would take fifty percent of all of our supplies and everything we grow or produce."

"They declared an 8 p.m. curfew," Wade added. "To protect the good citizens of Baker City against *dangerous criminals* roaming the streets at night."

"And the penalty for breaking curfew?" Rocco asked.

"You need to ask?" Wade's voice was heavy with sarcasm. "Death."

"They went door-to-door, making a list of all the survivors' names and ages," J.R. said. "Again, at first they said it was to make sure that everybody got what they needed. Then they told us that fifty percent of our people between the ages of eighteen and thirty would be conscripted for the Allsop security forces."

"A couple of days ago, I heard Mr. Allsop talk about *culling the herd*," I said. "He wasn't talking about cattle." I glanced toward the open door to the children's room. Mrs. B. was bent over the table, chatting with Ever. Still, I dropped my voice. "They plan to starve everybody over the age of sixty-five. Unless you're a doctor or engineer or somebody especially *valuable*."

Horrified gasps met my words.

"Well, shit," J.R. said. "According to the Allsops, I got only a couple of good years left before I'm officially a waste of resources."

"They ordered us to turn in all our weapons. Gave us one week to comply," Wade said. "Again, for our *protection*. To make sure no criminals broke in and got their hands on them. They said we could check out a hunting rifle for a day or two—which I suspect was totally a bullshit offer—but all the weapons needed to be kept safely at a central location."

"You can imagine how that went over," J.R. put in. "We got a lot of second amendment enthusiasts around these parts. Our councilman Larry Schultz, along with two other good men—a high school coach and a local rancher—went to talk to Mr. Allsop."

"What happened?" Kyle asked, his hand tightening on mine.

Three men went to talk to Elliot Allsop. A gallows with three ropes stood in the city park. It wasn't hard to imagine what happened.

"You saw." J.R. waved a hand in the direction of the park.

"I'm sorry." Kyle shook his head.

"Where are the Allsop people now?" Rocco asked. "Did they just pack up and leave town?"

"Oh, they're coming back," Wade answered. "They said they'd give us time to think about the error of our ways. Told us they had business to attend to in Boise, but once things were settled there, we could expect to see them again. It's like living with a ticking bomb that could go off any second."

"And they said if they didn't get one hundred percent cooperation when they returned, they'd string up more people," J.R. added.

"They must be planning to do in Boise what they did here," Rocco muttered. "Centralizing supplies. Conscription. Curfew. Seizing weapons. Then once they stabilize their hold over the big city, they'll mop up problems in the smaller towns."

"Makes sense," Kyle agreed.

"We thought you might be spying for them." J.R. leaned forward. "That's why we stopped your truck."

Throwing a spike strip in the path of an Allsop vehicle would be a declaration of war.

"Are you saying that you decided not to cooperate?" I asked. "You plan to take on the Allsop organization, with all of their resources, their weapons, and their soldiers? They chased us out of Boise with a freaking helicopter."

"Talk about David versus Goliath," Sara muttered.

"Let me remind you who came out on top in that battle," J.R. said. "Baker City won't roll over and play dead for nobody."

Brave words, but I couldn't imagine a scenario where this turned out well for the townspeople. What were they going to do? Take to the hills and engage in guerilla warfare against the invaders? With winter coming in a couple of months? Their only hope was outside help. I glanced at Kyle and lifted my brows in a silent question.

He inclined his head, catching my drift. "Have you guys heard about Major Marcus Havoc in Pendleton?"

"He's organizing a resistance to the Allsops," I said. "We're on our way to talk to him."

J.R. leaned back in his chair. "A guy passed through town last week. Told us somebody new was setting up shop in Pendleton, but he didn't know who or why. How sure are you about this?"

"Completely sure," Kyle said. "Havoc sent a spy to infiltrate Allsop's organization. A damned good man. He blew his cover to help us escape and got caught for his troubles."

J.R. drummed his fingers on the table, clearly deep in thought. "Would you folks give us the room, so I can talk to my people in private?"

"Of course," Kyle said. Our group stood and filed into the children's playroom, shutting the door behind us.

"Come look at my puzzle," Ever called. I sat beside her and admired her handiwork while Kyle drew Mrs. B. aside and quietly filled her in on our conversation with the Baker City people. After about ten minutes, Wade called us back into the hall.

We took our places around the table. "I'm coming to Pendleton with you," J.R. announced. "To meet this major and find out what he's up to. Maybe we can work together, maybe not. In any case, I need to hear the man out."

"Good," I said. "After the most inauspicious introduction ever, maybe we'll end up allies."

"Maybe," J.R. agreed.

"I'm curious about one thing." Kyle scrubbed a hand across his jaw.

"What's that?" J.R. asked.

"A couple of months back, I helped defeat a group of neo-Nazis. They planned to take over an armory in central Oregon. They wanted the weapons and equipment for their white army." Kyle rolled his eyes in disgust. "Makes me wonder. What happened to all the weapons and equipment stored here, in this armory? Did the Allsops clear it out?"

Silence greeted Kyle's question, and the local people swung their eyes to J.R., leaving their leader to answer.

"Well, now," he said. "The Allsops asked the same question. What happened to all the weapons and personal protection equipment stored in the armory? We told them that back in May—just after the pandemic got started—the army rolled into town and packed it all up and hauled it away."

"Is that what happened?" Sara asked.

J.R. shrugged. "Not exactly. I'm a long-haul trucker. Own and operate my own rig. I was on the road when things got really bad. I drove home with my trailer loaded for a delivery to a grocery store that had already been looted and burned. Mostly dry goods, shelf-stable stuff. After things settled down a bit, I showed Larry the goods. We distributed the food to our neighbors."

"Okay," Kyle said slowly. "What's this got to do with the armory?"

"I'm getting there." J.R. tapped his fingers on the table. "In July, we started to hear rumors about an organized group of men showing up in different towns and taking over. Guess it was early stories about the Allsops from people clearing out ahead of them. Larry and I knew the armory would likely be a target for people like that, so we loaded everything into my forty-eight-foot trailer. Parked it in a barn outside of town."

Rocco whistled. "Smart."

"You've hidden the weapons and equipment," Kyle marveled.

"Yep," J.R. folded his hands over his stomach, smiling. "If it comes to war, Baker City won't be showing up empty-handed."

TWENTY-SIX

Kyle

D*rive casual.*
　　To lend authenticity to the *nothing-to-see-here* image I was trying to convey, I rolled down the driver's widow and rested my elbow on the rubber lip. Arm bent, I tapped my fingers against the roof, like I was keeping time to a song. Nobody who was up to something would adopt such a casual pose.

By prior agreement, we kept our eyes straight ahead as we drove past Exit 213, the first exit to Pendleton off I-84 west. No crawling slowly past; no raising suspicions by rubbernecking the men blockading the freeway exit. Once out of sight of the off-ramp, I picked up the two-way radio and called J.R., whose beat-up old sedan followed a few car lengths behind my truck.

"I counted five men," he said. "All armed."

"Yeah, that's what I saw, too. And three cars blocking the ramp."

"Least we know what to expect," he said.

Exit 210 approached fast.

"Almost there. Out." I shoved the radio into the glove box, clicked on the turn signal, and pulled onto the exit ramp leading to downtown Pendleton, J.R. following close behind. One of the armed men stepped into the middle of the road, holding up his palm, ordering us to stop. Four others took positions behind the parked cars that blocked the ramp, guns drawn and aimed at our vehicles.

"Showtime," Rocco muttered from the back seat.

I killed the engine and raised my hands in the air. Everybody else in the truck followed suit, even Ever. My chest tightened. In what kind of world did a nine-year-old kid know to raise her hands in the presence of armed men? These men wouldn't hurt her, I was certain of it, but still... This was the last time, I silently vowed. Ever would stay safe within Pendleton until it was time to take her home to Valhalla. Mrs. B. and Sunny, too.

The man—a guy in his thirties sporting a short goatee—sauntered over to my window, his eyes scanning the inside of the truck. "What do you want in Pendleton?"

"We need to speak to Marcus Havoc," I said. "I have a message for him from Finn Rasmussen."

His already stony expression hardened further, the name clearly hitting a nerve. "Hold," he barked, stepping backward. He signaled for the other men to surround our vehicles, then pulled a radio from his vest and made a call. A minute later, he walked back to my window.

"Everybody out."

They jerked open the doors to the truck and the sedan. We unfastened our seat belts and climbed out. The man in charge divested me of my shoulder holster and Glock.

"I expect to get that back," I said, doing my best imitation of Ripper's hard-ass scowl.

"Yeah. We'll see." He snorted.

"I don't have a gun." Sunny's voice sounded from the opposite side of the truck. Ignoring the headman's signal to stay put, I strode around the front of the pickup. Sunny stood, arms in the air, as one of Havoc's men patted her down.

"You done?" I demanded, frowning as his hands skimmed over her hips and thighs.

He glanced at me and shrugged, his expression almost apologetic. "Almost. Rules, you know." He stood. "All done." Sunny stepped to my side, wrapping both arms around my waist.

The young man turned to Mrs. B. and Ever. Mrs. B. had hooked her purse over her left arm—like the queen of England—and her demeanor was almost as regal. Sighing, she raised both arms high in the air in an exaggerated pose of surrender. Was she trying to distract him so he wouldn't check the contents of her bag? Who would expect a little old lady to be carrying a .38 Special in her shiny purse?

Didn't work. After patting her down, he slipped the handbag from her arm and opened the clasp. His eyes widened, and he held up her Smith and Wesson revolver, looking between Mrs. B. and the gun. She batted her eyelashes and her bright-pink lips turned up in a charming smile. "You will return my late husband's service revolver to me, won't you, dear? After you determine that we're not troublemakers?"

He tucked the weapon in his waistband then turned to Ever. Clad in shorts and a tee, the girl obviously wasn't carrying a weapon. "I'm not a troublemaker," she said. "But sometimes Finn calls me a little rascal."

Finn's name obviously rang a bell with him, too. His eyes softened. He pointed at the cat Ever held in her arms. "How about your buddy? Is he a troublemaker?"

"Fitzwilliam is the best kitty in the world," she proclaimed.

On the opposite side of the truck, Havoc's men patted down Sara and Rocco, eyeing the big guy suspiciously, even though he didn't so much as twitch when they laid hands on him. Behind us, J.R. had handed over his pistol, and one of Havoc's men gingerly ran his hands over Lori's torso. At eight-and-a-half-months pregnant, suffering from high blood pressure and fluid retention, she'd decided to accompany us to Pendleton in order to stay close to the doctor and the obstetric nurse.

The men searched our vehicles and confiscated our radios. Goatee guy crossed his arms over his chest. "Havoc wants to see you. Pick one of your people to accompany you."

I pointed at J.R. "He's here representing Baker City. He needs to talk to the major, too."

The headman signaled J.R. to join us. "Topher." He called over the young man who'd patted down Sunny and Mrs. B. "These two are going to see Havoc. They'll follow you into town." He fixed me with a sharp, no-nonsense glare. "You can take your truck, but no funny business. Stay right behind Topher."

I almost rolled my eyes. Like I'd try something when I was leaving Sunny and my other friends behind in his care. Topher jumped into one of the cars parked sideways across the ramp. I glanced back at my people as J.R. and I followed his car onto the main road. The top man talked tough, but he was down on his haunches handing Ever a bottle of water.

These are the good guys, remember?

My family used to visit Pendleton every September for the big rodeo, so I was familiar with the city. Topher led us downtown, then toward the complex that housed the city hall and public library. We parked in front and walked through the double doors past a pair of armed guards

"Follow me," Topher said, leading the way into a conference room that Havoc had apparently turned into his headquarters. Piles of papers littered two conference tables that were placed end to end at the far side of the room. A row of free-standing whiteboards were positioned behind the tables. Several large windows overlooked an interior courtyard, filling the room with light while maintaining security. Somebody had tacked paper maps of Oregon, Washington, and Idaho to a wall. Thick black Xs covered the words Portland and Seattle.

"Damn," I said under my breath. We'd suspected that Pastor Bill's minions had burned Seattle, just like they had Portland, but as long as a man didn't know for sure, he could hope. The big X over Seattle dashed that hope once and for all.

I met the eyes of a dark-haired woman in her early forties who sat cross-legged atop one end of the table. Her hair was shorn in a pixie cut that accentuated her delicate, elfish features. Pale knees poked through holes in jeans that had seen better days, and a Portland Trailblazers tee swamped her tiny frame. She held a pistol in her right hand. She smiled brightly at me when she caught me looking, a smile that promised death if I made the wrong move.

Marcus Havoc kicked back in a black office chair, ankles crossed and feet resting on the edge of a table. The wary intensity of his gray eyes gave the lie to his nonchalant pose. His eagle-eyed gaze tracked our progress as we crossed the room and stood in front of his makeshift desk. A bowl of walnuts—still in their shells—sat at his elbow. Locking his eyes on mine, he reached into the bowl and snatched up a walnut, then casually crushed it—shell and all—between his fingers. My lips twitched. The movement was too self-consciously macho to be anything other than deliberate.

Frowning, he popped the nut into his mouth, chewed, and swallowed. "Why'd you say damn?" he asked idly.

"I was in Portland when the city burned," I said, tilting my head at the map. "We heard rumors that Pastor Bill's men started a fire in Seattle, too, but until now, I didn't know for sure."

"You knew Pastor Bill?" He tossed a walnut to the dark-haired woman, who caught it deftly with her left hand. She smashed it against the tabletop, cracking it open. Havoc reached for another walnut and closed a powerful fist around it, the muscles in his forearm—what Kenzie used to call arm porn—clenching.

Was he trying to impress me with his badassery? Okay. I'd badass right back at him. I shrugged. "My friends and I took care of Pastor Bill and his deacons. Helped put Pastor Derek back in place." Well, actually, it was Ripper. Ripper killed Bill and his sanctimonious gang of henchmen, but I was there and I helped.

Me, too. Me, too. What was I, five? Shit.

"Huh," Havoc said. "I sent envoys to meet with Derek Heywood. I take it you're one of Ripper's men?"

I prefer to think of myself as a partner, albeit a junior partner, but sure, I'd claim the moniker. "Yeah, I am."

He studied me, chewing thoughtfully on another walnut. After a long moment he swung his legs off the table and stood, extending a hand. "Marcus Havoc."

Marcus Havoc was freaking huge, as tall as Rocco, but somehow less... squishy. All hard chiseled muscle—his black tee stretched across wide shoulders and a flat stomach—he looked like he belonged on the cover of one of Kenzie's romance novels. He was, or rather he had been, a major in the US Army, so I placed his age in his mid-thirties. Not sure why I expected him to still be in uniform. He wore jeans and a T-shirt, and a short brown beard covered his face. Not exactly regulation, was it? But then, he was building a ragtag army made up of civilian survivors of the great pandemic. No reason for him to stay in uniform.

"Kyle Chamberlain." We shook hands and I tilted my head toward my companion. "This is J.R. Dreyer, representing Baker City." The men shook hands.

Havoc pointed to the woman perched on the table. "My second-in-command, Rachel Cross." She waved, but didn't speak.

He invited J.R. and me to take the two chairs facing his desk. "Heywood said that he had no idea what happened to you all after you moved on," Havoc said. "Where's Ripper now? He's a man I'd like to talk to."

There was no point in obfuscation. The answer to his question was sitting in his parking lot, a truck with the words Valhalla Ranch emblazoned across the door. Moreover, our association with the Rasmussens would go a long way toward explaining why Finn broke cover and helped us escape Boise.

"I met Bear Rasmussen early on in the pandemic," I said. "He told me to come to his family ranch in central Oregon if things went to hell in Portland. They did. We showed up at Valhalla and found out that a group of white supremacists had taken over the place."

Marcus Havoc nodded. No doubt he'd heard about the Wilcox Brigade from Finn.

"We took it back, kicked their Nazi-loving asses. Freed Bear. Now, we all live at the Rasmussen place. Bear has no idea what happened to Finn after the Wilcox Brigade ran him off."

"I found Finn in Ukiah, about fifty miles south of here," Havoc said. "His parents were dead. His ranch occupied. He figured his brother had probably died from the virus. He was recovering from both a gunshot wound and the flu. He's one tough son of a bitch. Been with me ever since."

Finn wasn't with him now, was he? That was the point of this meetup. "Finn's in trouble," I said. "He got caught helping my friends and me escape from the Allsops. I plan to go back to Boise to rescue him, and I'm hoping you'll send some people along to help."

I outlined everything I knew about the Allsop's occupation of Boise. J.R. chimed in with details about Baker City's experiences with the organization.

"Baker City wants to fight, even with the odds stacked in the Allsops' favor?" Marcus asked.

"You're damned right, we do." J.R. screwed up his mouth, like he was going to spit, then thought better of it, maybe remembering Mrs. B.'s horrified reaction.

"How many people still alive in town?"

"Last count, fifty-three. Fifty-six before the Allsops hanged three men." J.R. paused. "Of course, nine of the fifty-three are kids and old folks."

"Got to be real." Marcus leaned back in the chair and folded his arms over his chest. "If the Allsops send in a couple dozen well-armed, trained fighters, no matter how brave your people are, how willing they are to defend their homes, most likely they won't stand much of a chance against the Allsop organization."

"So we should just give up?" J.R. erupted, throwing his hands in the air. "Hand over our guns? Let 'em take half our young people? Work like slaves to keep 'em fat and happy while we starve? No thanks. I'd rather go down fighting. Besides, we have an ace up our sleeve."

"Yeah? What's that?" Marcus asked.

"I emptied out the National Guard armory and stashed everything away in my barn."

"I like him." Rachel spoke for the first time. She hopped off the table and approached J.R., pulling a box of mints from her pocket. Flipping open the lid, she held the mints out to J.R. "Take a chill pill, dude."

Marcus glanced at me. "She *must* like him. Rachel doesn't share her mints with just anybody."

J.R. stared at the second-in-command, his mouth hanging open.

"No?" Rachel shrugged. "Your loss."

She walked around the table and plopped into the chair next to Marcus. Shoving three mints into her mouth, she shaped her lips into an O, inhaled and shivered when the peppermint sting hit.

Marcus turned back to J.R. "I respect a person willing to take a stand to defend their home and their people. That's the type of person the world needs, the type of person we can't afford to lose on a fool's errand."

"You got a better idea?" J.R. demanded.

"Yeah, I do." Marcus leaned forward, resting his elbows on the table. "Pack up your people. Come to Pendleton. Those who want to fight can join my army. Those who don't can stay behind our defensive perimeter. We're taking the battle to Allsop—make no mistake about that—but we're doing it smart, on our terms. Once the war is won, your people can go back to Baker City and rebuild."

"What does victory over Allsop look like?" J.R. asked. "What's your endgame?"

"My endgame?" Havoc's expression grew serious. "I took an oath to support and defend the constitution against all enemies, foreign and domestic. If Elliot Allsop isn't an enemy to everything the constitution stands for, nobody is. We can reconstruct our corner of the world the right way—reestablish a constitutional republic—or we can stand back and let predators like the Allsops take over."

J.R. sat in silence as he mulled over Havoc's words. "That's a proposal I can take back to my people," he finally said.

"Good." Marcus slapped the table and sat upright, swinging his gaze to me. "Now let's talk about your plan to rescue Finn."

My plan to rescue Finn? I owed the man for rescuing Sunny. And I'd gladly do whatever it took to bring Bear's brother back home to Valhalla. But my plan? A nebulous thing at best. Go to Boise. Find Finn. Bring him home. I *had* no real plan.

"I'm in over my head," I confessed to a man who'd probably served a dozen years in the military. "I can handle myself in a gunfight. And I'm willing to risk my life to save Finn, but the truth is, I don't know how to stage a rescue. I have no idea where Finn's being held or the best way to get past Allsop's guards and break him out." I swallowed, suddenly conscious of everything I lacked, of how ill-prepared I was to plan a rescue mission. If only Ripper were here.

"A smart man knows his limits," Marcus Havoc said. "What are you, twenty, twenty-one?"

"Twenty-two." My birthday had passed and I hadn't even noticed.

"Twenty-two," he repeated. "You were a college student before the pandemic?"

"Yeah."

"Yet in the past four months you helped defeat a cult leader and you brought down a group of white supremacists. I'd say you're doing all right."

I nodded my head acknowledging his praise. "But how are we going to rescue Finn if we have no idea where the Allsops are holding him? Or even if he's still alive?"

Marcus Havoc smiled. "Good thing I have a second spy embedded with the Allsop organization, isn't it?"

TWENTY-SEVEN

Sunny

"Here you are. Home sweet home." Topher parked his car in front of the two-story motel across the street from city hall.

From the back seat, Ever giggled. She'd taken a fancy to the young soldier, especially after he fussed over Fitzwilliam. "Look, Fitzwilliam. Home sweet home," she repeated, holding the cat up to the window.

The meeting between Kyle and Marcus Havoc must have gone well, because his men received a call to drive us into town and help us move into the motel. We were assigned four rooms on the ground floor. Sara and Lori would share a room, Rocco and J.R., too. Mrs. B. and Ever were assigned a room next to the one I'd share with Kyle.

Mrs. B. sweet-talked Topher into fetching her boxes from the back of Kyle's truck. She and Ever spread pretty quilts on their beds and scattered pottery figures, books, and games around the room, lending the space a homey air that my unadorned room totally lacked. I didn't give two figs—as Grandma used to say—about the plain décor. I'd happily share a mud hut with Kyle. We had a queen-size bed under the plaid polyester spread, porta-potties in the parking lot, and a door that locked. I was good.

Twenty minutes after we arrived at the motel, Kyle and J.R. joined us.

"We're meeting Havoc and his lieutenants for dinner at six," Kyle said after he shut the door to our room. "They have only one doctor here, so he's especially interested in talking to Sara and Rocco about expanding their clinic." Kyle peeled back the bedspread—he remembered my squeamishness—and patted the blanket. "Sit with me."

I took a seat then turned to face him. "What did he say about Finn?"

Kyle shoved a hand through his hair. "He said a lot. Bottom line, he's not going to leave his man in enemy hands. The rescue is on. We'll talk more about it tonight."

"Good. The sooner the better."

The notion of returning to Boise, of putting ourselves back in Elliot Allsop's crosshairs, terrified me, but not as much as the prospect of abandoning Finn. If we played it safe, if we left him to his fate, I'd wake up every morning for the rest of my life haunted by guilt. *You're a chickenshit.* That's what I'd think every time I looked in a mirror. Who could live with that?

Kyle had risen to the occasion during the past months. He'd fought a cult leader and the Wilcox Brigade in order to protect his friends. He'd understand better than anybody why I had to step outside my comfort zone and do my part.

"I want to talk to you about something." Kyle brushed his knuckles over my cheek then pushed a strand of hair behind my ear. His expression wistful, he gently touched a diamond earring. "I remember your eighteenth birthday party, when your parents gave you these earrings."

"And you and Jake went together on a gift and bought new tires for Daisy." I smiled.

"We weren't going to have you driving around town on bald tires," he said.

"You two always watched out for me," I said. "You were a pain in the ass sometimes, but I hope Jake knew how much I—" I stopped, pain stabbing through my chest, Jake's loss hitting me afresh.

Strong fingers cupped my nape, and Kyle pressed his forehead against mine. "He knew, Sunny. He knew. And he was trying hard to get home to you all when he got sick."

I stilled, remembering Kyle's description of the night my brother died. "It was here, wasn't it?" I asked in a muted tone. How had I not made the association before? "He died in Pendleton."

"Yeah, he did." Kyle pulled his head back, his hazel eyes scanning my face. "I was wondering if you'd like to see Jake and Ali's grave. We're heading to Boise tomorrow. I plan to make it back, but if something goes wrong, this could be my only chance to show you where I buried your brother. Unless it would be too hard for you, which I'd totally understand."

He was right. We had to be real. We might not make it back from Boise. If I wanted to see Jake and Ali's grave, this was the time. "It's not too much. Let's do it," I said. "Let's go right now."

"All right." He pressed his lips against mine, a kiss more tender than passionate, and one imbued with a sense of shared loss.

We found Ever playing cards with Sara and Rocco while Mrs. B. and Lori napped.

"Play five-card draw with us," Ever begged, tugging on Kyle's hand.

"Sorry, sweet pea." Looked like Finn's nickname for the little girl had been universally adopted. "Sunny and I have an errand to run. We'll be back before you know it."

Hand in hand, Kyle and I walked to the truck. We drove north, crossed the Umatilla River, and headed into a posh neighborhood overlooking the city.

Glancing at Kyle, I drew in a breath and found the courage to ask the question that I'd shoved to the back of my mind for a long time. "What was it like that night? Did they suffer?"

"It happened really fast," Kyle said. "That was a blessing. Sometimes people linger for days. Their fever spikes and they're out of their heads. Then the fever drops and they're coherent and you think that maybe... just maybe... they're beating it."

"Like Miles?" I guessed.

"Yeah. Like Miles." Kyle fell silent for a moment, scowling, as if forcing himself to focus on my question. "Jake and Ali got sick during the drive from Portland. They were feverish and sleepy. They dozed until we got to the big house. I got them inside and in bed. They were able to drink a little ginger ale, take some pain pills. They fell asleep and they never woke up the next morning. It was horrible, but I know now that it could have been so much worse."

Images unspooled before my mind's eye as I imagined the events. My strapping big brother and his sweetheart of a girlfriend laid low by an implacable virus. Kyle in despair, helpless to change the outcome.

I rested my hand on Kyle's knee. "I know that you did everything you could to help them. I'm so glad that you were with them, that they didn't die alone."

He met my eyes, his face bleak. "That's just the thing, Sunny. I'm not sure I did everything that I could. Kenzie and I were able to get Miles's temperature down by putting him in a cold bath. He rallied for a while. It never occurred to me to try to lower Jake and Ali's fevers that way. If it had, maybe it would have made a difference."

Crap. He'd been carrying this guilt, too? I turned and faced him square on. "Did it make a difference for Miles?"

"No," he admitted. "Not in the long run."

"So cut it out with the maybes. You did the very best you could to save them, and I'll be grateful for the rest of my life that you were there."

"But—"

I laid fingers across his lips, cutting off his protests. "Enough, Kyle. Let it go."

He opened his mouth, as if to argue, then snapped it shut. We drove in silence the rest of the way. Kyle pulled into the driveway of a large, once upscale house. Shattered glass from broken windows and household items abandoned on the overgrown lawn gave it a derelict appearance.

"Mrs. Malcolm lived in an apartment over the garage. She rented out the big house for family vacations and corporate retreats," he said.

The door to the big house stood wide open.

"Do you want to see the room where they died?" Kyle asked.

Call me a masochist, but I did. I wasn't there the night Jake and Ali died, but somehow it felt right to see the place where it happened, as if I could ease their souls by accompanying them on their last journey, bearing witness even at a distance to what happened. Maybe it defied logic, but it made sense to me.

"I do want to see it," I replied.

Kyle and I picked our way to the front door. We stepped around a small flat-screen TV and a laptop, the same type of items looters

210

abandoned in Boise. While ransacking a place people must have loaded their arms with high-value items from the old world, only to realize that those things were worthless in the new.

Pendleton was supposed to be safe, occupied by survivors who had gathered together under Havoc's banner, still Kyle's hand automatically went to the gun the guards had returned to him.

"I'll go first," he said, stepping inside the house. Kyle cocked his head, listening, then led the way through a grand dining room, past a table that could easily seat twelve, into the large kitchen. The cupboards had been stripped bare of foodstuffs, and the walk-in pantry was empty.

"The pantry was stuffed to the rafters with food," Kyle said, hands on his hips as he surveyed the room. "Mrs. Malcolm used to charge visitors five dollars for a can of soup. I filled my backpack with crackers and nuts and cans of soda when I left." He pointed at a piece of paper. "I left that note, telling Mrs. Malcolm that my dad would pay for what I took. Feels surreal that it's still here." Straightening his shoulders, Kyle held out his hand. "Come on. I'll show you the bedroom."

We walked down a short hall, stopping outside a closed door. He hesitated for just a few seconds before pushing it open. We stepped into a dark, musty bedroom. Kyle crossed over to a window and pushed aside the curtains. Dust motes floated in the light that fell across a rumpled king-size bed. Cans of ginger ale and lemon-lime soda sat on the nightstands. The blankets lay in a heap at the foot of the bed. Only stained sheets and pillows covered the mattress, pillows still bearing the indentations of Jake and Ali's heads.

I swallowed.

"It's just like I left it," Kyle said. He pointed to an overstuffed chair positioned at an angle near the head of the bed. "I pulled that chair up to the side of the bed so I could hold Ali's hand while she fell asleep." He turned to me, his expression tight. "I've never told anybody this, but Ali hallucinated that night. She thought I was Jake. I went along with it. Called her ladybug, just like Jake did. I told her I loved her."

"Oh, Kyle." I slid both arms around his waist and buried my face in his neck. "You helped Ali. You made it easier for her to pass. Jake would've thanked you if he could." Dear God, Kyle was worried that coming here would be too much for me. I should've considered that revisiting that night would be too hard for him. "Let's go, baby. You've done enough."

He pulled back. "I'd rather see it through, unless you need to stop."

"I'm okay."

"All right. Let's go."

French doors led to a brick patio overlooking what was once a garden. Straight ahead, miniature boxwood formed a complex knot, like something out of an Elizabethan garden. White pebbles filled the lines between the small bushes. A summer without water left the boxwood half-dead and brittle, but I could still make out the convoluted pattern of the knot.

"The garden was Mrs. Malcolm's pride and joy," Kyle said. "It used to be beautiful." I followed Kyle down a path toward the roses. In September, rosebushes typically were spattered with blossoms. The rosebushes here had suffered from the same neglect as the boxwood; they were parched and crispy. Not a flower in sight. Just past the roses, near a small ornamental tree, I spied a mound of earth. I glanced at Kyle and he bobbed his head. That was it. My brother's final resting place.

I took Kyle's hand as we approached the grave.

"I buried them deep, so, you know..." His voice trailed off and I squeezed his hand.

He'd piled dirt high over the grave, then tamped it flat. Instead of a traditional cross to mark their resting place, he'd spelled out their names with white pebbles from the knot garden. Jake. Ali. A heart.

My throat constricted and I whirled, hugging him tight. I'd given my heart to a good man. Whatever the future brought, I could face it if I had him at my side. I swallowed twice before I found my voice. "You did good. Thank you."

Arms wrapped around each other, we stumbled back to the truck and drove in silence to the motel. In the parking lot, Kyle killed the engine, turned toward me, and hauled me close. His lips sought mine in a kiss that morphed from gentle to scorching. Desire sparked through every atom of my body, zinging from my lips to my breasts to my sex. I closed my fists in his hair and moaned, molding my body against his. He bit my lower lip, and I jerked my head back, panting.

Where did this sudden onslaught of lust come from? What were we doing? No way we'd give into temptation and maul each other in a motel parking lot. Not with—

The door to room 107 popped open, and Ever stuck her head out. She waved, her face alight with excitement. Kyle groaned, then laughed softly.

"Rain check?" I said through lips that still tingled from his kiss.

"Yeah. Rain check."

He opened the driver's side door and hopped out of the truck. Ever rushed toward him, jabbering a mile a minute about the card game. Smiling wide, he swung her into the air.

My ovaries exploded. I'd heard friends say that when ogling a particularly hot guy, but I always thought the phrase was kind of silly. Until now. Watching the man I love treat Ever with such affectionate care made all my girl parts sing.

Happiness has always come easily to me, almost as if it's my birthright. That's why my parents called me Sunny instead of my given name, Alexandra. Dad called me his *little ray of sunshine*. I'm hardwired for happy.

Yet only a week ago, I was going through the motions, determined to be useful, to be grateful for everything I still had, but hollowed out inside. True joy, genuine happiness, had withered and died along with the old world. And now? I'd returned to default. My fundamental nature reasserted itself. I was so happy, and it was all because of the miraculous return of the man who was nodding patiently at an excited little girl.

"Sunny, come on!" Ever yelled. "Kyle says we have time to play a round of poker before dinner."

Smiling at the pair, I climbed out of the truck. "I should warn you, my mom taught me how to play poker. I'm good. Just ask Mrs. B. She lost a box of cookies to me once on a bet."

Ever gasped. "You took Mrs. B.'s cookies?"

"I brought them back a few days later." I raised a finger to my lips. "Shhh. Don't tell."

I met Kyle's eyes.

"Rain check," he mouthed the words.

Oh yeah. Rain check.

TWENTY-EIGHT

Kyle

"What is she doing?" Marcus Havoc glanced toward Mrs. B., who had walked off into the library stacks, pink reading glasses balanced on the end of her nose and a flashlight in her hand. "She's muttering to herself."

"That's never a good sign." Sunny shook her head. "Mrs. B. is a retired librarian. She's probably checking out the condition of the library. God help anybody who's messed with the books. She'll give them what for."

Havoc's lips quirked. Mrs. B. had given him what for before dinner when he'd gallantly extended an arm and offered to escort her to the dining table. Mrs. B. might play the helpless old lady card when it suited her, but she chafed when treated like one.

"Young man, I was hell on wheels when I was your age," she said. She poked him in the chest. "You wouldn't have been able to keep up with me. I don't need help walking across the room." Over Havoc's shoulder, Rachel grinned.

I sense a mint in Mrs. B.'s future.

J.R. and Lori had stayed with Ever while the rest of us joined Havoc and his lieutenants. After a dinner of boxed macaroni and cheese and canned green beans, we gathered in what was clearly a rec center. A ping-pong table sat in one corner of another large conference room, a piano in the other. Four sofas had been dragged together to form a sort of conversation pit. Mrs. B. wandered off to inspect the library while the rest of us took seats on the sofas. Rachel passed around a bowl full of snack sized candy bars. Sunny took two peanut butter cups.

"Tell me about the Haven," Marcus said to Sara. He'd been eyeing the pretty doctor throughout dinner, and I'd caught her looking at him more than once. For the next fifteen minutes, they sat together on a sofa while she filled him in on the origin and operations of the organization she founded.

"We have something like that here, run by one of my lieutenants, Thanh." He pointed to a dark-haired young man on the opposite sofa. "Thanh sends out gophers—"

"Excuse me, did you say gophers?" Sara frowned.

"What you call scavengers," Thanh said. "People who go-for this or go-for that. Food, meds, household supplies, whatever we need. We use a church north of the river as a distribution center. The medical clinic is next door."

"I'd like you and Rocco to work at our clinic," Marcus continued. "We have a veterinarian running the place. Great guy, but we could use your expertise."

"We'd be happy to help," Rocco said.

Marcus studied the big man for a moment, clearly flummoxed by a baby nurse who looked like an MMA fighter. "Obstetric nurse, huh?"

"Yep," Rocco said easily, unrattled by the raised eyebrows. "I love taking care of the babies."

Marcus shrugged, then pointed to a sandy-haired man of about forty who was seated next to Thanh. "That's Justin Mrachek. He taught biology at a high school in Salem and served with the Oregon National Guard. He's in charge of operations, sanitation, and water."

"How you doing?" Justin lifted a hand.

"How many people are in Pendleton?" Sara asked.

"About seventy after the flu," Marcus said. "Almost a thousand now. We're getting the word out that we provide a safe haven for survivors. That I'm raising an army to fight the Allsops. People have been trickling in for the past few months."

"Do you think Allsop has sent spies?" I asked. It made sense that he'd infiltrate Havoc's camp the way Havoc had infiltrated his.

"I'm sure he has," Marcus said, settling back and swinging his black boots onto a battered coffee table. "Rachel runs security and keeps an eye on all the new people. She's sniffed out a couple of Allsop's agents."

"I can smell a line of bullshit a mile away." Rachel sat on Havoc's other side. She mimicked Marcus and planted her red canvas shoes on the table. She had to be a good foot shorter than the major, so the edge was as far as her legs could reach.

"What did you do before the pandemic?" Sunny asked the woman.

"Bounty hunter."

Sunny's brows drew together. I bet Rachel was the first bounty hunter Sunny met. "Did you work here in Oregon?" she asked.

"Nah. Bounty hunting is... well, was... illegal in Oregon. I was licensed in California. That's where I met this guy." She elbowed Marcus. "In Sacramento, about five weeks after the pandemic got started. He and a group of survivors from his base were heading north. We were all ambushed and pinned down at a roadblock on I-5. By the time it was over, I'd decided to stick with Havoc."

"Are you two—um—involved?" Sunny asked. I tossed her a sideways glance. I'd wondered the same thing myself. Marcus and Rachel seemed mighty comfortable together. Maybe fraternization rules had gone the way of uniforms. But who asks a question like that of perfect strangers? I bit back a smile. Sunny does.

Rachel's lip curled back. "Ew. No. Sleeping with Havoc would be like sleeping with my brother." She shuddered.

Sara looked down at her lap, but not before I spied a small smile on her face.

Interesting.

Marcus threw his hands in the air and shot me a *See what I have to put up with* look. I glanced around the room, my gaze moving from face to face. I'm not sure what I expected from Havoc's resistance movement, but this wasn't it. Of course, my knowledge of military operations came entirely from TV and the news. Did I expect a war room full of stiff, formal, grim-faced soldiers obsessed with protocol? Well, yeah.

"How about you two?" Rachel pointed to Sara and Rocco. "You guys hooking up?"

"No." Sara glanced at Marcus. "Rocco and I are just friends."

"Can we talk about the plan to rescue Finn?" Sunny asked. "Sara, Rocco, and I were held prisoner in the Women's Ward of the old penitentiary. Finn might be there. Or, I suppose, Mr. Allsop might keep him at the house. Or someplace entirely different."

"Assuming he's still alive," Sara said. "I watched Allsop's men kill Gavin in cold blood. I hate to say it, but it's possible that they've already executed Finn."

"Yeah, it's possible," Marcus said. "But it makes more sense to keep him alive. They'll want to extract information from him about our operation here."

Sunny shivered and I wrapped an arm around her shoulders, drawing her close.

"Kyle says you have a second spy in Boise who might know where he's being held," Sunny said.

"I do," Marcus said. "Allsop keeps a small security force with him at all times. No more than ten men. The bulk of his men are barracked in town, at what used to be a hotel. They have a support staff, recruited—well, recruited and commandeered—from the local survivors. People who do the cleaning, cooking, serving food. People who fade into the background. Georgia has been embedded with the support staff for the past two weeks. We're hoping the men will talk in front of her, and she'll pick up valuable intel about the organization."

"You don't know if she's heard anything about Finn?" Sunny frowned.

"It's been less than twenty-four hours since his capture," Marcus reminded her. "Boise is too far away for radio communication. Message drop isn't scheduled for another five days."

"So what's the plan?" Sunny persisted. "When do we go in?"

We? I jerked, whirling to face her. "*We're* not going anywhere, Sunny. You're staying put in Pendleton."

"What are you saying?" she sputtered, genuine confusion on her face. "Of course I'm going with you. We've been talking about it all day."

Huh? "We've been talking about *me* going, not you," I said, totally bewildered.

"Guess again." She snorted. "I'm not staying behind while you ride to the rescue. Finn is my friend. I want to help. And I don't want to be separated from you. Don't you get that?"

Sunny had no idea what she was suggesting. It wasn't her fault. Once upon a time I'd been just as clueless, just as sheltered as she was. She'd never stood toe-to-toe with a man intent on killing her. She'd never pulled a trigger and ended a life. Thank God.

"Sweetheart, you don't know what you're saying—" I started. Sunny's brows shot up almost to her forehead.

In the background, Rachel hooted. "Where's the popcorn?" She mimed plucking kernels from an invisible bowl.

I looked at Sunny, whose cheeks had flushed pink.

"Sweetheart, you don't know what you're saying," she repeated. "Are you *trying* to act like a patronizing dickhead?"

Patronizing dickhead? Because I knew more than she did about the dangers of the real world? Because I wanted to keep her safe? My temper flared, but I swallowed back my angry retort. "Listen, Sunny." I made a herculean effort to keep my tone reasonable. "I'm sure you have the best intentions in the world, but let's get real. You don't have the experience or the skill set to be helpful on a rescue mission."

My sensible words and rational tone didn't help one bit, not from the expression on her face or the way she crossed her arms and glowered at me.

"I'm gonna break in here," Marcus said. "Sunny, tell me why you think you should come along on the mission."

"All right, I will. Thank you for asking." She offered Marcus a small smile, then turned her back to me. "I've lived in Boise all my life, and I know every corner of the city. I've spent the past three months working for the Haven. I've been breaking into strangers' houses looking for food and medicine. It's true that I don't know how to shoot, but I'd bring other skills to the mission. I've kept my cool in some dicey situations. I'm smart and levelheaded. I know where other scavengers live. People who would help us if we got into trouble."

Marcus scratched his jaw, apparently considering her words.

"Tell me, how do you plan to reach out to Georgia if she works at the hotel?" Sunny continued. "I could walk in, pretending to be an old acquaintance of hers looking for a job. I could act all wide-eyed and innocent, nobody they'd suspect is a spy."

"This is crazy," I burst out, throwing my hands in the air and turning to Marcus. "Brody Allsop wants her to have his babies, a new generation of little Allsops. You can't send her to Boise and risk Brody getting his hands on her."

"My choice, Kyle," Sunny said quietly. "In order to save Finn, I'm willing to take the risk."

"They'll recognize you," I said. "Elliot Allsop, Brody, Jonesy, the team from the house, they all know what you look like. Any one of them could ID you."

"We could color her hair or slap a blond wig on her," Rachel said.

"I'm serious," I said, exasperation coloring my voice. "It's too dangerous."

"That's the thing about the new world," Sara spoke up. "It *is* a dangerous place, but we'll never get back what we lost without taking risks. The question isn't whether sending Sunny back to Boise is dangerous. It is. The question is whether she can do the job."

"You think Sunny can do the job?" Marcus asked the doctor.

"In the months I've known her, Sunny has never backed away from a commitment," Sara said. "She shows up day after day and does the work. She keeps her word. She never complains. She's created a network of people who care about her and would help her if she gets in trouble. Do I think she could keep her cool and get the job done? Yes, I do."

"Do you think the soldiers at the barracks would let their guard down around Sunny?" Marcus asked.

"Sunny could charm anybody," Rocco said. "She's got mad people skills. I say use them."

Marcus glanced at Rachel. "That wig shop downtown, you think you could find something there that would alter Sunny's looks enough that nobody would recognize her?"

"From a distance, yes," Rachel said. "Up close, probably not, unless they weren't paying attention. But chances are none of Allsop's personal team would come to the hotel."

"Bring a few wigs here for her to try on tomorrow morning," Marcus ordered.

That was it? The man in charge gave his approval and Sunny was going? I sat back, at a loss for words. How could Sunny—how could any of them—be so damned blasé about the risks she'd face? Possessiveness roared through me.

What would Ripper do?

Shit. I already know the answer to that question. When Ripper infiltrated the Wilcox Brigade, Kenzie accompanied him on his undercover mission. Ripper hadn't liked it. It went against all his protective instincts, but he'd gritted his teeth and brought her along. Because she could help him do his job. Because she refused to be separated from him again in an uncertain world.

Marcus had agreed to take Sunny along on the rescue. Not only was I beat, I'd drive a wedge between Sunny and me if I continued to argue. I glanced at her. She sat perfectly still, her back stiff and her jaw tight, like she was bracing for a fight. I didn't want to fight. If the rescue went awry, tonight might be our last night together.

I laid a hand on her arm. She turned wary eyes toward me. "I'm sorry," I said. "I let worry get the better of me, and I handled it badly."

Her eyes narrowed. "What are you saying?"

"I won't lie," I said. "I'd much prefer that you stay safe in Pendleton, but I understand that it's not my call. If I could spare you from danger, from experiencing the crap that I have, I would. But Sara's right. The world's a dangerous place, and we all have to do our part to make it better."

"I'll be careful," she said. "I don't want to lose my chance at a life with you. And I need you to be careful, too."

"I will," I promised. I wove my fingers through hers, stroking the center of her palm with my thumb. "We have an early start tomorrow. Let's go back to our room."

She smiled, sunlight breaking through storm clouds. "Yeah, let's." Jumping to her feet, she tugged on my hand. "We're going to bed," she announced to the group. "Good night, everybody."

Rachel flashed a thumbs-up, and a chorus of good nights accompanied our exit from the room.

"Be back here at eight," Marcus called.

"Will do," I replied.

Arms slung around each other's waists, we dashed across the parking lot to the motel. Once inside our room, Sunny switched on the solar lantern sitting on the dresser. She unwound the scarf from around her neck and kicked off her shoes, then padded barefoot toward me, halting mere inches from my body.

"Can I do whatever I like?" she asked with a smile that made my heart flip-flop. "Because I've been fantasizing all day about all the things I want to do to you."

She had?

"Sure," I croaked, my voice catching in my throat like a prepubescent teenager.

Smooth, Chamberlain. Real smooth.

"Thank you," she said sweetly, her eyes shining. Rising up on her toes, she kissed me, her lips soft against mine. She gently bit my lower lip and sucked it into her mouth. The tip of her tongue brushed over mine, and I tasted chocolate and peanut butter. Moaning, Sunny swayed, splaying her fingers against my shoulders. She caught her balance, then slid her hands down my chest and scraped fingernails across my nipples.

"Off," she ordered, tugging at the hem of my tee. I peeled off my shirt and dropped it onto the floor. "Much better," she breathed.

She touched my chest once again, her face alight with wonder as she petted my pecs. If the hard-won muscles made Sunny smile, all the hours I'd spent in the gym during the past few years were definitely worthwhile. Her fingers trailed over my stomach, and my abs tightened. Her hand slid lower, cupping my denim-covered cock. Sunny sank to her knees, holding onto my hips as she pressed her mouth against my groin. She blew out a slow, warm breath, an exhalation that speared through the fabric and heated my cock.

I closed my eyes against the sight of Sunny kneeling before me, her eyelids heavy with desire as she caressed the bulge with her cheek. I threaded the fingers of one hand through her hair. With the other, I gripped the edge of the table behind me. No way I'd let myself topple over like some overstimulated virgin.

One by one, Sunny lifted my feet and pulled off my shoes. Her fingers slipped under the waistband of my jeans, then worked the buttons on my fly. She dragged my boxers and jeans down my hips, then paused. The cool air kissed my newly bared skin, then her lips bestowed a similar benediction. She caught the waistband again and tugged, pulling the jeans down to my ankles. Again, she lifted my feet one by one, then tossed the pants aside.

Naked and sightless, I strained to hear the slightest sound. My skin tingled with anticipation. This voluntary blindness rendered me oddly vulnerable, with no idea when or where Sunny would touch me next.

She ran her hand over the length of my cock, the touch tentative, uncertain. "I've been thinking about tasting you all day. May I?"

My head bobbed enthusiastically, almost as if it had a life of its own.

With a wide, flat tongue, she slowly licked the underside of my cock from base to tip. My eyes flew open, and I gaped at her upturned face.

"Was that okay?" she asked.

"Mm-hmm." My voice was a rasp. "That was good."

With a happy wriggle, Sunny acquainted herself with my cock. She brushed her cheek over the shaft, inhaling deeply, before licking again. Her fingers circled the base as her tongue flicked back and forth on the underside. Rising up on her knees, she sucked the head into her mouth. Her tongue swirled around the tip, and she slid her hand up and down the shaft.

I wallowed in pleasure for a good five minutes, savoring every stroke of her tongue, every glide of her fingers over slippery skin, every sound she made as she sucked and licked and hummed.

"Hey." I touched her face. She lifted bleary eyes to mine. "I want to finish inside of you, unless you're too sore after yesterday."

"I've been thinking about *that* all day, too," she said, wiping her hand across her chin.

I pulled her to her feet and shoved down her black yoga pants. Laughing, she kicked them across the room and peeled off her shirt. I'd planned ahead, hopeful lech that I am, and a condom was within easy reach on the nightstand. We climbed between the sheets and lay side by side, facing each other. Her racing pulse tapped against the thin skin at the base of her throat. A sheen of perspiration glistened on her chest and shoulders. Sunny sidled close to me and threw a leg across my hips.

"Would you indulge me—" she began.

"Yes." I cut her query off.

"But you don't know what—"

"Whatever it is, the answer is yes. I'll indulge any fantasy you have." With my thumb, I traced the outline of the most perfect, most kissable mouth ever.

She laughed and rolled on top of me. Sitting up, she straddled my waist. "Careful, Chamberlain." Her lips curved in a sly smile. "I've had years to fantasize about all the depraved things I want to do with you." She tapped a finger to her lips, studying me through narrowed eyes. "You know," she said slowly. "When I used to lie in bed at night, thinking about you—"

SUSANNA STROM

"I already know I'm going to like this," I interrupted.

"Shhh." She bent over and laid a finger across my lips. Her soft pink nipples grazed my chest, and I swear to God that electricity sparked across my skin from the contact. Shivering, I raised my hips. "Ohhhh, that's nice," Sunny moaned, gliding her wet sex up and down my hard and ready cock.

I fought the urge to grab hold of her hips, to drive my cock deep inside her heated core. I'd promised. Her fantasy. Balling my hands into fists, I forced my protesting limbs to hold still.

"You used to lie in your bed, thinking about me," I prompted her to continue.

"Yes." With a wanton smile, Sunny rose up on her knees. She slipped a finger into her mouth. Her lips parted and her tongue swirled around the digit, wetting it. She dragged her fingertip across her full lower lip, down her throat and between her breasts, pausing at her navel. She toyed with the gold-and-diamond piercing, then slid her flat palm down her belly. Her fingers parted slick, swollen folds. Closing her eyes, she arched her back, her perfect breasts jutting into the air.

"What are you doing?" I choked out, my body rioting.

"I'd touch myself." Rocking gently back and forth, her finger sketching lazy circles around her clit, she gazed at me through slitted eyes. "I'd fantasize that you were watching me. I'd play with myself. For you." Her lips parted, and she drew in air, then she exhaled slowly. "You'd watch my skin flush, hear my breath catch. You'd scent how turned on I was. You could almost taste it. Then I'd come. For you."

Jesus Christ, the woman was killing me.

"Would I only watch?" My hips rose and fell as I mimicked her rocking motion.

"No," she breathed. "You'd touch my breasts."

That was all the permission I needed. I slid my palms up her thighs and over her ass before gliding across her ribs. I cupped her breasts. The soft mounds filled my hands as I gently squeezed, brushing my thumbs across the tips. No longer soft and smooth, her nipples had puckered into rigid peaks.

"Like this?" I asked.

"Yes," she gasped. Her head fell back, and her chest rose and fell beneath my hands. "And then..."

"Then... what?" I demanded, my voice hoarse.

Her finger moved more quickly now, going round and round that supersensitive bundle of nerves. "Then you'd roll my nipples between your fingers."

I pinched her nipples between my thumbs and forefingers, twisting and elongating the taut nubs. She moaned, and a pretty pink blush spread across her cheeks and chest.

"Come for me, Sunshine," I ordered.

As if on command, her body bucked and spasmed. She cried out, then slumped forward, collapsing over my chest. I stroked her back, from the curve of her ass to her shoulders.

"I like your fantasies," I murmured into her ear.

She turned her head to meet my eyes, her expression sleepy and sated. "Baby, we've barely scratched the surface of my fantasies. There's a lot more I want to do with you."

"I'm glad you see it that way." I reached for the condom and tore open the foil packet.

I rolled Sunny onto her back and knelt between her legs.

"Kyle?"

"If you remember, I told you I got some fantasies of my own." I slid the condom over my still-hard cock.

She smiled, her sleepy expression replaced by curiosity. "Is that right?"

"Yeah, that's right." I covered her body with mine, supporting my weight on my forearms as I gazed down at her face.

Her eyes widened, and I saw the instant she remembered what I'd promised to do.

"You good?" I asked. If she told me she was too tired or too sore, I'd stop.

Sunny nodded. "I'm perfect, remember?"

She truly was. I laughed softly, my shoulders shaking. "Sunny, where have you been all my life?"

She rolled her eyes. "That's easy. Right next door. Waiting for you to notice me."

"You got my full attention now," I said.

Beneath me, she arched her hips. I pressed the head of my cock against her entrance. She locked her ankles behind my back. With one smooth thrust, I slid all the way home. Home.

Sunny lifted her head, seeking my mouth. Instead of kissing me, she sank her teeth into my lower lip. Releasing my lip, she met my startled gaze, her expression full of challenge. "I believe, Kyle Chamberlain, that you promised to wreck me."

What's a guy to do?

I wrecked her.

TWENTY-NINE

Sunny

"No." I gawked at my reflection in the bathroom mirror. "Just no."

Standing behind me, Rachel gave my shoulders an encouraging squeeze. "C'mon. It's not that bad. Bet Kyle will like it. Let's show him." She took my hand and tugged me out of the bathroom into the library, where Kyle, Marcus, Justin, and J.R. lounged against tables, waiting for me to get ready.

Silence greeted my arrival.

"Well, what do you think?" Rachel asked brightly.

Kyle scratched his head, frowning.

J.R. waved his hand at the platinum-blond wig. Bouncy curls cascaded down my back, past my butt, halfway to my knees "I suppose if it's part of a sexy Lady Godiva costume, it would be all right. The long hair would cover all her bits, you know..." His voice trailed off and he blushed.

Laughter burst from Marcus and Justin.

I stomped back into the bathroom, followed by a giggling Rachel.

"Now that you've had your fun, do you have any serious contenders?" I asked, yanking the offending wig off my head.

We tried a sleek black bob and a layered auburn shag. Both earned a resounding no. If I wanted to call attention to myself with hair that looked unnatural against my complexion, they might work, but blending into the crowd was the point.

"Close your eyes," Rachel ordered.

Grumbling, I complied. She attached another wig to my head.

"Open up."

I did. Leaning forward, I studied my reflection. Loose beach waves—dark blond hair with caramel highlights—skimmed my shoulders. Longer and lighter than my real hair, it changed my look without screaming *fake*. "Not bad," I said, twisting my head back and forth, checking the look from different angles.

"Yeah, this was my number one choice," Rachel confessed.

"Then why did you have me put on that platinum thing?"

She shrugged. "Havoc's heading straight into enemy territory. We're all on edge. I thought if I could make the boys laugh, it might cut the tension for a minute."

I touched her arm. "Are you trying to tell me that behind all that snark and attitude beats a heart of gold?"

"Shut up." Rachel made a face. "I'm a scary badass and don't you forget it."

"Your secret is safe with me." I laughed, then sobered. "Will you do me a favor?"

"Sure, if I can."

I undid the clasp on my gold charm bracelet. "This belonged to my grandma. Ask Mrs. B. to hold onto it for me. And if anything goes wrong, tell her that I'd like her to give it to Ever someday."

"Oh, shit." Rachel screwed up her face and took the bracelet. "Don't jinx it. Marcus knows what he's doing. He'll get you in and out, and you're going to bring Finn back home."

"Yeah, I know," I said. "But just in case..."

"Okay." Rachel shoved the bracelet into her pocket. "I promise."

We walked back into the library. Rachel, Marcus, and Justin huddled together, deep in a last-minute conversation while the rest of us loaded backpacks and weapons into the trunk of an older, blue, four-door muscle car.

Marcus and Justin jogged out of the building.

"J.R., sit up front with me," Marcus said. "Before we drop you off in Baker City, we need to go over our plans one more time."

Kyle, Justin, and I piled into the back of the car. Thankfully, three adults fit comfortably on the seat, although I took pity on the men and offered to sit in the middle. Ninety minutes after we left Pendleton, we pulled into the parking lot of the Baker City National Guard Armory. J.R. radioed his top people to assemble for a meeting with Marcus. An hour later, we were on the road again.

"How well do you know the Nampa Boys?" Marcus asked as we flew east on I-84.

"I never met any of them," Kyle said. "Except maybe the second-in-command, Robbie. He came at us swearing and waving a gun, and the Allsops shot him down before he got close."

"Fuckers," Marcus said. "Killed him before you could compare stories and then took credit for rescuing you."

"I've met David, the head of the Nampa Boys, and a few of their scavengers," I said. "I have no idea if any of them survived the Allsops' attack on their headquarters."

"You know the location of their headquarters in Nampa?" Marcus asked.

"Yes. I went there once with Sara and Gavin. They set up shop at a local skating rink."

"Allsops probably left it a burned-out hull," Marcus said. "But if anyone from their organization survived, I want to talk to them. Their HQ might be a good place to start looking."

"Are you thinking of allying with the Nampa Boys?" Kyle asked.

"If anybody wants payback against the Allsops, it's them," Marcus said. "Definitely be worthwhile to approach them. See if they have any interest in working together."

A little before one in the afternoon, we exited the freeway and drove to the skating rink. Bullet holes pockmarked the stone-and-stucco facade, and the front doors had been blasted off their hinges. Three torched cars sat in the parking lot.

"Doesn't look good, boss," Justin said in a low voice.

"Nope," Marcus agreed.

The men all drew their weapons as we climbed out of the car and cautiously approached the entrance. Marcus and Justin led the way. I followed, with Kyle bringing up the rear. Marcus and Justin swept flashlight beams over the skating rink, which—like the hospital in Boise and the armory in Baker City—had once been transformed into a survivors central. Folding chairs and tables littered the floor, probably overturned during the mad scramble when the Allsops hit the place. Empty metal shelving units lined a wall. Splotches of dried blood stained the hardwood floor, and more bullet holes pitted the walls. I shuddered, imagining the attack.

Marcus and Justin stalked through the snack bar, the game room, and the party room, while Kyle and I circled around past the lockers and restrooms. Evidence of a firefight, of death and destruction, surrounded us on every side, but there was no sign of life in the place.

Dejected, we walked outside, blinking against the bright afternoon sunlight. Across the street from the skating rink, a dumpster hugged the wall of a tire store. A flash of movement caught my eye.

"I think there's somebody hiding behind that dumpster," I said in a low voice.

"Play it cool," Marcus ordered. We stood next to our car as if engaged in conversation, but ready to take cover if anybody opened fire. A minute later, a face peeked out from the side of the dumpster, the familiar blue baseball cap on their head.

"A Nampa Boy," Kyle whispered.

THIRTY

Kyle

"**G**otta take a piss," Marcus announced in a loud voice. "Gimme a minute." He ambled toward the side of the building. Once out of sight of the dumpster, he darted across the street, then headed toward the back of the tire store. A minute later, the Nampa Boy was face-down on the asphalt, Marcus's knee on his back. We jogged across the street and formed a circle around Marcus and his prisoner.

Marcus locked a hand around the Nampa Boy's wrists and pulled him into a seated position. During their brief scuffle, the cap had been knocked from the boy's head. Sunny gasped. The person glaring defiantly at us couldn't have been more than twelve years old.

"I radioed in a report." The kid tilted his head at a black device on the ground next to the dumpster. "If you're smart, you'll get out of here before my guys show up." The words were brave, but his voice quivered.

"Nah. I think we'll wait and meet the guys," Marcus said easily.

I crouched down next to the boy. "Do you know who attacked your headquarters?"

"Yeah." The boy sat upright, anger twisting his features. "It was the Allsops. They tried to make us think it was the Haven, but it was them. They killed a whole lot of people. They killed *old ladie*s. Bunch of fucking pussies."

"Language," Justin said. Old habits must die hard in a former high school teacher.

"Sorry," the kid mumbled.

Sunny knelt next to me and gave the boy her most engaging smile, the one that always worked miracles on crabby neighbors. "My name's Sunny. I used to work for the Haven. These are my friends. What's your name?"

He hesitated. "Ethan."

"If you know about the Allsops, Ethan, you know that they drive around in black SUVs and they wear gray T-shirts." She pointed to our bright blue muscle car.

His gaze followed her finger. He whistled. "Sweet ride."

"Yeah, it is. And look at us," Sunny said. "We aren't wearing gray tees. We aren't working for the Allsops. We're the good guys."

"The good guys?" He snorted. "Tell that to David. See if he buys it."

Finally, some good news. David was alive. Marcus and I exchanged a glance.

"We want to talk to David," she said. "That's why we're here." Ethan shrugged, not losing his petulant expression.

A red car careened around the corner, its tires squealing. Marcus yanked Ethan to his feet as we all stood to face the approaching vehicle. With one hand, Marcus secured Ethan's wrists, with the other, he held a pistol. Justin and I drew our weapons, too.

The red car braked hard. Doors flew open and three men jumped out. For half a minute no one said a word and no one moved. We were inside a moment in time, a turning point when things could either go off the rails or somehow work out for the best.

"You okay, Ethan?" a man called.

"Yeah, I'm okay."

"David," Sunny called, stepping forward and addressing the leader of the group. Tall and lean, he was barely out of his teens. "We've met. My name's Sunny. I worked with Sara and Gavin at the Haven."

He squinted, studying her from a distance. "You don't look familiar."

Sunny touched her hair. "I'm wearing a disguise. A wig. My friends and I are going into Boise, and I don't want the Allsops to recognize me."

"Why are you going into Boise?" he asked. "Allsop and his goons are running the place."

Marcus released Ethan. "Go on, kid."

Ethan scrambled back to his friends. David grabbed his shoulders and looked the boy up and down, probably searching for signs of injuries. "Get in the car," he told the boy before turning his attention back to us.

"My name is Marcus Havoc," the leader of the resistance said. "You may have heard of me."

David rubbed a jaw speckled with skimpy whiskers, his expression thoughtful. "We've heard stories about a dude named Marcus Havoc taking over in Pendleton, but we've had to deal with so much shit lately that we haven't given the stories much thought."

"No? Well, think about this. Elliot Allsop is trying to carve out a personal kingdom in the northwest, a place where his rule is law, and he lives like a king. He'll destroy anybody who gets in his way."

"No news there," David said, scowling. "He tried to crush us like a bug."

"My people are going to stop him from creating his little kingdom. Rebuild the right way, with a new government that protects the constitution and civil rights. Simple as that," Marcus said. "Survivors are pouring into Pendleton. I have soldiers and weapons. Baker City just signed on to join our cause. The Tri-cities, Walla Walla, and La Grande, they've signed on, too."

"If you're Allsop's number one enemy, why are you sneaking into Boise?" David scoffed. "Why risk placing yourself in his hands? He's a shoot first and ask questions later kind of man."

"He took one of my men, and I aim to get him back. Maybe do a little damage while I'm in town."

"So what do you want from me?" David asked, throwing his hands in the air. "He hit us hard less than a week ago, took out a third of my crew. I want to go after the fucker, I really do, but I'm in no position to attack Allsop. Not yet. And I got folks counting on me to take care of them."

Marcus took one step toward David. "I'm not asking you to come along on our rescue mission. We got that covered. I'm here to invite the Nampa Boys to join our cause, to help us stop Allsop from

233

making life hell for good people who are just trying to get by after the pandemic."

David held up a hand, then huddled with his two companions, glancing back over his shoulder at Marcus once or twice as they quietly spoke. After a few minutes, he turned back to us. "What does that mean exactly? Join your cause?"

"Baker City is refusing to knuckle under to Allsop's demands. They're evacuating the town—temporarily—and are withdrawing to Pendleton. Those who can fight are joining our army. Those who can't will stay safe inside our defense perimeter. You could do the same."

"They're abandoning their city?" David asked.

"They've got no choice. There aren't enough survivors in Baker City to make a stand against Allsop."

"Baker City is a small town," David conceded. "We had hundreds of thousands of people in Nampa, Meridian, and Caldwell before the flu, almost as many as Boise."

"You plan to stand your ground and fight Allsop here?" Marcus asked.

David sighed, kicking at the asphalt. "A few days ago we had a run-in with a couple of Allsop's men. My boys managed to take out one of his guys. The next day, those damned black SUVs hit the streets in our towns, shooting everybody they came across. They plastered the town with posters warning that for every Allsop man the Nampa Boys kill, they'll shoot twenty of our people."

"Like what the Nazis did in occupied Europe," I muttered, shaking my head in disgust. "Murdering civilians as retribution. That's a powerful deterrent."

"After the pandemic, we found almost three hundred survivors in our communities," David said. "Providing them with food and water was hard enough before the Allsops came along. Now it's almost impossible. And the Allsops are going door-to-door searching for people, making promises, making threats. Folks are scared and don't know what to believe. My crew wants to fight, but not if it means putting the people who count on us in the Allsops' crosshairs."

"Would you consider evacuating your people to Pendleton and having the Nampa Boys join our army?" Marcus asked.

"How the hell would you evacuate close to three hundred people? Assuming they want to go and not take their chances with

Allsop?" David asked. "The logistics would be a nightmare. People would need some warning to be ready, but we'd have to make sure that the Allsops didn't catch wind of it. How'd we do it? Cars? Buses. How many people fit into a city bus or school bus?"

"About fifty," Justin answered.

"We're talking six buses. How much fuel would that take? Sneaking all those people out of town under the Allsops' noses. Shit, how would it be possible?"

"If you want to make it happen, we'll find a way," Havoc said.

David shoved both hands through his hair. He blew out a slow breath. "I gotta be honest with you, Havoc. If you evacuated our civilians, me and some of my boys would stay behind to fight. Guerilla warfare shit. Ambushes. Bombs. Hit-and-run attacks. We'd make them bleed. You'd be taking on the responsibility for civilians and be getting nothing in return."

"We're here to open a dialogue," Marcus said. "We don't need to decide anything today. Talk to your people. Consider your options. It's only going to get worse here as Allsop consolidates his hold over the territory."

David crossed the distance between them and extended his hand. "I will. I'll send a message to Pendleton when we're ready to talk."

They shook hands, an incongruous pair. One, an experienced soldier in his mid-thirties, battle-hardened, muscle-bound. The other, a lanky young man sporting a wispy mustache. Both carried the weight of the world on their shoulders. Both were determined to do right by their people.

David and his men climbed back into their car. As they drove away, Ethan pressed his face against a window and waved. Sunny waved back.

Justin whistled. "David's only a couple of years older than my students, and he held the Nampa Boys together. He's tough, but with Allsop's resources, the bastard will chew him up and spit him out."

Marcus planted his hands on his hips, his eyes tracking the retreating car. "The world needs men like him. Got to hope he reaches out." The car disappeared around a corner. Marcus turned back to us. "Let's go get Finn."

We jogged back to the car.

No matter how you slice it, sneaking into an occupied city is a high-risk venture. Good news? The Allsops had around two hundred men to cover eighty square miles. Nobody could work twenty-four, seven, so at best Elliot Allsop had a hundred men patrolling the metropolitan area at any one time. Bad news? No matter how careful we were, at any moment we could run out of luck and chance across a black SUV.

We approached the city from the foothills northeast of town. Our luck held as we cautiously made our way into the city.

"Boise is lousy with empty houses," I told Marcus. "We need to make our base camp in a spot that we know for sure is unoccupied. If the Allsops catch wind that we're in town, it needs to be a place where they wouldn't think to look for us."

"Northumberland Heights is out of the question. Brody knows where we used to live," Sunny said. "Mrs. B.'s house is out, too, because Jonesy's been there."

"You got some place in mind?" Marcus asked, swiveling his neck to scan the roads in every direction.

"Yeah, I do." I directed him to an older residential neighborhood in west Boise. Following my instructions, he turned down a side street and parked in the driveway of a blue bungalow.

"Ever's grandma's house," Sunny exclaimed.

"Yep. It's an easy choice. We know for sure the house is vacant. Ever said her grandma sold her car years ago, so there's room in her garage to hide our car. It's centrally located, close to major roads if we have to book it out of town."

I hopped out and rolled up the garage door. Marcus parked inside. We emptied the trunk and carried our backpacks and weapons into the house. Grandma had pulled down the Venetian blinds and drawn the curtains closed over every window before she left her home for the last time. Nobody from the outside could see us as we settled into the front room.

Marcus sprawled on a gold velvet couch, his large frame dwarfing the dainty furniture. He swung his feet up—as if to plant them on the glass-topped coffee table—then apparently thought better of it. Justin elbowed him. "Make room." With a grunt of protest, Marcus tossed a brocade pillow onto the floor and wedged himself into a corner of the sofa. Sunny and I took the two floral chairs facing the sofa.

Justin spread a map of Boise across the coffee table. He pointed at a downtown location. "Allsop houses his men here. The hotel has two hundred guest rooms. Each soldier gets his own room. The hotel had an on-site restaurant, so the dining room is large enough for the men to be served meals together. It's basically a fancy-ass barracks, although with limited electricity. They fire up the generators for only a few hours per day, to cook dinner and provide lights during the evening."

"What's the plan?" Sunny asked, clasping her hands together on her lap.

"The plan is for you to walk into the hotel tomorrow morning," Marcus said. "Tell them you want a job. Tell them you heard that your old friend Georgia works there, and that she'll vouch for you."

"Georgia doesn't know Sunny from Adam," I pointed out. "How's that going to work?"

"No problem," Marcus lifted the lid of an antique glass candy dish. He briefly studied the piece of hard butterscotch candy, then tore open the wrapper and tossed it in his mouth. His jaw worked as he rolled the butterscotch on his tongue. If Ever's grandma was anything like mine, the candy could've been sitting in that bowl for years. "Sunny will use a code phrase that will let Georgia know I sent her."

He made a face and spat the candy across the room. It bounced with a ping off a crystal lamp base and landed on a lace doily.

"You got no couth, man," Justin said, wrinkling his face in disgust.

Marcus shrugged.

"Seriously. You're asking Sunny to march into the lion's den," I said. Sunny shot me a warning glance. "I'm not arguing against the plan," I added quickly. *That* had backfired in a spectacular way, hadn't it? "I just want to know if there's a way to extract her if something goes wrong."

"Nothing's going to go wrong," Sunny said. "Have a little faith."

Marcus leaned forward, resting his elbows on his knees. "I won't lie to you. The operation is not without risk, but I promise that we won't send Sunny in without a contingency plan."

"That's good enough for me," Sunny said.

Optimism had always been Sunny's default. Mine, too, once upon a time. Maybe she was deliberately minimizing the danger she faced. Maybe she needed to put on a brave face in order to see it through. Whatever the case, filling her head with self-doubt wouldn't do a damned bit of good.

I reached over and took her hand. "You got this, Sunshine." She offered me a small smile. I turned to Havoc. "Let's hear the plan."

THIRTY-ONE

Sunny

I crossed the street under the watchful eye of the two armed men who flanked the entry to the hotel. Hands on their guns, they scrutinized my approach. My nerves got the better of me. I stumbled and the strap on my pack slipped off my shoulder and slid down my arm. I paused and shifted the pack to my other shoulder, which must have looked as suspicious as hell to the two men. They went on high alert. One of them lifted a radio to his mouth.

Crap. The mission was off to a promising start, wasn't it? I was marching up to the hotel with all the finesse of a jittery suicide bomber.

One of the men held up his hand. "Stop. Drop the backpack. Raise your arms."

I did, resisting the urge to look back over my shoulder at the window a block away where Marcus waited with a rifle in his hands. Two men burst through the hotel doors and ran toward me. One of the men patted me down, dispassionately running his hands over my arms, torso, hips, and legs. The other dumped the contents of my pack onto the sidewalk. He sifted through my clothes, tossing aside tees, yoga pants, sleep shorts, panties, a hoodie. He unzipped my toiletry bag and tipped the contents onto the cement. A toothbrush and toothpaste fell out. Hairbrush. Deodorant. Lip balm. Hand lotion. Tampons.

Worst start to a job interview ever.

"You can pack up your things."

I stuffed everything back into the bag, then clutched it to my chest. "I was hoping to see somebody about a job."

"Captain Mataraci is in charge," one of the men said. "We'll escort you to his office."

One led the way and the other trailed behind me as we walked into the hotel and past the former reception desk. We turned right and followed a hallway lined along one side with floor-to-ceiling windows that overlooked an interior courtyard. The leadman knocked at the door to the former manager's office.

"Come in," the captain barked.

I did, and my two escorts retreated.

Before the pandemic, a laptop probably would have sat on his desk. Now the surface was littered with piles of papers and manila file folders. Captain Mataraci kept his eyes fixed on the papers on his desk for a good thirty seconds after I entered the room. Instead of jacking up my anxiety—which was probably his intention with such a blatant power play—the lull gave me time to calm down.

"Yes?" He glanced up at me, his expression that of a man far too important to be bothered with piddling affairs.

"Hi." I smiled my most winsome smile. "Thank you for seeing me, Captain Mataraci."

He sat back in his chair and folded his hands over his stomach. "Have a seat."

"Thank you, sir." I dropped my pack on the floor and sat down opposite him. "I'm afraid that I did something to alarm your men when I walked up to the hotel. And here I was trying so hard to make a good impression." I rolled my eyes at my boneheaded move.

"Why do you want to make a good impression?" he asked.

"The truth is, I want a safe place to sleep at night and regular meals. I heard that one of my old friends works here in exchange for room and board. I'm hoping that you might have more openings."

"You have any skills that might make me consider employing you?"

"I've been working part-time since I was in high school. Let's see. I've worked as a waitress at a pancake restaurant. I worked in the laundry at a swim center. Man, I must've washed and dried a mountain of towels. I've worked retail. One summer I worked at a bed and breakfast, cleaning up rooms after guests checked out and changing the sheets. I know you can't exactly check references any more, but I promise that I'm a hard worker. My friend will vouch for me."

"Who's your friend?'

"Her name is Georgia Abbott. We went to high school together here in Boise. I was away at college in Pocatello when the pandemic hit. My parents were killed in a car accident two years ago, so I had no reason to rush back to Boise. Not at first."

"Something happened to change your mind?" the captain asked.

"I kept waiting for somebody from the government to show up and take charge. You know, make sure everybody got food and water. Get the police up and running again so we could feel safe. Make life normal again. But nobody came, and scary things started happening around town. I decided to get out of Pocatello."

"What made you come back to Boise?" he asked.

"Two things. First, I heard that Mr. Allsop was in town and that he was working really hard to make Boise a safe place to live. And second, I wanted to see if anybody I knew had survived the flu. That was a big fat no, until one of Georgia's neighbors saw me knocking on her door and told me she was alive and working here at the hotel taking care of Mr. Allsop's soldiers. So I thought I'd come here and see if you're hiring."

"What's your name?"

"Bonnie. Bonnie Bernard. Pleased to meet you, sir." I hopped to my feet and extended my hand across his desk. After a moment, he stood and shook my hand.

"Trask," he bellowed.

A young man stuck his head in the door. "Yes, sir?"

"Find Georgia Abbott. Tell her that her old friend Bonnie Bernard is here."

"Yes, sir."

The captain gestured for me to sit again. I did, wriggling with fake excitement.

"Does this mean you're considering offering me a job?"

"Perhaps. Don't you want to hear what you'd be expected to do?" he asked.

"I assume that it would be housekeeping or laundry or helping out in the kitchen or serving food," I said. "Any of those are fine with me." I paused, a frown crossing my face. "Although, if the job requires me to—um, entertain the troops, so to speak—I'm not down with that."

"No, no." He waved his hand. "Mr. Allsop is a man of old-fashioned virtues. He would never require a young woman to do anything sordid or unseemly. In fact, he has strict rules about fraternization. And rape is a crime that is punishable by death. You'd have absolutely no reason to fear for your safety if you work for the Allsop organization."

I pressed my hands to my chest. "That is such a relief, sir. A woman can't take her safety for granted anymore. Thank God that Mr. Allsop is working so hard to restore order and protect us all."

Liar, liar, pants on fire.

My jeans didn't spontaneously burst into flames, and Captain Mataraci actually smiled at me. I must have sounded more sincere than I felt.

So rape was punishable by death in the Allsop organization? Somebody needed to tell that to Brody because no way could he believe I'd bear "a passel of Brody juniors" willingly. In fact, my horror at the prospect had seemed to excite him. What would Elliot Allsop make of his son and heir's predilection for rape? Would Brody get a pass because he was family? Were the rules just for the common folk, or would Mr. Allsop truly disapprove?

Somebody rapped on the door. I turned around in my chair, then leaped to my feet, squealing with excitement when a blond young woman entered the room.

"Georgia," I cried, rushing toward the stranger with arms outstretched.

"Bonnie," she sobbed, throwing herself at me. We hugged and shrieked, hopping up and down as if we could barely contain our joy.

I clasped her cheeks between my hands. "It's so good to see you. I can't believe somebody from the old days is still alive."

"I know." Tears spilled down her cheeks. "Me, too."

Marcus picked the right woman for the job. Georgia was a natural actress, or maybe she was genuinely happy to see what must be a friendly face in the enemy camp. We turned toward the captain, our arms wrapped around each other's waists. Georgia sniffed back tears and wiped her nose on her arm.

"I take it you'll vouch for Miss Bernard?" he asked dryly.

She nodded enthusiastically. "I will, sir. I promise that Bonnie will work just as hard for you all as I do."

"All right. Bonnie can start right away. She can share your room. Take an hour to tell her how things work around here. Put her things away, then show her around." He glanced down at his watch. "It's 9:30. I'll send word to your supervisor that you'll be back at work at 10:30."

"Thank you so much, Captain Mataraci," I said. "I'll work my butt off. You won't be sorry."

He made a shooing gesture with his hands.

I grabbed my pack and slung it over a shoulder. Hand in hand, Georgia and I walked from the room. Shoot, we actually skipped for a good ten seconds, as if we couldn't believe our luck. Nobody watching us behave like giddy fools would believe that we were spies for the dreaded Marcus Havoc.

Smiling broadly at everybody we came across, Georgia and I crossed the lobby. We passed elevators that had been out of commission since the power grid collapsed and pushed open a swinging door leading to a dark stairwell.

"This hotel doesn't have penthouse suites, so staff stays on the top floor," Georgia said, pulling a flashlight from her pocket. "Hope you don't mind the climb." By the time we arrived at the sixth floor, I was breathing hard. She led me down a long hallway to a room overlooking the inner courtyard. She pointed at the single queen-sized bed. "We'll have to share."

"With any luck, it should just be for a night or two," I said. "My mission is time critical."

We sat cross-legged on the bed, facing each other. "When they told me my old friend Bonnie Bernard was in the office, I almost laughed," she said in a low voice.

"Why?" I asked.

"Didn't Marcus tell you why you had to use that name?"

I shook my head. "Nope."

Georgia smiled. "When I was a little girl, I had a St. Bernard dog named Bonnie. If somebody struck up a conversation with me and asked about pets, I was supposed to say that I had a St. Bernard when I was a kid. Anybody Marcus sent to contact me would say, 'What a coincidence. I had a St. Bernard, too. Her name was Bonnie.' When they told me that my friend Bonnie Bernard was here, I was startled. Luckily, I recovered fast."

I smiled, then sobered, clutching her hand. "Listen, have you heard anything about the Allsops capturing one of the major's spies? A man named Finn Rasmussen?"

"No." Her eyes widened. "I had no idea that Marcus had sent a second spy into Boise. And I haven't heard a word about anybody being taken into custody."

"Damn." I sighed. "I should've known that it wouldn't be that easy." I shoved my hair behind my ears—an old nervous habit. My fingers tangled through unfamiliar hair. Afraid that I'd knocked the wig askew, I tugged it into place.

"What are you doing?" she whispered.

"It's a wig. A disguise," I explained. "I know Brody and Elliot Allsop, and I've met the men stationed at the Allsop house. I don't want them to recognize me."

"I haven't seen the Allsops at the hotel," Georgia said. "But their head of security, Jonesy, has popped in a few times. You'll need to be careful."

"I will. Are you friendly with any of the soldiers? Anybody you could casually chat up for information?"

"No way. Captain Mataraci forbids any socializing between the soldiers and the staff. When I first got here, I acted all friendly and sweet as pie. Couldn't even get the men to smile back at me. Mataraci must've put the fear of God into them."

"Okay, that's out." I tapped my chin, deep in thought. "How about the men who guard the prisoners? Do they live at the hotel?"

"They do," Georgia said.

"Crap," I muttered. Georgia lifted her brows in a silent question. "I was held prisoner at the Women's Ward. The guards might recognize me." She opened her mouth to say something, and I waved a hand. "That's a story for another time."

Nobody in their right mind would escape from prison—evading capture by the skin of their teeth—then turn right around and come back to town. And I was wearing a disguise. Still, I'd need to keep my distance.

"The guards stick together," she said. "During meals, they always sit at the big round table closest to the windows. I'll offer to take that table during lunch today and try to get you stationed across the room. And I'll listen for any mention of Finn."

"If that doesn't work, we'll have to try something else," I said. "Finn is a good guy, and Marcus is counting on us."

BEDLAM

"I'm supposed to be showing you around the place," Georgia said. "You should know how things work, in case a supervisor asks."

"Yeah. We should get moving," I agreed.

"Most of the men have their own rooms," she said as we descended the stairs. "Once a week we wipe down their rooms and run a carpet sweeper over the rug. To cut down on laundry, the sheets are changed every two weeks. Laundry is a *major* pain in the ass. We load grocery shopping carts with dirty clothes and sheets, then roll the carts down to the greenbelt to wash everything in the river. Then comes the fun part, hauling baskets of wet laundry to the roof to hang it all out on clotheslines."

"I hope I dodge that bullet," I said.

"We also help prepare and serve food, then clean up after meals."

"Sanitation?" I asked, making a face.

"There're a dozen porta-potties next to the hotel. Somebody else deals with them, thank the lord. Somebody takes away the trash and burns it, too."

Georgia led me to the kitchen and introduced me to the supervisor. We helped the cooks finish lunch prep. At noon, men filed into the restaurant and took their seats. The servers loaded rolling food service carts with bowls of chili and boxes of soda crackers. We passed out the food and brought the men cans of room-temperature soda. Allsop fed his men, but they weren't exactly living large.

Eight men sat at the round table by the window. Out of the corner of my eye, I watched Georgia dispense their food and drinks. One of the men threw back his head and laughed at something somebody said. Recognizing the guard who'd delivered my teriyaki jerky dinner just three days ago, I turned my back on the group.

Georgia disappeared into the kitchen. Commotion at the guards' table drew my eye. One of the men had knocked over a can of soda, and the liquid poured over the side of the table onto the floor. He jumped to his feet and pointed at me, snapping his fingers.

I grabbed a pile of napkins and rushed over to them. Dropping to my knees, I wiped up the puddle on the floor.

"Get the table, too," a man said.

Holding my breath, I stood. I lowered my head, so the wig's longish blond hair fell over my face as I swiped at the sticky soda.

"You're just spreading it around." I glanced up at the pissed-off face of my guard. He scowled at me, and my breath caught in my throat. "Go get a towel."

"Yes, sir." I wheeled around and dashed for the kitchen.

"Hey, you," he called. "Hold up."

Shit. I halted in place, fighting the impulse to bolt. What could be more incriminating than fleeing the scene? Not to mention that if I ran, I'd be abandoning Georgia. As if I could escape a room full of armed soldiers anyway.

"Jesus Christ, are you ignoring me?" he called.

"Sorry, sir." I turned around to face him.

He held up a sleeve of crackers. "Crackers got wet. Bring another box."

Relief made me light-headed. "Yes, sir."

I ran into the kitchen and told Georgia what had happened. She brought the crackers to the guards' table.

"That was a total bust." I sighed when the last man walked away from the restaurant. "We need a plan B."

We spent the next hour cleaning up after lunch, then were given a half hour break to eat our own bowls of chili. We carried our bowls to the courtyard and sat on the edge of a three-tiered stone fountain. The fountain was dry as dirt, of course, the bottom level filled with cigarette butts. The courtyard must be a popular place for the men to take their breaks, but we had it all to ourselves now.

"Plan B," Georgia repeated my earlier words. "You have any ideas?"

"I have one, but you might not like it," I said, glancing around the courtyard to make absolutely certain that it was deserted.

"Try me." She took a bite of chili.

"The skeleton key you use when you clean the rooms, does it unlock the office doors on the main floor?"

She dropped her spoon into the bowl. "Are you suggesting that we..." Instead of saying the words out loud, she raised her brows and mimicked putting a key in the lock.

"Mm-hmm."

"Mataraci's office?" she whispered.

"If anybody here knows something about Finn, it'll be the top man," I said. "His desk is covered with files and reports. We need to check out his papers. It's high risk, but it's our only shot."

"Let me think." Georgia stared off into the distance, her mind clearly racing a mile a minute. "Guards are stationed at the hotel's entrances twenty-four, seven. At the front desk, too. Lights out for the men is at 10 p.m. Overnight, two-man patrols circulate throughout the building. They pass by my door every twenty minutes."

"What happens if you're caught outside of your room after 10?" I asked.

"Nobody's allowed to smoke in their rooms," Georgia said. "Last week one of the staff snuck down to the courtyard in the middle of the night for a cigarette. The patrol stopped her and put a strike in her file. The policy is two strikes and you're out. And by out I mean you disappear and nobody knows where you went."

I blew out a slow breath. "So even if we get caught supposedly sneaking out for a smoke, it wouldn't be the end of the world if it's our first strike?" Yeah. I was putting a positive spin on a dire situation. Kyle would call that my default.

"*That* wouldn't be the end of the world," Georgia answered. "But getting caught snooping in Mataraci's office definitely would. There's a list of offenses punishable by death posted in the staff lounge. Being caught in a restricted area without supervision is near the top of the list."

"The operative word is *caught*," I said. "We won't get caught."

"How are we going to manage that?" she asked.

"We're intelligent women," I said. "We've got the rest of the day to come up with a plan."

At a little past 3 a.m., clutching a couple of cigarettes and a book of matches that we'd bummed off a cook, Georgia and I crept silently down a dark stairwell to the ground floor. We pressed our backs against the wall just inside the swinging door and waited until we heard a patrol pass by in the hallway on the opposite side of the door. Counting off the seconds, we lingered for four minutes, then slipped into the corridor. Mataraci's office was the second door on the right. No light shone from the crack under the door. The captain wasn't working late. Georgia slipped the skeleton key into the lock and twisted it. A click, and the door handle turned. Georgia handed me a penlight.

"Ten minutes," she mouthed. Ten minutes would give us time to get back to the stairwell before the next patrol. I stepped inside the office, quietly shutting the door behind me. I spread my hoodie out along the bottom of the door, to block the glow from my flashlight. Georgia would retreat to the courtyard. If anybody unexpected approached the office door before the next patrol, she'd light up, the flame drawing attention to her illicit presence in the courtyard. I'd slip from the room while she kept the interloper occupied dealing with her infraction.

I wasn't kidding when I called it a high-risk operation.

Leaning against the door, I counted to five while I steeled myself for the task ahead. If I allowed myself to think about Kyle or how much I wanted a future with him, I might wimp out. No way would I wimp out. Not when Finn's life was at stake.

I tiptoed across the office and clicked on my flashlight. Mataraci's desk appeared a jumbled mess, with no obvious order to the files and papers scattered across the top. Just because it was messy, didn't mean that he wouldn't notice if a file or paper shifted location. There might be an idiosyncratic method to his apparent madness.

I carefully shuffled through all the papers and files, taking care not to displace anything. A lot of the information would be of interest to Marcus, but with only minutes to search, I had to stay laser focused on any reference to Finn. I skimmed rapidly over every document on the desk, but found no reference to a spy or Finn Rasmussen. Acid burned in my stomach and my hands began to shake.

Dammit.

I whirled around and leaned dejectedly on the edge of the desk. My flashlight beam fell across a small cork bulletin board hanging on the wall.

The Pleasure of Your Company Is Requested

A tasteful invitation—gilt lettering on cream paper—was tacked to the bulletin board. Some inexplicable impulse led me to pull out the tack and open the invitation.

Inside the card, a handwritten message scrawled in black ink.

I blinked three times, scarcely able to fathom what I was reading. With shaking hands, I pinned the invitation to the board once again. I padded across the room, picked up my hoodie, cracked open the door, peeked outside, then stepped into the hallway, checking to make sure the door locked behind me. Georgia immediately joined me and we stole up the corridor to the stairwell. Two minutes later, the patrol passed by. We dashed up the stairs and snuck back into her room.

"What did you find out?" she whispered.

I bit the knuckles of my hand, stifling hysterical laughter, before choking out the words.

Georgia pulled me into her arms, hugging me tight. I gulped in air, willing my hysteria to subside. Too ludicrous to be real. In any sane world, this should be too ludicrous to be real. Not in the Allsops' world.

I hiccuped and got a grip.

"Can we walk away from the hotel early tomorrow morning?" I asked.

"Thursday mornings is when my team takes laundry down to the greenbelt," Georgia said.

"We need to report to Marcus ASAP. When does your team leave?"

"Usually around 9 a.m., but if you and I take off with our carts earlier, my supervisor would probably pat us on the back for showing initiative."

"Okay." That was good. "We'll get an early start. We'll ditch the laundry, and meet up with Marcus and Kyle."

We laid out our clothes for the morning, then crawled into bed. At most, we'd get two or three hours of sleep, although I was so worked up that any sleep seemed unlikely. I stared at the ceiling for a long time. Georgia's rhythmic breathing told me that she finally drifted off. I was just starting to feel groggy when muffled voices sounded from the hallway. The staff was starting to rise. I rolled over and poked Georgia.

"Wake up," I whispered. "It's D-Day."

THIRTY-TWO

Kyle

I was going to call this the longest twenty-four hours of my life, but glancing at my watch, I amended that thought. Longest twenty-*two* hours of my life. Less than a day since Sunny marched by herself into the lion's den, but it felt like freaking forever. It had killed me to let her go, but she was the right person for the job. And like Ripper always said, the new world doesn't coddle anybody.

Marcus Havoc stretched out on the floor across the room, arms crossed under his head, catching a few z's. Ripper could do that, too, seize any downtime to grab a nap. I stood at the window, binoculars held to my eyes, scanning the street for signs of Sunny or Georgia. Georgia was one of the handful of survivors from Havoc's army base in California. He'd shown me her military ID, so I'd know what she looked like.

The radio squawked. "Sunny and Georgia just exited the hotel, pushing what looks like two shopping carts," Justin reported from his position two blocks to the east. "They turned a corner and they're heading south."

Marcus appeared at my side and held out his hand for the radio. "Are they alone?" he asked.

"Yes."

"Intercept them," Marcus ordered. "If they have something to report, meet us at the car. Over." He grabbed his rifle and strode toward the door. I followed close behind as we dashed down the stairs and ran to the parking lot of a Chinese restaurant, where we'd hidden the car under a tarp behind a pair of dumpsters. A few minutes later, Sunny, Justin, and Georgia jogged into sight. Sunny clutched a bundle of something gray to her chest.

Marcus threw open the car's back door. Sunny, Georgia, and I clambered in. Marcus and Justin hopped into the front. Sunny threw her arms around me, squashing a pile of smelly gray T-shirts between us.

"It's good to see you," I said, almost choking on my relief. I cleared my throat, then tapped on the bundle of clothes. "What you got there?"

"I grabbed a bunch of T-shirts from the laundry," she said. "Just in case you guys need to disguise yourselves as official Allsop men."

"Good thinking." She laid her head on my shoulder, and I held her close, despite the stink from the dirty tees.

"What do you have to report?" Marcus asked, pulling out onto the road.

"Last night, we broke into Captain Mataraci's office," Georgia said.

My stomach clenched. Jesus. If they'd been caught, they would have been shot. No, they would have been tortured and then shot. I swallowed back bile.

"And?"

"Brody sent Mataraci an engraved invitation to Finn's execution. It was tacked to the bulletin board behind the captain's desk," Sunny said. "On the front it said, 'The pleasure of your company is requested' in gold letters. Very formal. Inside, Brody wrote that the festivities start at 8 tonight with appetizers and drinks. The main event is at 9. Followed by billiards and more drinks in his man cave."

"An engraved invitation to Finn's execution? Un-fucking-believable." Justin shook his head.

Treating an execution—hell, a murder—like a party. This had to be the most cold-blooded thing I'd ever heard of. How had my old buddy gone so totally off the rails?

"Where?" Marcus asked.

"Cell House 5 at the old penitentiary. Apparently it has a built-in gallows that the state used only once. Brody is excited about bringing it back," Sunny said.

Marcus was silent for a minute. "Sunny and Georgia discovered the what, the where, and the when," he finally said. "I'd call that a successful reconnaissance mission." He stopped the car at an intersection and leaned forward, scanning the road in both directions.

"And we've got about twelve hours to plan a rescue." Justin scrubbed a hand across his chin.

Our luck held, and we arrived back at grandma's place without incident. We hid the car in the garage and traipsed into the house, settling down in the living room again to devise our plan.

"Appetizers and drinks. Sounds like Brody is planning quite the bash." Georgia sat in one of the floral chairs.

"We don't know what went down at the Allsop house on the night Finn was captured," I sat in the other chair and pulled Sunny onto my lap. "He was going back in to rescue their private chef, Hildy. She may or may not have been compromised that night."

"If the Allsops aren't aware that Hildy turned on them—if it's business as usual—I bet Brody will have her prepare the appetizers for the party," Sunny surmised. "She's a fabulous chef, and he obviously is trying to impress his guests."

"You think he'll bring over food from the Allsop kitchen?" Marcus asked.

"Food. Booze. Crystal glassware. Probably linen tablecloths," Sunny listed. "He wouldn't serve beer and pretzels if he went to all the trouble of sending gilded invitations. He's trying to make an impression."

"Huh." Marcus planted his boots on the glass-topped coffee table. It wobbled on its spindly legs, but held up under the weight. "I can work with that."

After playing cat and mouse across town, dodging Allsop SUVs, we cautiously approached the penitentiary. High stone walls surrounded the entire facility. We parked in the back lot of a nearby community center, where trees and buildings hid the car from view.

Hid the car *and* Sunny. She grumbled, but when Marcus Havoc told her that he wasn't taking an untrained civilian into a potential firefight, even Sunny knew better than to argue with the major. Marcus, Justin, and I donned jeans and the dirty gray T-shirts. We'd pass for members of Allsop's team.

The Allsop organization was strictly a boys club. Georgia didn't roll her eyes or complain when Marcus ordered her to dress up like a caterer. Luckily, Grandma and Georgia were about the same size. Sunny and Georgia rooted around in Grandma's closet and found a pair of black slacks and a simple white blouse that would pass for a caterer's uniform. A black-and-white-checked apron they found hanging on a hook in the pantry completed the ensemble.

According to Sunny, Ever said her grandma liked to hold fancy dinner parties for her friends. A search of the basement revealed several silver serving trays, chafing dishes, and champagne flutes, all useful props for the mission.

A few minutes past 7 p.m., I kissed Sunny goodbye.

"Be careful," she said, hugging me around the waist. "And come back to me."

"Always."

I picked up a box holding a dozen champagne glasses and a silver ice bucket. Justin lugged an insulated cooler, supposedly packed full of ice and cold champagne, but in reality holding extra magazines, a fragmentation grenade, and a couple of wrenches. Georgia's pistol was stuffed inside the steel chafing dish she carried. Marcus tucked several silver serving trays under one arm and carried another cooler, this one holding an extra pistol for Finn.

I took a last look at Sunny before the operation, then followed Marcus up to the prison's administration building, the only exit and entrance to the facility. One of the two guards stationed outside the entrance shook his head as we passed. "More food for the party? Really?"

"You want to tell Brody Allsop how to throw a party, be my guest." Marcus snorted.

The guard raised both hands in the air, acknowledging defeat.

"Yeah, me neither," Justin said, grinning at the man.

Inside the entrance, another soldier sat behind a desk. He shook his head as we passed, clearly sharing the first guard's opinion on

Brody's excesses, but not challenging our right to pass through. Once through the administration building, we took a hard right, heading directly for Cell House 5. We jogged past the sally port—an entryway into the prison grounds built into the high wall and secured by a locked rolling gate.

"Three guards at the entry to the prison," Justin said. "Wonder how many are at Cell House 5?"

"We'll see," Marcus responded.

"They said *more* food. Somebody's already here." I shot a look at Marcus. "If Brody came early to supervise the setup, we're in trouble. He'll recognize me, then the jig is up."

"Hang back," Marcus said. "Justin, Georgia, and I will go first. The Allsops know *about* me, but they have no idea what I look like."

We hurried toward the execution site. A two-story building designed for function not beauty, Cell House 5 resembled a concrete box with narrow barred windows. We pushed through the entry door and stepped into a passageway that led to both the ground floor cells and a staircase.

Glancing to our right, I recoiled. It was easy to forget that before the Allsops resurrected the place as a functioning prison, this used to be a historic site, complete with handy-dandy placards telling visitors what was what. I stared into the small room directly below the indoor gallows. There was nothing remarkable about the bare walls and floor, but the ceiling—shit—the ceiling gave me chills. A hinged trapdoor was built into the rafters and under it, an odd wood-and-rubber contraption with a dangling counterweight. *Gallows Trap Door Weight and Stop*, the sign pronounced. If Brody had his way, in two hours Finn's lifeless body would hang there.

Marcus followed my gaze. "Not going to happen," he reassured me before jogging up the stairs. Justin and Georgia followed close behind. I waited at the bottom, listening for any indication of trouble. "Where do we set up?" Marcus called out. Somebody answered, then Marcus laughed and leaned over the stairwell. "Stop gawking at the trapdoor and get your ass up here."

The all clear. Brody was nowhere in sight.

"Yes, sir," I called. I took the steps two at a time, emerging onto a wide landing. Dear God, this place was bleak. Once upon a time, the cement floor had been painted red, but over the decades, the paint had worn away. Now the red color clung only to the very edges of the floor, places where few people had trod. Scuffed, dirty white paint covered the walls. Gray metal doors were propped open, leading to what placards identified as the *Witness Room* and *Death Row*.

I glanced through the open door into death row. Four dismal cells occupied the center of the room. A guard sat in a folding chair facing the cells. Finn had to be there, but I couldn't see him from the open doorway.

"In here." Marcus jerked his head toward the witness room, a simple, square room with a large picture window installed in the end wall. I knew what lay on the opposite side of that window. The execution chamber. A trapdoor over which the condemned man stood while a noose was attached to his neck. A lever in the floor, that the executioner pulled, would release the trapdoor. I'd gaped at the sight while on a school field trip. I had absolutely no desire to see it again.

On the wall across from the window, two banquet tables covered with linen tablecloths had been set up. Steel chafing dishes, silver serving platters, and crystal glassware covered one table. A woman stood with her back to me, arranging a platter of appetizers. She turned around, spied me, and her eyes widened.

Hildy. So she hadn't been busted on the night the Allsops arrested Finn. I flashed a smile, then titled my head toward death row. She bobbed her head once, understanding glittering in her eyes. Good. With advanced warning maybe she'd have a chance to duck out of the way if bullets started flying.

Three armed Allsop guards lounged against the wall. If they were expecting trouble, nothing in their demeanor conveyed that. So, four guards were stationed in Cell House 5, three at the entrance to the prison. Not an insurmountable number. Not with the element of surprise on our side.

Hildy glanced at her watch. "Oh, dear," she said. "Mr. Brody should be here in fifteen minutes, and he'll expect everything to be ready when he and his men arrive. If you boys help me set up, I'll fix you each a nice plate. Our little secret." She winked at the guards, then looked at me. "You and your friends need to make yourselves useful, too."

"Yes, ma'am," I said, exchanging a glance with Marcus. She gave us a timeline for Brody's arrival, but what did she mean by make ourselves useful?

"I promised Jimmy in the next room an eclair," Hildy said. She took the pastry from a box and placed it in the middle of a silver tray. "I'll be back in just a minute." She pointed at the guard standing closest to the table. "Could you put the bacon-wrapped water chestnuts into the largest chafing dish? They're in the rectangular container in the bottom of that insulated tote." She pointed at the second guard. "And could you plate the mini quiches? Put them on the three-tiered tray." As two of the three Allsop men busied themselves removing containers from the totes, she glanced at me again, frowning. "I mean it. You boys need to step up." She rolled her eyes in the direction of the guards.

Georgia placed the chafing dish holding her gun on the floor and squatted down next to it, her hand resting on the lid. Marcus and Justin ambled over to the tables. My team was ready to rumble.

Silver tray in hand, Hildy bustled out the door. Following her into death row, I glanced into a cell. A figure lay on a bunk, curled on his side, motionless as a corpse.

THIRTY-THREE

Sunny

Before my friends rounded a corner and disappeared from sight, Kyle turned around and walked backward for a few steps, his gaze locked on my face, as if committing my features to memory. Shifting the box to one arm, he pressed his fingers to his lips and blew me a kiss, then pivoted and trotted after the others.

He was being romantic, right? There was nothing ominous about the way he looked at me. As if he wasn't sure we'd see other again. As if he wanted the image of him blowing me a kiss—reaching out to me with love—to be my last memory of him.

I had to get a grip and not let my fears get the better of me.

Marcus was right to leave me behind. I wouldn't be a damned bit of use in a gunfight. Far better to send three trained soldiers and a man who'd already proven that he could handle himself in battle. I got it, but it stung to feel useless, especially after yesterday when my actions had made a difference.

On the last day of his life—hours before he went down in a hail of bullets—Ed had told me that it was past time for me to learn how to shoot. When this was over, when we made it to Valhalla, I'd ask Kyle or Ripper to teach me. I couldn't afford to be a liability, somebody who had to be tucked safely out of the way when things got dangerous.

If all went well tonight—the absolute best-case scenario—my friends would incapacitate the guards, liberate Finn, and race back to the car without firing a single shot. We'd head out of town before the Allsops knew anything was amiss. With both Georgia and Finn in the back seat, it would be a tight squeeze. I'd have to wedge in next to Kyle or sit on his lap, but we could manage until we secured another vehicle. We could manage, but it would be a cramped and bouncy ride.

My back twinged at the prospect. A little preemptive stretching might be in order, and it might help to calm my nerves. Back before the pandemic, I used to practice yoga. Maybe it was time to start that up again, too, once we got to Valhalla. I stepped out of the car into the golden light of a balmy September evening. Lifting both arms over my head, I reached for the sky, then bent over and lay my palms flat on the asphalt.

Gunfire fractured the quiet evening. My spine snapped straight, and I whirled toward the direction of the prison.

Please, God, please, God, please, God...

Holding my breath, I listened for more sounds of battle, but a deceptive quiet crept across the neighborhood.

"Kyle," I whispered. Without conscious thought, I stumbled toward the street, toward the route my friends would take in any mad dash back to the car. Within a minute, rational thought overruled impulse. I dropped to my knees behind a tree, within sight of the road.

Three black SUVs hurtled past the community center's parking lot. I flattened my body against the ground. The SUVs screeched to a halt, and men poured out. Angry voices filled the night. Doors slammed. Feet pounded over the pavement. The tumult retreated and silence, a fleeting interlude of calm, reclaimed the evening.

I lifted my head, my mind racing. The guards had called in reinforcements. If—when—my friends fought their way past the Allsop soldiers, we'd pile into our car. We'd race out of the city. If any of our enemies survived the skirmish, they'd give chase in those black SUVs.

Unless I somehow managed to disable the vehicles.

How do you disable a car? Sugar in the gas tank? Yanking out some wires or a spark plug? I'd never looked under a hood and had no freaking clue how to stop a vehicle in its tracks. Its tracks. Its tires. Scrambling to my feet, I dashed back to the car and fumbled frantically in the glove compartment. There. My fingers closed around a leather sheath holding a fixed-blade knife, a weapon Justin had tossed in the glove compartment *just in case.*

Knife in hand, I sprinted to the cluster of SUVs parked next to the prison wall. I dropped to my knees next to the first one and slashed at the front driver's-side tire. The blade barely sliced into the rubber. Almost sobbing with frustration, I pressed the tip into one of the shallow cuts and hammered the end of the hilt with my fist. The tip popped through the rubber, followed by a gratifying hiss of air. This SUV wasn't going anyplace.

"What the fuck are you doing?" a familiar voice demanded.

I rose to my feet on trembling legs, then turned toward the voice.

The front passenger door of the middle SUV stood open, Brody Allsop next to it. He stomped to the front of the vehicle. I shuffled backward, glanced down at the knife clutched in my hand, then at Brody. He slowly pulled a gun from his shoulder holster.

"You." He pointed the gun in my direction. "It all went to shit once you showed up." With each word, he shook the gun for emphasis.

Bending my elbow, I placed the tip of the blade against the driver's door. I kept my eyes firmly on Brody while I surreptitiously scratched at the black paint. I couldn't risk looking down at my handiwork, had no idea if Kyle would ever spot it. But I had to try.

"What are you doing here?" I asked.

He laughed, a bitter sound devoid of any humor. "Didn't you hear my dad? 'Stay in the car, Brody.'" He mimicked his father's sonorous voice. "'You're a total fuckup, Brody.'" He threw back his head and shouted at the sky. "Fuck you, Dad." He turned his gaze back to me, his eyes gleaming. "You know what? Dad's right. He's got this. He doesn't need my help. Maybe you and I should head back to the house. Got everything set up for a party in the man cave. Fuck, let's have us a party."

Never take a knife to a gunfight. If I rushed Brody, could I stab him before he shot me? Probably not. It'd be a suicide charge, and I wasn't ready to throw away my life. Not yet. *Where there's life, there's hope.* A Roman statesman said that. And then he got his head chopped off. Crap. I was full to the brim with useless sayings, wasn't I?

Focus, damn it. I dragged the tip of the blade across the door panel again, then dropped the knife and kicked it under the SUV. I wasn't giving up, not by a long shot, but I'd find a better opportunity than knife versus gun.

A muffled explosion, then gunfire erupted from the prison. Both Brody and I spun around to look, but the tall walls hid any muzzle flashes.

"Time's a wasting," Brody said cheerfully.

He tucked his gun back into the holster and strode toward me. Grabbing my upper arm, he hauled me to the open passenger door of the second SUV. He reached into the glove compartment, pulled out a zip tie, and secured my wrists behind my back. He half lifted me into the seat and fastened the seat belt around my waist.

"Safety first," he said with a wink. "Don't want anything to happen to you before we get a chance to party."

THIRTY-FOUR

Kyle

Hildy waved the silver tray at the guard. "See! I didn't forget your eclair."

Jimmy stood, smiling as Hildy approached. Without missing a beat, she swung the tray, clocking Jimmy on the side of the head. He staggered, his expression morphing from delight to confusion. Hildy brought the tray down again, and he dropped to his knees, fumbling for his gun.

From the witness room, the sounds of a scuffle.

"What the—" somebody shouted.

Gunfire rang out from the witness room.

Jimmy wobbled on his knees, his hands scrabbling for his gun. I lunged at the guard while Hildy stood by, posed to clobber him again with the tray. I knocked the stunned man face-down onto the floor then knelt on him while I snatched the handcuffs from his belt. Adding insult to injury, I restrained him with his own cuffs.

I spared a second to glance toward Finn, who hadn't moved on his cot. My chest tightened. Shit. How badly was he hurt if all this commotion hadn't roused him?

"Keep an eye on him." I handed Jimmy's gun to Hildy, then ran back to the witness room. "Anybody hit?" I asked, my gaze darting from person to person. Marcus, Justin, and Georgia were on their feet. All three Allsop men were down on the floor, like Jimmy, shackled with their own cuffs. No time to ask what went down. I whirled and raced back into death row.

Jimmy had crawled over to the wall and now leaned heavily against it, panting for air and blinking rapidly. I unclipped the keys from his belt and rushed to the cell holding Finn.

Slumped on his side, facing the wall, Finn lay motionless as a corpse. I reached out. My hand paused an inch from his shoulder, as if I was afraid to close the distance, afraid to discover that all our efforts to save him had come to nothing.

"C'mon man," I said through gritted teeth, forcing my hand to touch his shoulder. He groaned—thank God—and rolled onto his back. "Shit," I breathed. Allsop's men had really gone to town on Finn. His right eye was swollen shut, the lid puffy and purple. Dried blood crusted the side of his face, and a gaping crack split his lower lip. "Finn." No reaction. "Finn," I tried again, this time with more force.

The lid over his left eye fluttered, then slid partially open. He squinted up at me through the slit.

Marcus Havoc appeared at my side. "We're getting you out of here, brother," he said, bending over Finn. "How bad are you hurt?"

"Ribs," Finn croaked. Marcus carefully lifted Finn's shirt. Mottled red and purple bruises covered the side of his torso.

"Broken?" Marcus asked.

"Dunno." Finn choked out. He blinked, his bloodshot eye struggling to stay open. "Drugged... me."

Marcus and I exchanged a glance. Clinging to consciousness, with injured ribs, would Finn be able to walk, or would we have to carry him? Whatever the case, we had to move. No doubt the guards at the entrance had heard the shots and had called for reinforcements.

Footsteps sounded behind us. The four Allsop soldiers shuffled past. Georgia and Hildy stood nearby, weapons trained on the men. Justin stuck his head into Finn's cell and held out his hand toward me.

"Key." I passed it to him. A clink and rattle followed as he locked the soldiers into a death row cell. Justin stepped up to Marcus. "We gotta book, boss."

"Yeah," Marcus agreed. Sliding an arm under Finn's shoulders, he lifted him into a seated position. Finn groaned and swayed, his head lolling back against Marcus's arm. He paled, the skin under the dried blood on his face turning pasty white. "Can you walk?" Marcus demanded.

"I'll try."

"One, two, three." Marcus hauled Finn to his feet and slung the injured man's arm across his shoulders. Marcus wrapped an arm around Finn's waist, and the men lumbered out of the cell, the major's body acting as a crutch to support Finn's weight. They stumbled toward the stairs, Finn's feet dragging cockeyed across the cement. "Fuck it. Sorry, brother," Marcus said, bending over and throwing Finn across his shoulders.

Finn hissed and I winced. Within seconds, he passed out, going limp against the major's back, a pure mercy if you asked me.

Justin and Georgia led the way down the stairs, guns drawn. Marcus followed, with Hildy and me bringing up the rear. We jogged toward the administrative building and the exit from the prison.

Every step brought us closer to an inevitable firefight. My pulse ratcheted up and dread curdled in my gut. I wasn't a soldier—not like Marcus, Justin, and Georgia—but this wouldn't be my first gunfight. Chaos and cacophony ruled when bullets flew. The best laid plans went haywire, and as far as I knew, our only plan was to blast our way out past the guards.

Marcus halted at the entrance to the old sally port. The opening in the wall offered a tantalizing view of the land outside the prison walls. Unfortunately, thick metal bars and a sliding gate blocked access to the outside world. We could blast or bash our way through the metal bars, but the clamor would bring the guards running. Marcus gently laid Finn on the ground, pulled two wrenches from his back pocket, and handed them to me.

"Justin, Georgia, and I will engage the guards inside the administration building," he said in a low, urgent voice. "You and Hildy will get Finn out through the sally port. As soon as you hear gunfire, take the wrenches to the padlock on the gate. The thing's almost a hundred years old. You should be able to bust it open. Head to the car. Give us a few minutes to follow. If we don't show, or if you're pursued, take off for Pendleton."

This made absolutely no sense. Marcus Havoc was the leader of the resistance, Justin one of his lieutenants, Georgia a soldier he trusted enough to send as a spy. None of them were dispensable. Shaking my head, I opened my mouth to protest.

Marcus gripped my shoulder and gave me a hard look. "You come on a mission with me, you follow orders." Without waiting for me to reply, he wheeled around and led Justin and Georgia toward the administration building, where God-knows how many Allsop men waited for them.

"I'll keep watch while you break the lock," Hildy said, Jimmy's gun still gripped in her hand.

I clutched the wrenches in sweaty palms. All the spit in my mouth dried up. Seconds ticked by, the wait interminable. Without warning, an explosion ripped through the air, followed by a barrage of bullets.

I hammered the wrench against the lock. It held. Frustrated, I inserted the heads of the two wrenches through the metal loop at the top of the padlock, then squeezed. The padlock popped apart. I threw my weight against the heavy metal gate. It shrieked and protested as I muscled it along its tracks. Without the cover of gunfire, no way could we have escaped covertly through this gate.

Hildy held the gun in both hands, swinging her head from side to side as she stood lookout.

More gunfire erupted from the admin building.

I glanced down at Finn, who was sprawled on the ground hovering between consciousness and unconsciousness. The cowboy stood an inch or two taller than me—when he could stand, that is—and years of hard work on the ranch had packed muscle onto his frame. Good thing the weight bench and I were old friends.

When we were teenagers, Jake and I had watched videos and practiced something called the Ranger roll. Surprised the hell out of Ripper when I demonstrated it to him this summer. I stood by Finn's feet, grabbed his right leg, and did a sort of somersault, swinging him across my shoulders. I pinned his leg and arm against my chest, then lifted up on one knee. Pushing off against my bent thigh, I stood, two hundred pounds of deadweight across my shoulders.

"Nicely done," Hildy said.

I broke into a shambling run, heading down the Old Penitentiary Road toward our car. We jogged passed two black SUVs. The front tire on one of them had lost its air. Nice. Maybe luck was on our side. I smiled with grim satisfaction.

Footsteps pounded on the pavement behind us. I pivoted, balancing Finn on my shoulders while I reached for my Glock. Marcus, Justin, and Georgia caught up with us.

"What happened?" I asked, as we jogged toward the community center.

"Most of the Allsop men had taken cover in a small room just inside the admin building," Marcus said. "Probably planned to hit us as we ran in. Justin lobbed a frag into the room. While we engaged with the rest of the guards, two Allsop men ran and locked themselves in the armory."

"Probably Elliot and Jonesy, his number one," I guessed. "They'll radio for reinforcements and be after us."

"Yep." Marcus nodded at Finn. "You good?"

I was staggering under Finn's weight, but we couldn't afford the time to switch him from my shoulders to Havoc's. "I'm good."

We turned off the main road, running toward the back of the community center. Dying sunlight glinted off the windows of our getaway car. I'd never been so glad to see a vehicle in my life. Within a minute, we'd be racing out of the city, heading to safety in Pendleton.

In my mind's eye, I could see what came next. Rolling up to Valhalla with Sunny, Finn, Mrs. B., and Ever in tow. Bear's gobsmacked joy at being reunited with his brother. Introducing the woman I love to my friends. Watching Mrs. B. and Ever settle into life on the ranch. After everything that had gone wrong during the past ten days, finally everything was going right. I could almost taste our happy ending. Impending victory gave me a last burst of energy, and my feet flew across the parking lot.

I came to a stop, panting, next to the car. Marcus and Justin slid Finn from my shoulders and held him up against the car. I peered into the empty back seat.

My world came to a screeching halt. Where the hell was Sunny?

"Sunny?" I yelled. Maybe she'd needed to piss and was hunkered down behind a bush next to the car. No. If she'd heard us run to the car, she'd call out or pop up from behind a bush. I turned my gaze to Marcus. "She wouldn't just wander off."

Headlight beams sliced through the twilight, and tires squealed. From the main road, someone shouted.

"Go," I said. "I'll stay behind and find Sunny. We'll steal a car and meet up with you in Pendleton." No way would I leave Boise without Sunny, but neither would I deny reality. Marcus Havoc and his people were the only things standing between the Allsops and victory. This time, he *had* to see sense and flee.

"Havoc," Justin said, his expression grim.

"Get Finn and Hildy to safety," I continued. "Raise an army. Stop the Allsops. That's your job. My job is to find Sunny."

Justin opened the rear car door and dumped Finn onto the seat. Hildy scrambled in the other side and squeezed in next to Finn. Georgia sat next to Hildy.

"With Hildy, there's no room for Sunny and me anyway," I pointed out.

"Fuck." Marcus shoved his hands through his hair.

"Go," I urged. "I want you to." I hesitated. Haste was essential, but I'd face whatever the next few hours brought with peace of mind if I could tell him one more thing. "Listen, if we don't make it back, ask Finn to tell my friends at the ranch that I'm good. Tell them I found love, and that I'd risk anything to bring her back home to Valhalla."

Marcus clapped me on the shoulder. "Will do. You have extra magazines for the Glock?"

"Yep." I stepped back, signaling the end to our conversation. Justin lifted a hand in farewell, then hopped into the front of the car. With a shake of his head—a man clearly going against his instincts—Marcus climbed into the driver's seat and started the engine. Headlights off, the car crept across the parking lot, then turned right onto the street.

Alone. I was alone. The night pressed in from every side. Somewhere in that dark expanse, Sunny waited for me.

"Where are you, Sunshine?" I whispered into the quiet.

THIRTY-FIVE

Sunny

Brody punched the gas. I twisted around in the SUV's seat, desperate for one last look at the prison.

Please God, let Kyle be okay. Let all my friends be okay.

If Kyle were hurt or dead, I'd sense it somehow, wouldn't I? I buried my fear in the darkest corner of my mind.

Maybe they survived the gun battle unscathed. Maybe they'd come running out the prison's entrance, see Brody carting me off, and give chase.

No matter what, Kyle wouldn't leave me behind. My higher self—the better angels of my nature—would tell Kyle not to risk himself, to flee to Pendleton with the others. But I knew down to my bones that the man I loved would try to save me. In fact, I was counting on it. He'd see my scrawled message on the SUV door, and he'd follow.

That didn't mean that I wouldn't try to save myself first, or that I wouldn't do everything in my power to make things easier for Kyle when he showed up. Hands tied behind my back, there was little I could do physically to bring Brody down. But maybe I could get inside his head.

I glanced sideways at the Allsop scion. Spoiled and petulant, he shouldered an outsized sense of entitlement and grievance. Daddy had humiliated Brody tonight, and he was incandescent with both rage and embarrassment. Could I parlay that to my advantage? Psychological machinations had never been my strong suit. I'd rather just tell people what I think without running everything through a filter, but my options were limited. At the very least, maybe I could buy some time before Brody got down to *partying*. Shudder.

The five minute drive from the prison to the Allsops' ridgetop estate flew by. Before I had time to catch my breath, we pulled up in front of a house I'd never expected to see again. Daisy—my faithful old van—was parked on a gravel strip alongside the garage. Brody parked the SUV, threw open my door, and unfastened my seat belt. His fingers bit hard into my elbow as he hauled me from the vehicle.

I wobbled, my balance unsteady. He jerked my arm and strode quickly up the cobblestone walk to the front door. Two armed guards, their faces impassive, watched us approach. Were they used to seeing Brody drag bound women into the house? So much for Mataraci's lie that women had nothing to fear from the Allsops.

I stumbled along beside Brody as he strong-armed me through the door and across the foyer. If I threw myself down onto the floor, made myself a deadweight, it would slow him down. Or he might simply order the guards to carry me to his stupid man cave. If it came to it, I'd rather deal with one man than three. I kept to my feet, moving slowly and clumsily down the stairway and long hallway leading to the basement room.

Brody shoved open the double doors and flicked on the overhead lights. Light reflected from the glass eyes of murdered animals. They stared at me from every direction, beautiful creatures who'd been captured, killed, and mounted as trophies. Like them, I'd been captured. Would I, too, be mounted and killed? Crap. If I thought Brody's man cave was a chamber of horrors the first time I saw it, it was waaay worse this time.

In preparation for the post-execution soiree, a long table covered with bottles of booze and crystal glassware had been set up along one wall. Brody shoved me into a deep, leather club chair, then pointed a finger at me, a clear warning to stay put. He ambled over to a small refrigerator next to the bar table and pulled out a cold bottle of beer.

"You want a beer?" he asked.

I needed to keep my wits about me. I definitely did *not* want a beer, but he'd have to free my hands in order for me to hold the bottle, wouldn't he? "Yes, please," I said. "A beer would hit the spot."

He twisted the cap off a bottle of lager, then crouched next to my chair, holding the bottle to my lips. No help for it. I said I wanted the beer, and I couldn't be caught lying. Not yet. I parted my lips and he upended the bottle into my mouth. Choking against the flood of foamy lager, I pressed my lips together and shook my head.

He'd dumped half the bottle down the front of my shirt. "Why did you do that?" I sputtered, my eyes watering.

"See, that's the problem," Brody said. "You all think I'm stupid, but I'm not stupid. I know what I'm doing, and I know exactly what you're up to. 'Yes, please, Brody, a beer would hit the spot.'" His voice rose to a falsetto as he mocked me. "You actually thought I'd cut the zip tie so you could hold the bottle. I'm not a moron." He glanced at the ceiling. "You hear that, Dad?"

"Has your father always been so hard on you?" I asked. "I felt bad when he was rude to you at dinner the other night. You were just kidding around—Kyle and I knew that—and he sent you to your room like a naughty ten-year-old."

Brody's jaw clenched and his eyes spit fire. I'd hit a nerve. "He's always been like that, always had a fucking stick up his ass. Never could lighten up."

I offered a small, sympathetic smile, afraid to overplay my hand.

"Nothing I did was ever good enough. You'd think a C in geometry was the end of the world. 'No son of mine is going to be average.'" He imitated his father again. I felt a reluctant flash of pity for Brody. Carrying the weight of Elliot Allsop's unforgiving expectations would be a crippling burden for any child.

"I got a C in geometry, too," I lied. "Life's too short to knock yourself out getting an A in a subject you'll never use."

"I know, right?" Brody threw his hands in the air. "But did Dad see it that way? Fuck, no."

I wrinkled my brow in sympathy. Brody frowned, his overwrought expression giving way to suspicion. "You playing me, Sunny? You've always had that sweet, innocent act down pat. *Everybody* likes you. You're *everybody's* friend. But when I asked you for a simple favor—when I asked you to get me another beer at that party—you showed what a stuck-up bitch you really are."

Brody *had* been holding onto that grudge.

"Made me look like a fool in front of my boys," he continued.

271

There it was again. Humiliation and disrespect propelled Brody's rage. What could I do to derail that anger now?

"I'm sorry," I said quietly. "I'd had a fight with my date that night, and I was in a crappy mood. I shouldn't have taken it out on you. That was my bad."

Would a lightning bolt strike me dead after that string of bald-faced lies? Even if lightning didn't kill me, my self-esteem would take a hit after that phony, groveling apology. Brody was right, though. I *was* playing him, and that knowledge allowed me to hang onto the tattered shreds of my dignity.

He lowered his chin and studied me, his eyes filled with skepticism. "You look different." He waved at my hair. "I like it. You look hot with blond hair."

"It's a wig," I blurted out, thrown by the word hot. Definitely not where I wanted Brody's mind to go.

"A wig, huh?" He tilted his head, then snorted. "You and Kyle thought you could outsmart the Allsops by wearing a stupid wig?"

Didn't just think it, I knew it, although there was nothing to be gained by rubbing that in Brody's face. Despite my best efforts, Brody must have read the thought on my face.

"You really are a stuck-up bitch, aren't you?" he accused me for the second time. "You want to know what's going on right now? Odds are, your boyfriend and the traitor are both dead, shot during their lame-ass escape attempt. If by some miracle they got away, Dad and Jonesy and a bunch of our men are hot on their tails." With a smile of pure malice, he tapped the tip of my nose. "Either way, you're screwed, Sunny McAllister. Kyle ditched you and now it's just you and me."

In his triumph, Brody stood too close to my chair. I couldn't use my hands, but my feet were free. I bent my right leg, then kicked out, nailing him on the thigh with the flat of my boot. Crap. I'd been aiming at his knee, but he shifted position just before my foot made contact.

He laughed, rubbing his thigh. "Oh, sweetheart, you'll be sorry you tried that." His lips curved in a mirthless sneer. "Before we're done, I'm going to make you scream."

THIRTY-SIX

Kyle

D*on't count your chickens before they hatch.*
Mom had a gift for spouting trite sayings. Her voice reverberated in my head now. Less than five minutes ago, I had begun to breathe easy, sure we were posed on the brink of success.

Don't get cocky. Another Mom-ism.

Luck, kismet, whatever you want to call it, once again fate kicked me in the balls.

Where the hell was Sunny?

Think.

What did I know? At some point during our rescue mission—probably alerted by guards who heard the first gunshot—Allsop reinforcements had arrived on the scene. I'd carried Finn past the two black SUVs that had brought the men here. I cautiously approached the main road. Only one SUV remained, and because of the flat tire, it wasn't going anywhere.

Huh. Damned odd that the SUV got a flat tire right after the Allsop men parked it. I jogged over to the vehicle, pulled a penlight from my pocket, and examined the tire. Shallow slashes marred its surface, and at their center, a puncture the size of a knife tip.

"What did you do, Sunny?" I breathed, pride battling with fear when I touched the gash. So Sunny had disabled the SUV, then what happened? I stood and marched around the front of the vehicle. Two SUVs had been stopped here when we ran past, the second one parked a good twelve feet away from the first. Why park so far away? Unless... had a third SUV been parked between the other two? Had somebody taken Sunny away in it? Who?

Frustrated, I kicked at the pavement. I paced back around to the flat tire. My flashlight beam swept over the side of the vehicle, throwing light on the driver's door. I bent over, my fingers tracing over the lines Sunny's knife had scratched onto the panel. BRODY, and beneath that, CAVE.

The words had barely registered before I took off at a dead run. The Allsop estate was a little more than a mile from the penitentiary. By the time I got to the bottom of the long, curving driveway, I stopped to catch my breath and go over my plan. The house sat on a rocky, arid ridge, surrounded by hardy trees and shrubs. Elliot Allsop stationed two guards at the entrance to the house and another patrolled the grounds. Even if he took most of his security team with him in pursuit of my friends, Mr. Allsop would leave behind at least three guards.

I touched my Glock. Anybody who got in my way was shit out of luck. I loped up the driveway, darting into the trees before the roadway straightened out in front of the house. Holding my breath, I listened for any sign of a guard. An owl hooted from a nearby tree, and something skittered through the underbrush. The moon slid behind a cloud as I crept closer to the front of the house.

There. A man jogged around the garage, heading into the trees. If he kept to his course, all I had to do was sit pretty, and he'd come to me. Sticks snapped as he advanced. I stood, my back to a tree trunk, hidden from his view. He passed by and I sprang. Locking my elbow around his neck, I compressed his carotid artery and cut off blood flow to his brain. He bucked, but I held tight. Within ten seconds, he slumped in my arms. Moving quickly—before he regained consciousness—I tore his T-shirt over his head and fashioned a gag. I took the handcuffs from his belt and secured his wrists behind his back. He groaned, the sound muffled by the cloth in his mouth. I yanked off his belt, slipped it around the chain linking the handcuffs, and fastened it to the tree trunk.

One down.

Slinking between the bushes, I drew closer to the front door. Instead of flanking the front door and staring straight ahead into the night—like guards in movies—the two men huddled together, laughing softly while one lit the other's cigarette. Maybe fortune decided it owed me one. Arm extended, Glock in hand, I advanced on the men. I fired four times, dropping the men before they caught sight of me.

When the hell did I become a man who shoots down men in cold blood?

Six months ago, my conscience would have bothered me; now, not so much. Men who signed up for Elliot Allsop's private army deserved none of my sympathy. Besides, these goons had probably stood to one side while Brody dragged Sunny into the house. Fury roiled in my gut as I imagined the scene. I checked to make sure they were down before stepping into the foyer.

The mansion was built on the side of a hill. Tons of rock and dirt surrounded Brody's private retreat in the windowless basement. Odds were he hadn't heard the gunshots. Pausing inside the front door, I listened for voices, footsteps, anything that indicated other people were in the house. Nothing.

Gun in hand, I raced to the stairs.

THIRTY-SEVEN

Sunny

I*'m going to make you scream.*

Brody's cheerful tone while delivering the threat raised goose bumps across my shoulders. He pointed at the ceiling and walls. "And don't imagine anybody will hear you and come to your rescue. The guy who built the house used the man cave as his music room. It's totally soundproofed." He shrugged. "Not that anybody would come even if they heard you. The men know better than to disturb me when I'm having my fun."

I held still for a good ten seconds, my breath frozen in my lungs, then I exploded into action. Twisting my hands, I tugged frantically on the zip tie binding my wrists behind my back. I was nestled deep in a soft, oversized leather chair, so deep that my feet didn't touch the plush carpet. I absolutely couldn't get the leverage necessary to hoist myself out of the chair. Swinging both feet up into the air and down, I hurtled my body back and forth, trying to rock into a position where I could stand.

Brody stood with both hands on his hips, smiling down at me. "You're adorable when you put up a fight."

Anger overrode my panic. I wanted to smack that smug smirk off his face. With an *oomph,* I threw myself forward with such force that my feet finally made contact with the floor. I stood, breathing hard.

"Adorable," he repeated, reaching out to cup my nape. I jerked away. "No, Sunny," he chided. "You don't get to push me away."

The doors burst open. I whirled around. Kyle advanced into the room like an avenging angel, pistol drawn, and murder in his eyes. Brody snaked his left arm out and pulled me against his chest. In his right hand, he held his gun. He tapped the barrel against my temple.

"Glad you joined the party," Brody called. "Put down the gun and kick it across the floor, or I'll splatter your pretty girlfriend's brains across the room."

There had to be some evasive move I could make. Twist and roll out of the way, maybe. Or some slick trick with my hands like people do in the movies, but if there was a way out of this, I didn't know it.

If Kyle dropped his weapon and Brody shot him, I couldn't live with the guilt. I couldn't continue to draw breath in a world where Kyle threw away his life to save mine. My eyes sought his. "Don't do it," I said quietly. Kyle's eyes met mine for an instant. I jerked my head in a shaky nod, trying to convey a world of meaning with one small gesture.

I mean it, baby. Don't put down your gun.

"What's it going to be?" Brody demanded.

Kyle dropped his Glock onto the carpet, then kicked it across the room. It came to a stop at the feet of the brown bear, whose fierce eyes seemed to glint with reproach.

Why did you give that asshole your gun?

THIRTY-EIGHT

Kyle

"Glad to see you've still got some brains," Brody sneered. "I was starting to doubt it after you hooked up with her."

White hot rage surged through my body. I tamped it down. In a crisis, strong emotions make for stupid mistakes.

"You okay?" I asked Sunny, ignoring Brody's taunt.

"Yes."

Brody shoved Sunny into a leather chair so deep that her feet couldn't touch the carpet. "You should see her try to get out of the chair with her hands tied behind her back. Fucking adorable the way she swings her feet."

I swallowed back my angry retort and fought the impulse to smash in Brody's face. He smiled and waggled his gun, reminding me who had the upper hand. For now.

"Seriously, man." Brody dropped into a chair and waved a hand, indicating that I should do the same. I took the leather chair opposite him, next to Sunny. "Look how we live," he continued. "Electricity. Hot water. Great food. Gas for our cars. Security. And we invited you in. Because you're one of us. A gentleman. Born and bred to lead, like Dad says. We offered you the keys to the kingdom, and you spit in our face. Because of her." He scowled at Sunny, who jutted her chin out defiantly.

SUSANNA STROM

"I didn't turn you down because of Sunny," I snorted, deliberately drawing his eyes away from her. If his attention wandered for just a moment, I could lunge for the gun. "I turned you down because I want no part of your batshit crazy regime."

"Batshit crazy regime?" Brody pulled a face. "I'm pissed at Dad myself right now, but I wouldn't call his plans batshit crazy."

I sat forward in the chair, resting my forearms on my knees, ready to jump. "Why are you pissed at your dad?"

Brody shrugged. "He didn't like the little party I planned for the execution. Said I created the opportunity for somebody to try to break Finn out. Told me to wait in the car like a fucking kid." Brody shook his head. "But you know what? When he catches up to the traitor, when he finds out that you two were involved and that I captured you both single-handed, all will be forgiven. Me. Brody Allsop, *I* brought down the quarry." Brody stood and pointed his gun at the mounted giraffe. "Pow. Pow. Pow," he said, imitating the sound of gunfire.

I sprang up and dove at Brody, knocking the gun from his hand. We tumbled sideways onto the carpet. Brody kicked, missing me but sending the gun skittering under the sofa. He drove an elbow into my nose. Pain exploded and my eyes watered. I shook my head, trying to clear my vision. Brody scuttled backwards and managed to haul himself to his feet. He grabbed an antique sword from the display rack—one he'd stolen from a museum—and brandished it in my direction, standing between me and the wall of swords.

"How about we settle this like gentlemen?" I suggested, gesturing at the weapons. He'd used the word first. The Allsops had twisted the meaning of gentleman to something unrecognizable, but he might fall for my challenge. I climbed to my feet, wiping blood off on the back of my arm and positioning myself between Brody and Sunny. "I propose a duel."

"To the death?" Brody's startled expression quickly gave way to enthusiasm. "It would impress the hell out of my dad if I killed you in mortal combat, and we'd still have Sunny." Brody spun his sword around in a flashy move that looked like something out of a video game. "Yeah." He gave an exaggerated nod, obviously impressed with his own snazzy sword spinning skills. "I've been practicing."

The two of us going at each other with antique swords in the middle of his man cave was probably the closest thing to combat Brody would ever see.

"I can tell you've been practicing," I said, fake admiration coloring my voice.

"I've been training with some of the men," he said. "I haven't lost a contest yet. Jonesy says I'm a natural swordsman."

Wow. Elliot Allsop's men hadn't handed Brody his ass when they played at sword fighting with him. Had it occurred to him to wonder why he always won against daddy's men?

"A duel to the death," I repeated.

He spun the sword again. It had to be centuries old, but the blade looked sharp. No way I'd permit him to get close to Sunny with that thing.

"Yeah, to the death," Brody said excitedly. "Pick a sword."

Turn my back on Brody while I peruse the selection? No thanks.

"I challenged you to the duel," I reminded him, scrambling for an appropriate response. "That means that you have the right to choose the weapons. You're a gentleman. I trust you to select my sword."

Still better than turning my back on Brody.

"Okay." Glancing away for only a few seconds, he chose a sword and slid it across the rug to me.

"We'll be fighting with eighteenth-century cutlasses," he said. "Like pirates on the Spanish Main."

I picked up the short sword with a curved blade and a simple knuckle-bow hilt. Slashing at the air, I tested its balance. I'd been on my college fencing team for years, but sword fighting and fencing are different animals. My reflexes were good. I'd mastered speed, timing and footwork, but I was no swordsman, and unlike Brody, I knew it.

"Fighting makes me horny," Brody said cheerfully. "After I kill you, Sunny and I are going to get to know each other."

The threat against Sunny could have left me sputtering with rage, ready to rush headlong at the bastard. Maybe that's what he intended. Instead of fury, a blanket of calm dropped down over me, smothering all violent emotion. I looked at Brody with cool, dispassionate eyes, full of quiet resolve. He'd never get past me to hurt Sunny. Regret and sadness mingled in my blood. After all the advantages life had bestowed on him, Brody had ended up a clueless, blustering bully. And now he was going to die.

My body automatically assumed the en garde position I learned from fencing, my right leg forward, knee bent, foot pointed at Brody.

Brody faced me, grinning and bouncing on his toes. He lifted his sword in a mock salute.

"To the death," he repeated, lifting the cutlass over his head and lunging forward, swinging the sword down in a vertical cut aimed at my head.

Raising my sword above my head and holding it parallel to the ground, I blocked the strike. Brody danced back, then struck again, a horizontal cut aimed at my shoulder. I parried, my sword in a vertical position as I deflected the blow. He tried again, aiming at the opposite shoulder. Once again, I parried the strike.

I was no expert swordsman, but even I could tell that the months of practice had taught Brody little more than the basic offensive strikes. He was like a man who learned how to waltz, then counted the steps one, two, three in his head, moving to the music in a graceless and plodding fashion. He'd probably be more dangerous if he was an absolute newbie, his movements less predictable. A natural swordsman? Jonesy hadn't done Brody any favors with his unearned praise.

There was no honor in this, no glory in defeating such an opponent, but the bastard had left me no choice. The longer I kept evading his attacks, the greater the chance that I'd wear myself out or that he'd somehow land a lucky blow. Time to end this.

Brody lifted his sword above his head, practically inviting me to attack his vulnerable midsection. Certain of victory, I swung my sword. Instead of completing the downward arc, Brody blocked my strike with his sword, holding my sword in place while he lifted his foot and kicked toward my groin.

Fuck! He faked me out. All that practice with Allsop's men had taught the little shit some tricks after all. Guess I was the one who was too cocky and sure of myself.

I twisted in the nick of time, so his foot struck my hip instead of my groin. Staggering back, I fought to regain my balance.

Brody threw back his head and laughed, delighted by his little trick.

Couldn't resist gloating, could you, buddy?

That was all the opening I needed. I feinted left, aiming a downward swinging cut to Brody's left leg. When he swung his sword down to parry the attack, I shifted direction. Lunging forward, I thrust my sword into Brody's chest. I threw all of my weight into it, hoping to slice the major arteries that supplied blood to his liver.

A slow and painful death wasn't my goal. I wanted Brody dead, but I didn't want him to suffer.

My blade disappeared into his upper torso and blood spurted from the wound—a sight so fundamentally wrong that I gaped at his chest and then at the sword clutched in my hand. He'd left me no choice, but I'd done this. This was my handiwork. Nausea tickled the back of my throat.

Eyes wide with shock, Brody collapsed to the floor.

I stepped backward, breathing hard as I looked down at Brody's crumpled body. What a fucking waste.

"Kyle." I turned my head and shifted my attention to Sunny. "We need to get out of here before Mr. Allsop comes back," she said gently.

Shit. "Yeah. You're right." I pulled her out of the deep chair. She turned her back to me and held out her bound hands. I wiped the cutlass blade on my jeans, carefully sliced open the zip tie, and pulled the plastic strips from her wrists.

"Better. Thanks." Sunny rubbed the red marks left behind by the zip ties.

I dropped the sword onto the carpet, then touched the abrasions on her wrists. "Are you all right? Did he hurt you?"

"I'm okay. I kept him talking about his favorite subject, all the ways the world had done him wrong." Her smiled faded and she clutched at my arms. "I was scared, but I knew you'd come for me."

I cupped her cheeks, staring into her beautiful amber eyes. "Always. I'll always come for you. You're my world, Sunshine."

She pulled my head down and kissed me, a quick celebratory kiss full of the promise of many more to come.

"Finn? Is he okay?" she asked.

"He's beat up, but he'll survive."

"Thank God," she breathed. "But now we really need to jet." She grabbed my hand. We ran from the room and up the stairs to the main floor. On the landing, Sunny paused and turned to me, her eyes bright with excitement. "I just thought of something. If we have time, we should grab some of Mr. Allsop's files. Anything we can bring back to Marcus would help his war against the Allsops."

"You're a genius, Sunny." I ran to the deck and scanned the surrounding streets. I couldn't see any moving lights. That was no guarantee that we were safe, of course, but Elliot Allsop and his men weren't bearing down on us. "The war room is right across the hall from the armory. Let's take five minutes. You go into the war room and grab anything that looks promising. I'll go into the armory and pack up a few weapons and as much ammo as I can carry."

We grabbed a few empty hampers from the laundry room and rushed toward the war room and armory. While Sunny stuffed files and maps into her hamper, I swept box after box of ammo into mine. When both of my hampers were full, I tucked two AK-47s under my arm and stepped into the hall.

"Time's up," I called.

Sunny emerged from the war room, dragging a hamper filled to the brim with papers.

"Let's go out through the garage," I suggested. Sunny didn't need to see the bodies on the front porch.

"There's gasoline in the garage. We could set a fire," Sunny said. "Losing his headquarters would be a real setback for Mr. Allsop."

Burn down the Allsop headquarters? For five seconds, I indulged in the fantasy of setting the place ablaze, imagining Elliot Allsop's helpless fury as he watched his castle burn. Memory squashed that happy fantasy.

"I saw Portland burn," I said. "Odds are the fire wouldn't spread beyond the ridge, but there's a chance embers might carry the flames to other structures. We can't risk setting the city on fire."

"You're right," Sunny conceded. "We don't want to be responsible for hurting innocent survivors. I feel bad enough already about leaving people behind in the city."

We lugged the hampers through the kitchen and down the hallway leading to the garage. Outside of Hildy's room, Sunny paused. "Was Hildy at the prison? Did you guys rescue her, too?"

"Yeah. Hildy is on her way to Pendleton with the others."

Sunny held up a finger. "Ten seconds. I promise." She dashed into Hildy's room and emerged a moment later carrying a Bible, a rosary, and a framed photo of a smiling family. "These were on Hildy's nightstand," Sunny said, dragging the hamper over the hardwood again. "She should have something to remember her old life."

"You're a sweetheart, Sunny McAllister," I said, grateful beyond words that fate had brought this kind woman back into my life.

I headed toward the SUV that was parked in the driveway, the one Brody had used to bring Sunny to the house.

"Can we take Daisy?" Sunny asked. "It feels wrong to abandon her to the Allsops if we have a choice."

I opened the driver's door on the SUV and felt around for the keys. No sign of them. Shit. They must be in Brody's pocket.

"I threw Daisy's keys into the cup holder," Sunny said. "She's good to go."

If I was going to pick my dream getaway vehicle, it wouldn't be a twenty-year-old, blindingly white van covered with flower decals. The late model black SUV was a much wiser choice, but maybe it held bad memories for Sunny. And I really didn't want to take the time to run downstairs and dig through Brody's pockets for the SUV keys.

"All right," I said.

Sunny opened the door to the Refrigerator and waved the keys at me. I put the hampers into the back of the van, then quickly grabbed a few five-gallon gas cans from the garage. It was tempting to take more, but Daisy had trouble accelerating under the best of circumstances.

"You mind driving?" Sunny asked. "I didn't sleep last night and I'm too tired to be safe behind the wheel."

I held out my hand and she tossed me the keys. We buckled in and I fired up the engine.

"I don't want to go into the city," I said. "How about we head into the hills on Highway 21, then work our way west? It'll be slower, especially in Daisy, but we'll be less likely to run into Allsop's people."

"Sounds good," she said, stifling a yawn.

At the bottom of the driveway, I peered to the right. Still no sign of the SUVs, thank God. I turned left, navigating toward Highway 21.

"We've got a long drive ahead of us," I said. "Why don't you take a nap?"

"No way," Sunny said. "I'm going to stay awake and keep you company."

Ten minutes later, her head lolled to one side and she was snoring.

I grinned into the darkness, so happy that I thought my heart might burst.

THIRTY-NINE

Sunny

Driven by a potent mix of sleep deprivation, giddy relief, and a body worn out by too many adrenaline spikes, I fell headfirst into deep sleep. When I awoke, jostled by Daisy coming to a stop, the first rays of pink-hued morning light were brightening the horizon.

My eyelids slid open, and I turned groggy eyes toward Kyle.

"Good morning," he said, smiling. "We just pulled onto the exit for downtown Pendleton."

I sat up straight, rubbing the sleep from my eyes. "Oh, crap. You mean I slept the entire trip?"

"Yep." Kyle rolled down his window. I squinted at the armed man jogging toward us from the cars blocking the exit ramp. "Not a problem. You needed it." Kyle leaned out the window and spoke to the guard. "Kyle Chamberlain and Sunny McAllister to see Marcus Havoc."

The man lifted a radio to his mouth. "They're here." Whoops of joy sounded through the radio. Smiling, he signaled for the cars to clear a path for us. "Havoc wants to see you at HQ."

We drove downtown and parked in front of city hall. The double doors to the building flew open. Marcus, Justin, Rachel, and Georgia rushed outside. I jumped from the van and ran to Georgia.

"Holy shit, I was afraid I'd never see you again," she cried, throwing her arms around me. We'd known each other for only two days, but we'd bonded during our mission, and I hugged her like the long-lost friend she'd pretended to be.

"Me, too," I whispered. Over Georgia's shoulder, hands tucked in her jeans pockets, a grinning Rachel watched our reunion. I detached from Georgia and held out my arms to Rachel. "Come on. You know you want a hug."

"Do I look like a sentimental sap?" Rachel rolled her eyes, but didn't protest when I wrapped my arms around her shoulders and drew her close. She returned the hug, her arms locking around my waist. "Glad you made it back," she whispered fiercely in my ear. After a moment, she pulled away. "I saved the sexy Lady Godiva wig for you." She wiggled her brows. "Thought you might surprise Kyle with it sometime, if you know what I mean."

I laughed, pure happiness zinging through my veins.

Kyle stepped away from the cluster of men and slid open the van's passenger door. "Got something you'll want to see," he called to Marcus, lifting the hamper full of documents from the van. "We only had five minutes, but before we took off, Sunny grabbed files and maps from the Allsop war room." He hauled out two more hampers and set them next to the first. "I raided their armory. Took a few AK-47s, but I figured extra ammo was the priority."

Marcus whistled low, touching a box of cartridges. "You figured right. Damn." He picked up a file folder and rifled through the papers. Looking up, he met my eyes. "You did good, too, Sunny." He swept out his hand at the three hampers. "This is invaluable."

"You need to know that I killed Brody," Kyle said, his expression hard. "I killed Elliot Allsop's son and heir. He'll blame both you and me, and he'll be gunning for us."

"Once we decided to make a stand, we were both in his crosshairs." Marcus squeezed Kyle's shoulder. "And the world's a better place without Brody Allsop in it."

Kyle nodded in agreement, but I saw the pain in his eyes. However justified his actions, he'd killed a man he once considered a friend. Another bloody memory, another ghost to haunt his dreams. I took his hand. He'd never again face the nightmares alone.

"How's Finn?" I asked Marcus.

"Finn's going to be fine," Marcus said. "He's bruised and battered, but he'll make a full recovery. He's at the clinic with Sara and Rocco, sleeping off the drugs the Allsops pumped into him."

"I'm taking Finn back to Valhalla." Kyle straightened his spine as if he expected a fight. "He's your soldier, but he's Bear's brother. They're family. They need to see each other."

"I agree," Marcus said. "Take Finn to Valhalla. Let the brothers reunite. But you've got to know that a war's coming, and you can't hide from it, not even on a ranch that's—what's that phrase you used—at the ass end of nowhere."

"I know." Kyle sighed. "A war is the last thing I want, but there'll be no peace until Elliot Allsop is in the ground."

Marcus crossed his arms over his chest. "Before you leave for Valhalla, I want to sit down and talk about my plans for the campaign against Allsop. I'm going to ask you to carry a message to Ripper."

"Yeah, Ripper needs to be brought in." He sighed again. "Kenzie is going to kill me. She thought they were finally living their happily ever after."

I squeezed his hand. "If Kenzie is anything like me, she'll want to help bring down Allsop."

Kyle offered a small smile. "Bet you're right, Sunny. It won't be the first time Kenz helps bring down the bad guys. She took on a skeezy cult leader and a bunch of Nazis. A simple megalomaniac won't stand a chance." He turned back to Marcus. "I want to check on Finn, and find out when it will be safe for him to travel. Sunny and I need to talk to Mrs. B. and Ever about our plans, then get ready for the trip home. How about you and I meet this afternoon?"

"That'll be fine. We'll start going over Allsop's papers." He picked up the heavy hamper full of ammunition and signaled for Justin to get the other. Rachel dragged the third while Georgia took the rifles from the back of the van, then followed the men back into headquarters.

Kyle and I drove across the river to the clinic. Rocco sat behind the reception desk. A huge smile broke out across his face when he saw us. He jumped up and swept me into his arms, lifting me off the floor and spinning me around.

"You had me scared for awhile. It's good to see you, Sunny. You, too, Kyle." He gently set me down, then looked out the window into the clinic's parking lot. "I'm glad you didn't have to leave Daisy behind in Boise. I love that van."

"You do?" Kyle asked, clearly surprised.

"Sure. Who wants a boring ride when you can drive something with personality?"

I shot Kyle a look. *Don't answer that.*

Kyle and I hadn't talked about it, but I had no plans to drive Daisy over the narrow and rutted roads to Valhalla. She was a city girl through and through, doing best on wide, flat streets. "Would you like to keep Daisy?" I asked my friend. "I can't think of anybody else I'd rather give her to."

"You kidding?" Rocco asked. "Hell, yes, I want Daisy. Can you imagine it, me riding around town in style?"

"Then it's settled. Kyle and I will be leaving town as soon as Finn can travel. I'll leave Daisy in the parking lot of the motel with the keys in the cup holder."

"How is Finn?" Kyle asked.

Rocco sobered. "Sons of bitches beat him up bad, but he's young and strong, and he'll heal. He's more alert now that the sedative is working its way out of his system."

"Can we see him?" Kyle asked.

"Sara is with him. Second door on the left." Rocco pointed down the corridor. "Knock. She'll let you know if he's up to visitors. She told Marcus to wait till this afternoon to talk to him, but since you're here, she might allow a visit."

"Will do," Kyle said. "Thanks, Rocco."

Kyle rapped on the door. Within seconds, Sara cracked it open, then stepped into the hall, closing the door behind her with a soft snick.

"Finn will be fine," she assured us in a low voice. "His ribs are bruised, but not broken. He's dehydrated. Still a bit groggy, but he's lucid. He's been asking about you two." She opened the door. "You have visitors." Sara touched my arm. "I'm so happy that you made it back."

Kyle and I walked into a small room furnished only with a hospital bed and a chair. Morning light filtered into the space through a window on the far wall. When he saw us, Finn raised his head and lifted up on his elbows. Suppressing a groan, he dropped back onto his pillow.

"Not a good idea," he said. "Not till the blasted headache goes away."

"I am so sorry," Kyle said, approaching the bed. "I feel like a shit for leaving you behind."

"No need for an apology. No need for guilt. We both did what we had to do, and we're both still standing." His lips twisted in a wry smile. "Least I *will* be standing as soon as the doc gives me the all clear."

"Oh, Finn." I reached out, then stilled, my hand hovering in the air. His face, his arms, even his hands were bruised, his knuckles bloody. He'd gone down fighting. There was no place I could touch him that wouldn't hurt. My eyes filled with tears.

"No, sweetheart, none of that." He frowned and took my hand, wrapping black-and-blue fingers around mine. "Don't cry for me. I've been hurt worse plenty of times. When we get to Valhalla, ask my brother to tell you about the time I tussled with a goose. I tripped and rolled down a hill trying to get away from it."

Laughter burst from my throat at the unexpected mental image.

"You think I'm fooling?" he asked, opening his eyes wide. "You ain't seen nothing till you've dealt with a hopping mad goose."

"Speaking of Valhalla," Kyle said. Finn and I fell silent and turned our eyes to Kyle. "Did Sara say when you'll be able to travel?"

"Doc said she wants me to take a day to rest and drink fluids. If the headache is gone and I can stand without getting dizzy, she'll clear me to leave tomorrow."

"If you're up to it," Kyle said, "I'd like to head out in the late morning."

"You sneak me to the car, I'll leave right now," Finn said. "Never thought I'd see my brother or Valhalla again. Now that I know Bear's alive, the waiting is killing me."

"You're not going anywhere until the doctor says it's okay," I said in my best mom voice.

"Yes, ma'am." Finn glanced at Kyle. "Bossy little thing, isn't she?"

Kyle was waaay too smart to answer that question, especially after I stepped on his toe.

"If Sara says you're good to go, we'll leave around eleven tomorrow," Kyle said, wriggling his foot out from under mine. "That'll get us to Valhalla by evening."

"I'll be ready."

We visited with Finn for another fifteen minutes, telling him about what went down in Boise and Brody's death.

"Let's head back to the motel," I suggested as we walked to Daisy. "If Mrs. B. and Ever are up, we can see them. If not, it wouldn't hurt you to lie down for a while."

"I should be tired, but I'm too wired to sleep," Kyle said.

No sooner had we parked in front of our motel room than the door to the neighboring room flew open. A nine-year-old dynamo charged at the van, waving her arms in the air. Mrs. B. stood in the doorway, pressing a hand to her heart. Kyle jumped out of the driver's seat and lifted Ever up into his arms. Round and round they spun, until he carefully deposited her on the concrete. She flung herself at him again, wrapping her arms around his waist.

"I knew you and Sunny were okay." She raised a beaming face to his. "I just knew it."

"Yeah, we're okay. And tomorrow we're all going to Valhalla," he said, ruffling her strawberry-blond curls. "Do you think you'll like living on a ranch with Sunny and Mrs. B. and Finn and me and all our friends?"

"Yes," she shouted, hopping up and down. "And Fitzwilliam, too."

"Fitzwilliam, too," he agreed.

I walked up to Mrs. B. Her bright-pink lips turned up in a welcoming smile, but her eyes were awash with tears. "You are never to frighten me like that again, Sunny McAllister," she scolded, clutching me to her chest. "My poor heart can't take it."

"I'm sorry you were scared," I murmured. I couldn't promise her that we'd never face danger again or risk separation—not with a war brewing—but I'd offer her what comfort my conscience would allow. "I love you, Mrs. B. And I'm happy you're coming to Valhalla with us."

"You're my family, sweet girl," she said. "Where you go, I go."

"Sunny!" Ever released Kyle and rushed toward me. I dropped down onto my haunches and held out my arms. Ever threw herself on me, toppling us both over. "Whoops-a-daisy," she laughed, settling on my lap. She reared back, pointing at my head. "What's wrong with your hair?"

I touched the blond wig that I'd forgotten I was wearing. "It's a wig," I said in a conspiratorial whisper. "Part of my super-secret spy costume."

Her eyes widened. "You were a spy?"

"I was. I'll tell you all about it someday, when you're older."

She made a face. "Why does all the good stuff have to wait until I'm older?"

I dropped a kiss on the top of her head. "Don't be in such a hurry to grow up."

As soon as I said the words, I regretted them. Ever's childhood—what was left of it—would be nothing like the idyllic childhood Kyle and I enjoyed. The world had changed. We'd love her. We'd do our best to keep her safe, but we couldn't wrap her in a cocoon or coddle her. Doing right by a child in the new world meant teaching her how to fight and how to survive. I swallowed hard. Was I up to the task?

I glanced at Kyle, who was deep in conversation with Mrs. B. His eyes met mine. He smiled and I felt the warmth of that smile down to my bones. My fears evaporated. Kyle loved me—he loved Ever—and he'd do whatever was necessary to keep us from harm. He'd proven that time and time again. And I'd do the same for all the people I loved.

"Sunny, are you listening?" Ever asked.

"Sorry, sweet pea." Finn's nickname for the girl was official. "My mind wandered."

"I said, yesterday Thanh took us to the place where they keep stuff people need. He packed up a couple of boxes of schoolbooks for me to take to the ranch. And lots of paper and pencils and crayons. I got a new winter coat and clothes and shoes that are big enough for me to grow into."

"That's nice," I said. "You'll need all that at Valhalla."

"And Mrs. B. got a big bag of yarn and knitting needles and a pair of boots to wear on the ranch. They're pink and she loves them. She called them Wellingtons, but I think she made the name up."

"No, Wellingtons are real," I said. "Just like Jammie Dodgers and toad-in-the-hole."

"Toad-in-the-hole? Now *you're* making things up," Ever said.

"Nope. It's a real food. Ask Mrs. B."

Ever hopped out of my lap and tugged on Mrs. B.'s floral blouse. Kyle took my hand and pulled me to my feet. I laid both palms on his chest. The muscles twitched under my fingertips, and I smiled up at him.

"You're doing that on purpose," I whispered. "Popping your pecs like a male stripper."

"They got nothing on me," he growled in my ear. "I got moves that would make your panties melt."

"Really?" I said. "You planning on showing them to me someday?"

"Count on it." Laughing, he slid both arms around my waist and pulled me close. "Tomorrow we go to Valhalla. Are you ready to see your new home?"

"I didn't think—" My voice caught, so I tried again. "I didn't think I'd ever feel this happy again."

"Me, too, Sunshine. Me, too."

FORTY

Bear

Valhalla

Hannah's laughter rang out, filling the front room from one side to the other. Sahdev might have taught her how to play Parcheesi, but the student had become the master. The girl took to Parcheesi like a duck to water. Sounds like she'd got all her pieces into the home square, winning the game yet again.

My mama taught me to be gracious in victory, no whooping and hollering when I won. *A cowboy doesn't gloat*, she'd say. I glanced over at the girl, who threw her arms in the air and jumped up to dance a little jig. Mama might disapprove of Hannah's victory celebration, but I couldn't find it in my heart to judge. Hannah and her boyfriend Levi were young, but they both had a lot of guts, grit, and try.

Levi sat back at the game table and grinned at his girlfriend's victory. Don't think the boy genius had a competitive bone in his body. Sahdev stood and stuck out his hand, offering his congratulations. I suspect his mother taught the same good manners mine had, but he didn't look put out by Hannah's glee. If anything, he beamed with pride. The doc was a good man. Steady, kind, brave.

Just the sort of fellow you want on your side when the world goes kittywampus.

We'd rearranged the furniture in the front room first thing after we beat the Wilcox Brigade. Well… no… the *very* first thing we did was to rip down that blamed Nazi flag they'd tacked to the wall and stomp on the thing. *Then* we shifted furniture around, setting up a game table to one side of the stone hearth and another small table next to the window, where it could catch the sunlight, a place for Nyx to work on her drawings. Grandma's rocking chair sat by the fireplace now, too, hauled from a back bedroom because both Hannah and Kenzie loved it. The front room looked different from when I grew up in this house, but that was all right. A home wasn't a museum. Change comes, whether you want it to or not.

Hector dozed on a sheepskin rug in front of the fireplace, the German shepherd's legs twitching like he was chasing rabbits in his sleep. We hadn't lit a fire yet this season, but he'd staked a claim to the spot nonetheless.

Kenzie looked up from her book and smiled at Hannah's antics. Kenzie and Ripper sprawled at opposite ends of the leather couch, their feet on each other's laps, both of their noses stuck in books. If tonight went like most, before long Ripper would peel off her socks and massage her feet. The man knew how to reduce his woman to putty. Kenzie would sigh and close both her book and her eyes. After a few minutes, she'd open her eyes back up and give him *that look*. He'd take her by the hand, wish us all goodnight, and lead her back to their room.

Only a petty man was jealous of another man's happiness. I didn't begrudge Ripper and Kenzie the contentment and joy they'd found. Shoot, it was good to see that not even the end of the world could stop men and women from falling in love and building a life together.

My eyes strayed to Nyx. She bent over her drawing, working by lantern light since it was evening. Colored pencils were scattered across the tabletop. Her wild burgundy hair tumbled down her back, and she frowned with concentration. Giving in to an impulse, I crossed the room and stood behind her, studying her artwork.

A pair of skeletons—a man and a woman—danced in the moonlight. A crown of roses sat atop the woman's skull, her white bones gleaming beneath her long, red hair. The man wore a top hat on his bony skull. Under its brim, his empty eye sockets were circles of black.

Nyx glanced up at me. "Day of the dead art," she explained. The reference went right over my head, but I nodded anyway. The ghoulish figures should have given me the creeps. Dancing corpses was the stuff of nightmares. Somehow, under Nyx's hand, the image was beautiful, almost—what's that word—ethereal.

"Nice," I said. The inadequacy of the compliment struck me right away. "Real nice," I added.

Nyx tossed a smile over her shoulder, her expression full of amusement, like she saw right through me. "Why thank you, cowboy."

I squirmed. The woman had a knack for flustering me, for making me feel like a raw sixteen-year-old who didn't have a clue how to talk to a woman.

Over Nyx's head, something caught my eye. Looking out the window, I saw two bouncing lights poke holes in the darkness. "Somebody's coming up the drive," I said.

Instantly, Ripper was on his feet and at my side, his Colt in hand, peering at the advancing lights. "Weapons," he ordered in a low voice.

Our guns were always within reach; that was the way of the world nowadays. Ripper and I stood on opposite sides of the window, tracking the vehicle's progress. It stopped in front of the house. There was just enough moonlight to pick out its shape. A pickup.

My heart started to beat faster. Kyle had driven a pickup to Boise. He was overdue. Made sense that Kyle had returned, but I saw the shadowy forms of multiple people inside the truck's cab.

"Can you tell who is it?" Kenzie whispered.

"Might be Kyle," Ripper answered.

Kenzie took a step toward the door. Ripper held up a hand. "I said *might* be Kyle. Don't know for sure. Till we do, stay back, darlin'."

Both front doors of the truck swung open. Moonlight reflected off the words Valhalla Ranch painted on the door panel. A woman stepped out of the passenger side. Kyle loped around the front of the truck, kissed her, then threw open the back passenger door.

"Well, I'll be," I muttered. So Kyle had brought back a woman. The man moved fast. Couldn't wait to hear *that* story.

"It's him," Ripper said to the others, leading the charge out the door.

By unspoken agreement, we waited on the porch for Kyle to help his passengers out of the cab. No sense in making them skittish by having a group of strangers stampede down the steps toward them. Kyle lifted a little girl from the back. The girl looked at us, her eyes wide in a pale face. Something squirmed in her arms. A cat. All right. We could always use a mouser in the barn. Next, Kyle helped a tiny old lady climb out. She smiled and waved at us. Kyle trotted around to the far side of the truck and opened the door. A man slowly climbed out, moving like his bones hurt. Kyle stuck by his side as they came around the back of the truck. The man was unsteady on his feet, but shook off Kyle's hand when he tried to help. Instead of stopping and standing with the other passengers, he walked straight toward the porch.

"Sweet Jesus," I breathed.

The blood drained from my face, leaving my lips numb and tingly. If I hadn't grabbed ahold of the porch rail, I'd have fallen. Soon as I caught my breath, I tripped down the stairs, my legs wobbling like a newborn foal.

"Finn?" I lurched toward my brother. I patted his face, his arms, his chest, like my fingers had to prove that my eyes weren't fooling me. Finally certain that he was real, I crushed him in my arms.

He grunted. Shoot. I forgot. He'd been walking funny. I let go, but kept my hands on his shoulders, just in case he needed support.

Kenzie had run into the house and fetched a solar lantern. The light fell across Finn's face, and I jerked back. Somebody had beat the crap out of my little brother. His right eye was swollen clean shut. Bruises covered his face and his lip was split wide open. Finn pressed one hand against his ribs. Damn, that hug must've hurt him something fierce.

"What happened to you?" I choked out.

"I'll tell you all about it later, big brother," he said. "For now, all you got to know is that Kyle helped saved my ass, and he brought me home."

I glanced at my friend, who stood with one arm around the young woman. I mouthed my thanks. He smiled back at me.

"Are you Bear?" the little girl piped up.

"I am," I answered.

298

She walked up to me and held out her hand, pretty as you please. "Hi, Bear. I'm Ever van der Linden." We shook hands, then she held up the fluffiest cat I ever seen. "This is Fitzwilliam. And that's Mrs. B." She pointed to the old lady, who smiled and waved again. "We're Kyle and Finn's friends."

"Happy to meet you, Ever," I said solemnly. "If you're Kyle and Finn's friends, you're my friends, too. Welcome to Valhalla."

"Thank you." She glanced up at Finn. "Is that a real porch swing?"

"Yes, it is," he said.

"Is it okay if I sit on it?"

"Sure thing, sweet pea," Finn answered.

Ever skipped up the steps, saying hi to everyone she passed. Plopping down on the swing, she set her cat on her lap, then pushed off with her feet. "We're going to like it here, Fitzwilliam," she declared.

I turned back to my brother. "Let's get you inside and get a load off, then introduce me to your friends."

Finn climbed the steps on his own steam. I walked behind him, close enough to help out if he stumbled, but not so close that he'd shoo me away. Little brother is a tough son of a bitch. He marched into the house without a hitch. Dropping down onto the couch, he looked around the room. "It sure is good to be home." He sighed. "Never thought I'd see this place again."

Kenzie took Ripper's hand and walked over to Kyle and his pretty friend, who stood together next to the fireplace. "You were gone so long," Kenzie cried, throwing her arms around him. "I was afraid something happened to you."

"Looks like something *did* happen to him," Ripper observed, glancing at the young woman.

Kyle returned the hug, then slung his arm around his companion. "Ripper, Kenzie, this is Sunny," Kyle said.

"Jake's sister Sunny?" Kenzie exclaimed. "I met you last Easter."

Last Easter, when Kenzie and Kyle were dating. This could be all kinds of awkward, but Sunny just smiled. "Nice to see you again, Kenzie. And it's nice to meet you, Ripper."

I sat down next to Finn while everybody introduced themselves to Sunny and Mrs. B., who had claimed a spot in the rocking chair and appropriated the fancy cat from Ever.

Hector ambled into the room and trotted right over to Kyle's side, who dropped down into a squat and hugged the dog. One hand on Hector's collar, Kyle pointed at the fluffy cat. "Hector, meet Fitzwilliam."

The cat sat up and lifted one paw, a clear warning of trouble if the German shepherd got too close. It didn't hiss or howl—it didn't look one bit scared—but the cat meant business. Hector swung his head around and fixed mournful eyes on Ripper. If a dog could look betrayed, Hector did.

"It's gonna be all right, Hector." Ripper laid a hand on his dog's head.

"I'm sure that in no time they'll be the best of friends," Mrs. B. said. "Isn't that right, Fitzwilliam?"

The cat coughed like he was hawking up a furball.

This was going to be all kinds of fun.

I looked back at Finn. "Seriously, brother," I said in a voice that wouldn't carry. "Are you all right?"

Finn shook his head, looking like he was at a loss for words. "Got so much to tell you, Bear, and so many questions of my own about what went down here. But we got time to catch up. What you need to know now is that a war's heading our way, and there's no way we can steer clear of it."

FORTY-ONE

Sunny

One week later

"Fitzwilliam Darcy does not sleep in a barn," Mrs. B. said emphatically. She sat up straight in the rocking chair, her erect posture telegraphing her serious intent.

Bear scratched his head. "Well, ma'am. I don't see how it can hurt a cat to sleep in a barn at night. He could make himself useful hunting mice."

"Are you familiar with the Bible, Bear?" Mrs. B. inquired.

"I don't quite see the—"

"The Book of Matthew. 'Consider the lilies of the field, they neither toil nor spin.' Think of Fitzwilliam as a feline lily of the field."

"I don't rightly think—"

Mrs. B. patted his hand and smiled sweetly up at him. "Fitzwilliam isn't a mouser. His only job is to provide an old woman with company during her declining years."

I suppressed a groan. The woman was shameless.

"Fitzwilliam is my best friend," Ever added, looking up from the picture of a chicken that she was coloring. "He sleeps next to me at night. If I have a scary dream, I hug him."

SUSANNA STROM

Bear knew when he was beat. "Yes, ma'am. It was just an idea." He retreated to the front porch, where Kyle and Ripper were drinking beer—a once a week treat—and shooting the breeze.

"Really, Mrs. B.," I said. "Keeping you company during your declining years? Don't you think you're laying it on a little thick?"

She blinked, her eyes wide and innocent. "I'm merely helping the dear boy see reason."

Nyx snorted and took a sip of her beer.

"Can I have a taste?" Ever asked, reaching for the bottle.

She sat across the art table from Nyx, who'd graciously agreed to share the space with the little girl. The two of them had taken to traipsing across the property together. Nyx would draw a black-and-white picture of whatever struck Ever's fancy, and Ever would later sit at the table and color the image.

Nyx snatched up the bottle and placed it out of reach. "Mitts off the beer, pip-squeak."

Ever giggled and returned to her coloring. Kenzie and Hannah padded barefoot into the living room. After dinner, they'd warmed water and helped each other wash their hair, which now lay damp against their shoulders.

"Spa night," Kenzie announced, holding up a basket. "Who wants to paint their toenails?"

Ever shot up out of her seat. "I do."

"I'm good," Nyx said, wiggling bare toes adorned with black polish. "I did mine yesterday."

Of course she did. It might be the end of the world, but Nyx always sported perfect makeup and polish. She must have laid in a supply of that purple-burgundy hair dye, too, because I saw no sign of her natural color at her roots.

Mrs. B. sighed and held up her hands. "I'm afraid my fingers are too stiff tonight to paint my toenails."

"I'll do it for you," Kenzie offered before I could. She set the basket of pedicure supplies on Mrs. B.'s lap. "Pick out the color you want while I go get a towel."

Mrs. B. selected a vivid pink—no surprise there—then passed the basket off to Hannah and Ever, who dumped the bottles onto the rug and pawed through the pile, exclaiming over the colors. Hannah selected a turquoise polish. Ever lined ten bottles up in a row. "I want one of each," she declared. "Like a rainbow."

"Okay, kiddo. Let's do you first," Hannah said, laughing.

I picked out a shimmery lavender polish and took a spot on the floor next to Ever and Hannah to paint my nails.

Kenzie sat cross-legged on the floor in front of the rocker and spread a towel over a pillow on her lap. She slipped off Mrs. B.'s shoes and gently lifted her feet onto the pillow. "Has the arthritis spread to your toes?" she asked.

"Thankfully, no. Only my fingers so far."

Kenzie massaged Mrs. B.'s arch. "You know, I've learned a lot about foot rubs from Ripper. The man is very good with his hands."

Mrs. B. lifted her brows. "Yes, dear, I imagine he is."

Instead of blushing, Kenzie threw back her head and laughed. With both hands, she rubbed circles against the sole of Mrs. B.'s foot. Mrs. B. sighed happily and leaned back against the chair.

"I've always had a soft spot for men who look like big, scary bruisers," Mrs. B. continued. "Like your Ripper and my Jack. Tough exterior, heart of gold."

"Well... in all honesty... sometimes Ripper *can* be a big, scary bruiser," Kenzie said.

"But never with you?" Mrs. B. asked.

"That's right. Never with me." She flashed a smile. "Except when I want him to be." Kenzie carefully set Mrs. B.'s foot on the pillow, picked up the other one, and began massaging it.

"What did Ripper do before the pandemic, dear?"

Kenzie was silent for a moment, seemingly intent on her task. "He served in the army, and later he was in a motorcycle club. The Janissaries."

"Ripper was a biker?" Mrs. B. exclaimed. "I've read romance novels about some truly yummy bikers."

Nyx choked on her beer.

"You read motorcycle club romances?" Kenzie asked.

"Oh, yes. I read everything. Do you like romance novels?"

Kenzie nodded. "I have quite a collection."

Mrs. B. patted Kenzie's shoulder. "I knew we were going to be great friends."

Kenzie was finishing painting Mrs. B.'s toenails when Finn, Sahdev, and Levi came in from a game of horseshoes, Hector on their heels.

The German shepherd stared at his sheepskin rug. Fitzwilliam was curled up in the middle, napping. All eyes followed Hector as he trudged across the room to his bed. He whined. Fitzwilliam slept on, or ignored the dog, which I wouldn't put past the supercilious feline. With a long-suffering sigh, Hector carefully positioned himself around the sleeping cat, hugging the perimeter of his sheepskin rug.

"See, the best of friends," Mrs. B. said with a delighted smile.

Kyle, Bear, and Ripper wandered in from the porch. Kyle dropped down on the carpet next to me.

He lifted my hand and kissed my knuckles, then pointed at my freshly painted toenails. "Pretty." He slung an arm around my shoulders and drew me to his side. "With so many of us living here now, we should look for another couch," he suggested, glancing around the crowded room.

"Good idea," Ripper agreed. "You wanna take the truck tomorrow and hunt one down with me?"

"It's a plan," Kyle said.

We hung out until the sun slipped below the horizon, and Mrs. B. dozed in the rocking chair. When Ever started to yawn, Hannah offered to tuck her into bed and to read a few chapters of *Beezus and Ramona* to the girl. Kenzie stood up and gave an exaggerated yawn.

"Take me to bed, Mr. Solis."

"With pleasure, Mrs. Solis." Instead of accepting the hand she held out, Ripper bent forward and threw Kenzie over his shoulder. She yelped and wriggled. Clamping his hand across her thighs, he met my startled expression with a grin before striding out of the room.

"Mrs. B." Finn touched her shoulder. "Folks are heading to bed. How about I walk you to your room?"

Mrs. B.'s eyes fluttered open and she looked confused for a few seconds, then her disorientation cleared and she smiled at Finn. I half expected her to refuse his overture—the way she'd rejected Marcus Havoc's similar offer—but this time she smiled and took his arm. "I'm happy to see chivalry isn't dead. Good night, dear ones." She blew Kyle and me a kiss and waved at Bear. Pausing at the doorway, she nodded to Nyx, who had resumed her drawing, and to Sahdev and Levi, who were setting up the Parcheesi board.

"Take me to bed, Mr. Chamberlain." I appropriated Kenzie's line.

"With pleasure, Miss McAllister." Kyle hopped up and pulled me to my feet. He may have borrowed Ripper's response, but instead of tossing me over his shoulder like a caveman, he swept me up into his arms. Definitely more my style.

Kyle took a lantern from a hook on the wall and carried me down the hallway toward our room. Finn's parents had added a wing to the old family ranch and rented out vacation rooms to people who wanted to experience life on a working ranch. The extra bedrooms came in handy now with twelve of us in the house.

Our room wasn't as spacious as the guest suite at the Allsop estate, but what it lacked in luxury it more than made up for in coziness and comfort. The creamy yellow paint glowed in the lantern light. A queen-sized maple bed topped with a beautiful hand-stitched quilt occupied one wall. A maple dresser and overstuffed chair took up the other. For the chilly nights to come, a colorful Pendleton blanket was folded over the back of the chair. An old-fashioned braided rag rug covered the floor. Framed photographs of Valhalla in the late 1800s dotted the walls. Over the dresser hung a photo of Finn and Bear's Norwegian-born great-great-grandparents, Erick and Borghild, a handsome couple standing proudly on the porch of their American home.

"I love this place," I said as Kyle deposited me on the floor. "This room. This ranch. These people." Kyle set the lantern on the dresser and locked the door. Two steps brought him to my side. He slid his hands around my hips and tugged me close. "But most of all," I whispered, "I love you, Kyle Chamberlain."

No painful memories haunted his eyes as he gazed down at me. No ghosts from his past lingered on the outskirts of his consciousness. At least not tonight. Kyle was happy and at peace. He was all mine. He traced the outline of my lips, his expression unutterably tender.

"And I love you, Sunny McAllister."

It had been less than two weeks since Kyle and I first made love, but I'd already discovered that sex wore many faces. Sometimes it was frenzied and animalistic, leaving me wrecked, just the way Kyle had promised. Sometimes it was giggly and slaphappy. Sometimes lazy and languid. Tonight, I sensed, it would be something new.

Kyle retrieved a condom from the nightstand drawer and tossed it onto the bed. He loosened the tie at the neckline of my peasant top, his nimble fingers pushing aside the gauzy fabric to expose my throat. He pressed a line of soft kisses across my collarbone, then he pulled the blouse off over my head. Fingertips skimmed over my shoulders and down to my wrists. Lifting my hand, he kissed my upturned palm.

He dropped down on his knees and worked the button on my jeans, his eyes locked on mine and filled with unguarded emotion, his heart laid bare. For a few seconds, I could scarcely breathe. I closed my eyes and sent a prayer of thanks to the universe. The cocky, charismatic teenage boy I'd fantasized about for years—my unattainable crush—had grown into this brave, compassionate, sexy man. And he loved me. Sometimes dreams came true. Even now.

I opened my eyes. His hands were warm against my skin as he dragged my jeans down my legs. One by one, he lifted my feet, then tossed the jeans aside. He slipped his fingers into the sides of my panties and slowly pushed them down to the floor. Kyle undid the front clasp of my bra and slid the straps down my arms. It fell to the rug, and I stood nude before him except for the gold charm bracelet that once again encircled my wrist.

Kyle sat back on his heels, his eyes gleaming. "You are so beautiful, Sunshine," he breathed.

I *felt* beautiful. Adored. His dream come true, too.

In one fluid movement, he rose to his feet and peeled his T-shirt over his head. "Lie back on the bed," he ordered. I willingly complied, my fingers aching to touch him. A small smile played at the corners of his mouth as he stripped. Naked, he planted one knee on the mattress. He snatched up the condom and the foil crinkled as he tore it open, then rolled it over his rigid shaft. I wriggled, anticipation heating my blood.

Lifting my foot, he kissed the arch. His lips sketched a chain of kisses from my ankle to my knee. His fingers gentle, but insistent, he pressed my knees apart, widening my thighs. Kyle crawled up between my spread legs until we were face-to-face. Supporting his weight on his bent arms, he gazed down at me, his eyes incandescent.

"I'm yours," he vowed. "And I will love you every day for the rest of my life."

For the rest of his life. I shivered at this allusion to mortality, at this reminder of the peril we still faced. My lips trembled. "We still have to fight Elliot Allsop."

He touched my cheek. "Yeah, we do. And when the battle comes, we'll face it with our friends, and we'll come out intact on the other side. I know it. But tonight it's just us. Together. Safe. So stay with me, Sunny. Stay in the moment."

I gasped and arched my hips as he pushed inside of me. I locked my ankles around his waist. We rocked together in a leisurely rhythm, taking our time, in no hurry to reach culmination. Kyle rained kisses on my face, murmuring gentle words of love. Every brush of his fingers and lips over my skin was imbued with reverence and devotion.

Sex wore many faces. Tonight I discovered that sometimes sex was a sacrament, a communion of spirits, a vow exchanged with touch and sighs.

Afterward, we lay sated in each other's arms. Kyle fell asleep first. I curled against him, my fingers splayed against the sculpted chest I loved to caress. Was it wrong to feel so happy when our world stood on the brink of another cataclysm?

When the battle comes, we'll face it with our friends, and we'll come out intact on the other side. I know it.

Kyle had faith in tomorrow and all the tomorrows to come. I had faith, too. We'd persevere and build a future with our friends. We'd help raise Ever. Maybe someday we'd have children of our own, too. I smiled at that thought, my eyes growing heavy as sleep rushed in to claim me.

EPILOGUE

Bear

Never understood why some people avoid cemeteries at night. Why would anybody get spooked by treading on consecrated ground that holds the bones of their nearest and dearest?

I visited the Rasmussen family plot most nights before I went to bed. Sitting on a cement bench facing the gravestones, I talked to my parents and grandparents. I'd tell them about my day and ask for their advice, as if I expected them to drop pearls of wisdom from the great beyond. Which I didn't. I wasn't delusional. They didn't actually talk to me. But sometimes when I posed a question, it triggered something in my memory, and I recalled the lessons my folks taught me growing up.

"Trouble's coming," I said to the boulder that marked my parents' grave. Everybody else buried in the cemetery had a fancy marble or granite stone etched with their name to mark their spot in the soil. The Rasmussens did right by their dead. Only my folks had to make due with a plain old boulder that Ripper had helped me wrestle into position.

The wrought iron gate creaked. I glanced over and watched Finn pick his way between the graves, careful to avoid stepping on the ground above the coffins because that'd be disrespectful to the dead.

"Make room," he said.

I scooted over, and he dropped down beside me on the bench, a beer in his hand.

"Not sure Mama would approve." I pointed at the bottle.

"Are you kidding?" Finn demanded. "That woman liked nothing more than to have a beer on a Saturday night."

"True enough, but in a cemetery?"

Finn shrugged. "I don't think she'd hold it against me." He took a sip, then tipped the bottle over the grave, spilling a few drops of the amber liquid. "Cheers, Mama. Sure do miss you."

I twisted sideways on the bench, studying my brother's face in the moonlight. The swelling had gone down, and he could see out of his right eye. The split lip had sewn back together. His bruised ribs were healing, too. He walked funny only at the end of the day when he thought nobody was looking.

"You're healing," I remarked.

"Yep," Finn agreed. A minute of silence passed. He took another pull on his beer. "I think the folks would like Nyx."

"What?" I reared back. Where did *that* come from?

"Nyx," he said. "You know, the woman with the wild hair and all the tattoos. The one you get all fidgety and flummoxed around."

"Humph," I said, refusing to engage in such nonsense.

"Yeah, her." Finn grinned, his teeth flashing white in the dim light.

I ignored him. Closing my eyes, I tilted back my head and listened to the familiar sounds of the night. Above our heads, branches scraped against each other. An owl hooted nearby. In the distance, a coyote yipped.

"I'm healed," Finn said. "It's getting to be time for you and me and Ripper to go to Pendleton to meet with Marcus Havoc and his people. Kyle and the rest can hold down the place for a couple of days while we're gone. Got to make plans to take the war to Allsop."

I sighed, my heart sinking. "I don't want this war," I confessed.

"Me neither, brother," Finn said. "But I've seen Elliot Allsop up close. The man is just plain evil."

I nodded, remembering the Wilcox Brigade. "Won't be the first time we dealt with just plain evil."

"True," Finn said. "And remember what our parents taught us. The Rasmussens never back down from a good fight."

I looked down the hill at the dark ranch house. Our friends slept safe and secure inside our home tonight. Beyond the low hills surrounding the house and barns lay more than three thousand acres of land that generations of Rasmussens had worked, protected, and bled for. Valhalla.

I laid a hand on my brother's shoulder and looked him square in the eyes. "You're right. Nobody is ever going to kill our people or take our land again."

The World Fallen series continues in *Cataclysm*, Bear's story.

Thank you for reading *Bedlam*. I hope you enjoyed it. If you have the time and inclination, please visit the site where you purchased it and leave a brief review.

ACKNOWLEDGMENTS

I'm grateful to the many people who made the publication of *Bedlam* possible.

Christina Trevaskis—my brilliant developmental editor—brings decades of experience and expertise to our collaboration. Her knowledge and skills are second to none.

Raven Dark—a gifted author and dear friend—lends an ear whenever I need advice or encouragement.

I couldn't ask for better proofreaders than Brittany Meyer-Strom and Sharon Shook, women whose eyes light up with excitement at the prospect of hunting down typos and errors.

The wonderful Lori Jackson designed the gorgeous cover for *Bedlam*.

Wander Aguiar shot the perfect cover image.

When my writing mojo needed a boost, I turned to author and Better Faster Academy coach Milana Jacks, who helped me right my course.

A big shout out to my wonderful friend, Debbie Morley, who always takes my call when I need I need to bounce ideas off someone.

Thanks to the lovely Korrie Noelle for her friendship, encouragement and support.

And finally, a big thank you to my husband, John Hoefer, who always encourages me to follow my dreams.

Made in the USA
Coppell, TX
23 August 2021